What _____ _____
a happily-ever-after?

Just Add Children

All little Timmy wants is a capable baby-sitter.
He has no idea he has to play Cupid to get one.

Scott, Julie and Josh need a home. But it isn't long
before they decide what they *really* want is a family.

Davey and Ginger already have a new mother picked
out. Now all they have to do is convince their father.

Just Add Children
The sure way to spice up a romance

Relive the romance...

**Three complete novels by your
favorite authors!**

About the Authors

Elise Title

Elise Title, author of more than fifty-five novels, has always had a soft spot for the "classics"—Hepburn and Tracy, Bogart and Bacall. So, it was only a matter of time before she decided to try her hand at creating her own unforgettable love stories. This prolific author lives in Massachusetts with her husband, Jeff.

Cathy Gillen Thacker

Cathy Gillen Thacker believes that love and laughter go hand in hand. A charter member of the Romance Writers of America, she is the author of over forty novels and numerous nonfiction articles. Cathy, a native midwesterner, lives in Texas with her husband and three children.

Eva Rutland

Eva Rutland began writing when her four children, now all successful professionals, were growing up. She has become a regular—and very popular—contributor to Harlequin's Romance and Regency lines. Eva lives in California with her husband, Bill, who actively supports and encourages her writing career.

Just Add Children

Elise Title
Cathy Gillen Thacker
Eva Rutland

Harlequin Books

TORONTO • NEW YORK • LONDON
AMSTERDAM • PARIS • SYDNEY • HAMBURG
STOCKHOLM • ATHENS • TOKYO • MILAN
MADRID • WARSAW • BUDAPEST • AUCKLAND

HARLEQUIN BOOKS

by Request—Just Add Children

Copyright © 1995 by Harlequin Enterprises B.V.

ISBN 0-373-20111-7

The publisher acknowledges the copyright holders of the individual works as follows:

BABY, IT'S YOU
Copyright © 1988 by Elise Title

NATURAL TOUCH
Copyright © 1988 by Cathy Gillen Thacker

TO LOVE THEM ALL
Copyright © 1988 by Eva Rutland

CONTENTS

Little Timmy saved her account—
Michael Harrington saved her sanity!

BABY, IT'S YOU

Elise Title

1

MADDIE SARGENT GRIPPED the phone, quivering in rage, her knuckles white.

"Yes," she said tightly. "That's exactly what I said. It shrank."

She listened to the clerk at the other end of the line for only a moment before her rage heightened. "I could have swallowed a horse for lunch and the dress wouldn't be this tight. And more to the point, I did not ask to have the dress dry-cleaned. I said pressed. Pressed. It's brand-new. I've never even worn it. It was just a bit creased, that's all. I bought this dress expressly for a very important dinner meeting tonight. The last thing I need at this moment is this kind of aggravation."

In the midst of her tirade the doorbell rang. She dragged the phone across the living room and went to see who was there. "Oh, what's the use," she muttered into the receiver. "I don't have time to argue about it now."

At the door she took a quick look through the peephole and then opened it with her free hand. A plump young woman entered, giving Maddie a wry smile as she scanned her outfit. Maddie raised her hazel eyes toward the ceiling and strode back to the telephone table, talking all the way. "I'll be down to see the manager of your dry-cleaning establishment first thing Monday morning. And you might inform him that this dress cost me two hundred and thirty-four dollars, and I intend to get full reparation."

Maddie hung up the phone, her outraged expression turning to despair as she stared down at her dress and then across to her friend and administrative assistant, Liz Cooper.

"It shrank," Liz said with a humorous grimace.

"I know I'm foolishly superstitious—" Maddie sighed "—but something tells me the Fates are trying to warn me of bad tidings."

Liz grinned. "Buck up. I've actually managed to get a bit of helpful information for you on our Mr. Harrington."

Maddie returned a halfhearted smile. "Good. You can fill me in while I try to dig up something else to wear." She walked into her bedroom and wriggled out of the red jersey dress that had once fit her lithe, one hundred and fifteen pound, five-foot-five body to perfection. It would now look better on a scrawny ten-year-old.

Liz followed, watching Maddie pull dresses out of her closet, frown and then hang them up again.

"How about that little black number you wore to the Christmas party last month?" Liz suggested, slipping off her blue down parka.

"You mean the one that our eminent dermatologist, Kevin Gleason, spilled punch on?" Maddie slipped on a gray crepe de chine, took a quick look in the mirror and immediately proceeded to strip it off.

Liz smiled at her attractive, blond-haired boss. "Maddie, relax. I've never seen you so frazzled. You'll look terrific in whatever you wear. And you'll do great with Harrington."

"Need I remind you, Liz Cooper, how crucial this deal is? If we land this new line of skin-care products for a luxury chain like Barrett's, it's not only going to mean fabulous visibility for the whole Sargent line, but it will also put an end to all our cash-flow and reinvestment worries. This undercapitalized baby of mine that I've nursed through infancy and seven years of growing pains just might finally be able to start standing on its own two feet."

"Look, Maddie, no one knows better than me how hard you've worked to make Sargent one of the finest companies of its kind around. You're twenty-eight and look how far you've come in seven years. Okay, we're small, but we've got a fabulous product line and a dedicated staff. Harrington is going to be bowled over. Besides, Barrett's came to us with the idea for this exclusive, not the other way around. I'll bet anything Harrington's up here to talk turkey."

Maddie grinned. "You're right. I should be optimistic. I need to get a grip on myself. This is just so important." She held up a cognac-colored wool dress.

Liz nodded. "That's a good one."

"I'll need to press the skirt a bit," she said, examining it. "Okay, tell me about Harrington."

Liz pulled a small notepad out of her purse. "Let's see. Harrington, Michael. Thirty-four years old. Single. Worked his way up the ranks at Barrett's to VP in charge of Marketing and New Product Development. A real Horatio Alger, it seems. Rumor has it he started out as a stock boy at the Barrett's store here in Boston." She flicked a page in a businesslike fashion. "He grew up here in Beantown, by the way. South End. Large family. He's the oldest. There's a sister at Wellesley College and a brother at Tufts. Premed. Three sisters who are married. Oh, and there's another sister who's getting married over in Watertown next Sunday. Harrington will be staying in town for the week to attend the nuptials."

"How did you manage to dig all that up on two days' notice?"

"I have an old college buddy who works in personnel at the Barrett's store here."

Maddie smiled. "What would I do without you?"

"Go insane probably."

Maddie laughed. "You're right." She bent down and started searching for her black pumps. "Where did Harrington go to school?"

"He never went to college. I do believe he's the only top exec at Barrett's who doesn't have a fancy business degree from some prestigious university. He rose to VP the blood, sweat and tears way."

Maddie tossed one black pump into the room but continued searching for its mate.

"You'd better wear boots," Liz said. "It's starting to snow."

"Oh, great."

"Actually—" Liz hesitated "—they're predicting a possible blizzard by late tonight."

"Wonderful. Harrington would have to choose Simeoni's clear across town for dinner," Maddie said as she slipped on her flannel robe.

"At least Simeoni's has valet parking."

"If I can get my car started. It doesn't like cold weather any more than I do." She glanced at her watch. "Damn, look at the time. I've got to step on it, or I'll be late."

"I've got to dash off, too. I've got to go to that baby shower for my sister-in-law tonight."

"What's this baby? Number three?"

Liz laughed. "Four."

Maddie shook her head. "And I think *I* have my hands full."

Liz grabbed her parka and headed for the door. "Well, I'm off. Good luck. I'll speak to you tomorrow."

"Thanks again, Liz." Maddie saw Liz out and then hurried to the kitchen with her dress to set up the ironing board and plug in the iron.

Leaving the iron to heat up, she ran into the bathroom to comb her hair and apply some of her favorite Sargent moisturizing lotion, a light Sargent foundation, a touch of green eye shadow and a peach-toned lipstick.

She was back in the kitchen a couple of minutes later, fretting because the iron was still cold, when the doorbell rang insistently.

"Okay, okay. Hold on a minute," she shouted, giving the iron one frustrated scowl before she set it down and rushed for the door.

A cacophony of knocks and muted sobs accompanied the shrill, persistent rings.

"What the . . . ?" Maddie peered quickly through the peephole and then hastily flung open the door. Her cousin Linda was standing there, her infant son, Timmy, bundled up in her arms. It was Timmy doing the crying at the moment, but tears were rolling down the young woman's wan face. Her reddened eyes indicated that she'd been crying for a while.

"Good heavens, Linda. What is it? What's happened?" Maddie tried to usher her cousin inside, but the distraught woman wouldn't budge.

"It's Donald. He's gone."

Maddie gasped. "Gone?"

"He's . . . left me, Maddie. He's left me and Timmy." As soon as she got the words out, Linda began crying in earnest along with her infant.

"Oh, Linda," Maddie said, feeling at a complete loss, "that's awful."

"Don...went to Vale, Colorado...for an engineering conference. He...he was supposed to be back this morning. Only...he called and said he wants a...trial separation. It's Timmy...the pressures of being a father...it's all so different since the baby..."

Maddie missed half of what Linda was saying because of the infant's bellowing, but she got the gist of it. "Look, come inside and sit down for a while. I'm afraid I have to rush out for a meeting. I'm late already. But you stay here, and...and we'll talk later...when I get back."

Linda remained firmly planted in the hallway. "I must go to him and try to save my marriage, Maddie."

Before Maddie could respond, Linda thrust the wailing baby into her arms.

"You've got to look after Tim...just for a couple of days. There's no one else I can turn to."

"But...but...I can't," Maddie stammered, her voice drowned out by the baby's shrieks, heightened now that he found himself being held awkwardly in strange arms. She tried to give him back to his mother, but Linda was reaching down for a small overnight bag and a plaid canvas car bed.

"Here. Timmy's clothes, bottles, some diapers, and he can sleep in this," she said rapidly between quick, shallow breaths, dumping the tote and car bed at Maddie's feet. "Oh, God, Maddie, I can't tell you what a lifesaver you are. What would I ever have done without you? I love him so, Maddie. And Timmy needs his father. It's just...such an adjustment. For me, too." She clutched Maddie's shoulder. "I'll be back Monday morning. I'll repay you somehow. I have to hurry. I've got just enough time to catch my plane."

After a quick hug that encompassed both Timmy and Maddie, Linda was gone.

The door swung shut in Maddie's stunned face. A moment later Maddie jerked the door back open only to witness the elevator doors sliding closed. Maddie stared down the empty hall and then at the screeching baby in her arms.

Panic set in. It was bad enough that she didn't know the slightest thing about babies. But of all the times in the world, there couldn't be a worse one than this to have to start learning. "No, no, this can't be happening. I don't believe this."

Poor Timmy seemed none too happy with the situation, either. He began writhing in outrage, his ear-shattering shrieks reaching new heights.

"Please . . . please stop crying," Maddie implored. "I can't think. What am I going to do?"

She began pacing frantically in her hallway, holding the nearly apoplectic infant and wondering what she'd ever done to deserve this.

"Call the restaurant. That's the first thing," she mumbled. "Leave a message for Harrington that . . . that I'm having a little car trouble, but I'll be there as soon as I can. Okay. Then all I have to figure out is what to do with *you*." She stared down at the bundled-up baby, his crinkled face a bright scarlet as he took a gulp of air before breaking into new wails.

"Don't think I'm thrilled, either, kid," she said, blinking away some of her own tears.

Squealing babe in arms, Maddie headed for the kitchen phone but picked up a decidedly unpleasant scent as soon as she stepped into the room. An instant later her eyes fell on the smoking iron, and she let out a shriek to rival Timmy's. The iron that she'd thought was broken and had therefore set down mindlessly on top of her cognac wool dress had decided to function after all.

"Oh, no. No. Why me?" she moaned, lifting the iron to reveal a large singed hole on the front panel of her dress.

The only good part was that Timmy seemed to find her newest predicament soothing. He stopped crying and stared up at her, a little smile on his face as he emitted a soft cooing sound.

"Oh, I see. A child who smiles at others' adversities." But Maddie's lips curved up faintly. "Okay, kid. Just keep it down until I make my call."

It was too much to ask. The minute Maddie got the maître d' at Simeoni's on the phone, Timmy began bellowing again. Maddie gave him the message but couldn't really hear the maître d's response with Timmy screeching in her ear. Of course, the instant she hung up, Timmy's squeals came to an abrupt stop.

"So that's the game you're going to play, is it? Do you have any idea how bad it's going to look for me to show up late for this meeting with Harrington? And now I not only have to find someone to look after you, I've got to dig up something else to wear, too. This has got to be one of the most impossible evenings of my life."

Timmy cooed.

Maddie sighed, using this moment of silence to ring Liz and hopefully enlist her aid. After a half-dozen rings, Maddie realized that Liz must have gone straight over to her sister-in-law's shower.

"Okay, think, Maddie. Think. Who else can you try?" She considered the occupants of the other five apartments in her brownstone building. She only knew them well enough to exchange pleasantries. How could she ask one of them to watch a strange baby?

After exhausting her list of friends, all of whom were either not at home or on their way out, she was desperate enough to ring up all of her neighbors.

Only one of them was home—Mrs. Johnston on the first floor. And she was just on her way out to visit her niece in Marblehead for the night. She did, however, offer Maddie a helpful suggestion. Mrs. Johnston's daughter sometimes used a baby-sitting service.

"Now let me think. Was it Wee Folks or Wee Love? Something like that. Oh, I remember. It was Wee Care. Isn't that cute?" Mrs. Johnston chuckled while Maddie forced a polite little laugh. "They have branches all over the area."

"Well, anyway," Mrs. Johnston went on, "there are quite a few of those services in the yellow pages. I believe they are all licensed and quite professional. You should be able to find a nice, capable person to look after your baby. Oh, that's right. It isn't your baby, is it? It's your nephew. No, no. Cousin. That's it. Well, good luck, my dear. Oh, that's my niece tooting outside. I must go. I'm sorry I couldn't be of more help. I do feel neighbors should help each other out. Now that we've gotten acquainted, you must stop in to have a cup of tea with me sometime."

Maddie was thumbing through the yellow pages before she even hung up the phone. It turned out that there were seven child-care services listed in the Boston area. The Wee Care Agency was the last one on the list. Crossing her fingers Maddie started there.

MICHAEL HARRINGTON DROVE down Storrow Drive with snow swirling in front of his windshield. The temperature was dropping rapidly, and the roads were icing up. The cars in front of him were slipping and sliding all over the place. Michael, on the other hand, maneuvered his Lamborghini expertly, the sleek sports car gripping the road solidly. He'd driven the car from New York to Bos-

ton, leaving it parked in his mother's driveway for a week
while he flew down to Palm Beach. Despite sitting idle
all that time in the cold weather, the engine purred like
a contented tiger. He patted the steering wheel affectionately as he pulled off the Government Center exit.

A young man in a blue parka with a Simeoni's em-
blem on the breast pocket darted out of the restaurant
with an umbrella as Michael drove up. Stepping out of
the car, Michael waved away the umbrella. The young
man closed it, tossed it over by the curb and gave the
Lamborghini an appreciative smile before driving it off
to the parking lot.

Another man, this one middle-aged and dressed in
formal livery, opened the large brass-and-glass door for
Michael, greeting him by name. A pretty brunette stood
behind the counter of the coat checkroom and beamed
as Michael approached.

"It's nice to see you again, Mr. Harrington. It's been a
long time." She gave him the same kind of appreciative
smile the young man outside had given his sports car.

"It has been a while." He smiled back, slipping off his
Italian black cashmere coat.

"Where'd you get that divine tan?" she asked, surveying a broad, angular bronzed face that wasn't so much
handsome as imposing, with its wide, square jaw,
slightly hooked nose and dark brows and lashes that
framed eyes the color of midnight blue. It was his eyes
that held her. Those midnight-blue eyes were capable of
making a woman believe she was the only person on
earth.

"I had some business in Palm Beach this past week."
He smoothed back his thick hair, damp from the snow,
with careless fingers.

"Mmm. Lucky guy."

The corners of his mouth lifted in a slightly tired smile. That Palm Beach trip had been exhausting—a week spent discussing, evaluating and surveying the L'Amour Skin-Care Company, one of two he'd narrowed his choice down to for the Barrett's special new line. He'd left Palm Beach convinced he'd found the right company. Which made his meeting tonight with Madeline Sargent of Sargent Skin-Care Products rather superfluous. Only a sense of fair play and the knowledge that the Sargent woman had gone to a lot of trouble sending him a detailed portfolio on the company made him decide to keep the engagement. He wasn't looking forward to having to tell her that he'd already made his selection. But those were the breaks. The least he figured he could do was treat her to a great dinner first.

"Ah, Mr. Harrington. It's good to see you." The maître d' greeted him warmly.

"Good to see you, too, Charles. How's the family?"

"They're fine. My son just got accepted at Annapolis. My daughter, on the other hand ... well, she's a teenager. What can I say? My wife says most teenagers go through a stage."

"Tell me about it," Michael replied. "With six younger brothers and sisters I've seen every variation on that stage you could imagine."

The two men shared compatriotic smiles.

"Shall I show you to your table, or would you prefer stopping at the bar first? Your guest, Miss Sargent, telephoned to say she would be delayed because of some car trouble."

Michael rubbed his jaw thoughtfully. He could telephone her and suggest they postpone the dinner. He'd much prefer to cancel it altogether, but he never conducted business that way. He finally opted for the bar.

He'd give her a few minutes to get here. Better to resolve everything now.

"Looks like a bad storm moving in off the coast," the bartender said, setting a bourbon and soda down in front of Michael.

"It's coming down pretty heavily already," Michael commented. "The roads are slick."

He nursed his drink for a few minutes and then decided to give Maddie Sargent a call after all. If she was still in, he'd offer to pick her up. His efficient secretary had noted the woman's home number and address in his appointment book. He checked it and then dialed a couple of times, but the line was busy. He finished his drink, left a tip and stopped on his way out to tell Charles he was going to see if he could catch Miss Sargent at home and give her a lift. If she'd already left, he would meet her back at the restaurant. "Unless," Harrington added, "I get stuck out there."

MADDIE WAS GROWING increasingly frantic. Wee Care was all booked up. So was the TLC Agency, Baby's Best, Mary Poppins, Les Petits and Goosey Gander. Maddie had one last hope—Hugs Plus. She'd already tried them a couple of times, but their line was busy. This time she finally got a ring, only to be put on hold with a medley of Muzak lullabies.

Crossing her fingers, she sat on the couch, Timmy squirming, but quiet, on her lap. Once it had dawned on her that the poor kid was probably boiling under all the layers of clothes Linda had put on him, she'd managed to strip him down to his terry playsuit. He'd rewarded her with blissful silence.

Maddie was considering this momentary good fortune when she felt her lap grow decidedly damp. Of course she'd already thrown on that little black number Liz had suggested earlier, deciding that the faint stain from the punch wasn't really noticeable. This stain was not only going to be visible but was also going to make her smell about as aromatic as a skunk.

While Maddie muttered some very unmaternal words under her breath, Timmy cooed happily.

"Good evening. Hugs Plus. Can I help you?"

"I hope so," Maddie said with such a note of desperation in her voice that the woman on the other end of the line laughed softly. "I need a sitter. Right away. It's really crucial. Just for a couple of hours."

"Right away?" The woman paused. "Saturday nights are always so busy. I do believe all of our people are booked, but let me check for you. Perhaps due to the storm someone has canceled. Can you hold a minute?"

"Yes, but please, please try to find someone for me."

As soon as she was put back on hold, Timmy began to cry again. Maddie put the phone next to his ear. Maybe he'd like the canned rendition of "Rock-a-bye-baby" better than she did. He didn't. "Well—" she sighed wearily "—at least you have good taste in music."

The compliment didn't help any more than the Muzak.

"Come on, Timmy. Give me a break. With any luck, a nice Hugs Plus nanny will zip over here and rescue us both from torment."

She lifted the soaked child gingerly in her arms, clutching the receiver between her chin and her shoulder. "I know you need your diaper changed. As soon as I finish this call, I'll see what I can do. Don't expect much, though. I've never changed a diaper in my life. And to tell you the truth, it isn't one of those must-do things I had on my list of life goals."

Her words offered little solace. Timmy cried louder until he discovered her silver necklace. Fascinated, he stopped crying a moment before the Muzak clicked off. Maddie waited with bated breath.

"You're in luck. We do have a cancellation. One of our best young men is available. You don't mind a male nanny, do you? He's exceptional. Now some of our clients prefer—"

"No, no, that's fine. Wonderful," Maddie interrupted hurriedly, giving her name and address. "How soon can he get here?"

"Well, the weather is getting worse. But he doesn't live that far from you. He should be able to be there within fifteen minutes or so. I just need a little information first."

Maddie gave her Timmy's name, said that, as she recalled, he was about six months old . . . and yes, he was in great health. Judging from his fine pair of lungs, anyway.

"That should do it. You will leave our sitter your location and phone number, one other person to phone in an emergency, Timmy's physician's name—"

"Yes, I'll leave whatever information I can."

"That should do it, then."

"Oh, thank you. I can't tell you how much I appreciate it."

"We hope you'll become a regular customer."

Maddie smiled dryly. Not in a million years.

As soon as she hung up the phone, she scooped Timmy up from her lap, dug through the overnight case and pulled out a cloth diaper.

"Oh, great. Doesn't your mother believe in those nifty little disposable ones that they're always advertising on TV?" She stared morosely at the large rectangular strip of cloth. "Well, like I said, kid, don't expect any miracles."

She laid him down on the couch, realizing too late that she should have placed something absorbent under him. Gritting her teeth, she hastily set about her task. Timmy didn't make it easy, but she finally managed to remove his wet playsuit and the soaked diaper.

Timmy cooed. He also chose just that moment to relieve himself once more. Maddie screamed, leaping back. Timmy seemed to find her reaction positively amusing.

"Did your mother mention that you have a demented sense of humor, kid? But I'll get even with you," Maddie muttered as she hastily and haphazardly folded and pinned the new diaper on him. "Eighteen or so years from now you're going to be sitting at some family function with your girlfriend, trying to look cool, and I'm going to tell her just what you did to me, you little imp. Go on and laugh now if you want."

Which Timmy did until Maddie set him down on her rug so that she could quickly change her clothes—again. She pulled out a much worn print challis dress from the closet and glanced at Timmy. "What do you think, kid?"

Timmy burped.

"Yeah, well, it's clean and dry. That counts for something."

Not for much, according to Timmy. As soon as she slipped the dress on, he once again started exercising his vocal cords vociferously.

"Hey, what are you—a connoisseur of high fashion?"

When her doorbell rang twenty minutes later, Maddie had her coat on, her car keys in her hand and was wearing out her hall carpet pacing frantically with the howling infant. Timmy, par for the course, once again had a damp bottom, but she'd leave the next diaper change to a professional.

At the first ring she darted to the door and flung it open, practically throwing Timmy into the arms of the man standing there.

"Oh, thank God. I thought you'd never get here." She was out the door, talking fast as she raced down the hall to the still-open elevator. "His stuff is on the living-room couch," she called out. "My number's there, too. I won't be late."

"Hey, wait. Hold on a second—"

She was already in the elevator. "I can't. I'm late."

The man dashed down the hall with the screaming infant, but the elevator doors swished closed before he got there.

MADDIE ARRIVED AT SIMEONI'S thirty-five minutes late with a pounding headache and frozen toes, her car heater having chosen this opportune time to conk out. The Fates not only seemed to be against her, but they were also obviously conspiring to do her in.

Maddie's hazel eyes glinted with determination. It was going to take more than a wardrobe of ruined dresses, a recalcitrant iron, a malfunctioning heater and even a hysterical, uncontrollable infant to defeat her. At least that's what she told herself as she handed her coat over to the brunette in the coat checkroom.

She smoothed down her hair, which she wore in a neat, stylish blunt cut to her shoulders; then she took a deep breath to steady herself and proceeded to the maître d's station.

"I'm Maddie Sargent, Mr. Harrington's guest."

The maître d' looked over her shoulder. "Is Mr. Harrington with you?"

Maddie shrugged. "No. Isn't he here yet?"

The man picked up a couple of menus. "He should be back shortly. Shall I show you to your table, or would you prefer to wait in the bar?"

"The table, please."

He smiled pleasantly and led the way through the candlelit main dining room. Maddie had never been here before, although she knew that the restaurant was considered one of the finest in Boston. She was, however, too keyed up to appreciate the elegant decor and the savory aromas wafting up from the well-spaced tables she passed. Right now the thought of eating dinner left her feeling slightly queasy.

As the maître d' pulled out a beautiful mahogany table so she could slide onto the plush gray banquette, Maddie asked, "Did you say Mr. Harrington would be back shortly?"

"Yes, that's right."

"Oh," Maddie said, taking her seat, "then he was here earlier."

"Oh, yes. At a few minutes past eight," the maître d' said, smiling pleasantly as he slid the table back into place. "Would you care to order a cocktail while you wait?"

"You're sure he's coming back?" Maddie queried worriedly. "He did get my message?"

"Oh, yes, I gave it to him myself. Car trouble, correct?"

Maddie grimaced. "Right. Car trouble."

"Actually, Mr. Harrington went to see if he could offer you a ride here, but it seems your paths didn't cross."

"He left to pick me up?"

"Don't worry. He said he would return if he discovered you'd already left. Can I get you a cocktail while you're waiting? Or a glass of wine?"

"Wine," Maddie muttered absently, a most disturbing sensation creeping into the pit of her stomach. The man who'd shown up at her door to watch Timmy... he *had* shown up to watch Timmy, hadn't he? He *was* from Hugs Plus, wasn't he? Of course he was. He had to be. It couldn't have been ...

"Excuse me, Miss Sargent. Will that be red wine or white? We have a very nice Chablis Premier Cruor—"

"What?" Her hazel eyes had lost their glint of determination. They were slightly glazed now.

No, she told herself. No, it was impossible. It couldn't have been Harrington's arms she'd dumped Timmy into. She tried to picture what the man had looked like. What he'd been wearing. But it had happened in a flash, and she'd been so preoccupied that the man was a complete blur.

"Would you prefer red or white wine, Miss Sargent?"

"Oh ... white." But what if it had been Harrington? Hadn't everything else that could possibly have gone wrong tonight gone wrong? No, she repeated silently. Surely he would have said something. Wouldn't he? Then again, she *had* raced out of there.

Just sit tight, she told herself reassuringly. *Don't jump the gun.* It was just as likely that Harrington arrived at her apartment after she'd left and the sitter from Hugs Plus had told him that she'd already gone. Any minute now Harrington would come walking into the restaurant.

She sipped the chilled white wine slowly. Twenty minutes later the wine was gone and Maddie was growing increasingly edgy.

As she stared blankly at her empty glass a few minutes later, the maître d' came over. "I'm sorry, Miss Sargent. Mr. Harrington just telephoned. He asked me to offer his apologies. He tried to phone earlier, but the lines were down temporarily because of the storm. He will not be able to keep his dinner engagement after all." The maître d' paused. "He said to tell you he's been unexpectedly detained."

"Unexpectedly detained?"

"He might have gotten stuck on the road."

"Stuck . . . right."

IT TOOK MADDIE nearly an hour to get back home. More than a mile from her street her car stalled, and she couldn't start it again. She walked the remaining distance, a good five blocks, in what had now become a raging blizzard. Oblivious to the cold or any fear of frostbite, Maddie's mind was obsessed by a far more catastrophic worry. Namely that the man she'd so cavalierly taken for the sitter from Hugs Plus was none other than Michael Harrington. The man who held her future in his hands.

Her future . . . and a soaked, howling baby.

2

WHEN MADDIE OPENED the front door, she heard a soothing male voice coming from the kitchen.

"Okay, Scout. Dinner's just about set. Ready to chow down?"

Maddie quietly slipped off her coat and took off her boots. She stood in the foyer shivering. It took a minute for her circulation to return, her frozen fingers and toes burning as she began to warm up.

She took a few steps in her stockinged feet into the living room until she reached a spot where she had a direct view into the kitchen. She remained silent as she watched the tall, dark-haired man, his back to her, standing by the stove. Timmy was slung casually and contentedly over the man's broad right shoulder as he expertly tested a heated bottle of milk by shaking a few drops onto his wrist.

"Perfect," he announced in a deep baritone, cradling the baby in the crook of one arm. He laughed softly as Timmy reached out with his hands to help guide the bottle to his lips.

"When's the last time your mama fed you, Scout?" He walked over to the kitchen sink and, letting Timmy manage the bottle for a moment, turned on the taps. "I'll get a nice bath ready for you, and then you'll be set to sack out. And as soon as your mama gets back here, she can tuck you in."

The man's move to the sink put him in profile. A strong, rugged and attractive profile at that. As he looked down at Timmy, his tanned face creased in a smile, crinkled lines deepening about his eyes and the corners of his mouth. His shirtsleeves were rolled up above his elbows, the muscles in his forearms rippling as he moved.

When he shut off the taps and turned away from the sink, he spotted Maddie. He was startled for a moment but quickly composed himself.

"Where'd you learn how to diaper a baby? In a war zone?" The corners of his mouth twitched in a faint smile; his dark blue eyes held her transfixed.

Maddie stared at him for a long moment. And then she threw her head back and broke into a soft peel of laughter.

The man continued to regard her as he walked with the still-contented Timmy in his arms into the living room and waited for her to calm down.

"Care to share the joke?"

Maddie sank onto the soft cushions of her sofa. "I'm sorry," she said as soon as she got the laughter down to a giggle. "It's just . . . for a while back at the restaurant I thought I'd made the supreme mistake of my life."

"And what mistake is that?"

Maddie didn't answer immediately. Instead, she watched the man remove the nearly empty bottle from Timmy's mouth, swing the infant over his shoulder and rhythmically pat his back until Timmy let out a resounding burp.

"That's better, Scout. Now you can finish up your dinner." He swung the baby back into the crook of his arm again and stuck the bottle in his mouth. All this without a cry, a whimper of protest or even a scowl from Timmy.

"You're terrific," Maddie exclaimed, hastily adding, "with babies. You must have been at this line for some time."

The man smiled enigmatically. "I've had my share of experience." He surveyed her face closely, and then his gaze dropped for a moment to take in her long, shapely legs. "So tell me about the mistake you almost made."

Maddie uncrossed her legs, self-consciously pulling her dress down over her knees, and sat up straighter. She cast the man a demure glance only to find his smile tinged with amusement. Maddie was dismayed to feel herself blushing.

"It's just . . . well, for a minute or two back at the restaurant I thought I'd actually . . . left Timmy with the wrong man."

"The wrong man?"

"I was afraid that you weren't the male baby-sitter from Hugs Plus. That instead you were my dinner date who'd come to pick me up. Well, not exactly my date. I was meeting the man on business. I've never even set eyes on Michael Harrington. And since I'd never met either one of you . . . well, it was certainly possible that I'd made a walloping boo-boo. And then, when he called the restaurant and left a message for me that he'd been unexpectedly detained . . . I started to think . . . Well, that's one worry off my mind. Not that I don't have plenty enough to still worry about. I've probably messed up my big chance with Harrington by not showing up on time." Maddie sighed wearily, her gaze on Timmy, who was now asleep in the man's arms.

"Why is it," she pondered half to herself, "that the one time in my life I'm desperate for everything to go right, nothing, absolutely nothing, does." She paused, then managed a weak smile. "Except for you showing up and calming Timmy down . . . and taking such good care of him."

Her compliment seemed to disconcert him. Maddie could even make out a telltale hint of redness rising from his neck. His reaction surprised her. With his looks, his build, his self-assured style, Maddie took him to be the type to get lots of compliments from women all the time. And the type who took them in his stride. This unexpected show of vulnerability in him touched her. And, in turn, left her feeling embarrassingly adolescent. Could she actually be developing a schoolgirl crush on her baby cousin's sitter?

"Well, anyway," she went on hastily, trying to dispel the disturbing reaction she was having to him, "once I walked in and saw you with Timmy . . . well, I was positively relieved to see my worst fears hadn't been realized after all. Michael Harrington certainly wouldn't have been standing in the kitchen with an infant in his arms, cooing to him, testing his milk, running his bath." Maddie wished the sitter wouldn't keep studying her with those incredible, hypnotic blue-black eyes. "So, uh, do you do this kind of work . . . full-time?"

It was his turn to laugh. "No, not anymore. Truth is, I'm out of practice."

"Oh. They told me at Hugs Plus that you were one of their best."

"Hugs Plus said that, did they? One of their best?"

He was playing with her, she realized. And the game was clearly seductive. Well, she'd have to put an end to that right this minute. She stood up abruptly. "So how much do I owe you? I never did ask about the rates." She started across the room for her purse.

Timmy woke and began squirming. "Take it easy, Scout. Your mama's here. She'll give you your bath and tuck you in."

Maddie stopped in her tracks. "Oh, his bath." She turned slowly. "Look, since you're here anyway and were just about to bathe him when I came in...why don't you do it?"

He cocked his head. "Still a nervous new mom, huh?"

"I'm not a mom." She gave Timmy a rueful glance. "He's . . . on loan."

"On loan?"

Maddie's eyes narrowed. "My cousin arrived on my doorstep about a half hour before you did. She was in hysterics, begging me to look after Timmy while she raced off to Colorado to try to save her marriage. Her husband is having a hard time coping with being a father, and he's having serious second thoughts about the whole thing. Believe me, twenty minutes with this kid and I can see daddy's point. I've never taken care of a baby in my life. And that kid in your arms scares the living daylights out of me."

He grinned at her. "This kid? Hey, Timmy's a great kid." He walked over to Maddie. "You two must have just gotten off to a bad start."

Maddie laughed dryly. "You've got a gift for understatement."

"Come on. Take him in your arms and hold him."

Maddie backed off. "No . . . really. Every time I touch him, he starts to wail."

"I'm the pro, right? Go on. Take him. I'll give you a few pointers."

Maddie pressed her lips together and stared at the baby. She was sure Timmy was eyeing her as warily as she was eyeing him.

"Just relax. Babies can pick up all kinds of vibes. Just like adults can." He reached out and rested his free hand on her shoulder.

A tiny shiver went through Maddie at his touch. She pressed her lips together tighter.

"See. You're tense." He gently massaged the curved area where her neck and shoulder met.

His ministrations only made her tenser. "Okay, okay," she said, a tinge of desperation in her voice, "give me Timmy."

The minute the baby was in her arms, his face reddened and he broke into an outraged scream.

"See. See, I told you. He does this every time." She tried to return Timmy, but the sitter merely gripped her arm.

"Come on. We'll bathe him together." He had to bend very close to her ear to be heard.

His warm breath only served to agitate Maddie more, which in turn heightened Timmy's agitation. She gave the sitter a panicked look. He finally relented when they got to the kitchen and took the now-hysterical Timmy from her.

A couple of tosses in the air, a playful nuzzle on his belly, and Timmy was actually giggling.

"Dr. Jeckyll and Mr. Hyde," Maddie muttered sardonically.

"I guess I've just got the magic touch." He tested the water with his elbow. "Warm it up a little."

"Why not put him in the bathtub?"

Michael grinned. "He might get lost in it."

Maddie managed a begrudging smile. "He is kind of little." She started to turn on the tap.

"Whoa. Pull out the stopper first, or we'll all be having a bath." His hand was over hers. "I bet you could use a nice, hot bath yourself. Your hand's like ice."

"My car conked out about a mile from here. I had to walk the rest of the way home from the restaurant." His hand was still over hers, rubbing some warmth into it. His caress gave her a deep, unexpected sexual thrill.

Take your hand away, Maddie, she commanded herself. *This is crazy. Get a grip on yourself. You're just temporarily deranged. You don't want to do anything foolish. Anything you're bound to regret later.*

"Are you okay?"

Maddie nodded. She pulled her hand away, stuck it into the tepid water and pulled out the rubber stopper.

"Okay, that's enough." He caught her wrist, plunging both their hands back into the water again as he guided the stopper back over the drain. "You're trembling. You aren't that scared of bathing this tyke, are you?"

She continued to feel that sharp sexual tug. "I'm just . . . cold still."

"Maybe we ought to hold off on Timmy and look after you first."

She nervously turned on the tap.

"Please don't do this." Maddie had trouble getting her voice much above a whisper. "Don't . . . come on to me. I'll be perfectly straight with you. I've had a lousy night. And somewhere in this city Michael Harrington is, no doubt, also having a lousy night. Chances are he's holding me responsible for it. What I'm trying to say is . . . I think you'd better leave. I'll give Hugs Plus a call first thing tomorrow and tell them you were . . . great."

He stared at her, a sharp tug of conscience causing his throat to turn raw. "Maddie . . ." His voice was a note deeper.

She looked up at him, surprised and disoriented to hear him call her by her first name. She realized she couldn't even remember his name although the woman from Hugs Plus had given it to her. The disastrous events of the evening really had left her temporarily crazy.

"Maddie," he repeated soberly, no hint of seduction in his voice now. "There's something I'd better tell you."

She stared at him. "What is it?"

He saw that she was flushed, knew that she found him disturbingly attractive. Just as he knew he was equally attracted to her.

His brow beaded with sweat. He felt like a first-class heel, even though he hadn't been the one to start the ball rolling. Maddie had done that. But he'd played along. He had to take responsibility for carrying the ball as far as he had. It was that devilish streak in him. He could be an incorrigible tease if given half a chance. And Maddie had left herself wide open. Having taken advantage of her vulnerability made him feel even crummier.

He took a deep breath. "Maddie, I'm not a baby-sitter. The fact is, the sitter from Hugs Plus called five minutes after you flew out of here like you were running the fifty-yard dash. He said he couldn't make it, that someone in his family was sick. I tried to call the restaurant, but I couldn't get through. To tell you the truth, I was steaming there for a while. Getting an infant suddenly dumped in my lap wasn't exactly how I'd planned to spend my evening. I felt trapped, and believe me, that's not a feeling I cotton to. But I couldn't very well leave Timmy here alone. And I knew that once you got my message, you'd be home soon. There was nothing else to do but sit tight. It's a good thing Timmy here was such a good sport."

Maddie nodded inanely. The truth was slowly registering.

"Anyway, when you walked in and still mistook me for the sitter, I got this urge to teach you a little lesson. Without really meaning to I guess I let myself get a little carried away."

"You're Michael Harrington." She gave him such a look of abject despair that he felt like digging a hole for himself on the spot.

"I'm sorry. It was a rotten stunt to pull on you. But I thought Timmy was yours, that you were just some ditsy dame who couldn't get her act together and..." He watched her pretty hazel-green eyes narrow, hostility emanating from them like burning sparks.

"You aren't the least bit ditsy." His throat was dry. "Not ditsy at all."

Maddie took a step back, slowly shaking her head, her arms clutched across her chest as the whole charade came sharply into focus. "What you're saying is that you deliberately made a complete fool out of me." Her voice was quavering with rage. "And what's more, you had a grand old time doing it."

"Maddie..."

"Don't call me Maddie," she shot back. "Only my friends call me Maddie. And another thing..." She stopped abruptly, realizing that she was sounding off to the man who still held her future in his hands. Had she gone irrevocably insane? Was she really about to simply toss her future out the window because of foolish pride? Anyway, she reasoned, hadn't she done to Michael Harrington exactly what Linda had done to her? He'd come out in a raging blizzard to pick her up and what did she get in exchange for his kindness? A bouncing baby boy. Could she really blame him for wanting to even the score a little?

Tears stung her eyes. "Oh, Lord, when is this nightmare going to end? Why are the Fates out to destroy me?" she moaned, crumpling into a kitchen chair and dropping her head onto her arms, which were folded on the table.

Michael walked over with Timmy still snug against his chest. He felt rotten. Not only did he feel like a heel for misleading her, but on top of that he was also going to have to tell her she was no longer in line for the Barrett's account. He knew he shouldn't prolong her agony. Get it all on the table and then bid a hasty, if guilty, retreat.

But he couldn't bring himself to do it, not now, not when the poor woman was already feeling so low, no small part thanks to him. How much could she handle in one night? And a small voice inside him asked how much he could handle. Maddie Sargent was proving to be far more than he'd bargained for. Maybe, he told himself, the best thing to do was put off any further bad news until he got back to New York, where he could have his secretary write her a nice, businesslike Dear John letter.

He put his hand lightly on her back and felt the muscles beneath her skin tighten at his touch. "Look, I don't blame you for feeling angry. Or upset. I don't blame you at all. Maybe I'd better just take off now and let you get some sleep. I'm sorry, Maddie."

Maddie didn't say a word. Nor did she look up.

Michael removed his hand and straightened. He felt at a complete loss. He stared down at Timmy, who had once again fallen asleep, his tiny body curled contentedly in the crook of his large arm. "You'll have to take him now," he said softly.

Maddie lifted her head so that only her eyes were visible. They held such a vulnerable, unprotected look that

Michael felt an urge to take her in his arms. Instead, he stood there awkwardly.

"You're leaving?" She raised her head a little higher, her voice anxious.

He broke into a slow smile. "It's been a tough night for you. And I'm sorry to think I made it even tougher." He tried to sound sympathetic, but he was distracted by a quick flash of desire. Maddie Sargent was very appealing, and he found himself wishing he'd met her under altogether different circumstances. He made it a rule never to mix business and pleasure. Then again, he reminded himself, he wouldn't actually be doing business with Maddie. Not that that gave him a viable edge. Once she learned that he'd not only humiliated her but was turning her company down for the new skin-care line at Barrett's, as well, he seriously doubted he'd have much luck wooing the woman. Michael frowned, realizing that he was in a no-win situation, a rare place to find himself these days.

Maddie lifted her head fully and stared at Michael with a pleading expression. "But . . . but you can't leave. Not like this. Give me a break, Harrington. Your walking out now would just top off this nightmare. You've got to give me a second chance," she said with a melancholy smile.

She saw Michael step back, and her voice took on a frantic note. "Look, it's still early. We can have that meeting here. I have this whole great pitch to give you about the line we want to work on for Barrett's. It's a knockout. I don't think that portfolio I sent you gives you more than a hint of where my company is heading, how fantastic our products are."

She had to stop to catch her breath, but she continued to watch him closely. She was afraid she wasn't making any headway and quickly decided to switch tactics.

"Besides, you promised to help me give Timmy his bath. You owe me, Harrington. You admitted yourself it was a dirty trick to pull on me. I didn't deserve it."

Michael's smile was tender. "No, you didn't deserve it." He squinted down at Timmy. "I guess he can skip his bath. Why don't you take him now that he's fast asleep and tuck him in?" He met her gaze levelly. "Then I guess we can talk for a little while. But, to be honest, I'm bushed. I really am out of practice with babies. They can wear you out sometimes."

"Believe me, I know." She watched anxiously as Michael carefully transferred the sleeping infant into her arms. She held her breath as Timmy squirmed for a moment and then sighed with relief when he nuzzled against her breast, still sound asleep.

Her relief lasted all of two steps. The moment Timmy started to cry, Maddie froze. "Oh, not again," she moaned.

Michael came up to her. "Just rock him a little."

"He's allergic to me, I swear. Or else he just plain hates me. Here, you take him," she said, thrusting Timmy back into Michael's arms.

Michael grinned as his hand moved under the baby's bottom to support him. "He's wet, that's all. He's just letting you know he wants his diaper changed."

"When do they learn to ask politely?" Maddie quipped. "And how come he isn't screeching in your arm? For you he coos about his wet diaper. For me he hollers bloody murder."

He kissed Timmy affectionately on the top of his head. "Like I said, babies are sensitive creatures."

And, Maddie recalled, he'd also said that he'd had a lot of experience with babies. Did that mean babies of his own? She frowned. Hadn't Liz told her Harrington was single? Did she mean single *now*? As in once married?

"Where do you want to put him?" Michael's voice broke into her ruminations.

"Put him? Oh, put him. Um, I guess in the spare bedroom. Wait, Linda left me some sort of crib for him." She went ahead of Michael into the living room. The little plaid canvas car bed was beside the couch. She picked it up by its metal handles.

When she turned back to Michael, he was already heading down the hall with Timmy.

"It's the second door on the left." She hurried after him, the car bed knocking against her calf and causing a major run in her last good pair of panty hose. Well, it was par for the course.

Michael entered the small, not entirely tidy room that served more as a home office than a spare bedroom for Maddie. She dropped the car bed on the floor and scurried about the room, picking up. "I'm afraid I wasn't expecting . . . company in here," Maddie said, flushing. She'd given up worrying about her cheeks reddening. It was out of her control.

Michael watched her with a glint of amusement in his eyes. And a feeling of empathy. She really was having a tough time of it.

"Relax, Maddie. I'm no Mr. Clean myself."

She was bending over, picking up a pile of papers on the floor near her cluttered rolltop desk. Michael couldn't help letting his gaze wander down her lovely rounded bottom to those slender, beautifully shaped calves and ankles. She rose quickly and whirled around to face him. He felt a little like a small boy who'd got his hand caught in the cookie jar.

But Maddie was oblivious to Michael Harrington's intimate survey. "Oh, believe me, the room is clean. It's spotless. Just messy. I have a regular cleaning service. It's just . . . I do a lot of work in here." She ran her fingers nervously through her honey-blond hair, caught for a moment between anxiety and distraction as she finally took in Michael's warm, enticing smile. She stared at him. He was at least six feet two, and her fingers just itched to smooth his thick, dark, ruffled hair. He had the darkest blue eyes she'd ever seen, eyes that Maddie thought capable of being hard and cold, but which also could, like now, look heart melting.

Michael was the one to pull his gaze away first. He only managed it with difficulty. He set Timmy down on the narrow spare bed, but not before he slipped a magazine under the baby's wet bottom. "We're going to need another diaper." He could see Maddie out of the corner of his eye. She didn't make a move. "A new diaper," he repeated.

Maddie pulled herself together. "Right. Diaper." She hurried out of the room, returning a moment later waving the diaper like a white flag in one hand, the tote filled with the rest of Timmy's belongings in the other. "I thought everyone used disposable diapers these days. Now those make some sense. Or at least it looks that way on TV commercials." She walked up to Michael.

He'd already removed Timmy's diaper but was wisely holding it on top of him to avoid the kind of accident Maddie had earlier learned about the hard way.

She laughed softly, handing Michael the clean diaper. "I really am impressed. You are a pro. Is that because you have some kids of your own?"

"Me? Are you kidding? That's a definite no. And I have absolutely no plans in that area." He said it so emphatically that Maddie laughed.

"I see we have that in common, anyway. But I'm baffled. How come you're so great with babies?" And then before Michael could respond, she said, "Oh, all those brothers and sisters of yours."

Michael was smiling again. "I see you've been doing some research."

She flushed, but then she smiled back. "Okay, I know that you're thirty-four, you didn't make it to where you are by resting on any university laurels, you have six brothers and sisters, and you grew up in the South End." She took a breath. "What do you know about me, Mr. Harrington?"

His smile was sensual, generous, all male. It warmed Maddie to her bones. "I know I'd prefer if you called me Michael."

There was an awkward silence. Both of them were disconcerted by how easily they could slip into a relationship that was more intimate and complex than either of them wanted under the circumstances. Maddie had a rule that matched Michael's about separating her professional and private life. She also prided herself on never becoming too emotionally attached to any man. Raised by a divorced and fiercely independent mother whose work as an artist's rep kept her on the road a great deal, Maddie had learned at a young age to look after her own needs. She had grown into a self-assured, self-contained young woman. So why, she wondered despairingly, was she feeling so utterly inept and nervous since setting eyes on the sublimely appealing Mr. Harrington?

The tension Maddie and Michael were feeling got to Timmy, as well. Or else he was getting impatient to have his needs attended to. He broke into a loud wail and began wildly flailing his arms and legs.

Michael was relieved to have something less complicated to focus on. He pulled his key ring from his trousers pocket and jangled it above Timmy's face. Timmy's crying stopped midtear.

"I'd better teach you how to change a diaper. Tomorrow you're on your own." He could feel the tightness in his throat, hear the hint of gruffness in his tone. All at once he was feeling claustrophobic, panicky. Maddie Sargent was setting off too many sparks. Sparks, nothing. High-voltage charges.

He concentrated on the diaper, folding it diagonally and slipping it under Timmy's bottom. "It's perfectly simple. Just bring up the bottom flap," he muttered, safety pins stuck in one corner of his mouth, "grab the two ends on one side, pull, pin . . . be sure to keep your fingers behind the cloth as you stick the pin in . . . you'll cry a lot less than Timmy here if you get stuck . . . then the other side and . . . voilà." He lifted the baby and held him in his outstretched arms for Maddie's inspection. "Got it?"

Maddie grinned. "I doubt it."

"You will with practice." He rummaged through the baby's tote for a terry sleeper. "You want to try putting this on?" He held up the tiny stretch suit.

Maddie laughed. "I don't think it would fit."

Michael laughed back, his gaze instinctively trailing down her shapely body, the simple shirtwaist dress in no way inhibiting his vivid imagination. And in no way curbing his rapidly escalating pulse rate.

Their eyes met and then they each glanced away. Michael busily attended to Timmy, adeptly dressing him in the stretch suit.

"There," he said, straightening and clearing his throat. "You can have the fun part of tucking him in."

Maddie looked doubtful, but she gingerly held out her arms as Michael handed Timmy over. When the baby didn't shriek, Maddie smiled cautiously. "Hey, will you look at this. Not bad. Okay, Scout," she murmured, unconsciously adopting Michael's nickname for the infant, "we've got this under control." Carefully she pivoted, her long, slender fingers encircling Timmy's little waist. She took a few steps toward the car bed and placed Timmy down in it as if he was a delicate bomb that would go off if there was one false move.

She hovered over the bed after she released him. "Which way? On his back like this, or on his stomach, his side?"

She sounded so earnest that Michael had to smile. "He looks pretty happy just the way he is."

Maddie straightened slowly. "Yes, he does, doesn't he? He is kind of cute." She laughed softly. "I remember my mother telling me that I always looked beautiful when I was asleep."

She turned to him as she spoke. Michael fixed her with his dark blue eyes. "You're beautiful when you're wide awake."

Maddie gave him a heart-crushing smile. But she didn't say anything.

Michael came over to her. She could feel her whole body change as he approached, a tightening of her muscles, an alteration in her breathing. But when he was within touching distance, he merely glanced down at

Timmy, winked at him and then headed for the door. "Come on. Let's get out of here while the going's good."

Michael's suddenly brusque tone threw Maddie, and it took a couple of moments for her to regain her equilibrium.

When she stepped out of the room after Michael, she saw that he was heading straight down the hall, picking up his suit jacket and overcoat from the entryway bench.

"Where are you going?" she asked, running up to him. "I thought we were going to talk . . . business."

Go on, Michael, say it now. Tell her there is no business to discuss. Go ahead. Really make her day.

"The snow's coming down hard. I'd better get going before I get stuck. Look, I'll be in touch with you. This isn't a good time, anyway. And . . ."

An eruption of wails from down the hall made him stop talking. But not walking. He really had to get out of here.

"It's Timmy." There was a note of panic in Maddie's voice.

"Just give him a couple of minutes. He'll settle down." Michael's hand was on the doorknob.

"But what if he doesn't?"

He had the door open. "Have faith."

Maddie smiled ruefully. "Oh, yeah, sure. Look where it's gotten me so far tonight."

He glanced back over his shoulder at her. For one optimistic moment Maddie thought he was going to change his mind about leaving. She even heard what she took to be a capitulative sigh.

Instead, it turned out to be a sign of resignation. "Look, I'm sorry, Maddie. I'll be in touch."

Maddie watched the door close. She stared at if for a long moment. Then she turned and looked down the hall toward where Timmy was exercising his vocal cords full force.

"How could you do this to me, Michael?" she muttered as she folded her arms across her chest, hugging herself tightly. It was bad enough that he was deserting a sinking ship. But having to figure out how to cope with Timmy was only half her problem.

Maddie was far more perplexed about how she was going to cope with the disturbingly unsettling emotions Mr. Harrington set off in her. She could not remember ever being thrown so completely off guard by any man. But Michael Harrington, she was forced to admit, wasn't just any man. He was tantalizingly good-looking, he had an incredible body, he was shrewd, self-assured, impossibly sexy. He was even good with babies.

In short, Michael Harrington had a lot going for him.

Including, lest she forget, the opportunity for her to put Sargent Skin-Care Products on the map.

3

WHEN MADDIE'S DOORBELL RANG a few minutes later, she dashed down the hall, a bright smile on her face.

I knew he wouldn't just walk out on me, she told herself as she unlocked the door. *The man's got a heart.*

She was still smiling as she opened the door, but her smile faded quickly as she saw the scowl on Michael's face.

"My car's been towed." He shook the snow out of his dark hair and entered the foyer, his scowl deepening. "I didn't pay any attention to the Snow Tow Zone sign when I pulled in to pick you up because I was only going to be gone for a minute."

Maddie felt a sinking sensation in the pit of her stomach. She couldn't have done more tonight to ruin her chances of winning over Harrington if she'd intentionally set her mind to it.

"You wouldn't happen to ever have had your car towed from here and know which lot the police take the cars to?" Michael absently smoothed back his damp hair from his forehead.

Maddie shook her head. "Sorry. I have a parking spot behind the building."

"I need to use your phone." Michael's voice remained gruff.

"Fine. I'll go check on Timmy. There's a phone...well, you know where the phone is," she said stiffly.

Of course, Timmy who had miraculously stopped crying just after the doorbell had rung, immediately began fussing again when Maddie peeked in on him.

"Terrific," Maddie grumbled, lifting Timmy up to check his diaper and praying fervently that her cousin Linda's plane hadn't been able to take off in the storm after all and that she'd show up at any moment to rescue her.

"See if there's a pacifier in that tote," Michael called out. "That should work."

A look of intense annoyance flashed across her features. "You think you know everything there is to know about babies," she muttered under her breath, her sense of pride rising to the fore. "Timmy is my responsibility. I'll manage on my own just fine." She gave Timmy a determined look, but the baby clearly doubted her word.

Two minutes later she'd pulled every item out of the tote. There was nothing that resembled a pacifier. She did find a rattle, and she shook it over Timmy's red face as he lay shrieking in the car bed.

She wasn't aware that Michael was standing in the doorway until he spoke. "The line's busy. I'll bet half of Boston is calling in to the police to ask where their cars have been towed to."

Maddie's failed ministrations with Timmy had caused her to break out in a sweat. She wiped her damp brow and shook her hair back out of her eyes.

"I'm sorry about the car. I'll pay for the towing." She looked away from Michael and stared down at Timmy. "Maybe he's hungry again."

Michael hesitated for a moment and then unbuttoned his coat and walked over to her. "Here, let me show you something," he said, taking the rattle from her hand.

Maddie watched, chagrined, as he turned it over and stuck the specially designed handle against Timmy's mouth. Like magic, the baby's lips parted, and he began contentedly sucking on it.

"Oh," Maddie said dejectedly. "I didn't realize . . ."

Michael was struck by the despairing look in her shimmering hazel eyes and felt himself involuntarily tremble a little.

"You'll get the hang of it." He reached out and gently touched her cheek.

Her lips parted in a tremulous smile. "I guess so. Anyway, Linda's due back on Monday."

Michael's hand slid from her cheek to her golden hair. "Then it won't be so bad." The timbre of his voice lowered. His free hand moved up to the other side of her face. He saw the despairing look disappear from her features, but not the vulnerability.

Maddie stood there motionless, lost in Michael's midnight-blue eyes. She could feel herself melting at his touch, but she had no desire to move away. "I usually have...everything under control. I...I'm just...so new at this. I mean...babies." Her voice was raspy. And none too steady.

Michael felt his heart pound. He smoothed back her hair from both sides of her face. "You're doing okay." He could smell her perfume, a spicy floral scent that made him feel light-headed.

"I am?"

Slowly he nodded. In spite of all his honorable intentions, he drew her closer. Her lovely mouth promised all kinds of pleasures.

Maddie tried to grasp any last remnant of common sense. But there wasn't any to be found. Besides, her body wasn't paying attention. It was letting Michael

Harrington fold her against his firm, strong frame. She tilted her head back.

He grazed her lips lightly, tentatively, unsure if he was testing something out about her or about himself.

That barest kiss made her feel woozy. She smiled crookedly up at him.

Something in Michael exploded. He found her lips again. This time there was nothing tentative in his kiss. It was reckless, dangerous, exciting.

The way she kissed him back openly revealed her desire. And her panic. She broke away breathlessly, feeling far more disheveled than she looked. She was about to give Michael a speech that was bound to sound ridiculously arch when, fortunately, she was saved by some shrieks from Timmy, who had misplaced his pacifier.

Maddie and Michael grabbed for the rattle at the same time. They both laughed nervously. Kissing Maddie had shaken Michael more than he'd realized. His hand was trembling. So, he saw, was hers.

He moved his hand away, letting Maddie put the pacifier handle back into Timmy's mouth. The baby shot them both a look that seemed to say, "Just don't forget I'm here, too." As if Maddie could!

"He sure is a handful," she said awkwardly. "Do you want to try again?"

Michael eyed her with speculative humor.

Maddie felt her cheeks blaze. "I mean . . . the phone. The precinct. Your car," she stammered in a flustered rush of confusion and embarrassment. Seeing Michael look equally shook-up made her relax a little, and she broke into a warm laugh. "What a night."

Michael grinned, relaxing a little, too. "Definitely a night to remember."

Her gaze locked with his. "Will you give me another chance?" And then, seeing his lips curve into a sensual smile, she hastily added, "I mean the chance to show you that I'm really a perfectly levelheaded businesswoman with just the right product for Barrett's?"

Michael felt a stab of guilt. His potent attraction to Maddie had let him forget, at least temporarily, about that all-too-disturbing matter. "About the account, Maddie..."

She raised her hand. "Wait, we can talk business later." She glanced down at Timmy. "Let's tiptoe out of here, and maybe he'll go to sleep."

Michael nodded. "Good idea."

They left the room, Maddie closing the door very carefully behind her, praying Timmy would not break into an outraged cry at their departure. Or at Michael's departure, anyway.

"So far, so good," she whispered.

Her stomach gurgled as she and Michael walked down the hall, and it dawned on her that she never had gotten around to eating dinner. And then she realized that Michael hadn't eaten either. "Why don't I make us something to eat while you try to track down your car?"

She turned into the kitchen, Michael following her. "I figured I'd just grab a bite back at my hotel."

"You don't stay with your family when you're in town?"

"No. I'm big on privacy. If you grew up in a house like mine, full of a half-dozen noisy, intrusive little kids who got into everything, you'd understand."

Maddie smiled wistfully. "I was an only child. It was just me and my mother. And she was gone a lot. She had a friend who lived next door who'd come over and look after me. And then I went off to boarding school starting when I was twelve." She shrugged. "Actually, there wasn't much privacy there. I have a thing about that, too."

Michael gave the wall phone near the stove a fleeting glance and then he slipped off his coat. "I think it's going to be awhile before I track down my car. Something to eat sounds good."

"Steak?"

"I'll help."

Maddie smiled. "Oh, no. I want to prove to you I can do something right. I happen to broil a mean steak. And I'll show you my expert skill with a salad, too. I even have a bottle of white wine in the fridge."

Michael removed his jacket, casually folding it over the back of a kitchen chair. "You have to let me do something. I'll set the table."

"Okay. Silverware's in the top drawer next to the sink. Plates are in the cupboard next to the fridge."

Michael glanced over at the kitchen table. "Shall we eat in here?"

Maddie shrugged. "What about the living room? We could make a fire and eat at the coffee table, if that's all right with you. I never have gotten around to picking up a real dining-room table. The truth is, I don't entertain very much. I'm so busy with work. I keep a punishing schedule. But don't get me wrong. I love it."

"Eating by the fireside sounds perfect," Michael said softly. For some reason, which he didn't want to analyze, he was pleased that Maddie was too busy to do a lot of entertaining. And it confirmed a feeling he'd had during their kiss that while Maddie had a very definite passionate streak, it seemed to come as more of a surprise to her than it had to him.

He gathered the plates, silverware and a couple of wineglasses and took them into the living room. After setting them on the coffee table, he took on the task of starting a fire. As he watched the newspaper and kindling take, he realized he hadn't tried the police station again. He glanced out the window at the snow, then at the phone and shrugged. No harm in waiting until after dinner.

"Can I do anything else?" he called out.

Maddie appeared at the kitchen doorway. "Yes," she whispered sotto voce. "You can keep your voice down. Do you realize this is the first five minutes of lovely silence I've had all evening?" They grinned at each other.

After a moment's hesitation Michael walked over to her. He leaned very close, sending Maddie's heart immediately into an erratic gallop. "Can I do anything else?" he repeated, this time in a murmur, his warm breath against her ear vibrating clear through her.

Her eyes widened. She smiled tremulously. From behind her came a sizzling sound. And as she stared into Michael's mesmerizing eyes, trying to decide whether, for once in her life, to throw caution to the winds, she picked up the scent of something burning for the second time that night. "Oh, no," she shrieked, whipping around. "The steaks."

Racing to the stove, she jerked open the door, a blast of smoke hitting her in the face. "They're burnt."

Michael was behind her, catching hold of her hand as she went to pull out the broiler tray. "Watch it. You need a glove. Here, let me." He reached over her for the pot holder at the side of the stove and lifted out the charred steaks. "Forget it, Maddie. They don't look so bad. I like my meat well-done." He set the broiler tray on top of the stove and put down the pot holder.

Maddie stared at him. She had a hard smile on her face, but Michael knew she was close to tears. "You'd better run while you can," she said, looking away. "Trust me, the way my luck's gone tonight, anything could happen. You're treading on dangerous turf."

Michael surveyed her face, taking in her heightened coloring, her honey hair, her soft, wonderfully shaped mouth. Maddie exuded a combination of strength and beguiling innocence that both intrigued and challenged him. "I'm beginning to realize just how boringly uneventful my life's been these past few years."

Maddie found herself wanting to know every uneventful detail. In fact, she wanted to know everything she could about Michael Harrington.

He kissed her and a small, welcoming sigh escaped her lips. His tongue slipped between her teeth, warm and sensual, exploring her palate, the backs of her teeth. The sensation ignited her, and she captured his tongue with her own. He pulled her hard against him, and she could feel the heat of his body.

When they pulled apart, they were both a little unsteady. Maddie's breathing was shallow and irregular, her heart racing.

He took hold of her trembling hand, bringing it to his lips. He kissed each finger, then ran his tongue lightly over the tips.

Maddie shivered, her eyelids fluttering closed. "I'm not good at this, Michael. In fact, next to looking after babies . . ." She opened her eyes. "I'm very conventional. And pragmatic. Mostly, I'm an all-work, no-play type of gal." She stared as Michael continued his erotic ministrations on her hand. "I could count all of my mad, passionate flings on that one hand you're so fascinated by, and we could skip a finger or two without any problem."

His free hand pressed against her back, his fingers lightly massaging each small bone along her spine.

"Oh, that feels good." The words escaped her lips just before she snapped back to reality. "I think we'd better slow things down a little." He pulled her closer. "We'd better talk," she said with a gasp.

He frowned. The idea clearly didn't please him. Even though he knew she was right.

She took a steadying breath. "Look, Michael, I seem to have given you every wrong impression about me possible tonight. I so desperately wanted this evening to go off without a hitch. Instead, I've slammed into every hitch in the book. I'm on awfully shaky ground right now, and we haven't started negotiations. How about a rain check?" Some of the intensity left her face, and she gave him a wry smile. "A snow check might be more appropriate. What about Monday night? Linda will have collected Timmy, and I promise not to be the least bit . . . ditsy." She stared down at her hand, still securely clasped in Michael's.

He followed her gaze, reluctant to release his hold on her, although he had to agree that her suggestion made good sense. He was hoping to figure out a way to graciously turn her down for the Barrett's deal and not come out of it smelling like a skunk. He told himself he had no reason to feel guilty about selecting another company for the Barrett's line. He'd been leaning toward L'Amour even before he made that trip to Palm Beach. It was a larger, more established operation, and Barrett's had done business with them before. He blamed this whole sorry mess on his executive secretary, Ruth Arnow. If she hadn't raved about some new Sargent products she was using, Michael would never have contacted Maddie at all. But Ruth had made him curious. So he'd asked Maddie to send him some information on the company, and he'd set up this business date. Another mistake, this one his. He should have waited until after he'd talked with Helen Dennis of L'Amour. Well, it was too late now to even hedge on this thing with Maddie. He and Helen Dennis had already shaken hands on the deal.

He let go of Maddie's hand. "Okay. Monday night. Shall we try Simeoni's again?" He'd have another go at it. Wine her, dine her. And break the news gently. Like she'd said before, he owed her.

She grinned. "Don't you think we'd be tempting fate?"

He had to laugh. "I'm willing to take the risk if you are." His laughter faded as he was once again swept up in a desire to pull the appealing Maddie Sargent back into his arms.

It was Timmy's sudden, shrill cry piercing the silence that brought Michael to his senses. "You want me to settle him back down?"

Maddie took a quick breath, a determined glint lighting her beautiful hazel eyes. "Nope. It's about time Timmy and I came to a little understanding. You go ahead and call the police about your car."

Maddie's determination faded as she approached Timmy's crib a minute later. He seemed to have reached new heights of unbridled indignation. And the sight of her was anything but soothing.

"What is it with you and me, Scout? Why do we always seem to rub each other the wrong way? You want your pacifier again?" Maddie dug it up from the side of the thin mattress. "Here you go." But Timmy was in no mood to be pacified. "Okay, okay. Wrong guess. How about your diaper? Are you wet again?" She lifted him out of the bed. A strong pungent odor assailing her nostrils left no doubt that Timmy most definitely needed another diaper change.

Maddie gritted her teeth. Holding him gingerly in her arms, she retrieved a clean diaper and some premoistened towelettes from the tote. "Okay, Timmy. This is going to be a little tricky, but if you stop wailing, I'll give it my best shot."

While Maddie was in the bedroom steeling her nerves for yet another first, Michael was in the living room breathing a sigh of relief after finally getting through to the local precinct.

"Yes, Officer, a 1988 Lamborghini, New York plates, parked outside of 1349 Commonwealth Avenue. Yes, I realize the snow-removal trucks have to clear the streets. I only meant to be parked there for a couple of minutes. Could you just tell me what the fine is and where I can pick up my car?"

Before he got his reply, Maddie heard a loud "Oh, no" coming from down the hall.

"Michael, come quick." Maddie's voice sounded panicky.

"Just a sec, officer. I'll be right back. Don't . . . don't hang up, please," he pleaded to the cop on the line, knowing, before he got the words out, that the line would be dead when he returned.

"This better be good," he muttered, dashing down the hall into the spare bedroom. Maddie looked anxious as she stood by the bed watching over Timmy, whose tears had changed to rather frantic hiccups.

"Oh, Michael, something's the matter with Timmy."

"For heaven's sake, Maddie, it's just hiccups. The kid's been crying so much."

Maddie shook her head impatiently. "No, Michael. I'm not talking about the hiccups. This is serious. He's got a terrible rash."

Michael gave her a questioning look and walked over. He bent down to survey the plump, naked baby, who, while still hiccuping, looked up at Michael with an angelic smile.

"Well . . . what do you think?" Maddie asked.

Michael straightened, rubbing his jaw thoughtfully. "Malaria, possibly. Tell me, has this little guy been crawling around any jungles recently?"

Maddie stared at him, dumbfounded. "Jungles? What are . . ." She gave him a fiery look. "Michael, this is no time for jokes. I'm responsible for this baby, like it or not. When Linda brought him here, he looked perfectly healthy. And now look at him. He's covered with welts. It almost looks like he's been beaten."

"Maddie." He put his hands lightly on her shoulders. "You really don't know a blessed thing about babies, do you?"

"Until Timmy arrived on my doorstep, I could count on one hand the number of times I've even held a baby in my arms."

Michael grinned. "And you could even skip a couple of fingers, right?"

Maddie frowned. "You are an incorrigible tease. Please be serious, Michael. Do you know what's wrong with Timmy?"

He smiled softly. "Timmy's going to be fine, Maddie. All he's got is a bad case of diaper rash. Babies get it all the time. You should have seen my brother, Alan, when he was a baby. He had it the worst. Very sensitive skin. But all the kids got diaper rash on occasion. It's not anything to worry about."

"It looks so awful, though. And it must be painful."

Michael winked at Timmy, who, rather than bemoaning his condition, seemed quite pleased with all the attention he was getting. Michael reached down and tickled the baby's tummy, and Timmy squealed in delight.

"You're wonderful with babies," Maddie said, a touch of envy creeping into her voice. "You know how to make them laugh, how to soothe them, even what ails them."

An enigmatic look darkened Michael's features. "I really didn't learn about babies by choice. I was fourteen when my dad died, and my mom took a job working nights. My sister Kelly was six months old. Alan was a little over a year and a half. Jessie was going on three and stubbornly uninterested in toilet training. Between me and my mom we had our hands full. And there were no helpful next-door neighbors. No money to hire babysitters. I was it. While my mom was off doing the night shift at a local bank, I was the chief diaper changer, bottle washer, nose wiper and arbiter of scrapes between the older ones. I had enough experience looking after kids to last a lifetime."

He stopped abruptly, giving Maddie an awkward smile. "Sorry, I didn't mean to give you some hard-luck story."

There was an underlying sadness in Michael's voice and she wanted to urge him to tell her more about himself, about what it was like for him growing up, bearing those weighty burdens of responsibility. It had been so different for her. Unlike Michael, who had so many ties holding him, she'd had none. Her only responsibility growing up was simply not to be a burden to her mother in any way or to hamper her mother's freedom. For a fleeting moment she found herself envying all of Michael's brothers and sisters for having had this remarkable older brother to look after them.

Michael misread the intensity in her eyes. "Don't get me wrong. There were plenty of fun times, too. They're really a great bunch of kids, all the hassles notwithstanding. I just don't plan to create any new hassles, if you know what I mean."

Maddie grinned. "I know exactly what you mean." Her expression turned serious as she looked down at Timmy. "No wonder my mother flew the nest as soon as she could. Just look at me. I've had a baby for one evening, and I'm a complete wreck. I've always seen myself as a woman who could do anything well if I set my mind to it. I've started my own business from scratch, I've put in more twenty-hour days at the plant than I can count on your hands, mine and Timmy's combined; I'm twenty-eight and I head a loyal staff of over thirty people...."

Her eyes misted slightly as her gaze continued to rest on Timmy. "Babies are so tiny, so vulnerable, so needy. I can't picture my mother coping with me when I was Timmy's age. My dad had already walked out on her by then. Felicity once told me he'd only stayed around to see her through the delivery and until she was on her feet again."

"That must have been tough."

"Felicity never really talked much about it."

Michael looked at her with compassion and tenderness. "Tough for you, too. Growing up without a father."

Maddie looked away. Her voice held an acid note. "I used to tell myself I couldn't very well miss someone I never knew. I never saw my father when I was a kid. He wrote me a few letters, but I never answered them. I hated him for deserting me. And later, when some of that hate gave way more to hurt, I thought it would be disloyal to Felicity to have any contact with him."

Absently she stroked the soft fuzz on Timmy's head. He smiled up at her, but her eyes, while fixed on him, were looking into the past. "Felicity isn't exactly the maternal type. I guess that's why I've called her by her first name rather than Mom since I was a teenager. She always seemed so awkward and uncomfortable when she had to play the role of mother. Not that I was all that great at playing the role of daughter. Neither of us ever really knew how to act with each other."

"Maybe you both were trying too hard," Michael said softly.

Maddie stared at him, a curious expression on her face. "I always thought it was because we didn't try hard enough. We didn't have much practice. We really didn't see each other all that much. Her work took her all over the world. Oh, I spent time with her during my school vacations and summers, but most of the time she was traveling, and I just got dragged along. She still travels a lot."

"What kind of work does she do?"

"She's a very successful artist's rep. Commercial art, mainly. And she acts as liaison between artists and big corporations. That kind of thing. It was exciting to go around with her once I was old enough not to be left in the care of one or another of mother's hired assistants. But still, we never really talked much. Not about anything personal. We still don't although we seem to have developed a reasonably comfortable relationship these days. She pops into town every few months, and we go on mad shopping sprees and eat ourselves sick in some of Boston's best restaurants. We really have a great time."

"Sounds like fun," Michael said, but there was something in his voice that led Maddie to think he didn't quite buy her enthusiasm. She didn't buy it completely herself. There were still moments when she wished she'd had the kind of mother who kissed her children's scratched knees, made them special treats when they had colds, read stories to them at night, sang lullabies. But she wasn't a little girl anymore. Surely she didn't need a mother's kisses for her hurts.

Michael surveyed Maddie's face. She seemed to him like a finely cut gemstone, faceted with myriad emotions. For a man who had always prided himself on never getting too involved with any woman, he could feel the intensity of Maddie's emotions with a depth of feeling that startled him.

Maddie felt unbidden stirrings in her body as their eyes held. Out of a growing discomfort, she turned away and glanced back down at Timmy, who seemed quite content for the moment as he paused in his survey of his tiny fingers to look up at her.

"Michael," Maddie whispered excitedly, clasping his wrist, her eyes still on Timmy. "Look, he's smiling. At me. He's smiling at me. This is a first." She glanced up at Michael. "Or is it gas? I remember my friend Sue Gardner told me that—"

"He's smiling at you, Maddie." Michael's hand moved over hers. "He's got good taste. Knows a beautiful woman when he sees one."

They smiled at each other. Maddie felt a warm glow suffuse her. Never before had she been so instantly charmed and thrilled by a man. Never before had she felt so overwhelmed.

Overwhelmed enough to be glad for once to have Timmy here to focus on. "So what do we do about diaper rash, Papa?" she asked, avoiding Michael's steadily intimate gaze.

Michael's thoughts were far removed from cures for diaper rash. He was caught up in wondering just what he was going to do about Maddie Sargent. He knew the wise thing to do, but he wasn't feeling very wise at the moment. He was feeling very aroused. He wanted to feel her warm, graceful body melt against him again; he wanted to experience the multitudinous pleasures of her lips, her tongue. . . .

Maddie's voice broke into his torrid thoughts. "Come on, Michael. You're the expert. What are we going to do about Timmy?"

Michael reluctantly pulled his gaze away from Maddie and concentrated on the baby, who was now busily examining his toes and having a grand time doing it.

Michael grinned. "Timmy looks perfectly content. I think he likes lying around naked." His grin broadened. "I like it myself . . . on certain occasions."

Maddie had a most maddening vision of Michael sprawled on her bed, his tanned, naked body against her lily-white sheets. Against her lily-white body.

"But I suppose we should put something on that rash before we diaper him again," Michael was saying.

It took a moment for his words to register. Michael broke into a grin, his fingers finding their way to her hair. "You weren't listening. What were you thinking about?"

"I was listening. You said. . .put something on his rash. What do we put on it?" she muttered, trying very hard to dispel the vivid picture of her stunning naked Adonis and the flash of arousal both the vision and his touch had ignited.

"Let's see if your cousin tossed some medicated lotion in that tote." He slid the palm of his hand sinuously down

Maddie's back before he reached over for the tote. They both dug their hands into the bag at the same time. Maddie withdrew hers first.

"No ointment," Michael said, smiling.

Maddie considered the problem for a moment. "I have an idea. Be right back."

A minute later she returned with a tube of her company's new hypo-allergenic treatment gel for dry skin. "We designed it for women, but there's nothing in the formula that could do him any harm."

Michael examined the tube. "Maybe it will help." He undid the cap. "I'll put the cream on his bottom. You can take care of the soiled diaper," he said, winking.

Maddie grimaced. "How about *I* do the anointing and you..." She caught his narrowed gaze. "No, I don't suppose that would be fair. I'm the volunteer mama, even if I didn't exactly volunteer." She eyed the folded diaper on the floor with dismay. "I don't know why Linda doesn't use those nifty disposable diapers. If it weren't snowing so hard, I'd traipse right down to the drugstore around the corner and buy some tonight. First thing tomorrow morning..."

"Go, Maddie. Take it to the bathroom and rinse it out."

"Right." Nose wrinkled, she lifted the soiled diaper from the floor and, holding it at arm's length, started for the door.

Michael laughed. "Ah, the joys of motherhood."

"I'll tell you one good thing about this whole experience," she said as she stopped to raise the window a crack. "It absolutely confirms my decision never to have one of my own."

"I agree wholeheartedly." There was a pause, and a slow smile settled across Michael's face. "They are awesome little creatures, though, aren't they?" He wriggled his fingers against Timmy's little hand, and the baby closed it tightly around two of Michael's fingers, his baby-blue eyes crinkling as he fixed on Michael and giggled with delight.

Before Maddie left the room, she looked back to see Michael doing another expert diapering job. Then he lifted Timmy in his arms and rubbed his back tenderly. Timmy cooed, settling his head in the spot where Michael's neck and shoulder met.

For a fleeting moment Maddie wondered what it would be like if Timmy were hers and Michael's. Then the pungent odor of his messy diaper cut sharply through the fantasy, and with a disgruntled sigh Maddie headed for the bathroom to cope with yet another first.

4

A HALF HOUR LATER Timmy was sound asleep, Maddie was dishing scrambled eggs out onto two plates in the kitchen and Michael was restoking the fire.

"Not quite steak," she said apologetically as she entered the living room.

"Eggs are fine." Michael was squatting in front of the fire. He pivoted to the coffee table and poured two glasses of wine. Maddie set the plates on the table and sat demurely on the couch.

Michael patted the carpet next to him. "Sit here. It's closer to the heat. You still look a little chilled."

But Maddie wasn't chilled at all. Quite the contrary—she felt uncomfortably warm. And nervous. Michael Harrington went very well with the decor. And he fit into her fantasies all too easily. Still, she rose and joined him on the floor, careful to leave a good two feet between them.

Michael smiled as he watched her settle beside him. "Better?"

Maddie popped a forkful of food into her mouth and nodded. She was on her second bite when she noticed Michael was watching her instead of eating.

"I thought you said eggs were fine. They're getting cold."

Michael smiled openly. He took a large bite. "Fantastic. Scrambled to perfection, Miss Sargent."

Maddie's brow creased. "Don't tease."

"It is a bad habit of mine," he admitted sheepishly. "I used to rib my siblings all the time. They always swore one day I'd get mine."

"And have you?" Maddie asked, raising one neat eyebrow.

Michael lifted his wineglass and took a sip. "I have a feeling my time is coming." His dark eyes sparkled as he gazed at her over the rim of the glass.

Maddie met his gaze for a moment, an amused smile on her face. But as they continued to stare at each other, her smile faded, and she grew increasingly uneasy. Michael Harrington, with his dark, mesmerizing eyes, had a way of looking at her that drummed at all her defenses. She chastised herself for allowing him to make her feel like a stricken schoolgirl.

She looked over at the fire, absently tucking her feet under her. The soft glow from the burning embers brought out red glints in her blond hair and made her flawless skin appear even more luminous, her hazel eyes almost amber.

Michael continued to watch her. Maddie was captivating. He wanted to tell her how lovely she looked, but instead, he drew his gaze away and focused on finishing his eggs. When he was done, he glanced over at Maddie's plate.

"Aren't you hungry?"

Maddie gave him a distracted look. "I was just thinking."

"About what?"

She looked at him wistfully. "Tell me about what it was like for you growing up, Michael. I . . . have this picture. . . ." She hesitated, laughing awkwardly. "Oh, you know. All those TV families where everyone squabbles, but deep down they're all very close. And there's always someone you can go to with your problems. Was it like that in your family, Michael?"

A soft smile tugged at the corners of his mouth. "I guess it was . . . sometimes. Especially before my father died. My dad and I were pretty close. He worked for the phone company as a linesman. He was a big, brawny guy with a gruff voice and a heart of gold. He was big on us toeing the line and keeping our noses clean."

"And did you keep your nose clean?" Maddie asked, thinking, even as she posed the question, that it wasn't very likely. Michael Harrington impressed her as having been a rough-and-tumble sort of boy.

He grinned. "I had my share of scrapes. And bloody noses. I'll never forget this one time when I was twelve, and I cut school and went down with a couple of buddies to an abandoned warehouse to smoke a cigar one of my pals had gotten his hands on. I was just getting my turn when who should arrive but my dad. Seems the school had called saying I hadn't shown up and wondering if I was sick. My dad took the call. He knew a bunch of us hung out at the warehouse."

"What did he do when he found you there?"

Michael laughed. "He tanned my hide when he got me home. A few well-placed smacks that hurt my pride more than my butt. The worst part was he made me and my three buddies finish that cigar before he dragged me home. I don't think I ever felt so sick to my stomach again in my life. It sure cured me of wanting to smoke after that. Which I'm sure was exactly what Dad had in mind."

Maddie smiled. "I think I would have liked your father."

Michael smiled back at her. "He was a good man." His smile faded as he looked into her eyes. "I still miss him. He was the kind of guy . . . you never thought would . . . die.

He was so full of life. He seemed so strong, so tough. I still remember the day it happened like it was yesterday. I was sitting in freshman Spanish class when a kid came in with a note for the teacher, Miss Alonzo. She read it very slowly and then she looked up. She had such a solemn expression on her face. I knew something bad had happened. I watched her gaze travel down my row of seats. I was the next to the last kid in that row. Tommy O'Shea sat behind me. And I remember thinking, poor Tommy. Something bad must have happened at the O'Shea home." Michael shook his head slowly.

"I'm sorry." Maddie looked at him with tears shining in her eyes.

Michael glanced over at her. He looked uncomfortable, as if he'd shared more about himself than he'd meant to. "Say, do you like basketball?"

Maddie blinked away her tears, thrown by the abrupt shift in the conversation.

"I have season seats. I used to go with my dad. I still manage to catch a few games, and my brothers use them a lot. They're big fans of the Celtics, too. I just thought . . . maybe you'd like to go to a game sometime."

Maddie wasn't sure if he was offering her the pass or asking her out on a date. She said vaguely, "That might be nice . . . sometime."

There was a prolonged silence as they both stared absently into the fire.

After a while Michael glanced at his watch. It was nearly midnight. "Damn. I'd better track down my car."

Maddie rose, gathering the plates. "Go ahead and try the police station again. I'll clear up."

Michael watched her for a moment. Then with a resigned shrug he got up and walked over to the phone.

It took several minutes to get through to the police station again. He was just writing down the information about where his car had been towed when Maddie looked in.

"Well?" she asked when he hung up.

He scowled. "It's over on Tremont near Government Center."

Maddie sighed. "If my car hadn't conked out on me, I'd drive you over. Which reminds me, I have to call my garage first thing in the morning and have them pick it up. Unless the police got to it first. I did manage to get the car over to the curb, but now that I think about it, I never even looked to see if I was leaving it in a no-parking zone. I was a little preoccupied with other problems at the time." Maddie grinned.

Michael, however, was not in a particularly cheerful mood as he stared morosely out the window. The snow was still coming down heavily. The idea of trekking across town didn't exactly thrill him. And he wasn't very optimistic about getting a cab, although he supposed he might as well try to ring up a few companies and see if he could get one to pick him up. "Any cab company you can recommend?"

Maddie shrugged and turned to stare out the window. "I think a dog-sled company might be a better bet."

Michael laughed dryly as he flipped open the yellow pages on the desk. Maddie returned to the kitchen to finish cleaning up.

She had just dried the last few dishes when Michael joined her.

"Any luck?" Maddie asked.

"Nope. Every cab company in town is tied up for hours." He picked up the forks and dried them.

They put the rest of the things away in silence.

"Nice and quiet in the place with Timmy finally settled down," Maddie said, slipping the last of the silverware into the drawer.

"Maybe that ointment of yours will do the trick, and Timmy will sleep through the night."

It was a perfect opening, and Maddie wasn't going to let it slip by. "We're working on a lot of new, exciting products now. I wrote you about that new skin toner we'd love to do for Barrett's. We've been doing a fragrance-free line, but for Barrett's I thought we'd come up with a product line with its own special scent. Something citrusy... kind of a cross between tangerine and lemon. It's unique, refreshing and different. And we've got a new moisturizing gel that you heat up and apply to puffy eyes and it miraculously chases away that fatigued look." She laughed and yawned at the same time. "I sound like a walking advertisement, don't I?"

Michael smiled uncomfortably as he fought back his own yawn. He'd conveniently put the whole business of the Barrett's contract, or more appropriately the lack thereof, on a back burner. But Maddie had reminded him that it was a pot with a strong potential to boil over and scald them both if he didn't attend to it. "Maddie... about the new line..."

Maddie yawned again and grinned. "I'm sorry. I guess I'm more exhausted than I thought. Look, Michael, I think the only sane solution to your problem is for you to stay the night. You can use the guest room," she quickly added. "I'll take Timmy into my room with me, and you can get a decent night's sleep. Tomorrow we can both cope with our errant cars. What do you say?"

Looking at her, smelling her floral fragrance, seeing the nervous set of those wonderful lips, Michael could feel the heat rise in his body. "I don't know, Maddie. I should go."

A whisper of a smile curved her lips. "If you're worried that you'll be bothered by Timmy waking you up...."

Michael laughed softly. Maddie'd hit on part of the problem, anyway. He was worried about being bothered, all right. But not because of a six-month-old baby. How did that old song go? "Bewitched, bothered and bewildered..."

Maddie's smile faded. She was certain he was laughing at her. "What is it? Are you afraid I'll panic again...like the diaper rash?"

He leaned forward a little, leveling his gaze on her eyes. "Aren't you afraid, Maddie?"

Maddie stared at him for several silent moments. "Oh." The word formed on her lips but was barely audible.

"Then again, there isn't a single listing for dog sleds in the yellow pages." He draped his arm lightly over Maddie's shoulder and steered her out of the kitchen. She came to an abrupt stop in the hallway, shifting her weight, uncomfortable with the sudden change in mood and with the seductive sensation of Michael's arm still around her shoulder. "I don't suppose we can just...start over again and forget what happened?"

"You don't mean only the comedy of errors, I presume."

She cast him a rueful smile. "You're not going to make this any easier for me, are you?"

He squeezed her shoulder and then released her, his expression tender. "Look, Maddie, I don't know about you, but I'm not likely to forget what it was like to kiss those warm, beautiful lips of yours. Nor am I likely to forget what it felt like to hold you in my arms. You're an incredibly appealing woman, Maddie. But I think we're both practical, sensible people. We just caught each other at a mutually vulnerable time back there. So . . . we lost our heads. Let's leave it at that."

Maddie straightened her shoulders. "I want you to know, Michael, that I don't lose my head very often." Her hand moved absently to her neck. "It's firmly secure now." Well, she was working at it, anyway, she thought, avoiding his gaze.

"Hey, so is mine." Without realizing it, Michael's hand moved to his neck, as well.

They looked at each other then, and both immediately dropped their hands to their sides.

Maddie grinned. "Now that we've cleared that up, I'll go move Timmy and you can get some sleep."

Michael caught hold of her wrist as she started to turn. "There's something else, Maddie. . . . Before I do stay the night, I feel I should make it clear that . . . well, that Sargent isn't the only company we're considering."

Maddie scowled. "Hold it, Michael. I don't want you to think for one instant that I'm trying to influence your decision because of my . . . my hospitality. It's a perfectly innocent invitation. And practical. I have a fantastic product line to offer Barrett's, Michael. Better than the competition. I don't need to use any other means to nab that contract. Staying here tonight in no way . . ."

Michael sighed. "Okay, okay. Let's just put business on hold for the night. What do you say?"

Her smile was tinged with relief. "Good idea." Her gaze drifted down to Michael's hand. His fingers were still wound around her narrow wrist.

He held on to her for another moment. Then he nodded faintly and released her.

"I'll carry Timmy into my bedroom, and then I'll come back and make up the guest bed."

"That's all right. Leave Timmy be. If you move him, you're likely to wake him up."

"But what if he . . ."

Michael grinned. "I'm a deep sleeper. If he squeals in the middle of the night, you can come get him and play mama."

"Play mama," she echoed, the notion making her grin. "Who would ever have thought . . ." Her voice trailed off as her eyes met Michael's. He was looking at her with a curious expression.

"And here I always thought that even devoted career gals secretly yearned to play that role . . . given half a chance."

Maddie laughed, but there was a hint of discomfort in the sound that she tried to ignore and that she hoped Michael would. "Well, this is one career gal who's never indulged that fantasy." She started down the hall to the linen closet. Michael followed her. "The only baby," she went on, pulling open the closet door and reaching for the bedding, "I'm interested in is my company. I've nursed it for a long time, and now I'm ready to see it take off and do me proud." She glanced at him as she piled a couple of pillows, a sheet and a blanket in his arms. "Sorry. We agreed not to talk business tonight. I just get carried away sometimes."

"But not too often," he couldn't resist saying, giving Maddie a broad grin.

She felt her cheeks redden, and she turned abruptly, fumbling with the towels, a precarious pile of them toppling to the floor. She muttered under her breath as she bent to pick them up. What was she doing? Gathering bedding for Michael Harrington had such an intimate feeling about it. Why hadn't she just let him go off into the night? He could have coped. He impressed her as a man who could cope with just about anything. He was certainly coping better with her foolishly offered invitation to spend the night than she was. She knew she wouldn't get a moment's sleep with Michael sleeping practically next door to her.

She stuffed the armful of towels haphazardly back on the shelf only to realize that she'd forgotten to keep one aside for Michael. She tugged one out, a couple of others falling to the floor. She gave them a firm kick into the bottom of the closet and slammed the door.

"There," she said tightly. "I'll just change your linens, and then we can both get some sleep."

"Maddie, relax." Michael shifted the pile of bedding under one large arm, his free hand lightly smoothing back her hair. "If you're having second thoughts, I could button up my overcoat, step out into that blinding blizzard and track down my car . . . or die trying, anyway."

She laughed. "Your siblings are right. You are an impossible tease."

"That's better." He plucked the towel from her hand and shoved it under his arm with the rest of his gear. "Okay. Now, I'll see to my bed, and you go get some sleep."

"You're sure you don't want me to help?"

"I'm a big boy, Maddie. Save the mothering for Timmy."

Maddie drew back with a little sigh. "Right. Sorry. I guess this mothering thing can be contagious if you're not careful. If I'm not careful." She walked backward a few steps as she spoke. "But I'm very careful. I'm not maternal by nature." She backed into the wall. "Well, I'll just go take my shower, and then you can have the bathroom." She hesitated for a moment and then started back down the hall. Stopping at the door to the bathroom, which separated the two bedrooms, she said, "If you need anything . . ."

Michael was at the guest-room door. "You don't happen to have an extra pair of men's pj's around."

"No . . . no, I don't."

He winked. "Glad to hear it."

With a half laugh she entered the bathroom. When she closed the door, she leaned against it and took a deep breath. She pressed her hand against her chest. Her heart was pounding. She could hear Michael shut his door. She could imagine him crossing the room, unbuttoning his shirt, moving to the very bed that had been hers before she'd splurged a few months ago on a new queen-size bed for her room.

She swallowed as she imagined hearing the thud of shoes. No, he'd taken his shoes off much earlier. They were in the front hall. *This is ridiculous*, she chastised herself.

She crossed her arms over her upper body, hugging herself, telling herself that she was overreacting, reminding herself that Michael Harrington was a potential business colleague. Okay, so he was a gorgeous, sexy, charming potential business colleague. Okay, so his kisses were inspired. Some men had talent. Michael was obviously one of them.

Who was she kidding? She couldn't remember ever feeling such intense desire for any man, let alone one she hardly knew. With a weary sigh Maddie pushed herself away from the door and turned on the shower taps.

Michael could hear the shower going as he made up the bed. He started to picture Maddie slipping out of her dress. Her undergarments would be silk and lace. White

against pale, smooth, flawless skin. He imagined away
the layer of silk and lace, envisioning her slender, shapely
body, her fine legs stepping into the shower. He imagined the spray falling over her rounded breasts, hardening the nipples. He could see her there in the steamy,
misty water, her skin glistening. He could feel the heat
rising.

Just then Timmy stirred, letting out two little coughs.
The sound shook Michael abruptly from his fantasy.
He was disconcerted to feel a thin bead of sweat across
his brow. And his heart was pounding. He hadn't had a
fantasy that vivid since he was a teen.

He heard the shower stop and forced himself not to
linger on a luscious, naked Maddie stepping out onto a
bath mat, reaching for a towel....

He shrugged off his shirt and undid his trousers. What
was the matter with him, anyway? She'd taken him by
surprise. That was it. There was a heat and passion in
Maddie that he hadn't expected. As well, there was a
softness and sweetness about her.

He knew what his problem was. Like Maddie, he'd
been so focused on his career lately that he hadn't given
enough time or attention to his more basic needs.

Not that he thought it wise to pursue those needs with
Maddie Sargent. Too much time with Maddie and he
knew damn well he'd have trouble putting her out of his
mind. And Michael Harrington was not a man who was
about to let a woman—any woman—interfere with his
concentration.

He folded his trousers over the desk chair, his car keys
falling to the floor. He picked them up and set them on
the desk, noticing, as he did, a rather provocative postcard lying there of a young, tanned, muscular fellow in
a manly pinup pose. Michael went to reach for it, shook

his head and peeled off his socks. He started to walk away from the desk, but then curiosity as to who would send Maddie a card like that got the better of him.

On the back was a brief note in flamboyant handwriting.

Darling,
Tell me this man isn't delicious. Greece is simply swarming with them....

Timmy started to cry. "Okay, okay. Settle down, Scout," Michael muttered, walking over to the baby and rubbing his back as he finished the note.

Next time you must tear yourself away from that sweatshop of yours and join me. Who knows? You might find the love of your life.

Viva l'amour,
Felicity

Michael grinned down at Timmy. "Mothers. They're all the same. They all want their children to find themselves a nice—"

There was a light rap on the door. Without thinking, Michael called out, "Yeah?"

Maddie took the "Yeah" for permission to open the door.

"Oh," she gasped as she stood at the open door, her eyes sweeping down Michael's body, naked save for a skimpy pair of navy-blue bikini shorts.

Michael gasped "Oh," at the same time, but he was so concerned about having been caught red-handed holding a piece of Maddie's mail that for a moment he didn't realize it wasn't the postcard she was staring at.

"Oh," he said again, feeling doubly exposed once the light dawned.

"I . . . I heard Timmy start to . . . fuss." Maddie made an effort to look past Michael, but her gaze kept straying. "I was just going to take him into my room."

Michael shoved the card behind his back. "He's okay. He's quieting down."

"I . . . I didn't mean to . . . walk in on you . . . like this."

Michael grinned. "It's okay."

"Well . . . I'll leave Timmy, then."

"Okay."

"Okay, then."

"Good night, Maddie."

She was halfway out the door when she stopped, her back to Michael. "Given the way the rest of my night has gone, I guess I should have expected to finish it with a flourish." She glanced over her shoulder at the near-naked man who was smiling broadly. A smile curved the corners of Maddie's mouth. "Well, good night, Michael."

She was standing there in a plaid flannel robe that did little to flatter her figure, but that fantasy vision of Maddie in the shower flashed through Michael's mind. For a moment a flood of heat overcame him, threatening to wipe out all sensible, rational thought. Only the soft, sweet vulnerability of her smile kept him from taking those few steps across the room and pulling her into his arms so that they could really finish the night with a flourish. Instead, he nodded, whispered, "Good night, Maddie. Sleep tight," and accepted the fact that visions of Maddie Sargent would drive him crazy for what little was left of the night.

5

LIKE A ROOSTER, Timmy was awake at dawn. It took a minute for Maddie to place the howling sound. Then, bleary-eyed, she began rummaging around for her slippers, gave up the search and struggled into her bathrobe as she hurried down the hall. She didn't care how sound a sleeper Michael Harrington was—Timmy's screeches could wake the dead.

Just as she knocked on the door, there was silence. And then Michael opened the door, a red-faced Timmy in his arms. Maddie's gaze dropped from Michael's bare chest, feeling a mixture of relief and disappointment as she saw that he had donned his trousers.

Timmy continued howling and began tugging on his ears.

"Is it his diaper rash?" she asked sleepily.

"Not a sign of redness there. That ointment of yours must be a regular wonder cream. He's probably just hungry."

"I'll feed him." She hesitated as she reached for Timmy.

Michael didn't release him. "I'm up, anyway." Their gazes met and held for a moment. A faint flush showed on Maddie's throat. She thought she must look a mess, her blond hair going every which way, no makeup, her eyes no doubt red from so little sleep. In contrast, she was struck by how good Michael looked, his dark hair tousled, a sleepy, sensual smile on his lips, his eyes...she had never seen eyes quite like Michael's. They had such extraordinary depth and feeling. His eyes were a mirror to his soul, she thought.

Michael's smile deepened. He wasn't the least bit put off by Maddie's wild honey-blond locks, her lack of makeup. He thought her skin luminous, almost velvety. It was the kind of skin that demanded caressing. He wanted to slide the palm of his hand along her warm, flushed cheek. He thought he knew where that touch would lead, and he wisely clutched Timmy with both hands.

"I'm sorry that you got so little sleep," Maddie said. There was a thickness to her voice, a quaver. "I should have taken Timmy into my room last night."

They walked together down the hall to the kitchen. "I always get up early," Michael said. "I like to put in a couple of hours of work before I get to the office. And...I don't know... since I was a kid, I always felt there was something kind of magical about dawn, the coming of a new day."

Maddie took the milk from the fridge and poured some of it into a saucepan to heat up. Then she poured some of the powdered baby cereal Linda had left for Timmy into a bowl. She smiled at Michael. "I wouldn't have guessed you to be a romantic."

"I don't give in to it very often," Michael said, a definite edge to his voice.

Maddie busied herself rinsing out a bottle. "I know what you mean," she muttered. "I guess when you're married to your work, like we are, there isn't much time for anything but blood, sweat and tears."

Michael laughed softly. "Old man Barrett has certainly extracted plenty of all three from me over the years. But it's been worth it. And the real payoff is yet to come."

Maddie lowered the heat under the saucepan and turned to Michael. "What's the payoff?"

"Jason Barrett is sixty-eight years old. He has no children. His only son died seven years ago. He plans to retire when he turns seventy. And he intends to pick one of his VPs to step into his shoes." Michael's dark blue eyes glinted with anticipation. "I'm the man to fill those shoes, Maddie. I've lived and breathed that company since I was fourteen. I know every nook and cranny of the business. And now, as VP in charge of creative marketing, I've expanded the scope of the operation beyond any of old man Barrett's dreams."

"Has he given you some indication that he intends to hand the reins over to you?" Maddie asked.

Michael's laugh was caustic. "You'd have to know Barrett to realize the folly of such a question. The old man gives nothing away. He's tightfisted, tough-minded, and he likes to keep his people guessing. It keeps us all on our toes. Barrett will play the waiting game with us right to the bitter end. But I'm as close to the old guy as they come. He took me under his wing way back when I was just starting out there. He thought I had the right combination of guts and ambition. He made me a department manager when I turned twenty. I was the youngest staff person put into a managerial position. And I'm the youngest vice president in the company now. Barrett has let me know all along that if I kept playing hardball, I could make it to the top. We've each kept our end of the deal so far. Barrett's a tough nut, but he's a straight shooter. I'm pretty fond of him. In a way, he's been a kind of father figure for me over the years."

Maddie set the bowl of cereal on the table, tilted her head and contemplated him. "I bet you'll make it to the top."

"Thanks for the vote of confidence. As long as I keep my wits about me and follow through on my strategic plans for the next two years, you just may be right."

Michael held Timmy in his lap while Maddie fed him the cereal. He couldn't help feeling touched by the warm, cozy scene—Maddie, in her flannel robe feeding the baby, the faint rays of sunlight filtering into the kitchen, the lingering scent of last night's fire, the muted sounds of snowplows outside.

"Shall I give him his bottle now?" Maddie asked after Timmy gobbled down the last spoonful of mush.

"In the living room. It's more comfortable."

Michael settled Timmy in Maddie's arms and sat down beside her on the velvety wine-colored couch as Timmy greedily drank his milk. Maddie smiled, then let her head lean back on the cushions. Michael put his arm around her to make her more comfortable. She stiffened for a moment and then let herself relax against him. She watched Timmy devour his milk, unaware of the warm smile of pleasure on her lips. She turned her head to look at Michael. His eyes were on her, intimate and absorbed. Neither of them said a word. Maddie's lids fluttered closed. A few moments later, when she looked up at Michael again, he was asleep. She smiled, glanced down at Timmy, whose head had lolled away from the empty bottle and come to rest against her breast. He sighed with pleasure, found his thumb and closed his eyes.

With a sigh of contentment unlike any she could ever remember feeling, Maddie closed her eyes again, snuggled more comfortably against Michael and fell asleep, too.

Sunlight was streaming into the room when she woke with a start, but as she began to rise, Michael's grip on her shoulder stopped her.

"Take it easy. Do you always wake up in a panic?"

Only, she thought silently, *when I've fallen asleep nestled in the arms of a bare-chested, near stranger.*

"Timmy... where's Timmy?" she said in alarm looking down to her empty lap, afraid that in her sleep she'd somehow dropped him.

"I put him back in his crib. He's fast asleep."

"Why... didn't you wake me?" She didn't, however, ask why he'd come back to take her in his arms again on the couch.

"You're a pretty sound sleeper."

"Please. Let me sit up."

He obliged and Maddie sat up ramrod straight. "How do real mothers do it?" She yawned, rubbing her scratchy eyes, trying her best to return her tangled hair to a modicum of order.

Michael smiled. "It isn't easy. I was always amazed at my mother's ability to juggle all us kids, look after the house and put in a full eight hours' work at the bank."

"She was lucky to have a son who was willing to help her so much. I bet a lot of kids in your position wouldn't have been so selfless."

"Whoa." Michael laughed, embarrassed. "I was no saint, Maddie. I did what I had to do, that's all. After my dad died, there was no one else my mother could turn to for help. Believe me, I wasn't thrilled about having to give up—" he paused, his voice lowering "—a lot of dreams."

Maddie turned to him. "What kinds of dreams?"

Michael shrugged. "Oh... kids' dreams, dumb dreams. I made out just fine without them. I can't complain." His expression tightened faintly. "Like I said before, I paid my dues with blood, sweat and tears. And, for the record, I'm certainly not the least bit selfless. I look after my own needs very well, Maddie. There's not a thing I'd change about my life at this moment." There was an unmistakable look of defiance in his dark blue eyes.

His words hung in the air. Maddie rose, adjusted her robe, tightening the tie belt. "Ditto." And then there was a whisper of a smile. "Except, of course, seeing a Sargent line at every Barrett's department store across the nation." She saw the hooded look in his eyes and was annoyed with herself for pushing at the wrong time. With Michael negotiations had to be according to his timing, his plans, his lead. That irritated her, but Maddie was a smart enough businesswoman to realize the goal was too important to get into a battle of wills with Michael. Besides, she wasn't at all confident that she'd come out the winner. She was not misled by Michael's tender, even vulnerable side. The other part of him, she knew, was tough as nails, shrewd, determined and, perhaps like his mentor, old man Barrett, intent on keeping hold of the reins until the very end.

With a sigh of resignation Maddie said, "I'll put on some coffee."

"I'll go shower, then, and finish getting dressed." Michael's hand moved down the ripple of muscles on his bare chest as he spoke. The gesture was innocently erotic, sending a flash of arousal through Maddie. It took a couple of moments to return her attention to his words. "I've got to settle on my car first thing. I've got this big family gathering this afternoon. I have to pick up a few things at my hotel for the nieces and nephews, change my clothes, that kind of thing. Listen, don't fuss with coffee on my account. I can get a cup on my way over to the garage."

His hand remained on his bronzed, muscular chest, and Maddie had a hard time pulling her gaze away. It took great effort to meet his eyes, and she was both certain and embarrassed that Michael could guess at her unbusinesslike thoughts. "I was going to make it for myself, anyway."

"Well, then, coffee would be great."

"Okay."

There was a tension in his features. He was being pushed by opposing forces—his head telling him to get out while the going was good, his heart telling him to stick around the captivating Maddie Sargent just awhile longer. Slowly he let out a breath. "I won't be more than a few minutes."

Ten minutes later, showered and dressed, his dark hair combed and still damp, Michael reappeared in the kitchen. Maddie poured two cups of coffee.

"Milk? Sugar?"

Michael shook his head. "Black is fine. I used your hairbrush. And the toothpaste." He smiled crookedly. "Not the brush, though." He held up his index finger.

Maddie smiled back, handing him a cup. She sat across from him at the table, noticing that, all dressed in his formal business suit, he looked suddenly cool and distant. The clothes were not the whole reason, though. It was more the expression on his face, the aloof look in his deep blue eyes. He was once more the suave, self-assured, consummate businessman. She felt a sudden longing to recreate that feeling of cozy intimacy between them, but she sensed that he had removed himself from those feelings as surely as if he had already removed himself physically from her presence. His mind, no doubt, was already on his plans for the day, his family... perhaps even his intimate faux pas of the night before.

They drank their coffee in silence. Maddie had made some buttered toast, but it remained untouched on the table.

When Michael finished the cup, he hesitated before taking a second one. Maddie poured herself another half cup.

They started talking at the same time.

Michael laughed. "You first."

"I just wanted to be sure our date... I mean our business meeting," she quickly amended, "is set for tomorrow night. I know you'll probably be busy with your family this whole week, what with your sister's wedding and all."

She was giving him a perfect opening to wheedle out of the dinner, but Michael merely said somberly, "Tomorrow night is fine."

"Good." She took a sip of coffee and then reached for a slice of toast.

Michael followed suit. He studied her thoughtfully as he chewed.

"What is it?"

"I was just thinking... that cream you used on Timmy... it really did the trick."

Maddie grinned. "You should see what it does for a woman's complexion. I hadn't actually thought of that cream for the Barrett's line since we've just come out with it, but we could work it in. What do you think?"

But Michael wasn't listening. Other thoughts were floating around in his head. "Huh?"

She decided the hell with playing by Michael's rules. Why not push a little? At least give him something to mull over. "I was saying we could add it to the Barrett's line."

Michael gulped down the rest of his coffee. "We'll . . . talk about it." He rose. "Well, I'd better get going. It isn't snowing now, and the plows have been out awhile. I shouldn't have too much trouble getting a cab."

Maddie glanced at the kitchen clock. It was nearly ten. "I'd better get dressed and go see about my car, as well. Maybe I can get it started again and not have to get it towed." Then she stopped, remembering Timmy. She couldn't leave him. But the idea of bundling him up, walking five blocks in the cold with him in her arms and then contending with her car was more than she could cope with.

Michael was able to read her mind. "I have an idea. Why don't I hike over to your car and see if I can get it started for you. If I can, I'll bring it back here."

Maddie wasn't about to refuse the offer. Instead, she thought of a perfect plan. "I'll get dressed in the meantime and get Timmy bundled up. If you can get the car back here, we can zip you over to pick up your car at the lot."

"No. That seems like more bother—"

"Hey, I owe you the ride. We both remember why your car got towed in the first place."

Michael laughed. "Okay. It's a deal."

Maddie's face lit up. "Only the first of many, I hope."

Michael continued to smile, but uncomfortably. "What kind of car and where did you leave it?"

Maddie gave him the particulars and the car keys, insisting he borrow one of her scarves, a dark blue one, for his trek.

"I'll phone you if I have a problem," he called out before stepping into the elevator.

When the telephone rang twenty minutes later, Maddie was sure it was Michael calling to tell her either he couldn't start the car or, worse still, couldn't find it.

It wasn't Michael. It was her assistant, Liz.

"Well, how did it go?" Liz asked without preamble.

"Don't ask."

"Bad?"

Maddie had to think about that.

"That bad?" Liz sucked in a breath.

"Well..."

"Maddie, come on. What happened?"

Maddie laughed. "Everything." She paused. "And nothing." Again she paused. "Well...not nothing. I mean...nothing in the way of a firm deal. But..."

"But! But what?"

Maddie picked a speck of lint off her caramel wool slacks. "He's a most unusual man."

"Unusual? As in strange?"

"No. No, not strange."

"Maddie, you don't sound like yourself. You're not making any sense. Maddie, what's wrong?"

Phone in hand, Maddie ambled over to the hall mirror. She gave herself a quick check, wondering if she should put on a bit more makeup. For a moment she forgot that Liz had asked her a question.

"Maddie?"

"Huh. Oh, nothing's wrong, Liz." She adjusted the cowl neck of her creamy-white sweater. "Well, unless we count having a baby to contend with."

Maddie thought she could almost hear Liz's mouth drop open. "A baby?" she gasped. "You're...pregnant?" Liz gulped down some air. "But, Maddie...I didn't even know you were dating anyone."

"What? Oh, Liz. Of course I'm not dating anyone. And I'm not pregnant. I've just . . . got this baby . . . temporarily. And let me tell you, Liz, having a baby is no picnic. If it weren't for Michael . . ."

"Michael, huh? My, my, we've moved to first names quickly."

Maddie couldn't help laughing. Or saying, "We've moved quicker than that."

"Maddie! You've got to be kidding."

Maddie scowled. "What does that mean? Do you think I'm . . . I'm a saint or something?"

"Maddie, come on. You've got . . . well, you've always talked a good line about never mixing business with pleasure."

"I wouldn't say mix." Maddie smoothed an invisible line at the corner of her mouth. "Let's say . . . stirred lightly."

"What does that mean?"

"It means . . ." Maddie stopped. She leaned closer to the mirror, scrutinizing herself. "What does it mean?" There was a worried tone in her voice. "I don't know what it means, Liz. I think . . . it means . . . I'm in trouble." She looked her reflection square in the eye. "Liz, I'm sorry to say I lost my perspective last night. I broke . . . well, I almost broke a cardinal rule. You're right. I mean I'm right. It's absolutely foolhardy to mix business with pleasure. At least Michael . . . Mr. Harrington . . ." How could she call him Mr. Harrington after she'd spent practically half the morning snuggled in his arms? "Michael feels the same way. He's as dedicated to his work as I am to mine. And he's not about to complicate matters by getting personally involved with one of his clients."

"Then he offered you a deal?"

"Not exactly. Not yet. But he's definitely taken with our products. I used one on Timmy and—"

"Who's Timmy?"

"The baby I'm minding," Maddie said impatiently. "Anyway, Michael was amazed at how well it worked on the baby's bottom."

"Hold on, Maddie. Aren't you working the wrong age group, to say nothing of the wrong end? We're not supposed to be selling Harrington on how well the Sargent formula works on a baby's tush."

Maddie laughed. "Well, Michael was impressed nonetheless. I'm sure he's thinking that if it does wonders for a baby, it can do as well, if not better, for the Barrett's customer." Maddie heard a car horn beep outside. "Listen, that may be Michael honking for me. I'd better go. I'll see you tomorrow morning."

Maddie hung up before Liz could ask any more questions. The truth was, she had very few answers. No. The truth was, she didn't even want to ponder the questions right now.

She ran to the living-room window, delighted to see Michael step out of her car and wave to her. She opened the window.

"Hurry on down. I'm in another tow-away zone."

Maddie waved back. "Be right there."

It actually took a good five minutes to bundle up a groggy Timmy and pack an extra diaper, an emergency bottle, his rattle and a change of clothes . . . just in case. By the time she was done, he was most unhappy and let her know it in no uncertain terms. And by the time she rode the elevator down to the lobby, a screaming Timmy in her arms, Maddie had a first-rate headache. Then she had her first piece of good luck. Who should be coming in the front door but Mrs. Johnston, home from her visit to her daughter.

Maddie must have looked desperate. Without a word her neighbor took Timmy in her arms. "Shhhh. Shhhh. What's the matter, sweetheart? What's the matter?"

"I don't think he likes the idea of taking a little trip. I've got a . . . friend outside I have to give a lift to."

"So what if I take the baby with me? I'll watch him while you're gone."

"Oh, Mrs. Johnston, that would be great. I won't be long."

"Long. Short. It's all right. I'll be happy to have the company. I don't have to be anywhere until later in the afternoon."

"Oh, I won't be more than forty-five minutes," Maddie assured her.

"Anytime."

"He's only with me until tomorrow," Maddie said, holding up her hand to reveal her crossed fingers.

Already Timmy seemed less upset. And as Mrs. Johnston unwrapped him from the blanket and unzipped the front of his snowsuit, he was practically smiling.

"Thanks, Mrs. Johnston," Maddie said, handing over the tote with Timmy's things, then running across the lobby when she heard her horn beeping again.

She smiled at Michael as she stepped into the car. "You got it started. I'm amazed."

"Where's Timmy?" Michael asked worriedly.

"Oh, my neighbor offered to watch him."

"What neighbor?"

Maddie gave Michael a teasing grin. "What's the matter, Dad? Worried about the little tyke not being well looked after?"

Michael frowned. "Very funny." As he gunned the engine and pulled away from the curb, the car fishtailed.

Maddie laughed softly. They rode in silence for a while, Maddie's thoughts drifting into fantasy. After a couple of minutes she commented, "It must be nice to have big family gatherings. Getting together for celebrations. Everyone excited, involved."

"Oh, they're involved, all right." Michael laughed dryly. "There's nothing the Harrington family loves more than a wedding. Let's see, today's the family gala. Tuesday night a bunch of the out-of-town relatives show up and we rent the back room at Steak and Stein for a pig out. Thursday night is the informal dinner with the groom's folks. And then there's the rehearsal dinner on Friday night." Michael grimaced. "And Jessie's only number four. That still leaves Kelly and Alan to go."

Maddie silently noted that he excluded himself from the single but eligible count. "How do you know they plan to get married?"

"Alan's already looking. He's made it clear he wants a wife by the time he finishes medical school. He'll find himself one, or my mother will. He's the only one of the kids that never minded Mom giving out his name and number to her friends' nieces or daughters." Michael laughed. "He's a mother's dream. And as for Kelly, the baby of the family, she's already making noises about getting hitched to this guy she's been seeing since her freshman year. The deal is, though, that she finishes college first."

"Who does she have that deal with?" Maddie asked.

"With me," Michael answered sharply. "Of all the kids, Kelly's got the most on the ball. She could really go places. I'm trying to get her to put marriage on extended hold and go to graduate school, get her MBA." He shook his head. "She's still such a baby sometimes. Spoiled rotten." He said the words with clear affection.

Maddie smiled wistfully, knowing it was Michael who'd spoiled her. She felt a flash of envy. How nice to be spoiled, protected and adored by a loving older brother. How nice to be a member of a large, close-knit family.

"What's the matter?" Michael asked, giving her a quick glance.

"I envy you, Michael," she said in a low voice.

Michael stole another look, nodded and maneuvered the car onto Storrow Drive. After a minute or two he said, "I have a confession to make."

"Oh?"

"I picked up a postcard that your mother sent to you. From Greece. The one with a Mr. Universe on the front. I guess curiosity got the best of me."

"She's funny," Maddie said thoughtfully, not the least bothered by Michael's admission. In a way, she liked the fact that he was curious about her. "Felicity is the most self-reliant, independent, contented career woman I've ever known. She loves gallivanting around the world, making her own decisions, being unencumbered. Oh, she's had men in her life, but they always came in a far second." She paused, wondering for a moment if that put her an even more distant third on her mother's list of priorities.

She shrugged. Those kinds of thoughts only depressed her. "I was raised to believe that being your own woman was the most important lesson to be learned. It was Felicity's idea that I start my own business. She backed me financially and emotionally. I don't mind telling you I was overwhelmed at first. She was terrific, though. One thing about Felicity. She knows how to run the show. And she taught me to be decisive, look confident even when I was shaking in my shoes, and believe in what I was doing. I don't think I could have pulled it off without her. It's the first time I remember her really coming through for me. But the crazy thing is, ever since the company really started taking off, just when you'd think she'd be cheering me on the most, she's been on my case to . . . well, you read the card."

"All mothers seem to have this natural instinct—"

"Not Felicity. She's not like other mothers, believe me. That's why I can't figure this new campaign she's on to get me fixed up. Sometimes I wonder if she's jealous of me. Maybe she figures a *good man* could drag me down a few notches."

Michael gave her a curious look. "Is that what having a man in your life would do?"

Maddie studied him as he returned his gaze to the road. "Don't you think so? I mean, aren't you just as worried that a personal involvement would drag you down?"

"Well, there's always that risk. But that's not what worries me. What worries me is having more demands made on me, having someone want things from me that I don't have the time or the inclination to give. I've got enough tugs on me, contending with my family. Barrett's been on me for the past year to move to the new offices here in Boston. No way. Having a nonstop diet of Harrington woes, dilemmas and hassles is just what I went to New York to escape."

"Maybe it's time to tell them you want out of the daddy role." She paused. "Or *do* you want out?"

Michael opened his mouth to protest but closed it without saying anything. A minute later they were exiting Storrow Drive. The car lot was just a block from the exit.

Maddie slid over to the driver's seat as Michael stepped out and closed the door. Rolling down the window, Maddie asked, "Shall I wait and make sure everything's okay?"

Michael pressed both hands on the window ledge and leaned down so he could see her face. "No, that's okay. Listen, Maddie, thanks." He tapped his fingers nervously against the metal.

"I should thank you. I mean, for helping me with Timmy. For not thinking I'm...ditsy. For giving me a second chance."

He stared at her in silence. "Well, I'll see you tomorrow night, then."

"I'll be there. Have a nice time today, Michael."

His brow furrowed. "Yeah. Thanks." He started to straighten up, then bent down again. "You, too." He smiled. "You should be okay. You've got down the bottle and the diapering bit. Yeah...you'll do great."

"Don't forget to pick up those gifts for your nieces and nephews."

He rapped lightly on the car door. "Right. I won't forget. Those kids would attack if their old uncle showed up empty-handed. They'll attack, anyway. Wrestling me to the floor is one of their favorite pastimes."

Maddie laughed softly. "Sounds like fun." She released the emergency brake. "Well, I'd better get back and see to Timmy."

Michael rapped lightly on the car again, gave her one more lingering look and then strode off at a vigorous pace.

An hour later Michael was driving toward his hotel. He kept thinking about Maddie, his fingers toying with her scarf. He knew they had dinner plans for the next night. He knew it was crazy to be thinking that tomorrow night seemed a long time away. Of course, he could stop by her place and give her back her scarf. But that was a pretty lame excuse, considering he could give it to her the next evening. He was just coming up to her exit on Storrow Drive. Okay, so it was a lame excuse. He couldn't come up with a better one.

Maddie was just finishing a very proficient diapering job on Timmy when she heard a horn beeping outside. She ignored the first few blasts and then peered out the window.

Michael stepped out of his red sports car and waved to her, the borrowed scarf in his hand.

She opened the window.

"I forgot to return this."

"You could have waited till tomorrow night. I have another one," Maddie called down.

He crossed his arms over his chest for warmth and stared up at her with a grim, perplexed look on his face, thinking that he must be crazy. He called out, "Hey, look, I've talked your ear off about the Harrington brood. You might as well come along and meet them."

Maddie felt like a schoolgirl who'd been asked to the prom just when she'd given up hope of ever getting there. "You want me to come to your family gathering?"

He looked up at Maddie, who was flushed, beautiful, excited. "Yeah, why not?"

"Well . . . okay . . . great." And then she remembered. "What about Timmy? I can't impose on Mrs. Johnston again."

"So bring him."

Maddie eyed him speculatively. But then, afraid he'd change his mind and not at all sure why she was making such a big deal of the invitation, she quickly shouted, "Okay, I'll be right down."

6

At two-fifteen Michael was edging into a tight spot in front of a newly painted, gray clapboard, two-story house on a street lined with houses of similar ilk and upkeep. Only the color of clapboard varied. A long driveway ran up the right side of each house. Most had one or two cars parked in them, safely off the recently plowed street. But Mrs. Harrington's driveway contained six cars, packed bumper-to-bumper or squeezed in sideways. The rear end of the last one, a large blue sedan, edged out into the street.

Michael managed after a couple of tries to fit into the small space. Maddie glanced over at him as he shut off the ignition. There were beads of sweat across his brow that she didn't think came from the exertion of maneuvering the powerful Lamborghini into the parking space.

She took a shaky breath, watching as Michael remained behind the wheel fidgeting with his keys.

Timmy enjoyed the demonstration, his baby-blue eyes watching the jingling keys with fascination. Maddie wasn't entranced.

"Look, Michael, if you're having second thoughts..." She paused for a moment hoping for a speedy contradiction, but none came. "I could tuck Timmy under my coat and trudge through a few ten-foot snowdrifts down to Dorchester Boulevard and try to hail a cab."

He slowly turned his head and stared at her, a faint smile on his lips that Maddie couldn't read.

"It's just . . . they're . . . likely to make a big fuss." He smiled a touch more broadly, but it was forced.

"A fuss about what?"

He merely sighed. "It's just the way they are. I don't . . . make it a habit of bringing women to family get-togethers. My family can get . . . carried away."

"Well, maybe when you bring a date. But this is different. I mean . . . I'm a . . . a business client. They can't make very much of that, can they?"

Michael stared at Timmy. "No, right."

Maddie tilted her head. "You think they'll mind about the baby?"

Michael raised his eyes to her face. "Mind? Last count there were five nieces and nephews, and you never know when another one is to arrive. Timmy will fit right into the baby set." He could feel himself relaxing a little. It was ridiculous to feel so uptight about bringing Maddie. She was right. How big a deal would they make over his inviting a business client along? Besides, he knew that Maddie would get a big kick out of an afternoon with the boisterous, affectionate Harrington clan. And when he thought about having to tell her tomorrow evening that he'd chosen to give L'Amour the contract, he hoped Maddie would be less likely to feel there was anything personal in his decision.

He smiled at her. "All set?"

She laughed nervously. "You're sure they won't feel I'm intruding?" She stared down at her camel wool slacks. "Maybe I should have changed. Put on a skirt . . ."

He leaned over, touched her cheek lightly and then squeezed Timmy's pudgy thigh, which was thickly wrapped in a blanket and his snowsuit. "You both look terrific, Maddie. It will be fine, you'll see."

Maddie swallowed, managing a not-too-convincing smile.

Michael got out of the car, sloshed through the wet snow near the curb around to Maddie's side, opened her door, reached in for Timmy, then helped her out with his free hand.

He watched Maddie's slender legs clad in trim slacks climb the steps to the front door as he followed with Timmy in his arms. She had beautiful legs, he thought. The kind of legs that look good in slacks. But he'd enjoyed his view of them more last night when she'd worn a dress. Great legs. He found himself wishing he'd stayed with her at her place today, given in to his erotic impulses, let his fingers glide languorously up and down those luscious legs....

Maddie stopped abruptly on the second last step. Michael, lost in illicit thoughts, nearly bumped into her.

"What's wrong?"

His voice sounded shaky. Maddie mistakenly read it as nerves.

"The packages. You left the packages for your family in the trunk." She could see little white puffs of breath drifting out of her mouth and Michael's as they spoke.

"Oh, right." He started to turn.

"Wait, let me take Timmy."

Michael nodded absently, passing the baby to her. He was still working at tempering those unbidden fantasies that kept springing up on him at the most unexpected times.

He hurried back to the car, and Maddie waited on the step. She watched Michael retrieve the packages. Then she glanced up at the front door to Mrs. Harrington's house. Her knees felt a little weak. She eyed Timmy, who seemed to be enjoying the crisp, cold air. And then she frowned.

Michael was coming back up the steps. "What is it?"

"I didn't bring any diapers for Timmy. I completely forgot."

"Don't worry. Lee or Debby will have some. They both still have kids in diapers."

"I feel so stupid."

She looked downcast. And Michael knew she was nervous. He smiled at her. "It's okay. You're new at the game."

Maddie shifted Timmy in her arms and smiled back.

For an instant Michael felt a funny sensation. *This is what it would be like to have a wife and kid and be arriving at Mom's for a family bash.* His own family. He caught Maddie's eye. Her smile deepened. He felt an urge to take her hand. But she was clutching Timmy, and he had an armload of packages. And then he heard the faint sounds of voices from inside the house. The warm feeling ended with a jolt. There was a thickening in his throat, a knot in his stomach. No, it was all wrong. A wife? A kid? Him? Michael Harrington? No. No way. What's wrong with this picture, folks? His eyes swept over Maddie and Timmy. Everything.

He scrambled up the rest of the steps and walked across the porch to the front door, leaving Maddie to follow his lead. His large frame just about blocked her and Timmy from view as he swung open the door. "Hey, the prodigal son has returned. Where is everybody?"

From down the hall came happy shouts from little children.

"It's Uncle Mike."

"Nana, Uncle Mike's finally here."

Two little boys and a little girl came bounding down the hall, trying to race each other to the prize—their uncle.

A young woman stepped out of the same room the children had come from and into the hall. "Hey, slow down, kids, don't bowl him over. Give the poor guy a chance...."

Michael bent, and Maddie and Timmy came into view for the first time. It was like someone had pulled out the plug of a movie projector in the middle of an action scene. Everyone froze, the children nearly tumbling over each other as they came to a grinding stop. The woman at the end of the hall didn't finish her sentence, didn't move.

The silence only lasted for a few moments, but to Maddie and Michael it felt endless.

"Cindy?" came a woman's voice from inside the room. "What's the matter?" As she finished her sentence, she, too, appeared in the hallway. She was an older woman with graying hair, tall and stocky, and she wore a blue-checked apron over her navy dress.

"Michael?" She smiled broadly. "You brought company?" She turned her head so she could speak to the people remaining in the room she'd just exited. "He brought company."

Maddie had to edge forward a few more steps just so she could close the door behind her. In tense silence she watched the mass arrival into the hall.

"You son of a gun, Mike." A younger, bulkier version of Michael was the first to stride down the hall. "I don't believe it."

"Believe what, Alan?" Michael retorted gruffly.

The rest of the family—Maddie saw them as a troop of hundreds, but there were less than twenty of them—

seemed to come to life at the sound of Michael's voice. They hurried down the hall en masse, and Maddie had a terrifying vision of being trampled by a horde of excited Harringtons.

Mrs. Harrington got to Maddie first. "Michael... yours?" Her voice quavered with anticipation as her large hand hovered over Timmy.

"Mine?" Michael's voice cracked. "Of course he's not mine." He stared at the wide-eyed sea of faces. "Whoa there, folks. Settle down. You're way off track here."

Maddie wasn't sure if Mrs. Harrington simply didn't hear Michael or if she chose not to believe him. Tears brimmed in her eyes. "A beautiful baby." And then she gazed at Maddie. "Beautiful."

"Mom!" Michael said, the word filled with exasperation. Then he roughly grabbed Maddie's jacket sleeve, edging her forward. "This is Maddie Sargent. A business client. We...were discussing...business this morning and...well, I just thought she might enjoy—" he stopped, scowled and then went on "—coming over."

"What a lovely baby," an attractive dark-haired woman with the Harrington blue eyes exclaimed. "Hi," she said, extending a hand to Maddie, "I'm Lee."

Maddie smiled nervously. "Hi."

"What's his name?" This came from a woman who introduced herself as Debby.

"Timmy."

"Here, let me take him," Mrs. Harrington said. "Set the packages down. You get your coats off. It's hot in here. You don't want to start sweating and come down with a cold."

They were both sweating plenty. Maddie gave Michael a wan smile, but he was busy eyeing his brother, Alan.

"Get that look off your face. I told you, Miss Sargent is a business client. Let's try to show her that the Harringtons are not a bunch of babbling idiots."

"Michael, such talk! Whoever she is, she's welcome. And so is her beautiful little boy."

Maddie cleared her throat. "Oh, he's not mine."

"No." Michael nodded. "I mean...she's right. He's not hers."

There were several awkward chuckles from the clan. "Hey, you two, relax." This from another blue-eyed Harrington woman. Then she addressed the brood. "You know Michael hates getting grilled, folks. Now let's just leave them be to get their bearings. Don't we have to get the table set, Mom?"

Mrs. Harrington was still beaming down at the baby in her arms. Then she smiled ruefully at her son. "Not yours. Not hers. What did you do? Pluck this sweet baby from a tree?"

Michael started to open his mouth to explain but merely sighed. "Please, Mom, just take Timmy inside and get his snowsuit off. He probably could use a diaper change...if there are any extras around." He looked awkwardly over at Maddie. "She...forgot to bring them."

Maddie grimaced. "I'm sorry."

"In a grandmother's house there are always plenty of diapers." She reached out and squeezed Maddie's arm. "It's like that with the first. You forget. One time when Michael was a baby, I went to visit a friend and I actually went back home without him. I forgot I had a baby altogether. Was I embarrassed when my friend Francine called. You remember that story, Michael?"

"You've told it enough times, Mom," he said dryly.

Maddie was unzipping her jacket. "Really, Mrs. Harrington . . ." She started to explain about Timmy.

But the woman was already cooing to Timmy and heading down the hall, the rest of the Harrington clan following suit.

When they were all out of sight, Maddie gripped Michael's wrist. "They don't believe us," she said in amazement. "They think—"

"I know what they think," Michael snapped. "They think I knocked you up. They think Timmy is mine." He shook his head slowly. "They probably think they've got another wedding to plan." His eyes narrowed ominously. "This was a bad idea."

"I could make a run for it," Maddie muttered.

"What about our *son*? Grandma down there is already performing the Harrington initiation rites on him."

"Michael, you have to explain."

"Just let it ride. I know them too well. Explain and they'll just think I'm getting cold feet. Then they'll be rushing to your side, telling you how to snare me. Oh, they're pros. And they've been waiting with bated breath for something like this."

"Didn't you realize they'd get the wrong impression when you asked me to come?"

Michael stared morosely at her. "I wasn't thinking about them when I invited you."

Maddie smiled a little. "Oh." She took off her coat and bent to unzip her boots. She had to grip Michael's arm so she wouldn't lose her balance. When she touched him, she could feel him stiffen. "Come on, Michael. I'm sure we can convince them they're barking up the wrong tree."

Michael slipped off his coat and hung it on a hook. "We're not going to be too convincing if we stay huddled together here." He cocked his head. "Ready, Ms Sargent?"

Maddie lifted her chin, threw her shoulders back and smiled. "Ready, Mr. Harrington, sir."

GOSSIP, LAUGHTER and devouring heaping plates of baked ham, mashed potatoes and other assorted nourishments were the order of the day. After the first tentative half hour or so Maddie found herself having a gay old time. Michael's family was warm, effusive, funny and welcomed her into the fold as if she was a new member.

Which was exactly why Michael Harrington sat in silence most of the afternoon, wondering what had ever possessed him to bring Maddie here today. Every time one of the family cooed at Timmy or smiled adoringly at Maddie, his brows shot up, a disgruntled expression darkening his features. The worst part, though, was enduring the ribbing, the little digs, the less-than-subtle innuendos about Maddie and Timmy that all of his siblings delighted in imparting. What had Michael told Maddie last night? That one of these days he'd get his comeuppance? He was getting it in spades.

Maddie was enjoying herself too much to pay Michael much mind. She was charmed by the Harrington brood, charmed by this wonderful feeling of warmth and acceptance she had never really known. She loved the attention, the feeling of belonging . . . even if it was only temporary.

When she took Timmy into one of the bedrooms to change his diaper after dinner, Cindy, the eldest sister, joined her.

"He's being impossible, isn't he?" Cindy commented idly while Maddie undressed Timmy and fumbled with the tabs of the disposable diaper Michael's sister handed her.

Maddie smiled uncomfortably. "I guess I shouldn't have come."

"Nonsense. Anyway, it's about time Michael faced the music. We all knew he'd get to this point one of these days."

"Cindy, really, you've got it wrong. We're not an item. And I swear, Timmy really is my cousin's baby. The last thing in the world I need is a baby." Timmy giggled and Cindy smiled indulgently at Maddie, neither of them apparently convinced.

"I catch the way he keeps looking at you," Cindy said.

"Timmy?"

Cindy laughed. "Michael. I'd say that brother of mine is smitten."

"Smitten? That's crazy. If looks could kill . . ."

Cindy laughed. "When Mike can't play it cool with a woman, believe me, she's gotten to him." Cindy's blue eyes shone. "You've got to him, I should say." Only her limited acquaintance with Maddie prevented Cindy from adding that Maddie looked equally beguiled. She settled for saying, "He's a great catch, that brother of mine."

"Cindy, I only met Michael last night. And then, through an unbelievable comedy of errors, we . . . well, we got to know each other . . . a little better than we might have. But I really am his client. His potential client, that is. Michael's a frustratingly cagey businessman. But I guess that's why he's so successful."

"Oh, he's frustrated, all right." Cindy grinned.

"You haven't bought a thing I've said." Maddie had gone from struggling with the diaper tabs to struggling with fitting the diaper on Timmy.

"Here, let me. With two kids, I'm a pro." Cindy nudged Maddie and took over, quickly diapering the baby and redressing him with equal speed. "There, nothing to it." Cindy picked up Timmy and smiled at Maddie. "It doesn't matter when the two of you met. Or whether you're a client of Mike's or not. I'm closer to Mike than anyone else in the family. I know the person behind that successful, cagey businessman facade. I know he's taken with you, just as I know about his tenderness, his commitment to all of us, his sacrifices and what they cost him. I even know about the resentment he tries to hide, the anger he feels at all his missed opportunities. Mike's biggest problem is that he holds everything in. He needs to let go, have some fun, stop taking life so seriously."

Maddie sat down on the edge of the bed. "He mentioned having had some dreams when he was growing up."

Cindy gave Maddie a sly look. "My, my. That reticent brother of mine is certainly loquacious around a woman he only just met."

"Aha," Maddie said smugly, "but he refused to tell me what those dreams were about."

Cindy laughed. "Give him time. I'm sure he'll get around to telling you. Mike was a star athlete in high school. Especially basketball."

"He used to go to all the Celtics games with your dad."

Cindy eyed Maddie shrewdly. "He told you that, too."

"Big deal. We both talked a little about our families, about growing up."

"Oh, but it *is* a big deal. Michael never talks about himself very much. And just about never about dad. We all took my father's death very hard, but no one as hard as Michael. He seemed to change overnight. He became so driven, so intense. He got it into his head that, single-handedly, he was going to make it up to all of us. For a long time he blamed himself. None of us could convince him that he wasn't somehow responsible for Dad's heart attack."

Maddie's brows knit. "Why would Michael feel responsible? He was at school when it happened." Maddie saw the look of surprise on Cindy's face. "I guess," Maddie admitted, "we both talked more openly to each other than we usually do. But why, Cindy? Why would Michael blame himself?"

Cindy regarded Maddie. "Mike and Dad were fooling around the day before, playing street hockey. When they came in for supper, Dad was real sweaty, and Mom bawled him out for carrying on like he was still a kid." Cindy looked down. "They fooled around like that all the time. Basketball was the main activity, though. Dad's biggest dream—and Mike's—was that Mike would play pro basketball one day. Mike was that good."

Timmy started to fuss a little, and Maddie took him from Cindy, absently rubbing his back, soothing him.

"Did Mike tell you that he won a full basketball scholarship to Northwestern?" Cindy asked.

Maddie shook her head.

"Then, until this moment, I'm probably the only person Mike told. He burned the letter the day it arrived, before Mom got home from work."

"But why?"

"Mom would have insisted he go, of course. And he didn't tell the rest of the kids because he never wanted them to feel that he was making any big sacrifices or anything by turning it down. That's the way Mike is."

"Michael told me that there wasn't money for college. But if he got a full scholarship . . ."

"Mom was barely making ends meet on her salary. Mike never considered going to college. He felt he had to get a full-time job and help support the family. He's still carrying more than his share. Who do you think paid off the mortgage on this house for Mom? Who do you think is paying for Alan's education? Kelly's? Who do you think is footing most of the bill for Jessie's wedding?"

So much for Michael Harrington's claim to not being selfless, Maddie thought. She said softly, "He's a special person."

Cindy observed her in silence for a few moments. "I know how terrified Mike is of taking on any more responsibilities. From the time he was seventeen or so, he swore he'd never get married, never get too involved with any woman. He's kept to that promise. Up to now. But there's not a single person in this house—except maybe you and Michael—who doesn't know something hot is brewing. You couldn't find a better man than Michael Harrington, Maddie. He was meant to be a husband and father."

"Look, don't get me wrong. I think Michael is a terrific man. But all I want from him is a contract to feature a line of my skin-care products at Barrett's. I'm not looking for a husband. And, believe me, I'm not looking for a father for my children. I mean . . . I don't want any children. I don't want a husband. I don't want to get . . . involved." She shook her head vigorously. "Michael and me? Never. We're both workaholics. I own a business that takes complete commitment, total dedication. There's no room in my life for anything else. Certainly not a husband or a baby."

Cindy merely smiled, and Maddie returned the gesture with a look of frustration. Maddie stood up, hoisting Timmy in her arms. "We'd better get back. Your mom said something about dessert."

Cindy nodded, taking silent note of the tender little smile that lit Maddie's face as Timmy giggled. She also noted the way Maddie tempered that smile when she realized she'd been caught in the act of being maternal.

There was coffee, several pies, cookies and a large chocolate cake on the dining-room table. When Maddie entered with Timmy, Kelly grabbed the baby and shooed all the children into the front parlor, where she was taking charge of handing out milk and cookies and giving the rest of the adults some peace and quiet.

Michael, leaning against the wall in a corner, had never been as quiet or felt as awkward at a family gathering. He turned down a slice of cake and mumbled something about having to get Maddie home. When he tried to turn down a slice of cake for Maddie, his mother wouldn't hear of it. And Maddie was no help. "Why, this looks delicious, Mrs. Harrington," she said brightly.

"Please, call me Anne."

Maddie smiled, catching the flicker of frustration in Michael's face. She knew Michael was eager to leave, but she refused to let him spoil the day for her. She wasn't likely to have another like this. From the uneasy look on Michael's face, she doubted she'd get a second invitation to a family gathering.

As it turned out she was wrong. But the second invitation didn't come from Michael. Before they left, Jessica insisted Maddie come to her wedding on Saturday. The rest of the family enthusiastically seconded the invitation.

IN THE CAR DRIVING BACK, Maddie glanced over at Michael. "It would have been rude to turn them down."

"Did I say anything?" he muttered.

Maddie shrugged. "I thought it was very nice of Jessica to invite me to her wedding."

Michael didn't respond, his eyes fixed straight ahead, his expression distant.

They drove the rest of the way in silence. That is, Maddie and Michael were silent. Timmy, on the other hand, counterpointed the silence with intermittent shrieks, cries and general irritation. Maybe the tension was getting to him, Maddie thought, almost envying the baby for being able to deal with his feelings so expressively. Then again, maybe it wasn't the tension in the car. Maybe it was his diaper rash. So much for her wonder cream.

Michael pulled up in front of her apartment building and glanced at her. "Can you manage?"

Maddie observed him. For all Cindy had said about her brother being tender, caring, sensitive, and for all that Maddie believed her, right now she thought Michael Harrington insufferable. "I can manage just fine, thank you."

He started to reach across her to open the door, but Maddie's hand got to the handle first. She swung her legs out.

"Wait." Michael's tone was low.

She turned expectantly, hoping for an apology. Or at least a kind word.

"Your scarf." He still had it stuffed in his coat pocket.

"That's all right," Maddie said, her hands full with Timmy. "Bring it tomorrow night."

"About tomorrow night . . ."

Maddie's eyes widened. She couldn't believe he'd renege on the meeting simply because of his family's positive reaction to her.

"The thing is—" Michael rubbed his neck "—there are still a few issues regarding the contract that haven't been resolved back at the home office. This...meeting...may be premature. Why don't I ... call you? I might even fly back to New York for a couple of days. Look into a few things."

"I see," Maddie said tightly.

Michael watched her struggle for a moment to hold on to a squirming Timmy and get out of the low-slung sports car.

"Here ... wait. Let me help you," Michael said, throwing open his car door.

"I don't need any help," Maddie muttered, managing with a lack of grace to extricate herself.

Michael got out, anyway, catching up to her and grabbing her arm as she trudged with Timmy, her purse and the tote bag over a pile of snow along the curb.

"Maddie ..."

They were at the front of the building. "Yes."

He stared at Timmy, and then at her, an unreadable expression on his face. "I will get back to you." Without another word he turned and headed for his car.

"PLEASE, MADDIE. I know it's asking a lot, but Donald and I need a little more time. I promise I'll be back no later than Friday."

"But, Linda, I've got to go to work. I have a business to run. I expected you back this morning. What do I do about Timmy?" Maddie picked up her dress from the bed and tried to slip it on over her head and hang on to the receiver at the same time.

"Couldn't you get someone in to watch him during the day? I'll pay for it."

"It's not the money," Maddie muttered, staring down at Timmy, who was rolling over onto his belly on the carpet, precariously close to the bookcase. "Oh, hold on a minute," Maddie said, dropping the receiver, grabbing Timmy and setting him on her queen-size bed. She gave him her key ring for amusement. Timmy giggled with delight, and Maddie grinned down at him, almost forgetting the discarded receiver for a moment.

"Sorry, Linda." She sat down at the edge of the bed. Timmy's little hands alternated between jingling the key ring and stroking the back of Maddie's silk dress. She winked at him over her shoulder. "Oh, well, I guess I could call a baby-sitting agency," she said slowly. "Timmy does seem to be settling down. But you might have told me he has colic."

"Colic? Timmy doesn't have colic. He's almost never cranky. Well, I guess he was pretty fussy when I handed him over to you, but I'm sure he was just picking up on my upset."

"He cried half of last night. It sounded like colic to me. Oh, and he had a bad case of diaper rash. I used one of my new skin-care products on him, though, and the rash cleared up completely."

"Timmy does get diaper rash sometimes. But to tell you the truth, I've tried half a dozen baby ointments on him, and none of them seems to work very well. You'll have to give me a tube of your stuff when I get back."

"Sure. Anyway, he's fine now," Maddie said, a touch of pride in her voice. She reached around and tickled Timmy's tummy, much to the baby's delight. "I'd better go. I'll have to phone my assistant and have her hold the fort till I track down a sitter for Timmy. Actually, I have a neighbor who might do it. If not," she said more to herself than to Linda, her eyes fixed on the smiling baby, "I guess I could stick around the house and catch up on some paperwork."

"Thanks, Maddie. You're an angel."

Timmy caught hold of Maddie's finger, gripping it in his little fist. "Well," Maddie told Timmy as she hung up, "I guess it won't be so bad playing mamma for a few more days."

Twenty minutes later Maddie wished she could eat her words. Timmy was crying hysterically and Maddie realized the brooch that had been pinned on her dress before she put it on was missing.

She hadn't put the two together until she checked Timmy's diaper to make sure the rash hadn't returned and the safety pins on his diaper were secure. Then she thoroughly searched her floor and her bed for the missing brooch.

"No, no," she muttered, her search growing more frantic as Timmy's shrieks grew louder. "Oh, God, no." There was a pleading note in her voice as she picked up Timmy, trying to comfort him. She grabbed his half-finished bottle from the bureau. "Come on, Timmy. You're just thirsty, right?"

Wrong. Timmy winced in pain as Maddie stuck the nipple in his mouth.

In her panic her first thought was to call Michael. Michael was an expert with kids. Michael would know what to do. *If only he's still at his hotel . . .* she thought, frantically looking up the number and then dialing, a flood of relief filling her when he answered the phone on the fourth ring. He'd barely gotten out a hello when she exploded into a rush of words.

"Maddie, calm down. I can't make out a word of what you're saying." Michael set his suitcase down. He'd been halfway out the door when he heard the phone ring. "What's Timmy screaming about?"

"That's what I'm trying to tell you," she shouted into the receiver, on the verge of hysterics herself as she paced with the sobbing baby. "He swallowed my brooch, Michael."

Michael frowned. "Your brooch?"

"It was on my dress. But it's not there now. I had the dress on the bed this morning before I started getting dressed. And then Linda called. And I was trying to get my dress on. She isn't coming back. I mean . . . not for a while. Oh, what am I going to do about Timmy, Michael? I'd better call the police. An ambulance."

"Maddie, calm down. Did you see Timmy swallow your brooch?" He spoke in a low, soothing voice, his chief concern at the moment to keep Maddie from panicking.

"No, no. But he did, Michael. I'm sure of it. I'd better take him to the hospital. Should I do something for him first?"

"The first thing to do is take a few deep breaths. If he's shrieking like that, we know he isn't choking. Just hold still. I'll drive over and get you. I was just on my way out the door, anyway, and my car's waiting out front. We'll take him down to Children's Hospital and let them check Timmy out. But look, Timmy could have indigestion or a cold or be cutting a tooth. It's not too likely he swallowed a piece of jewelry."

"Oh, Michael . . ."

"Keep looking for that brooch of yours, though. I'll be there as fast as I can."

Maddie was down in the lobby with a still-shrieking Timmy in her arms when Michael pulled up less than ten minutes later. She rushed out to the car, brushing away her own tears as she got in with the baby.

Michael put a comforting arm around her, gave Timmy a quick pat on the back and pulled out fast. Fifteen minutes later he was sitting with his arm around Maddie again, this time in the emergency waiting room, while a doctor examined Timmy.

"It's all my fault." Maddie used Michael's hanky to wipe her eyes.

"First of all, we don't know that Timmy swallowed the brooch. Second, it isn't as if you set Timmy down with the dress and let him merrily play with the brooch. You said you already had your dress on when you put Timmy on the bed."

"But I should have spotted that the brooch was missing. I should have been more careful. I should have watched him more closely. I should have—"

Michael cut her off sharply. "Maddie, there's no point in 'should haves.' Believe me, I know."

Maddie watched him take her hand. She met his dark blue eyes, so tender now, and she remembered her conversation yesterday with Michael's sister Cindy. Michael had blamed himself for his father's heart attack. No doubt he had been tormented by many "should haves," too. She squeezed his hand, her pale lips curving in a weak semblance of a smile.

"Thank you, Michael. You keep coming through for me. You probably think I'm a complete incompetent at this point."

He stroked her tear-stained cheek and then hugged her closer to him. "I don't think anything of the sort. I think you're terrific, Maddie Sargent."

A passing nurse caught Michael's remark and smiled, a clear touch of envy in her expression. Maddie smiled, too, her smile tinged with a mix of pleasure and trepidation. Michael pressed Maddie's head to his shoulder, his lips finding their way to her honey-hued hair.

They were still sitting like that when the doctor entered with Timmy, now subdued, in his arms.

Both Maddie and Michael sprang up from the plastic seats in unison, concerned expressions etched on their faces.

The doctor smiled. "We X-rayed him. No sign of a silver brooch. I have a feeling that it'll turn up one of these days."

"But . . . he was crying so hard. And he looked like he was in real pain," Maddie said.

The doctor handed Timmy over to her. "Oh, he *is* in pain. But not from swallowing a brooch."

Maddie stared at him, a look of terror on her face, waiting to hear the doctor's diagnosis.

Michael gripped Maddie's hand. "What's wrong with Timmy?"

The doctor's smile broadened. "Relax, it's just an ear infection. It's very likely been coming on for a few days now. Has he been fussier than usual, tugging at his ears? That's often the case."

Maddie nodded and smiled sheepishly. "I thought it might be an allergy . . . to me."

The doctor grinned. "You two must be new parents, right?"

Michael and Maddie shared a private look but said nothing.

"I'll write out a prescription for an antibiotic in liquid form. You'll have to give it to Timmy three times a day. He should be feeling much better in twenty-four hours. I already administered the first dose here, and he's starting to settle down. The only problem you may have is that some babies do get diarrhea from the medication and then develop a bad case of diaper rash."

Michael grinned at Maddie. "Don't worry, doc. We've got that end covered."

On the way home Michael stopped to fill the prescription while Maddie called Liz at the office to tell her she'd be working at home for the day. And yes, in answer to Liz's question, she was still playing mama.

When they arrived at Maddie's place, she started to thank Michael and say goodbye. He'd told her during the drive back that he'd planned to catch a plane to New York that morning, and she assumed he'd want to get out to the airport as soon as possible. While she was disappointed that it meant definitely canceling their business dinner for that night, she was feeling too grateful to Michael for helping her with Timmy to balk. He'd promised to return in a few days, and she was still hopeful they'd firm up a deal.

Michael, however, insisted on coming up with her, and Maddie didn't argue. Timmy was fussing again, pulling on his ears, and she felt that familiar helpless feeling. Michael took him from her, and when they entered her apartment, Michael slipped off his coat, undid Timmy's snowsuit and paced the hall with him in an attempt to settle the child down. Maddie was about to put on some coffee for them when the doorbell rang.

She opened the door to find Mrs. Johnston standing there. "I stopped by to see if you wanted me to watch Timmy until his mother comes back today. I thought you'd probably need to get to work. He's no trouble." Mrs. Johnston peered down the hall at Michael and the sobbing baby. "Oh, dear, still fussy."

"He's got an ear infection. I just got back from the doctor. He said Timmy needs to take an antibiotic, so I'm going to stay home with him." She chose not to mention her initial panic about Timmy swallowing the missing brooch.

"Oh, don't worry. It's not serious. My daughter's baby just got over an ear infection." Mrs. Johnston smiled at Maddie, who was still pale and frazzled. "You look like you could use a break. I'm home all day with nothing to do. Why don't you let me take Timmy for a few hours and give you a chance to relax?"

"I have to give him his medicine three times a day," Maddie said. "And he's so fussy. I'd feel better keeping an eye on him. But thanks, anyway. I appreciate the offer."

While she was thanking Mrs. Johnston, Michael went to change Timmy and tuck him in for a nap.

"There are only a couple of diapers left," he said when he walked into the kitchen. Maddie was trying to swallow a couple of aspirin.

"I'd better pick up some disposable ones," Maddie said after she got them down. "In a moment of sheer madness I promised my cousin Linda on the phone that I'd keep Timmy until Friday. She's still trying to patch things up with her husband."

Michael leaned against the wall. "You'll do fine with Timmy." He smiled. "Silence. Beautiful silence. I bet he's already out like a light."

Maddie grinned. "Let's hope he sleeps for a few hours."

Michael pushed away from the wall. "Did you eat anything this morning?"

Maddie shook her head.

"Go sit down in the living room, and I'll put on some coffee and toast."

He reached out to steady her as she stumbled a little. Without a word she leaned against him. She could feel the muscles in his shoulder flex, smell the freshness of his heathery tweed jacket. He pressed his hand against her back, and a feeling of expectation suddenly arced through her body.

Michael tilted her head back as he studied her face. His hands slid over her silk dress.

They swayed, as though dancing to a very slow tune. Michael's gaze didn't waver from her face. *Why don't I pull her closer still? Let the warmth of her body heat me? Move my hands along the glorious lines of her face, her body? Slip that silky dress off her?*

The same feeling of urgency that filled Michael filled Maddie—and frightened her. *This is crazy, reckless,* she told herself. *And I'm never reckless. I'm not good at this sort of thing. I don't know what I'm doing. I'm jumping into the deep end of the pool, and I can't swim to save myself.*

She felt his mouth against her throat. She closed her eyes, giving herself over to a feeling that was both sharp and sweet.

He drew her back a little. She opened her eyes, but her vision was a touch hazy.

"Maddie, we shouldn't start something we don't intend to finish."

His voice brought her vision back into focus. Her hand pressed against the front of his shirt, to steady her and give her a bit more distance.

She chose to misinterpret his meaning. "I almost forgot. You have a plane to catch. You shouldn't be bothering with my breakfast. You've done enough. And I'm really not very hungry." Maddie tried to keep her voice light, but all the while her mind was shouting, *Liar. You're starving. Ravenous. Why not let Michael feed your hunger? Why not let him draw you back into his arms, stroke you, caress you, make love to you?*

She shook her head as though she'd been speaking her thoughts. *Where can it go? Nowhere. I don't want it to go anywhere. Neither does Michael.*

She moved another step away, swaying slightly. "You'd better go. Your plane—"

"They run every hour."

"Michael." She paused and took a breath. "My life's been turned upside down this weekend. I keep trying to right it, but it . . . it isn't easy." She stared at him. "You don't make it easy."

"Neither do you," he admitted.

They stared at each other at length. Finally Maddie said, "I don't think we should start anything, Michael. I have my work. It's all I can handle. It's enough."

"Is it?"

"Isn't it for you?"

"Sometimes I'm lonely," he admitted. "Just like you."

Maddie didn't argue the point. "We're all lonely sometimes."

"The question is, what do we do about it?"

Maddie knew very well that Michael's question was not rhetorical. He was grinning boyishly, and Maddie felt a charge of excitement course through her. *Get a hold of yourself,* she chastised. *You can't just fall into the man's arms because you're suddenly feeling lonely and a little desperate for something you've managed to chase away all these years.*

"Maddie, you're a vibrant, beautiful, intelligent woman, and . . ."

"Stop it, Michael." Maddie laughed uncomfortably. "You'll give me a swelled head." She took a step back as she spoke.

Michael moved right along with her. "And I want you."

Of course she knew that's what he was thinking, but the actual words still caused a shock wave to run through her.

"It wouldn't work." Her voice was low and scared. "It would be complicated."

"Not if we don't make it complicated. Let's make it easy, Maddie. We're both strong, intelligent, realistic."

"It's dangerous," Maddie whispered. "I want to do business with you."

"You also want to make love with me."

"No." She hesitated. "Yes."

He smiled. "Good."

She backed up a few more steps. "No, it isn't good. I mean, even if it weren't complicated—and don't you dare say it's easy again—we have a professional relationship to uphold. Besides, I'm just not very good at this, Michael. I haven't been with a man for a long time. And when I was..." This was so damn hard. "I'm just not able to really let go. I get self-conscious. What I'm trying to tell you, Michael, is that I'd be a disappointment." She turned away. "This is so embarrassing. Don't you see, I've done nothing but make a fool of myself since we met. I've got to quit while I still have any vestige of dignity left."

He turned her around to face him, leaned toward her, brushing his lips against hers. "I wouldn't take you for a quitter, Maddie."

She looked at him with imploring eyes. "Michael, please...don't."

His mouth found hers again, this time covering her lips, his tongue forcing them open, probing the moist warmth of her mouth.

She felt a reckless, womanly excitement stir inside her even as she felt stricken by the excitement, like a young girl. Her knees were weak. Her heart was pounding.

"Look," he said softly, releasing her, "I've been fighting it, too. Arguments spinning in my head. My own fears, concerns, trepidations. But I want you, Maddie. And I'm tired of fighting it. And—" he drew her closer "—while I admit I do critical evaluations of my workers, I don't do the same with lovers. I want to make love to you, Maddie, not score your performance." A slow smile curved his lips. "You don't have to perform for me, Maddie. I'll take care of everything. Trust me."

If she had the right kind of style, she would have simply thrown her arms around Michael, wrapped her body around him, laughed throatily and said, "I'm all yours, darling." But she'd never had that kind of style.

He lowered his head to kiss her again, but she put out her hand. "No. Wait." She was desperately trying to rally.

But Michael had no intention of making that easy. Even as she held him at arm's length, his fingers found their way under the cuffs of her dress, sending shivers up her bare arms. She could feel her control slipping several notches. She could feel herself surrendering to his subtle ministrations, but her response was anything but subtle. She felt dizzy, hot, and her pulse raced.

Again he lowered his head, and this time, before she could protest again, his mouth was on hers, blocking her words, kissing her roughly, his tongue circling the inside of her mouth.

Maddie dissolved. She was melting, gripping the sleeves of Michael's jacket for support. His hands cupped her elbows as if he knew she'd sink to the floor in a heap if he didn't prop her up.

She leaned against him, and he slid one arm firmly around her narrow waist, his other hand stroking her face with just the tips of his fingers. Very softly.

Maddie expelled her breath in a little sigh. *Yes*, she thought, *just let it happen. Don't think. Don't do anything. Just let him take charge.*

But those very thoughts spinning in her mind distracted her, made her tense, self-conscious. Michael was holding her so tightly to him that he was crushing her arm against his chest. As she tried to wriggle it free, Michael laughed softly, relaxing his grip, guiding her arm around his neck. But she felt gangly, her whole body awkward as he swooped her up in his arms.

"Michael . . ."

He kissed her as he carried her down the hall. Before he made it to the door of her bedroom, he collided with the wall. He laughed, but Maddie was too nervous to laugh.

"Relax," he said softly as he let her down gently on the bed. "Just follow my lead."

Even though her tension mounted, her arousal, just at the prospect of making love with this strong, sensual, tender man, seemed to be melting her body from the inside out.

He stood over her. He slipped off his jacket, wiggled his tie loose and lifted it over his head. He started to unbutton his shirt.

"No," he whispered, "open your eyes. Watch me, Maddie."

Her lids fluttered open. She lifted her gaze to his face. Her eyes glistened. Michael could see a hint of emerald in them. Slowly she lowered her eyes and watched him undo each button of his shirt and then take it off. She had seen his bare chest the night before, but it had been different then.

Michael took greedy delight in watching her rising desire play across her face. He leaned on the bed with one knee and slid his hands down over the soft silk of her dress. Maddie moved slightly so that he could lift it off over her head. Yes, just as he had imagined, he thought with a smile as he unclasped her white, lacy bra to reveal the pale, silken skin of her breasts. He placed his hands lightly over them. The skin there was warm, her nipples already hard, and so sensitive that she uttered a little cry when he ran his thumbs over them.

She was sitting up and he gripped her shoulders, lowering her onto her back, her head on the pillow. Then he stood again, his hand moving to his belt. This time he didn't have to demand that Maddie watch him. Wide-eyed, entranced, she caught every movement he made.

He unfastened the buckle of his belt, undid the button of his trousers, lowered the zipper, his gaze moving from her face to her glorious breasts as her chest rose and fell with each quickened breath.

And then, just as he was about to slide his trousers over his hips, his expression turned thoughtful. "Maddie. You are on the pill, aren't you?"

She sat up like a shot. "No. I thought . . . You said . . . You told me you were going to take care of everything." She grabbed a pillow and pressed it against her chest. "We can't, Michael. I never bothered about the pill. I told you it's been a long time since . . ." She stared up at him. "I knew it. I warned you it wouldn't work. I feel so dumb. So . . . naked."

Michael smiled as he sat down next to her and yanked the pillow from her. "You look great naked."

"I don't suppose you have . . . anything on you."

His smile broadened. "You caught me unprepared. I feel so dumb. So . . . naked." Teasingly he thrust the pillow against his chest.

She pried the pillow away with little resistance from Michael. "You look good naked."

They both laughed, dispelling the discomfort they'd both been feeling.

"I think I noticed a drugstore just down the street," Michael said.

Maddie nodded.

He kissed her shoulder, then let his hands skim the sides of her breasts. She shivered.

"Don't move. Stay just as you are. I'll be right back." He zipped up his pants and pulled on his shirt as he spoke. He was just opening the door when she called his name.

He turned, fully expecting her to back out, desperately afraid the moment was going to slip away.

"What's the matter?" He hadn't meant to sound gruff, but he could hear the edge of disappointment in his voice.

There she was, sitting in the middle of the queen-size bed, her face flushed, her honey hair tousled, her beautiful bare breasts so delicious, so inviting. And there was so much more of her yet to discover, savor. *You can't do this to me, Maddie*, he thought. I'm in too deep.

"I just thought—" she smiled a smile that was at once innocent and erotic."—that since you're going to the drugstore anyway, you might pick up some Pampers."

He expelled a breath, only then realizing he'd been holding it in. "Pampers. Sure."

"Thanks."

He nodded. Then he started to turn, coming to a frozen stop as he heard his name again.

"You thought I was going to say we better forget it, didn't you?" Her smile was arresting.

"I'm so glad you didn't" was all he answered.

"Me, too," she whispered, falling back on the pillow in a most wanton pose. "Take my key. It's on the front-hall table."

He made it to the drugstore and back in record time, not able to dispel his worry that in his absence Maddie might have had some second thoughts. Michael, on the other hand, in his excitement, was way beyond any but the most heated thoughts.

Out of breath, he shrugged off his topcoat, and took off his shoes, and dropping the king-size box of Pampers on the hall table, hurried down the hall to Maddie's bedroom.

"I was a little chilly, so I crawled under the covers. Did you get everything?"

"I wasn't sure what size."

Maddie grinned. "Condoms?"

Michael laughed. "Pampers." He undid his shirt more rapidly than last time. "I bought a dozen."

"Pampers?"

He grinned. "Condoms."

"I think you're overestimating . . ."

"I just don't want to be caught unprepared again." He quickly shed the rest of his clothes and crawled under the covers beside her.

"Brrrr. You're cold."

"Only on the surface. Inside I'm burning, Maddie."

"Oh, Michael," she whispered, laying her head against his naked chest.

"I'm sorry for the delay, Maddie."

"It makes it all more real."

He looked down at her. "Is that bad or good?"

"Good," she murmured. "Very good. I want this to feel real, Michael. My few past flings were always couched in so much fantasy. Unfulfilled fantasy, if I'm going to be honest."

Maddie's admission struck a chord in Michael. Like Maddie, sex had never been real for him, either, but in a different way. It had always been more a physical than a deeply emotional experience. Not that he'd had all that many involvements himself. And not that he didn't care about the women he'd been involved with, so much as he'd been able to keep those feelings from spilling over into his real world. Maddie made that separation impossible. By all rights that realization should have scared the hell out of him. But at the moment he was far too caught up in the thrill of Maddie's unfolding passionate nature to ponder fears.

8

MADDIE HAD IMAGINED what Michael's body would feel like next to hers, but no fantasy came close to the sheer physical thrill of the real thing. The sensation of being pressed against his powerful, finely muscled frame while his cold fingers drifted down her neck, across her shoulders, caressing the sides of her breasts, drove Maddie wild. Her self-consciousness and worry about feeling awkward vanished. She felt wonderful.

It was only as Michael slowly edged the blanket down to her waist that Maddie's nervousness returned.

His eyes were fixed on her face, but as he started to lower his gaze, Maddie gripped the blanket and tried to tug it up over her again.

"Don't, Michael." Her voice sounded feeble.

"I want to look at you, Maddie," he said in a soft, slow way.

"I may not hold up under close scrutiny."

He lowered his head, his lips touching a taut nipple. Maddie held her breath. "Trust me," he murmured huskily against her breast. "You will."

Maddie let out a long, unsteady breath as she uncoiled her fingers from the blanket.

With his tongue Michael marked a whisper-soft trail downward over her stomach. He could feel the muscles beneath her silky skin tense, but he merely continued his maddeningly languorous exploration.

She could feel his fingers, still cool, against the heated flesh of her inner thigh. She could feel his mouth moving in intoxicating little circles across her stomach. The blanket no longer covered her body at all, and the sharp contrast of cold and warmth made her shiver. Her breath came unevenly. She squeezed her eyes shut.

"Maddie." His breath fanned her face.

"Mmm."

"Open your eyes."

She obeyed.

He smiled down at her. "You're beautiful, Maddie. Every inch. Every flawless inch."

"Oh, Michael." She let her gaze run all the way down to his feet. "You're beautiful, too."

They both laughed softly, and then his mouth locked with hers. She gripped his shoulders, her fingers digging into his corded muscles. Maddie loved the way Michael kissed her. He was so intent, so absorbed. So thorough. His mouth, his tongue, his lips were intoxicating. She could feel herself letting go, no longer trying to fight it. No longer wanting to. She wanted him to go on kissing her forever. She wanted to feel the weight of his body on her forever. In total abandon she reached down in between them and caught gentle hold of him, stroking.

When a low moan escaped his lips, Maddie thought it was one of pleasure. Only when he stopped abruptly with another moan, this one more clearly a grunt, did Maddie freeze, unaware until that instant that her body had been moving involuntarily in an instinctive rhythm of desire.

He rolled off her. The sudden separation sent a chill through her. She opened her eyes, confusion, embarrassment, unmasked desire in her expression as she stared up at Michael, whose own visage was caught between a smile and a grimace.

"What's wrong? Is it me? Did I hurt you? Did I do something you didn't like? I know . . . I'm a little tense. It's just . . ." She sighed wearily. "I'm trying, Michael. I knew this was a bad idea."

"Maddie." The smile won out.

She stared up at him wanly. "Yes?"

He leaned lower. His mouth moved to her ear. "I found your brooch. Or to be more accurate, my big toe found it."

"What?"

Michael sat up, reached down toward the end of the bed between the mattress and the wall and retrieved the brooch.

"Oh, Michael." She sat up beside him, watching as he closed what proved to be a faulty clasp and placed it in the palm of her hand.

"It must have landed there when I was flinging the covers back looking for it. Are you hurt? Let me see."

He grinned. "Only if you promise to kiss it better."

"Don't tease. Not now. The Fates really do have it in for me, I swear." She stared ruefully down at the brooch.

Michael took it back and set it on the bedside table. Then he cupped her shoulders and eased her back into a reclining position. He kissed her lips very gently. "This is fate, too, Maddie." He kissed her again, still tender but more demanding.

When he sought her lips this time, he plunged his tongue deep into her mouth, retreated, plunged again. His kisses were relentless, exploring her mouth in a tortuous rhythm that made her move involuntarily in accompaniment to his insistent onslaught.

There was nothing languorous about Michael's seduction now. His strong, sinewy body moved on top of
her, his weight forcing the air from her lungs so that she
let out a low gasp. He caught hold of her wrists and
stretched her arms over her head against the pillows. The
movement made her back arch, her high, firm breasts
thrust harder against his chest. He was all heat now. Heat
and fire.

Still holding her pinned, he gazed down at her. His
dark eyes were so bright they glistened. Maddie stared
up at him, mesmerized. When he lowered his mouth to
hers, they kissed in a timeless moment, capturing each
other's breath.

Maddie's mind shut down, instinct and desire her only
guide as her body moved beneath Michael's in an insin-
uating way. She thrilled to the rapid rise and fall of his
chest and abdomen as he quickly matched her rhythm,
and they breathed in unison.

When Michael released her wrists, her hands moved
greedily down over the hard, satiny skin of his back. He
shifted, his strong, muscular legs entwining her. This
time she sought his lips, her tongue eager to explore his
mouth. Her insides were turning to liquid as her hands
grew bolder, moving down over his firm buttocks,
pressing him more tightly to her.

Her hips moved against his. She ached to feel him inside her. She cried out his name. A fierce, restless yearning inflamed her. Boldly she stroked him, probing,
caressing, thrilling to the erotic intoxication of their
mingled gasps of pleasure. She felt his heat suffusing her.

"Oh, Michael, please..." she moaned against his neck.

He lifted his head slightly, looked down at her, saw the
fierce desire in her features. "Fate, Maddie." And then,
after a brief pause and the rustle of foil, he plunged deep

into the core of her. Maddie gasped, her head thrown back. His lips came down onto her neck, sucking there until she moaned with pleasure.

As his movements quickened, she writhed beneath him, never once allowing him to slow. Each scorching stroke merged them closer together until she was suspended in a sublime, precious ecstasy, trembling like a leaf, crying out his name with abandon. And all the while he made his claim on her.

He wanted to keep watching the play of pleasure on her face, but his fleeting control made him shut his eyes, letting himself get lost in a blur of time and space. He wanted to slow down, prolong the moment, but he'd moved beyond that possibility. His desire was like a tidal wave, washing over his body, sweeping into his head.

Feverishly he sought her lips at the very moment of release. He groaned deep into her mouth. Maddie felt her whole body quiver and then her own release came in a helpless, uncontrollable explosion of sheer pleasure that flooded her entire body.

She clung to him for long moments afterward, aware of herself and Michael only, linked by the ecstasy they had shared so completely. She could still feel the ripples of pleasure spreading through her.

"I've never done this before, you know."

Michael grinned. "You could have fooled me." He turned onto his side to face her, a tender smile softening his angular features, his dark eyes surveying her warmly.

"I mean I've never made love in the afternoon before. It feels . . . more wanton somehow."

"Just think what you might have missed," he said in a teasing tone that, while tender, reminded Maddie that in so many ways they were still strangers. A flash of guilt and nervousness overtook her. She started to reach for the covers.

"Don't," Michael said softly.

"It's chilly."

"Maddie," he said firmly, cupping her chin, "making love in the afternoon with you was wonderful. It was the best afternoon I can remember spending."

"But not the wisest," Maddie said. "For either one of us." She gave him a worried look. "What happens now, Michael? How do we put aside what happened and ever get down to business?"

Michael stared at her in silence for a long moment. "Listen, Maddie. I told you that we're considering another company. But putting that aside for now, I've got this new idea ticking away in my head about Sargent. It could prove to be a better deal all around. I'm going to need a little time to pursue it, though. I think we'll be able to work it all out, Maddie. Just as long as we don't put any undue pressure on each other."

Maddie wasn't sure if Michael was talking about their personal relationship or their professional one. She had the feeling, however, that he probably meant both. She was also very uneasy about this new idea of his.

"What new idea?" she asked warily.

"I'll tell you all about it as soon as details are firmer."

Maddie eyed him with a stubborn expression. "I'd just as soon push for the old deal, Michael. You know the saying, 'A bird in the hand . . .'" She frowned. "Look, if you really decide some other company is better, I don't need you to throw a few crumbs my way as compensation," she said angrily.

"I'm not talking crumbs here, Maddie." He sighed in frustration. No point in trying to convince her until he could show her something concrete and, he hoped, exonerate himself.

"How about if we go out and get something to eat?" Michael suggested.

"You have a frustrating habit of switching topics when it suits your purposes, Michael."

He smiled. "How do you think I made it to the top?"

She sighed. "Okay. I guess I am hungry. But what about Timmy?"

"We won't be away for more than an hour. I think it would be fine to leave him with Mrs. Johnston for that long, if she's still available."

"I'll go shower and then call her," she said, unaware of the controlled sound of her own voice but fully aware of the self-consciousness that she experienced, rising naked from the bed.

She didn't need to look at him to know that he was watching her closely. She hurried over to the closet, grabbed her robe, put it on and headed quickly for the bathroom.

She was just stepping into the shower when the bathroom door opened.

"Mind if I join you?"

"Join me?" She felt herself flush.

He was standing there naked. It had been one thing to lie beside his naked body in bed in the throes of passion, but it was quite another to find herself, just as naked, standing across from him under a bright fluorescent bathroom light.

He was smiling, which only heightened her discomfort.

"I bet this is something else you've never done."

"Michael . . ."

His smile deepened. "You've been around a little, though, Maddie. You must have heard the saying, 'One hand washes the other.'"

"Michael." This time her voice was sharp, indignant. If he thought . . .

"I'm teasing you, Maddie. Don't you know when I'm teasing and when I'm serious?" He took a few steps into the bathroom and shut the door. "You really think that's what I'm like?"

Slowly she shook her head. She was unable to keep her eyes from traveling down his tanned, lean yet muscular body.

The tiny room was growing smaller as he approached. He paused less than a foot from her, staring at her, not at all uneasy in his nudity.

She held her breath, then closed the gap. The feel of his body against hers was an aphrodisiac. He drew her tight for a moment, then reached past her and turned the shower on. "How hot do you like it?" he murmured against her ear.

Maddie's insides were already molten. "Very hot" was her husky answer.

They stepped into the shower and stood together under the pulsing jets, smoothing soap all over each other and then kissing, clinging in a slippery embrace. He lathered her hair, giving her scalp a fantastic massage, and kissed her while the water rinsed the lather off.

She gasped as he pressed her against the cold tiles of the shower, the contrast with the heated water and their heated bodies almost intolerably erotic. She could feel him hard, demanding, between her soapy thighs.

He lifted her up, gripping her buttocks, locking her legs around his hips. They made love with the water jetting down over them.

Afterward, as he toweled her off, she smiled. "You're right. I never did take a shower with a man before." A little laugh escaped her lips. "It was an exceptional experience."

He encircled her in the towel and pressed her to him, giving her a loud, greedy kiss.

Maddie wrapped her arms around his neck. It was impossible to believe so much had happened between them so quickly. But it didn't feel as though she had passed through ordinary time these past few days. No, it had all been quite extraordinary. She buried her face against his still-damp neck, her fingers skimming down his back. His body dazzled her. He was so strong, so powerful, so responsive. And so tender and loving.

He lifted her head, his gaze capturing hers, blinding her to everything else. His lips found hers, their tongues making electric contact. Yes, quite extraordinary, she thought happily. As for the personal and professional complications, this wasn't the time to talk of them or even to think about them.

They returned to Maddie's bedroom and dressed in an easy, unhurried fashion. Then Maddie phoned Mrs. Johnston, who said she'd be happy to watch Timmy.

Timmy seemed in better spirits, and Maddie guessed that the antibiotics were already working. She was relieved to hand a cheerful baby into Mrs. Johnston's care.

Conscious of not wanting to leave Timmy for too long, Maddie chose a steak house a couple of blocks from her place. They were both ravenous and chose king-size portions of T-bone steak, with french fries and salad, which they ate with relish.

Afterward they shared a hot-fudge sundae and finished off the bottle of Chianti Michael had ordered with lunch.

"That was terrific." Maddie sighed, after the last swallow of wine.

"I hope that covers more than the meal."

She grinned. "It does."

She watched him polish off the last of the sundae and then leaned forward a little. "Michael, I know you were teasing before about one hand washing the other, but I am concerned that what happened this afternoon won't influence your decision. Don't get me wrong. I want that account desperately."

"Maddie—"

"Oh, I know, you're still considering all your options. I just want you to know that I don't expect any favors."

The warmth and comfort Michael had been feeling vanished. "Maddie, believe me, there won't be anything personal in my decision. I don't do business that way. Ever." His tone was emphatic—perhaps to convince himself, even more than Maddie, that he couldn't allow his personal feelings to interfere with his business judgment, now more than ever. Even so, he found himself once again questioning whether he'd moved too quickly on the L'Amour deal, only to conclude that he knew damn well that it was the right company for the new Barrett's line. But he really did have a terrific new idea for Sargent. And if it panned out, he was sure Maddie would be thrilled. If it didn't pan out . . .

Maddie saw Michael's features darken. She reached across the table and placed her hand on top of his. "One more thing, Michael. If you're worried that I have any expectations—business dealings aside—you can relax. No strings, Michael. No strings, no obligations, no claims." Her smile was soft and far more vulnerable than she realized. "Agreed?"

He exhaled a little raggedly. "Agreed."

But when they walked back in the biting cold to Maddie's apartment, Michael was very quiet and seemed lost in his own thoughts. She wondered if he was still planning to fly back to New York, but she didn't want to ask. The truth was, she didn't want him to go. What she wanted was to crawl back into bed with him. If she was going to be liberated enough for a no-strings-attached fling, why not have it last just awhile longer?

But Michael had other pressing issues on his mind. He checked his watch. It was nearly three. He wanted to place a call to Barrett and toss around this new idea that was becoming more pressing. If the old man bit, he'd fly to New York so he could set some more wheels in motion first thing in the morning. With any luck he'd be back in Boston in time for his sister's wedding rehearsal and dinner on Friday night. And he'd be able to come clean with Maddie and sweeten her disappointment at the same time.

Lost in his own thoughts, he didn't hear what Maddie was saying.

"Sorry," he apologized. "I wasn't listening."

"Nothing important. I just remembered when we passed the cleaners that they owe me for ruining a new dress of mine."

"Oh." He nodded.

Maddie smiled halfheartedly, trying not to feel rejected. They were in front of her building.

"Will you come up?"

"No," Michael said. "I can't. I've got some calls to make. And I still plan to fly back to New York."

No strings, she reminded herself. Michael was merely emphasizing the point. It was, she went on silently, unfair to set the terms and then feel miserable when they were carried out.

"New York. Right. I almost forgot. You were heading there this morning. I really did throw you off schedule, didn't I?" She couldn't look at him, so she focused her attention on his hands. He wasn't wearing gloves, and he hadn't stuck his hands in his pockets for warmth. They were handsome hands, strong yet capable of such tenderness. She could feel them caressing her body.

A warm smile softened the tense lines in his face. "It was a wonderful detour."

Maddie didn't smile back. "What about the dinner with all your relatives Tuesday night?"

Michael shrugged. "I'll grab a shuttle in for the evening, if I can. Then fly back to New York afterward." He paused. "I still owe you a dinner."

"You still owe me a business meeting," Maddie corrected.

"We'll have it. How about if I come down to your plant on Friday? You can show me around. And we can talk."

"All right." She was getting cold standing still. "I guess I'd better go relieve Mrs. Johnston."

"Oh, Maddie, I almost forgot. Do you have another tube of that skin cream you used on Timmy? I'd like to add it to the product-line samples you sent us."

Maddie brightened, thinking Michael had abandoned that new idea for Sargent he'd brought up before. "You like the idea of including it, then. That's great, Michael. It could be part of a five-step facial program. It would fit perfectly with the cleanser, toner and mineral masque I already sent you. Plus there's a new facial spray we're working on in conjunction with the moisturizer. As soon as I get into work tomorrow, I'll get one off to you. Or we could even zip down there now."

"Slow down, Maddie. Let's take it one step at a time. I'll just come up with you and get the tube of skin cream for now."

Maddie smiled. "Right." Michael followed her into the building. As they waited for the elevator, Maddie couldn't resist adding one more idea. "What about a special travel kit for the collection? In Barrett's colors. Silver background with a print of Bs in maroon? We could use one of our designers, or if you'd rather use someone at your end . . ."

"The elevator."

Impatiently Michael ushered Maddie inside and stepped in behind her. He didn't want to think about how he was going to feel on Friday afternoon if his new idea didn't pan out.

BEFORE HEADING OUT to the airport, Michael made a call to his boss from Barrett's Boston store only to learn that Barrett would be out of town until Wednesday. He hung up, drumming his fingers on the desk of the store manager who had discreetly gone off to attend to other matters. After a few minutes he placed another call to Joel Epstein, a manufacturer who was one of Barrett's biggest suppliers. He spent thirty minutes on the phone, ending the conversation by setting up a meeting at Epstein's office on Thursday morning. When he hung up this time, he was feeling a little better. Epstein was a shrewd businessman, and he hadn't built his reputation or his bank account by being overly cautious. He had a knack for getting into the right markets at the right time. He was willing to take risks as long as he believed the odds were in his favor. Michael was banking on being able to convince him this time around.

When he left the Barrett's store, Michael encountered rush-hour traffic on his way to the airport. Sitting in traffic gave him some time to reflect on everything that had happened during the past few days. He couldn't get Maddie off his mind. When he found himself waiting to board his plane, he considered calling her but vetoed the idea quickly. No, he needed to get some distance from Maddie. Their relationship had gained momentum all too quickly. She had bowled him over. Confused him. He couldn't sort out how he felt. But he was clear enough to know that his feelings weren't casual. And he knew Maddie's weren't, either. She'd said no strings. And he believed she meant it. She wasn't playing it cool in some reverse psychological ploy. Still, strings had a way of sneaking up on a person and catching one off guard. He flashed on that vision he'd had yesterday arriving with Maddie and Timmy at his mother's house. The happy little family. A cold chill shot through him.

In the end he gave his sister Cindy a ring, but he soon realized it had been a bad idea.

"Damn it, Cindy. Drop the subject."

"What did I say? All I said was that she's a nice woman. A warm, attractive, intuitive, sensitive, nice woman."

"Fine. She's all those things. I agree. Okay. She's warm, sensitive, beautiful. And if she were interested—which she isn't—she'd make some guy, some *other* guy, a terrific wife. Do I make myself clear?"

"You're absolutely right, Mike." Cindy laughed. "Beautiful is a better description than attractive."

THE NEXT MORNING Maddie deposited Timmy once again with Mrs. Johnston, who'd clearly developed a genuine affection for the baby and wouldn't hear of Maddie hir-

ing a professional service to look after him. Maddie made
it to work just as the morning meeting she'd scheduled
was starting. Several times during the meeting with Liz
and three other key staff people she'd had to ask people
to repeat what they'd been saying. And with an embarrassed laugh she confessed that she hadn't had a chance
to go over Larry Gibbon's last market report. All four
stared at her with curious expressions. Reviewing the report had been the chief reason Maddie had called the
meeting.

As the foursome switched gears, getting into their
typical business-management discussions about target-
ing, strategy and new-product development, Maddie remained oddly distracted. Liz kept glancing over at her
with a bemused expression, especially after receiving a
vague response to her question about the status of the
Barrett's account.

When the meeting was over, Liz followed Maddie un-
invited into her boss's inner sanctum, a large, airy office
with a trestle-table desk, a cozy seating group done in
soft butter-cream velour in one corner and a bank of
windows along the far wall that looked out onto the
Charles River.

Maddie sat down at her desk and shot a quick glance
up at Liz, who had shoved aside some papers and
perched herself on a corner of the desk, facing Maddie.

"This is a first, Maddie."

Maddie looked alarmed. "What do you mean?"

"In almost seven years together, I have never seen you
unprepared for a meeting. Especially since you told me
you were staying home all day yesterday to catch up on
work."

"Well—" Maddie swallowed hard "—it was a hectic day. With Timmy. Taking care of a baby is a lot of work, Liz. A lot of work. It's . . . distracting."

"Mm-hmm."

"What does that mean?"

Liz grinned. "Something tells me Timmy wasn't your only distraction."

Maddie's eyes widened. "How did you know?"

Liz winked. "Lucky guess."

"Oh."

"No, it's more than that. You've got the classic signs, Maddie."

"What classic signs? I don't know what you're talking about, Liz." Maddie ran her hand through her hair and sighed. "I didn't sleep well last night."

Liz chuckled. "That's one of them. I bet you skipped breakfast, too. Weren't hungry, right?"

Maddie looked chagrined. "Right."

Liz leaned closer. "And you can't think straight."

Maddie smiled sheepishly. "It's only temporary. It'll pass." Her smile faded. "I'm the last woman in the world for this to happen to."

"What's happening, Maddie?" Liz didn't need the answer for her confirmation but for Maddie's.

"It's . . . an infatuation. I'm going to put Michael Harrington out of my mind."

"Does that mean quitting negotiations on the Barrett's deal?"

"No," Maddie answered quickly. "Thank God, Michael is a professional. Our business dealings are a separate issue."

"Then you won't exactly be able to put Michael out of your mind."

"You know what I mean, Liz," Maddie said impatiently, grabbing a pen and making little nervous doodles on a sheet of paper.

When Liz didn't say anything, Maddie dropped the pen and looked up at her. Her whole body ached from fatigue. She'd tossed and turned all night, unable to find a comfortable position, her bed never feeling wider or emptier. Ever since Michael had taken off yesterday, she hadn't been able to think about anything but him, her body in a frustrating state of semiarousal. But worse than the state of her body was the state of her mind. She had always been so clear-thinking, so sure of who she was, what she wanted, what she needed—and didn't need. She was sensible, independent, her own person. She'd spent practically her whole life alone. She'd never been really intimate—physically or emotionally—with anyone. Those few times she'd made a stab at closeness with Felicity had been awkward, embarrassing, ultimately disastrous.

But this weekend with Michael . . . she'd felt closer to him than she'd ever felt to anyone. Michael had transformed her awkwardness into abandon. He'd made her feel vibrant, alive. Michael made her imagine another world, a world of waking each morning with him, sitting across from him at the breakfast table, even taking turns making the bottle and feeding their own baby, singing little lullabies together. . . .

Maddie gripped her abdomen. "My stomach feels jumpy."

Liz laughed softly. "That's one of the classic signs, too."

9

MADDIE ARRIVED at Mrs. Johnston's door after work feeling chilled, frazzled and out of breath.

Mrs. Johnston insisted that she come in for a hot cup of tea. Maddie agreed out of gratitude, but she would have much preferred to go straight upstairs with Timmy, settle him for the night, take a hot shower and crawl into bed. It had been a tough day at work. She'd felt disorganized, disoriented, unable to concentrate. And her conversation with Liz had only made her more distracted.

While Maddie stepped out of her boots and slipped off her coat, Mrs. Johnston went to get Timmy, who was resting in the crib Mrs. Johnston kept for her granddaughter. As soon as Timmy saw Maddie, his face broke out in a big smile, his plump little arms stretching out in her direction. Maddie felt a rush of pleasure, and when she took him in her arms and he nuzzled her contentedly, she laughed.

"Hi, Scout. Looks like you had a nice, peaceful day." Which was more than she could say for herself.

Maddie followed Mrs. Johnston to the kitchen and sat at the table while she put on the kettle for tea.

"I really appreciate you watching Timmy while I was at work today, but I can't tie up your whole week, Mrs. Johnston. I should try to track down a baby-sitter."

"Nonsense. I wouldn't hear of it. I love looking after Timmy. He's an angel." Mrs. Johnston smiled as she looked over at the baby, who was busily playing with Maddie's hair. "He missed you today."

"No." The notion seemed impossible to Maddie.

"Oh, he did. You should have seen his face light up when I put him next to the telephone when you called me this afternoon to check on him."

"He did?" Maddie tenderly stroked Timmy's back. And then she flushed. "I wasn't checking on him. I knew you were taking wonderful care of him. I just . . ." Maddie wasn't really sure why she had called. Or why she, too, had brightened when she heard Timmy's soft cooing into the receiver.

"You just missed him," Mrs. Johnston said. "We get attached to babies so quickly. That's the way it should be. Hold a little bundle of joy in our arms and we all melt."

Maddie smiled down at Timmy. "Well, he is a sweet baby. As babies go, I mean."

"They're all sweet. Even the fussy ones. When you have your own, you'll see."

"No. Not me. Babies aren't in my plans. It's too hard to juggle a busy career and a family at the same time. I'm not looking for the superwoman award of the year," Maddie added emphatically.

"You just need a husband who'll pitch in. Plenty of men are doing it. My son-in-law, Garry, helps my daughter out all the time. She's a teacher and she went back to work when the baby was eight months old. She and Garry take turns getting up early to feed the baby and get her dressed. Garry changes her diapers and takes her to the doctor at the first sign of a sniffle. Half the time he's the one the baby-sitter calls when there's a problem with Jennifer."

Maddie couldn't help thinking, as Mrs. Johnston went on raving about her son-in-law, that Michael would be that kind of father—caring, attentive, involved. Not, she told herself quickly, that that was relevant. Michael might be a wiz with kids, but he didn't want any of his own any more than she did.

They drank their tea, and Maddie switched the conversation to more mundane chatter. Meanwhile Timmy munched contentedly on a teething cookie, although he was adamant about remaining in Maddie's lap, fussing each time she tried to set him in the small feeding seat Mrs. Johnston kept on hand for her granddaughter's visits. Maddie was certainly not going to admit it, but she felt a growing pleasure that Timmy was becoming attached to her. For a pair who'd started off on the wrong foot, they'd come a long way. That thought instantly led her to thoughts of Michael. Talk about starting off on the wrong foot. Talk about having come a long way. Unfortunately, she took little pleasure in that realization. She'd spent half the day at work chastising herself for her impetuous involvement with Michael, the other half fighting to make sense of her confused feelings.

On her way up to her own apartment fifteen minutes later, Maddie once again thought about her conversation with Liz that morning. Was her assistant right? Did she have the classic signs of a woman in love? It wasn't possible. It couldn't be possible. In love with Michael? After such a short time? It was ridiculous. Liz didn't think there was anything so astonishing about it, though. If love at first sight had become a cliché, she'd said, it must be because it had happened enough times to become one.

"Love at first sight," Maddie muttered aloud as she unlocked the door and stepped into her apartment. "Nonsense. It's merely an infatuation."

Timmy looked up at her, his cherubic face bearing a broad smile. Maddie found that smile surprisingly intimidating.

"Oh, so you don't believe me."

Timmy giggled.

"Well, Scout, it's true. And, I might add, a passing infatuation. And the same is true for Michael. Just look at the way he scooted out of here yesterday. I bet right this minute he's sorely regretting..." She stopped, gave Timmy a shrewd smile. "Well, never you mind what he's regretting. How about we change the subject? Let's talk about dinner. Cream of rice for you and a hamburger for me. What do you say?"

Timmy gave her a look that seemed to say he found the talk about her and Michael more interesting.

Maddie grimaced. "I don't know, Tim. I truly must be off my rocker to be having a conversation with a six-month-old. I'm beginning to get a little worried about my state of mind."

With single-minded determination Maddie busied herself making dinner, feeding Timmy, giving him his bath and tucking him in for the night. Only after she pulled the blanket up over Timmy did it dawn on her that she'd gone about the tasks of child care with an absent-minded ease. A slow smile curved her lips. *My, my,* she thought, *how much I've learned in such a short time.* And then, unbidden, came the thought, *How much Michael's taught me.*

The moment he snuck back into her mind, Maddie realized she'd lost the battle. She had to face it. Her senses were filled with thoughts of Michael. They exhausted her.

She decided to get to bed early, hoping sleep would come easier tonight, scared that if it didn't, it would only confirm one of Liz's classic signs. Those signs were beginning to take on a decidedly ominous cast for Maddie.

She undressed and went into the bathroom to shower. But as soon as she reached to turn on the water, she could see Michael reaching for the knob, asking in that low, sexy voice how hot she liked it.

Oh, God, she thought despairingly, *I must be in love. I can't even shower without him.* Tears filled her eyes.

Resolutely she decided on a bath, filling the tub with some bubble bath Felicity had brought her from Paris a few months ago.

Felicity. What would her mother make of her daughter's state of mind? Not for the first time Maddie found herself wishing she had the kind of mother she could confide in. She felt an urgent longing to be able to phone her mother, tell her to come over and help her sort out her confused feelings. She wanted motherly advice. She wanted a warm, nurturing caress, a gentle pat, a mother's understanding, knowing smile.

Fat chance she'd get that from the urbane Felicity, even if she could track her down. And if she were to confide in her mother, Felicity would no doubt give her a wry smile and tell her she was taking the whole matter far too seriously. Her advice would be to stick Michael in a tidy little cubbyhole, and if he became too bothersome, to cut him loose and go off and buy a new dress. For Felicity, love was carefree, unencumbered. She had certainly never let her personal relationships get too involved or allowed them to pull her off her own fast track. Maddie recalled that last postcard she'd received from Felicity, the one Michael had read.

"Well, Mom, I didn't have to fly off to Greece with you to find the man of my dreams. He walked right in my front door. I hope you're satisfied."

She sank deeper into the hot water, drawing her knees up to her chest, wriggling her toes among the bubbles. The fragrant, soapy heat was disturbingly sensual. Maddie closed her eyes, resting her chin on her wet knees. She wished she could take the advice Felicity would give. She wished she could be more detached, more casual about what had happened between her and Michael. She was angry at herself for falling in love so quickly, so impetuously.

She had to be very careful to keep her feelings under wraps. Michael must never know. Seen through his eyes, her feelings would appear traitorous. She was supposed to be a plucky lass with the same perspective on life and love as Michael. That was what he found so appealing about her. She wasn't threatening. She wasn't waiting with bated breath to snare him.

What was the matter with her? They'd made love together once—twice, she amended—and already she was thinking she wanted to marry him.

She stiffened. Who said anything about marriage? She looked around the bathroom in an absurd belief that some invisible being had heard her thoughts and would hold her to them.

Her panic gave way to relief. Nonsense. So she'd let herself get temporarily carried away by a few idle fantasies about Michael. Fantasies were a far cry from reality. She just wasn't used to them. She mustn't let herself dwell on them. She told herself that they were under her control. They were her secret. Thank God she hadn't said anything to Michael about being in love with him. No, she'd handled things very well. Nothing to feel awkward about. Nothing to worry about. She hadn't jeopardized anything. She felt confident she still had a clear shot at getting the contract for that exclusive line with

Barrett's. Even more than before. After all, Michael had even taken along that new moisturizer gel with him.

She stepped out of the tub, vowing once again to put Michael out of her mind. Of course, no sooner had she made the vow than she thought about him, this time surrounded by his family and relatives. Tonight was the big gathering at one of the local restaurants for his out-of-town relatives in for the wedding.

At the thought of that loud, gay get-together, Maddie felt a sudden intense loneliness and had to squeeze her eyes shut to stop the flow of tears. Her feelings angered her. Until Michael came along, she'd been perfectly content in her aloneness. Until Michael came along, she'd been undisturbed by fantasies of marriage, of having a baby. How dare he, she fumed, walk into her life and send it into such a complete turmoil?

The anger was refreshing. Maddie held on to it as she crawled into bed. It was only a little after nine o'clock, but Maddie was determined to get a good night's sleep. So much for Liz's classic signs! She flicked off the light, pulled the covers up over her head and shut her eyes.

Ten minutes later she flung the covers off. Timmy's antibiotic. She'd forgotten about his last dose. Damn.

She tiptoed into the spare bedroom. Timmy was sound asleep. Now what? Should she wake him and give him his medicine? Should she skip it tonight and give him a double dose in the morning? Was it too late to call Mrs. Johnston and ask her advice? What would Michael do? *I can't think straight. I'm not any good at this.*

The sound of the doorbell startled her and woke Timmy up. He started to cry. Maddie sniffed back tears, picked up Timmy and went to see who was there.

Her heart turned over as she looked through the peephole and then opened the door. "Michael."

Seeing her red eyes and Timmy's tear-drenched face, Michael's brow creased. "Maddie, what is it?"

She smiled and sniffed at the same time. "I forgot to give Timmy his last dose of medicine. And then he was asleep, and I didn't know if I should wake him."

A tender smile curved Michael's lips. "Well, he's up now." He walked in and shut the door. "Where's his medicine?"

Maddie laughed. "Oh, Michael, you've done it again. You've saved the day."

He put his arm around her and Timmy. "Think nothing of it."

But of course that wasn't possible, given Maddie's state of mind.

After Timmy had swallowed his medicine and Maddie had tucked him back into bed, she returned to the kitchen to find Michael putting on coffee.

Maddie stood watching him. "I thought you were at a dinner with your out-of-town relatives tonight."

"I was." He plugged in the coffee and turned around to her. "My family was disappointed that I didn't bring you along."

Maddie smiled awkwardly. "I guess they still have the wrong idea."

Michael's smile was just as awkward. "I guess so."

They stood a few feet apart. Their eyes met and held. "Why did you come here?" she asked finally, her voice weak.

He didn't answer immediately, but his gaze grew more intense. "I missed you," he admitted.

He hesitated for a moment and then, bridging the gap between them, cupped her face gently in his hands.

Maddie trembled at his touch. "I missed you, Michael."

He smiled for an instant at her words, and then he sobered. His eyes locked on hers. "We do have an understanding, Maddie. We do see things alike. No marriage. No family. No promises. We can handle this—don't you think?"

Maddie nodded silently, unaware that she'd lowered her eyes.

He tilted her head up and kissed her lips very gently. "I do want you, Maddie. I have never wanted any woman the way I want you."

She leaned into him, returning his kiss. She felt exhilarated and sad at the same time. As if from a distance she heard herself say, "I want you, too, Michael."

He kissed her again, this time more roughly and more possessively. She tensed at first, a reflexive response.

"Let go, Maddie," he whispered against her well-kissed lips. "I want to make love to you. Right here. Right now."

He opened her robe and drew her flannel nightgown up, kissing her breasts, her nipples growing hard beneath his lips. He gripped her hands tightly, drawing them behind her back, entwining his fingers with hers.

Maddie could feel an extraordinary tension emanating from her body. The fierce intensity of her own longing coupled with Michael's frightened her and excited her at the same time. She kissed him on the mouth, a hard, frenzied kiss.

Michael could feel her trembling race through her muscles. He released her hands, tugged off her robe, lifted her nightgown over her head. Then he pulled her to him, flattening her against his length with such force that she gasped.

The contrast between her nakedness and his fully clothed body flooded Maddie with a sexual wildness. She wound her arms around him possessively, her fingers pressing into the contours of his muscles. She could feel the outline of him, hard and hot, beneath the barrier of his trousers.

As Michael hoisted her up, her feet no longer touching the floor, and pressed her against the counter, a recklessness consumed her. She felt heat suffuse her as she stripped off his shirt, then snaked her hand down to free him from the confines of his trousers.

Michael's breath caught, then came in jagged, fiery exhalations as her hand engulfed him. He had never felt so aroused. He could feel his whole body quivering, his buttocks clenched tightly as he pushed up hard against her, frantic for union.

"Now," she said to him. "Yes, now." Her voice, husky with lust, filled Michael with promises of unsurpassed delight. A brief pause for a condom and then he penetrated her in one long, heated slide.

"Oh, Michael." Maddie clenched him fiercely, rhythmically, and she burned with passion, exquisitely joined to him. Her head went back, her eyelids fluttering, and she let go completely, Michael supporting her. Release burst inside of her, bringing her indescribable joy. She sighed with it, pleasure and ecstasy combining, filling her with a contentment unlike any she had ever known.

For Michael, release came as a surge of electricity, bringing with it deep, shuddering breaths. His fingers tangled in Maddie's hair as he brought his mouth to hers and they kissed long and hungrily, tongues caressing, lost within their shared ecstasy.

Later they made love again, more conventionally, but no less passionately, in Maddie's bed.

Maddie was half dozing when she felt Michael's weight shift away from her. She flung her arm out. "Don't go."

His hand moved caressingly over her bare breast. "I wasn't leaving. I was just going to check on Timmy. I thought I heard him wake up."

Fully awake now, Maddie squinted at the glowing dial of her alarm clock. It was four in the morning. "You stay in bed. You've got a flight to catch in the morning."

Michael shook his head. "You've got to go to work in the morning. I'll go."

They laughed. Then Maddie snuggled against him. "Okay—" she yawned and stretched languorously "—you can go this time. I'll go next time."

He pinched her bottom. "You could have put up a bigger fight," he teased, shivering as he rose from the bed.

Maddie rolled onto her stomach. "I feel too good to fight."

A few minutes later Michael scooted back under the covers, and Maddie moved against him, nestling into him.

"He's asleep," Michael murmured. "I must have been wrong."

"Mmm, let me warm you," she whispered, draping a long, slender leg over him, and thinking how wonderful it was to have a strong, reassuring body to curl up to.

"Anytime," Michael answered, his palms sliding down the satin smoothness of her naked back.

Does he mean that? Maddie wondered. *Anytime?* And then her thoughts changed abruptly. *Get a hold of yourself. Don't start reading more into this than he meant.*

His mouth found hers. His tongue circled inside the moist depths, then slid along her teeth. He urged her on top of him. "Yes," he whispered, "Warm me, Maddie, Warm me."

She knelt over him, supporting herself on her outstretched arms. Her thick honey-blond hair trailed across his chest as she lowered her head and captured his lips. Then she pressed the entire length of her body against him, reaching down between his thighs, catching gentle hold of him, stroking him. All the while she kissed him deeply, greedily. Then after quickly attending to birth control, she helped guide him inside her and began moving rhythmically, Michael matching her movements.

Oh, Michael, she thought, *I love you. I ache with love. I want to warm you. I want to go on warming you forever. How could I let this happen?*

Her fleeting despair vanished as she felt herself dissolving, melting, surrendering completely, currents of pleasure coursed down her spine.

The velvet darkness gave way to misty daylight before they fell asleep.

SURFACING RELUCTANTLY from a delightful dream-filled sleep, Maddie reached out for the alarm clock that was blaring. Michael, already out of bed, got to it before her.

"Sorry, I forgot to shut it off," he apologized. "I was going to let you sleep a little longer. I put on some fresh coffee, gave Timmy a bottle and took a shower."

She squinted at Michael, who was wearing only a towel wrapped around his waist and smiling down at her.

He looked wonderfully handsome, his dark hair damp, droplets of water still clinging to his broad chest. She rolled onto her stomach and pulled the covers up. "Don't look at me. I look a mess."

"Turn over." The side of the bed dipped as he sat beside her.

Slowly she moved onto her back. A muscle in his cheek moved, and his dark, intriguing eyes rested thoughtfully on her face. "You're beautiful in the morning, Maddie."

She smiled shyly.

He kissed the pulsating spot on her throat. "Do you know how long it's been since I made love to you?" His breath was hot against her skin, his damp hair sending a little shiver down her spine, a luxurious delight filling her.

But reason and practicality in the form of a baby's wail brought them both down to earth.

They looked at each other and grinned. "Ah, the joys of parenthood." Michael winked, pulling her up and pulling the covers off her at the same time. "Your turn, little mother."

His eyes traveled wickedly over the smooth curve of her breasts and hips and down the long, slender line of her legs as she rose from the bed. He got a secret thrill at the way she walked across the room this time for her robe. Unlike before, she seemed completely comfortable in her nakedness. They were making progress.

He felt a surge of desire twist in him like a bittersweet pain. Just what kind of progress was he hoping to make with Maddie? His brows knitted, his stomach performed a sudden unpleasant flip. Why think of the future at all? Maddie was quite content to take what was happening between them in stride. There'd been no weak moments during passion where she'd whispered words of undying love. She enjoyed him, enjoyed their lovemaking. She'd managed to keep the relationship in perspective. He had to do the same. But in a moment of complete honesty he admitted to himself that it was going to be a most difficult thing to do.

FEELINGS OF GUILT, discomfort and worry might have been floating around both Maddie and Michael's minds that morning, but on the surface the scene in her kitchen was one of pure domestic tranquility—Maddie, in her robe and slippers, adeptly toweling Timmy off after his bath in the kitchen sink; Michael barefoot, wearing his trousers and shirt, but not having bothered to button it, popping bread into the toaster; the radio tuned in to a weather station; the announcer promising a clear, crisp day.

"No problem getting to New York," Maddie said lightly, slipping a disposable diaper under Timmy, who was toying with one of the buttons on her robe.

"No. No problem."

She glanced over at the kitchen clock. "I should still be able to make my meeting with our chief chemist. It's not until ten."

"I can drop you off if you like."

"No, that won't be necessary. I should use my car. I think it stalled on me that night . . ." She smiled, remembering. "It stalls if I don't drive it every day."

"And conditions that night were rather . . . unusual."

Maddie's smile deepened for a moment. But then she busied herself finishing diapering Timmy.

Michael gingerly took out the steaming toast after it popped up and set the pieces down on a plate on the counter. "Butter or jam?"

"Butter." She picked up the diapered baby and turned with him to face Michael. "Well, what do you think? Not a bad job if I do say so myself."

Michael stopped buttering. "Terrific job. See that. It turns out you have a knack with babies, Miss Sargent."

"And no diaper rash, either, thanks to my wonder cream."

He walked over and kissed her cheek. "Maybe you're in the wrong line."

Maddie gave him a bemused smile. "Don't tease, Michael. I'm very proud of our products. And women, nationwide, love them. You saw some of our endorsements in that packet I sent. And if Barrett's features our exclusive line, we're both going to be in clover, Michael."

She saw a muscle work at his jaw, and she had to remind herself that Michael had already made it clear that Sargent wasn't the only company being considered for the contract. And that he didn't want her to press him. It was obvious to Maddie by now that Michael was not completely sold on her line, which was exactly why she couldn't let the opportunity pass to plug it. She would have liked to get in a few more plugs, but the doorbell rang.

Maddie grabbed a baby blanket and threw it around Timmy as she hurried with him to the front door. "That must be Mrs. Johnston."

Maddie turned the knob, opened the door—and her mouth dropped open, though no words escaped.

"Darling . . ." That was all the marvelously tailored, attractively coiffed woman said before her glance slid down to Timmy and *her* mouth dropped open. But Felicity Sargent was not a woman left speechless for too long. "Where did you get him?"

Before Maddie could answer, Michael popped out of the kitchen and into the hall, spotted Felicity and quickly started to button his shirt.

"And *him*?" Felicity smiled coquettishly. She patted Maddie's cheek softly, her smile deepening. "And here I thought I was going to bend your ear with *my* adventures."

Maddie couldn't help laughing. "For once I topped you, Felicity." And then, Maddie's eyes sparkling, an impish grin on her face, she added, "Say hi to Timmy. He's your newest relative."

"Madeline." Beneath the perfectly applied makeup Felicity blanched.

"Why, Mother, you haven't called me Madeline in years."

Felicity raised her eyebrows. "And you haven't called me Mother in years."

Maddie grinned. "A slip of the tongue."

Felicity watched Michael approach, eyeing him closely. "I suppose that means that he's a relative, too."

Michael put his arm around Maddie. "Hey, I thought I was the only tease in the family."

Felicity, not getting the joke, shook her head and brushed past the happy little threesome. "I think I need a drink."

"It's only eight in the morning," Maddie said, trying to contain a burst of laughter.

"I'm still functioning on European time." Felicity pulled off her Italian leather gloves, undid her black cashmere coat and flung them both on the couch, draping herself carelessly over them. "All right. I'll settle for coffee."

"Let me," Michael offered.

"Thanks, dear." Maddie winked.

Felicity narrowed her gaze. "When did all this happen?"

Maddie grinned. "Sometimes it feels like forever."

"How old is that baby, Maddie?"

"Timmy? Six months. Here, why don't you hold him."

"Wait a minute, Maddie," she muttered as her daughter placed the blanketed baby in her arms.

"He likes you, Felicity. He usually screams bloody murder when he's dumped into a stranger's arms. I guess he must sense that you're family."

A sheen of perspiration broke out across Felicity's brow. She looked terribly awkward and uncomfortable holding Timmy, but the baby truly didn't seem to mind, his eyes fixed on the glistening white strand of pearls Felicity was wearing.

"This isn't possible," Felicity went on, her hazel eyes, a deeper shade than Maddie's, resting on Timmy as she did some mental arithmetic. "I haven't been gone that long. When did I see you last, Maddie? It can't have been more than eight or nine months, can it?"

Before Maddie could answer, Michael entered with a cup of coffee for Felicity. "Here, let me take Timmy and get him dressed." They made an exchange. All the while Felicity took in the scene with baffled amazement.

As Michael brushed past her with Timmy, Maddie couldn't hold back her mirth any longer. Laughing, she crossed the room and sank down next to Felicity on the couch. "Oh, it's really a crazy story."

Felicity stared at her daughter, a wry smile on her lips. "I can imagine. Why, I never dreamed..." She scrutinized Maddie closely. "You do look radiant, though."

Maddie's laughter faded, a soft flush rising in her cheeks. "I do?" And then she did something she hadn't done in more years than she could remember. She suddenly threw her arms around her mother and hugged her tightly. "I'm so glad to see you," she whispered, tears seeping out the corners of her eyes.

Felicity, taken aback, stiffened for a moment. And then she did something she, too, hadn't done in years. She smoothed back her daughter's hair and kissed her tenderly on her cheek. "I'm glad, too, darling."

Demurely Felicity Sargent dabbed at her eyes when her daughter released her.

smoothed back her daughter's hair and kissed her forehead on her cheek. "I'm glad, too, darling."

Daniel watched Felicity Burgess declare at her eyes when her daughter released her.

10

"WHAT A DREADFUL THING to do. It's not like you to pull a prank like that, Maddie," Felicity said testily after Maddie explained the truth about Timmy's presence. As for the truth about Michael's presence, Maddie did not go into detail. Nor did Felicity press for any.

Maddie knew her mother was irritated by her little "prank," but she could also see the relief flooding Felicity's face. She felt a pang of disappointment, but not surprise at her mother's reaction. "Was the notion of being a grandmother that ghastly?"

Michael, sitting in an armchair with Timmy, observed mother and daughter thoughtfully. He had picked up Felicity's relief, too. But for a brief instant after Maddie's confession he could have sworn Felicity had cast Timmy a wistful glance. She'd regained her composure quickly, however, and Michael doubted Maddie had picked up that momentary flash of regret.

Felicity finished her second cup of coffee, set it down on the low glass-topped table and looked over at her daughter. "Well, darling, that kind of news does take some preparation. Why do you think nature gives us nine months?"

Maddie raised a brow. "I thought that was for the mother, not the grandmother. Anyway, you don't have to worry." Maddie shot a quick glance at Michael before looking back at her mother. "You won't have any little tykes running about calling you Nanny on my account."

Felicity smiled airily as she snapped open her purse and reached for a cigarette, rummaging around for her lighter. "You know my philosophy, Maddie. I've raised you to pursue any endeavor you so choose." She glanced at Timmy, a curious smile on her lips. "It's just that I never envisioned you as a mother, that's all." She gave up her search for her lighter and looked at Michael. "Do you have a light?"

Michael smiled pleasantly. "No, sorry. It's probably not such a good idea to smoke around the baby, anyway."

Felicity appeared a bit taken aback, but then she shrugged, setting her unlit cigarette on the coffee table beside her empty cup. "It has been ages since I've been around a baby." She smoothed back her short, stylishly coiffed, perfectly tinted blond hair. "I don't think I smoked when you were a baby, Maddie. I seem to recall it was that awful Rory Albertson who started me smoking about fifteen years ago. Do you recall him? A marvelous artist. I believe he was into mixed media when we first met."

Maddie couldn't recall him. But then, if Rory Albertson hadn't been around during her brief school vacations, it was unlikely Maddie would ever have learned of his existence.

Felicity hadn't bothered to wait for Maddie's response. "Such a talent, but really an impossible man. Self-destructive, I kept telling him. When I discover someone truly exceptional, I'll do everything in my power to bring him along. But Rory was terribly undisciplined, and he drank far too much. And carousing with his buddies . . . well, let me tell you, I had to bail him out

of jail more than once. I finally came to my senses and
realized that it was never going to work. If only he would
have pulled himself together and fulfilled the contracts
I'd lined up for him . . ."

Felicity sighed. "Oh, well, fortunately there haven't
been too many Albertsons in my life. I'm afraid I was
foolish enough to let myself get a little emotionally attached to him. It affected my usually astute judgment. I
can thank Rory for one thing, though. He taught me that
it's never a good idea to get personally involved with an
artist you intend to represent."

Michael and Maddie shared an uncomfortable glance,
both pulling their eyes away at the same time.

Felicity absently picked up her cigarette again and
then, remembering, put it back down, muttering, "I
should give them up, anyway."

The phone rang. Maddie rose from the couch and went
to answer it. It was Mrs. Johnston on the line. In a very
apologetic voice she explained to Maddie that she would
not be able to watch Timmy today as planned, and very
likely not for the rest of the week. A close friend, she
hurriedly went on, had suddenly taken ill, and she had
to go off to Newton, a suburb west of Boston, to take care
of her.

"That's all right, Mrs. Johnston." Maddie made an effort to keep the disappointment from her voice. "I understand. You've been wonderful. I'll work something
out. Don't worry. I hope your friend feels better."

"Problem?" Michael asked when Maddie hung up and
turned back to face her mother as she spoke.

A panicked look flashed across Felicity's face. "Don't
look at me, darling. I've got a thousand things to do
while I'm in town. And I'm completely out of practice
with babies, you know that."

Michael rose with Timmy from the chair. "I wish I could help, Maddie, but I've really got to get back to New York this morning. I've got several meetings. . . ."

Maddie raised a hand to silence him. "Of course, Michael. I understand. You've rescued me more than enough times already." She crossed to Michael and took Timmy in her arms. "Maybe I'll take him to work. Between me and Liz we should be able to cope. I'd better finish getting ready."

Felicity stood, carefully smoothing out invisible wrinkles in her skirt. "Well, I should be going, too, darling. I was about to suggest lunch, but if you will be busy with the baby. . ."

"Timmy has to eat lunch, too, Felicity."

To her credit, Felicity laughed. "See. I told you it's been ages. Well, why don't we meet at Ricco's, then. I imagine they can dig up a high chair or some such thing for the baby."

Maddie smiled. The idea of sitting with her elegant, urbane mother at the posh little Italian café while Timmy strung spaghetti over his high chair as if it were a Christmas tree greatly amused her.

Laughing at the image, Maddie walked over to her mother. "I think we'd be better off at the Waldorf Cafeteria. Why don't you ring me at the office, and we'll make a final decision. Here, hold Timmy for a minute, will you?"

Felicity stepped back abruptly as if Maddie were passing her a grenade.

"He doesn't bite, I promise."

Felicity gave a laugh that was decidedly false. "This is a brand-new outfit."

"Come on, Felicity. How much damage can one baby do in two minutes?" She and Michael shared a quick, private smile. "I just need to throw on some clothes and run a comb through my hair. Anyway, Timmy likes you."

Felicity acquiesced reluctantly, handling the infant like an unwieldy sack of potatoes.

This time around, Timmy, having lost his fascination with Felicity's necklace and not at all pleased with being passed about, broke into a loud wail. Maddie merely smiled reassuringly and turned to leave the room.

Felicity looked panic-stricken as she called after her daughter. "Maddie. Maddie, wait. You're wrong. I don't think he likes me one bit."

Maddie and Michael both grinned. "Just relax," they said in unison.

Before her mother could argue, Maddie dashed off for the bathroom. Michael called out to her that he'd wait until she came back to say goodbye.

"Why don't you take him, Michael." There was a pleading note in Felicity's voice as Timmy continued to cry.

"Just hoist him over one shoulder and pat his back. That usually settles him down."

Felicity looked doubtful, but she did what Michael suggested. It took a minute to calm Timmy down, but the change of position did the trick. Michael noted that the smile of accomplishment on Felicity's face was remarkably similar to the one he'd seen on Maddie's.

He smiled back at her and found himself beginning to like Felicity Sargent. While Maddie's mother was clearly a charming, vivacious and attractive woman, five minutes with her and he could see why Maddie and Felicity would not have a very close relationship. The woman was more than a little self-involved. Still, as he watched her soothing Timmy, once again observing that glimmer of wistfulness in her hazel eyes, he wondered if there wasn't more depth and feeling to Felicity than either he or Maddie imagined.

When Maddie came back to the living room a few minutes later, she stood quietly at the entry for a moment, unobserved. Michael and Felicity were sitting together on the couch chatting softly while Timmy was stretched out stomach down across Felicity's lap. She jogged the baby lightly, much to his delight.

"I used to do this with Maddie when she was fussy," Felicity was saying. "It was such a long time ago. How much we forget." And then, rubbing Timmy's back, she said more to herself than to Michael, "It went by so quickly. Too quickly."

Maddie was surprised and touched by Felicity's manner and words. A poignancy washed over her in a warm tide as she tried to imagine her mother holding, caressing, soothing her as an infant. She had always thought her mother couldn't wait for those days to pass, couldn't wait until her daughter was old enough to ship off to boarding school. Was it really possible she looked back on those days with a wistful remembrance?

Michael rose as he spotted Maddie standing silently in the entry. Their eyes met and held for an instant. Maddie had the distinct feeling that Michael could read her thoughts.

He smiled at her, then glanced down at Felicity. "It was a pleasure meeting you, Mrs. Sargent."

"Felicity, please. Mrs. Sargent sounds so formal. So old."

"Felicity," Michael repeated warmly. "I'm sure we'll meet again if you're going to be in Boston for a few days. I'll be back on Friday."

"I should be in town until the middle of next week. Then I fly to Paris." She rose, having a bit of trouble doing it gracefully as she struggled with the squirming baby. Both Maddie and Michael noted that she made no move to relinquish him, however. "I always stay at the Ritz. Perhaps you and Maddie will stop by and have a drink with me over the weekend."

Michael glanced at Maddie, trying to get a reading. She didn't seem averse to the idea. "Maybe Sunday. My sister is getting married on Saturday."

"Sunday would be fine."

Maddie walked over to her mother. "I'll take Timmy now. See—" her voice caught for a moment "—you did fine."

Felicity seemed pleased by the compliment. She gave Timmy's back an affectionate pat. "If Linda doesn't get back Sunday to retrieve her son, by all means bring Timmy along, darling. But do bring a bottle for him. I doubt the bartender specializes in infant cocktails."

Maddie laughed. "We don't have to worry about it. Linda swore she'd be back on Friday. And if she doesn't show up, I'm going to hop a plane to wherever she is and return her bundle of joy." She grinned at Timmy. "Nothing personal, Scout, but I do have other pressing matters to attend to."

Felicity tilted her head. "Well, I must say, Madeline, you do fit the maternal role far better than I would have imagined."

Maddie felt her cheeks warm, and she deliberately avoided Michael's eye.

Felicity, however, brought him into the conversation by asking his opinion.

Michael gave Maddie a pensive look. "She's quite wonderful at it."

Maddie felt an incredible warmth suffuse her. "So are you," she found herself saying, meeting his gaze at last. Maddie found it difficult to believe, but she spotted a flush rising in Michael's tanned face. She smiled at him, adding to his discomfort.

"I'd better get going," he said, his tone a little stiff.

"I'll walk you to the door." There was a touch of disappointment in her voice.

"Well, give me the child, then, while you say goodbye," Felicity offered.

"That's okay."

But Felicity pried him from her daughter's arms. "Go on."

At the front door Maddie and Michael stood awkwardly. After a few silent moments he leaned down and gave her a peck on the cheek.

"Friday, then?"

Maddie nodded. They both reached for the doorknob at the same time. Maddie drew her hand away, leaving Michael to open the door. He took a step out, stopped, then pivoted slightly.

Maddie smiled, bent on nonchalance. "See you." Damn those mesmerizing eyes of his. How was she supposed to play it cool when those dark eyes radiated such heat?

He touched her hair. Then after a brief hesitation he leaned forward, brushing her lips. That barest kiss made her feel woozy.

Just as she was swaying toward him, Michael impulsively grabbed her wrist, drew her out into the hall, slammed the door shut and kissed her fully, all in the same movement.

He left her leaning against the wall just outside her door, breathless, smiling dizzily. Not wanting to risk testing her balance, she stayed put until he gave her a final wave and stepped into the elevator.

Maddie let out a ragged breath. Then composing herself as best she could, she reached for the doorknob only to realize Michael had locked her out. Embarrassed and still a little flustered, she rang the bell.

"Who is it?" came Felicity's wry voice.

"Very amusing. Open the door, Felicity," Maddie replied sharply, her voice still husky from having been so thoroughly kissed.

Felicity was smiling broadly as she opened the door. Even Timmy wore an impish smile.

Maddie's composure, not completely stable, anyway, completely crumbled. She looked as if she might cry.

"Is being in love really that ghastly?" quipped Felicity.

This time Maddie didn't bother to deny it. She managed a wry smile. "Well, darling," she mimicked her mother, "it does take some preparation. Michael caught me completely unawares."

Felicity grinned. "It's about time. I can tell you now, Maddie, that I've been rather worried about you. It's all well and good to have a flourishing career, but there are no medals to be won for doing it alone."

"You've managed perfectly well alone. And so have I— until Michael arrived. Oh, I know you've had involvements with men, but you've always managed to stay levelheaded. My head has been spinning practically since I laid eyes on Michael."

"You're wrong about me, Maddie. Oh, it's been rare, but there have been one or two men in my life that made me reel. Your father, for one."

"My father?" Maddie looked at her mother curiously. "Really?"

Felicity's expression was a bit sad. "My problem is that I've always been attracted to the wrong men—men who fled responsibility, men who were too attuned to being fancy-free."

"Well, then I've inherited your problem, Felicity," Maddie said wearily. "Michael comes from a huge family. His father died when he was a boy, and he's been saddled with so many responsibilities that the very idea of taking on any new ones scares the living daylights out of him. And to further follow in your shoes, I've gone and allowed myself to fall for a man I very much hope to be working with." She went on to explain about the contract she was angling to get with Barrett's.

"I don't see why it can't work out, Maddie. I adore your line of skin-care products. If Michael needs any further proof, he can have my endorsement. I wouldn't worry about a thing if I were you."

Felicity sounded so optimistic that Maddie's spirits began to lift. Two minutes later they fell swiftly.

Just as she was putting on Timmy's snowsuit to take him with her to the office, the phone rang again.

This time it was Liz on the line, sounding frazzled and upset.

"You'd better get down here on the double, Maddie. A water pipe burst in one of the labs, and it's bedlam around her. I've already put in a half-dozen calls to the building maintenance crew, but it seems we aren't the only ones in the building with the problem. They say they're taking us all in turn. Meanwhile we're wading about in a couple of inches of water. Several experiments got fouled up in the process, and Crawford is having a bird."

"I get the picture," Maddie said wearily. "Just hold the fort. I'll soothe Crawford when I get there. Give me ten minutes."

"More problems?" Felicity asked, observing her daughter's morose expression as she hung up the phone.

"I've got to run. A pipe burst."

"Oh, dear."

Maddie was pulling on her coat. "I'll speak to you later." She threw a scarf around her neck and opened the front door.

Only as she saw her daughter start to leave did Felicity realize Maddie was leaving something—or more precisely some*one*—behind. "Maddie. Wait. Wait a minute. Timmy. You almost forgot Timmy."

Maddie came to an abrupt stop. "Oh..." She scowled. "Well, I can't take him now, Felicity. It's chaos down at the office. You'll just have to cope."

Felicity had difficulty taking in Maddie's words.

"No . . . you don't mean . . . cope with Timmy?"

Maddie hurried back and gave her mother a quick hug. "It's a cinch. I even have a supply of disposable diapers in the spare room. They're a breeze. Call me if you have any problems. I'll try to get back early."

"Any problems? Hold on, Maddie. Maddie. Get back here." She watched her daughter race down the hall. "Come back here this instant, Madeline."

Maddie waved without turning, quickly heading for the stairs to be sure her mother didn't corral her before the elevator came.

"Maddie. Please don't do this to me." Felicity watched the service door close and stared wanly down at Timmy. "She's gone."

"ONE CRISIS UNDER CONTROL." Maddie sighed, leaned back in her swivel chair and ran her fingers through her blond hair. When the phone rang, Liz motioned her to stay put and ran out to her office to pick it up, saying she was expecting a call.

Five minutes later Liz reappeared at the door.

"You're not going to like this," she said hesitantly.

"What now?" Maddie looked up from her paperwork. She was hardly in the mood for any further bad news.

"Actually, it's not confirmed."

"Liz."

"That was Colin Akers on the phone. One of our sales reps down in Palm Beach."

"And," Maddie prodded, although for the life of her, she didn't know why. She was sure that whatever Liz had to say was just going to add to her misery. Her only miscalculation was in degree.

"Akers happened to run into a salesman he knows from L'Amour this morning. And this salesman just happened to mention in passing that—" Liz took a deep breath "—Barrett's signed L'Amour for their exclusive skin-care line yesterday. This is all thirdhand, but it seems Harrington pretty much struck the deal with them last Friday."

Maddie couldn't absorb what Liz was saying. Meanwhile Liz was getting more and more fired up.

"The low-down bastard. Oh, I know Harrington told you we had some competition. But what he didn't mention was that he'd already made his choice before he got to Boston on Saturday. What I don't understand is why he didn't tell you Sargent didn't stand a chance. Why string you along?" Liz stopped abruptly, wishing she could swallow her words. "Oh, Maddie, I'm sorry."

A hundred different feelings and responses raced through Maddie's mind, but in the end she just stared at Liz, dazed.

"I can't believe he'd do that to me. Not Michael," she muttered to herself. "Just to get me in bed? He wouldn't. He isn't like that."

"What about that other deal he mentioned to you? Maybe he really does have something better in the works. Or maybe Akers got it wrong." Liz didn't sound convinced or convincing about either possibility.

Maddie never had bought Michael's line about a better deal. What deal could be better than an exclusive skin-care line with Barrett's? And if he thought she could be appeased by some third-rate consolation prize, he had another think coming.

She stared dolefully at Liz. "Maybe you're right. Maybe Akers got it wrong." But she didn't believe it for one instant.

FELICITY CALLED close to noon to check on Maddie's lunch plans.

"Why... she left over an hour ago. She said she was going home," Liz said, trying unsuccessfully to hide the worry in her voice.

"It only takes twenty minutes, even in traffic. And there isn't much traffic in the late morning."

"Maybe she stopped off to do some errands."

"Liz, what's wrong? Is Maddie all right? You sound odd."

"Oh... it's just that we found out that a deal Maddie was working on fell through."

"What deal?"

Liz clammed up. Maddie might not appreciate her spreading the news.

"Liz."

"I'm sorry, Mrs. Sargent. I'm swamped with work here. I'm sure Maddie will be home soon. She can tell you about it."

"You don't mean the Barrett's deal?" Felicity asked in disbelief.

"Please, Mrs. Sargent. I probably shouldn't have said anything. You know Maddie."

"Maddie's been surprising me lately."

Liz couldn't help smiling, despite her misery. "Me, too."

"Oh, I think I hear the key turning in the lock. That must be her now. Take care, Liz."

Maddie looked calm as she entered her apartment—deadly calm. Her complexion was the color of chalk. Felicity observed her closely, worriedly, but Maddie did not make eye contact.

"How about a cup of tea?" Felicity asked innocuously. Better to take this slow. She had never seen her daughter look more vulnerable. "It's bitter cold out today." She watched Maddie slowly, silently remove her coat, pull off her boots.

"I'll just go put on some water for tea," Felicity said after receiving no response from Maddie.

From the kitchen she called out, "You'll be pleased to know Timmy and I got along famously. You were right. Those disposable diapers are a snap. Oh, I gave him a bottle about an hour ago. He's been taking a nap ever since." She listened but couldn't hear Maddie moving about. After setting the kettle on the stove, she stuck her head out of the kitchen, but the living room was empty.

"Maddie, where are you?" Felicity started down the hall, peeked into the spare room to see Timmy sound asleep, then headed on to Maddie's room. She knocked softly.

When there was no answer, Felicity opened the door gingerly. "Maddie . . ."

Her daughter was sitting on her bed, a bright red dress crumpled in her arms. Head down, Maddie mumbled, "I'd almost forgotten. I've got to go down to the cleaners. They destroyed . . . my dress."

Felicity opened the door wider and crossed the room. She sat down on the bed beside her daughter. Gently she stroked her hair. "Tell me about it, Maddie. Don't hold it in." She could feel her daughter's whole body tense, but her face remained stoically calm.

"There's nothing to talk about, Felicity. It was just a . . . mad day at work."

"I see. Always the brave one, aren't you. So strong, so independent, so self-sufficient. You're going to handle this on your own, is that it?"

Maddie flinched. "I've been doing it all my life, haven't I? Just like you."

"It's been a mistake. For me. And for you. When we hold everything in, we only succeed in tying ourselves in knots. It makes the pain that much worse."

Felicity continued to stroke her daughter's hair, despite Maddie's stiffness.

"I'm all right, Felicity."

"It was the Barrett's account that fell through, wasn't it? And Michael didn't tell you."

Maddie's knuckles whitened as she fiercely gripped the red dress. "I've really got to take this dress to the dry cleaners and demand my money back. They had no right . . ." Her voice caught. "No right." She felt terribly cold. "I trusted him . . . them. The dry cleaners." Her head was ringing, her throat closing up. She gulped in some air, trying to fight back the sob she felt forming in her chest.

Felicity slipped her arm around her daughter's shoulders. "Poor baby," she whispered. "Poor baby."

Maddie lifted her head, looking at her mother, tears flooding her eyes, Felicity's face dissolving.

And then, throwing her arms around her mother, Maddie could hold the floodgates back no longer. Words spilled out through her sobs. "Oh, Felicity... I love him so. He lied to me. He deceived me. Oh, it hurts so much."

Felicity held her daughter tightly in her arms, rocking her, kissing the top of her head.

Maddie clung to her mother as she sobbed.

"I'm glad I'm here, baby." Felicity's voice was hardly more than a whisper. "I know how much you're hurting. I do. I truly do. I'll help you, darling. You'll see. It will be okay. I promise." Felicity felt her own tears stream down her face, felt the sting of mascara in her eyes. She paid it no mind. And Maddie, as angry as she'd always secretly been that her mother had never before been there for her, took great comfort from her nearness.

They sat together on the bed, both crying, holding each other, murmuring words that didn't have to be clearly heard to be understood. Finally Maddie took her mother's hand. "Thanks, Mom," she whispered. "This time it was not a slip of the tongue." There was more she wanted to say, but the words wouldn't come. And for the first time Maddie realized they weren't necessary.

"COME INTO THE KITCHEN." Felicity took her daughter's arm. "I'll make you a sandwich. You should eat something."

Maddie let her mother lead her from the bedroom, a wispy smile on her tear-streaked face.

Felicity caught the smile and grinned. "I know. I sound just like a mother, don't I?"

Maddie stopped and observed her mother closely. "I like it."

Felicity actually blushed. "Know something? So do I." She sniffed demurely.

Maddie gently rubbed her mother's cheek. "Your mascara ran."

"I must look a sight."

Maddie's hand moved to her own face. "Me, too."

Felicity put her arm around Maddie's shoulder. "Who cares?"

As they passed the spare room, they heard Timmy stirring. Instinctively Maddie turned toward the room. But Felicity stopped her. "You go into the kitchen and heat up a bottle. I'll see to Timmy."

Maddie tilted her head. "Are you sure?"

Felicity gave one of Maddie's ears an affectionate tug. "Some people get into having a second childhood. Why not a second motherhood?"

Maddie shook her head slowly. "You amaze me, Felicity. I never suspected . . ."

Felicity was pensive. "I'm not really sure I did, either." She opened the door to the spare room, pausing for a second to glance over her shoulder at Maddie. "He is a sweet baby."

Maddie nodded. "Yes, he is."

Felicity waved her on. "Don't make the milk too hot, now."

"No. No, I won't."

Five minutes later, while Maddie was pouring the bottle, Felicity entered with a cheerful, newly diapered and dressed baby in her arms.

Maddie screwed on the nipple. "He needs his medicine. When I rushed out this morning, I forgot to tell you."

"Is he ill?" Felicity's voice registered concern. She scrutinized Timmy. "He looks fine."

"Oh, it's just an ear infection."

Felicity pursed her lips. "You had them, too."

"I did?"

"Once the doctor even considered having these tubes inserted in your ears. It sounded so dreadful. I was horrified, even though he said everything he could to try to convince me you wouldn't feel a thing. I remember I was so relieved when he said it wouldn't be necessary after all."

Maddie didn't know what to say. It was astonishing to suddenly see and hear her mother talking and behaving just like . . . a mother.

Felicity handed Timmy over to Maddie for his medicine and then his bottle, and she headed for the refrigerator. "Are you hungry?"

"No, but you must be."

Felicity turned to her daughter. "How about if we share a sandwich. And then...if you like...we can talk about what happened."

Maddie stiffened immediately and was about to protest. She didn't want to talk about what had happened. She didn't want to talk about Michael. She didn't want to think about him. She didn't want to see him ever again.

Felicity turned to the refrigerator and examined the contents. "Now, let's see," she said before Maddie could say anything. "What shall I make?"

"There are some cold cuts in the meat section. And the bread is on top of the fridge."

"Wonderful." Felicity pulled out the bin and removed three deli-wrapped packages. Then she took out mustard and retrieved the loaf of bread.

As Felicity set busily to work, Maddie watched her mother with a mixture of wonder and sadness. She couldn't recall a single instance in her entire childhood that was in any way reminiscent of this scene. She remembered fantasies, sparked by TV shows, of her mother making her her favorite sandwiches, pouring her large glasses of milk, promising cookies if she ate everything on her plate. But for as long as Maddie could recall, it had always been baby-sitters, housekeepers and neighbors who'd actually fixed her lunches. Unless they'd gotten a dinner invitation from a friend or colleague of Felicity's, dinners when she and Felicity were together were always in restaurants. Restaurants were not luxuries with Felicity. They were a tradition.

Felicity generously piled meat on one slice of bread, got Maddie's approval for the mustard and spread it meticulously on another slice of bread, then made up the sandwich and cut it in two.

"Can you manage, holding Timmy?" Felicity asked as she put one part of the sandwich on a plate and carried it over to where Maddie was sitting.

"Nothing to it," Maddie replied. "Since I've had Timmy, I've discovered that mothers, even stand-ins, quickly learn how to be octopuses."

"Yes," Felicity concurred. "A definite requirement. I often wished, when you were a baby, that I had an extra pair of hands." She sat down across the table from Maddie, placing her own half sandwich on the colorful rainbow place mat. But she made no move toward it.

"Go on," Felicity urged. "Take a bite and tell me how it is."

Maddie had to smile. From the look of anxious concern on Felicity's face, her mother might have been asking her to sample a very tricky culinary masterpiece. Cradling Timmy in one arm, Maddie picked up the sandwich and took a bite. "Delicious," she said even before she'd finished chewing.

Felicity smiled, pride glistening in her eyes as she took a bite of her own sandwich. "Well, not quite Rossi's, but not bad."

Timmy gulped down the last of his bottle as Maddie and Felicity finished eating. Felicity rose. "Here, give me Timmy. He needs to be burped." She smiled at her daughter's bemused expression. "I know it probably comes as a surprise, Madeline, but I used to get quite a few hardy burps out of you."

Maddie grinned. "Never."

Felicity lifted Timmy against one shoulder, remembering at the last minute to squeeze a dish towel between Timmy and her shoulder in case he spit up. "It's amazing how it all comes back. Like riding a bike." She paused in the midst of a pat. "Not that I ever did learn how to ride a bike." She went back to rhythmically patting Timmy's back as she leaned against the counter, but her eyes rested a little sadly on her daughter. "I never did learn everything I should have about being a mother." There was regret in her voice. "I sometimes wish I could have been different."

"Different how?" Maddie asked softly.

"We both missed out on so many experiences together. I never went to one of your lacrosse games, and I missed all those school Christmas plays where you flitted about the stage as an angel, and where you once got to be one of the wise men."

Maddie stared at her mother. "I never thought you even knew I'd once been a wise man."

Felicity smiled wistfully. "I did keep track of all your activities. You probably never believed I wanted to be at any of them, but you were wrong. I did. But I couldn't. I suppose I could make a lot of excuses, but I won't. I may have had to have a career because of our circumstances. But I won't say I regretted it. I have always loved what I do. I was good at it from the start. But caring for a baby... I was so overwhelmed about the awesome responsibility of motherhood. You were so little, so helpless. And I was supposed to be strong, confident. I wasn't. I felt scared and helpless, too."

Maddie's eyes blurred with tears. "I was so lonely at all those dreary boarding schools. I felt so abandoned." The words burst forth from her so angrily that they startled her as much as they did Felicity.

Felicity nodded, not trying to defend herself, but refusing to make apologies, either. "I wish I'd been better at juggling a career and motherhood. Single motherhood, I should say. I did do my best. I was often very lonely, too. There was many a night when I sat in some silent, far-off hotel room fighting the impulse to simply call your school and demand they put you on the very next plane. Our times together were all too brief. But I felt it wasn't fair to disrupt your life. Maybe I was wrong."

Her mother's words mitigated some of Maddie's suffering. She could finally believe that her mother had truly cared about her. She had truly loved her. And her own experience with Timmy and, yes, with Michael this past week had helped Maddie see how difficult and painful love and motherhood could be.

Just then Timmy let out a loud, uninhibited burp. Both women laughed, diffusing the bittersweet mood.

Timmy looked at the two women and giggled.

"He is an adorable baby," Maddie said.

Felicity looked at her daughter with a tender smile. "Not nearly as adorable as you were." Abruptly she handed Timmy to her daughter and went out to the hall to retrieve her purse. She returned to the kitchen and plucked out her wallet, flipping it open to the picture section.

There was only one photo amidst the half-dozen plastic holders. It was old and frayed around the edges.

Felicity very carefully extracted it and handed it to Maddie.

Maddie stared down at the photo in silence for a long time as her mother stood behind her.

"See how darling you were," Felicity said softly. "You so loved to snuggle against me like that. You were just about Timmy's age when that was snapped. I'd just taken you from your crib. You were still a little sleepy, but the moment you saw me smile, you smiled back." Felicity reached into her purse, pulled out a handkerchief and swiped at her eyes. "See. You were a beautiful baby,

Maddie. A sweet, beautiful, perfect baby." Felicity put her arm around Maddie and drew her back against her heart.

"If I've taught you only one thing, darling," Felicity said soothingly, "it was to go after what you wanted. I never wanted you to deprive yourself of anything. I'm not just talking about having a career, Maddie. I'm talking about love. True love. Enduring love. A love you're willing to fight for. I know Michael's hurt you, but perhaps when he explains ..."

Maddie shook her head against her mother's breast. "No. I don't want his explanations. I don't want anything from him ever again."

Felicity stroked her daughter's hair. "We'll see," she said softly. "You may change your mind."

"No, I won't," Maddie said adamantly, straightening. She turned around to look up at her mother and grasped her hand. "You've got to help me, Mother. If he comes back on Friday, I can't see him. I can't. You will help me?"

Felicity bent and kissed the top of her daughter's head. "I promise, Maddie. You leave Michael Harrington to me." There was a glint of a mother hen in her hazel eyes. "You may not want to talk to him, my girl, but there are a few words I have to say to the man."

Maddie managed a faint smile. She might have lost a lover this morning, but she'd gained a mother.

MICHAEL LANDED IN BOSTON at five p.m. on Friday. He was feeling terrific. His meetings with Barrett and Epstein had gone better than he'd hoped. There was still a lot of groundwork to be done, but he had set the wheels in motion. And he was confident enough of the plan going through to finally be able to tell Maddie about the offer. That also meant it was time to tell her about

L'Amour, but he was sure this new offer would more than make up for any disappointment she'd feel at having lost out to the competition. Now everything Michael wanted for Maddie would work out.

He stepped into a phone booth at the terminal and called his sister Cindy.

"Hi! Listen, I just landed. What time is the rehearsal dinner?"

"Seven o'clock. Why don't you come straight over, have a drink and relax a little before the Mad Hatter tea begins?"

He laughed and glanced at his watch. "Mmm, no, I have a couple of stops to make. I'll be there at six forty-five."

"Are you coming alone?"

"Huh?"

Cindy laughed. "Are you bringing Maddie?"

Michael absently rubbed his jaw. "I...don't think so."

"Why don't we leave it open? We can always squeeze one more at the table. See how she feels about it when you stop over there now."

Michael laughed. "You don't miss a thing, do you, Cin?"

"I'd like to think I was a wiz at ESP, but the truth is, bro, you are about as transparent as a piece of plate glass."

"Don't get carried away, Cindy. Maddie's a terrific woman. And we do have... certain feelings for each other. But—"

"Skip the speech, Michael. You'll only be wasting your breath on my account. You can't convince me you're not hooked. And if you really think you can talk yourself out of your feelings, well, do it on your own time. I, for one, hope you fail. I like her. Tell her so when you see her."

Flustered, Michael muttered, "Yeah, right. I'll see you later."

After he hung up the phone, he stared at it for a minute. Should he call Maddie from here and tell her he planned to stop by for a few minutes before the rehearsal dinner? He'd hoped to get back to Boston earlier in the day, but it hadn't worked out. After checking his watch again, he decided she was probably en route home. Best to head straight for her apartment.

Getting out of the parking lot at the airport at rush hour was no easy matter. It took a certain amount of aggressiveness and cleverness, both of which, fortunately, Michael Harrington had plenty of.

Within five minutes he was heading down the expressway. He yawned suddenly. It had been a hectic three days. And, he admitted, part of his exhaustion had come from expending so much energy fending off enticing visions of Maddie. They sprang up at random, catching him unawares. At his apartment. At meetings with Barrett and Epstein. At restaurants. Waiting for cabs.

Maddie. He could see her so clearly. Laughing. Blushing. Holding Timmy soothingly in her arms. Lying naked on her bed, her fine, beautiful body glowing with warmth, passion. That body that was so perfectly in tune with his. Maddie.

He was stalled in traffic for over a half hour before finally making it through the Callahan Tunnel, but once he got on the Southeast Expressway, he adeptly weaved in and out of the traffic onto Storrow Drive and got to Maddie's place by six.

Damn, he thought, racing through the lobby, impatiently pressing the button for the elevator. He wasn't going to have much time with Maddie. And no time to shower or change before the dinner.

The elevator creaked to Maddie's floor. He hurried down the hall to her apartment, wondering if Timmy would still be there or if Linda had already come for him. He actually missed the tyke.

He rang the doorbell. What was taking her so long? Maybe she wasn't home yet. He pressed the bell again.

"Yes, who is it?"

A woman's voice, but not Maddie's. Felicity. Yes, that was who it was.

"It's me, Felicity. Michael Harrington."

"Oh."

Michael was puzzled by her tone, even more puzzled by how long it took Felicity to unlock and open the door. And then it was only a third of the way.

"Isn't Maddie home yet?" He gave Felicity a curious look. Where was all that charm and vivaciousness? Her face was as stoic and rigid as if it had been carved in granite.

"Maddie is home." Her voice was as cold as ice—like an icicle piercing Michael's buoyant feelings, collapsing them.

"What's wrong?"

"Maddie does not want to see you."

"What does that mean?"

"Really, Mr. Harrington, I believe you know perfectly well what that means."

"Okay, then why doesn't she want to see me?"

"I believe, Mr. Harrington, you know the answer to that question, as well."

Michael's dark eyes narrowed. "I don't know what's going on, Felicity—"

"Mrs. Sargent," she corrected archly.

"This is crazy. I want to see Maddie. Whatever's going on, I'd like to hear it from her."

"No, Mr. Harrington. You'll hear it from me. And you'll hear it in spades. You pulled a lousy trick on my daughter. You lied to her, deceived her and manipulated your way into her bed. That's bad enough, Mr. Harrington. But you also manipulated your way into her heart. And Maddie's heart happens to be very precious to me. You've broken it. She's in love with you. Not that that means much to someone like you. You, Mr. Harrington, define love as L'Amour, don't you? L'Amour. Personally—" she thrust back her shoulders "—I think they're a second-rate skin-care company." She started to slam the door, but Michael's hand shot out.

"Look, I can explain."

"I couldn't care less about your explanations."

Rage threatened to overtake him. He fought for control, nevertheless pushing at the door. "I want to explain to Maddie."

"You're no doubt stronger than I am, Mr. Harrington, and you can no doubt push your way in here. But I assure you, Maddie will not talk to you. And if you persist, I shall call the police and inform them that we have an intruder."

Michael stared at her, his hand still pressed against the door but no longer pushing on it. "I didn't mean to hurt her. Damn it, it's the last thing I wanted. Don't you know that?"

"I know that Maddie must have seen something special in you that she's never seen in another man." Felicity's voice softened a fraction. "That's the real tragedy of it. If the only crime you'd committed was in the name of business, Maddie would have been angry and hurt, but those wounds would have healed. In many ways, she's tough and determined. She'll find other deals, perhaps better ones. But the wounds you've inflicted go deeper, Mr. Harrington."

He leaned wearily against the doorjamb, his hand still on the door to prevent it being slammed in his face. "I need to talk to her, Feli—Mrs. Sargent. Okay, I should have told her about L'Amour straightaway. But . . . it just got so complicated. I wasn't trying to manipulate her. God, I was as far from being in control of a situation as I've ever been. It all happened so fast. I never dreamed . . ." He saw that Felicity wasn't really listening, that she'd already made up her mind, tried him and found him guilty. And from her perspective, why not? He was guilty.

It was getting late. Even if he did force his way in and get to Maddie, there wouldn't be time to explain, to sort it out with her.

A little vein pulsed in his temple. He took a deep breath. "Whether or not you believe it, Mrs. Sargent, I'm on Maddie's side. I told her I was working on a new angle for her. Well, it's really looking good. If I could just see her . . ."

Felicity remained stoic.

Michael swallowed his frustration. "Okay, Mrs. Sargent, you win this round. But the fight isn't over. Not by a long shot."

After Felicity closed the front door, Maddie stepped out of her room holding Timmy.

Felicity turned to her. "He'll be back."

Maddie shrugged.

"He wants to explain. He says he has a new deal for you."

Maddie laughed derisively.

"There is a chance you might be wrong about the man."

"I wish I'd never met him. I hate feeling like such a little fool."

Felicity walked over to her daughter. She could see circles under Maddie's eyes. "There's absolutely nothing foolish about being in love."

"Who said anything about love?" Maddie retorted too quickly.

"Maybe you should talk to him, Maddie."

"No."

Timmy began to fuss in Maddie's arms, and Felicity took him. "What time did Linda say she'd be here? She phoned almost an hour ago."

"By seven." Maddie stared at Timmy, an enigmatic expression on her face. "If it weren't for Timmy..." Maddie stopped, fighting back tears.

Felicity put her free arm around Maddie and held her close. "Come on. We'll bathe, feed and change Timmy so that Linda can take him straight home and tuck him into bed."

Maddie smiled faintly as she stepped back. "I do think you've grown quite fond of that baby, Mother."

Felicity smiled back. "I do believe you're right." There were tears in her eyes. "If you ever do marry and have children, Maddie, I rather think I'd make a more than satisfactory grandmother." She took her daughter's hand. "And you, darling, would make a wonderful mother."

"Don't. Please." There was helplessness and pleading in Maddie's voice.

"Talk to him, Maddie."

"I can't. I can't risk any more hurt."

"That's not the only possible outcome."

"Yes, it is," Maddie said so sharply that Timmy started to fuss. But Felicity had him under control very quickly.

"Don't you see?" Maddie went on, following her mother to the kitchen. "It isn't just that he lied about the L'Amour deal. Michael's made it perfectly clear from the start that he wasn't looking for anything lasting. No promises. No marriage. No strings."

"Oh, darling, they all say that at first."

"Michael means it. He's dead set against getting married and having kids."

Felicity ordered Maddie to run a bath for Timmy in the sink as she undressed him. "Last I remember, darling," she said casually, slipping the baby's terry suit off, "you felt exactly the same way. You have always been determined to take the world on by yourself."

Maddie dangled her fingers in the warm running water. *I don't need him. I'll stop feeling wretched without him.* It had happened so fast. That was the problem. One minute she had Michael, great plans for her company, laughter, passion, joy. The next minute everything had changed. Michael was gone, prospects were gone. A pain twisted through her middle . . . like a labor pain, she suddenly imagined.

She turned and stared wanly at her mother. In a voice that came out strangled, she whispered, "I'm tired of taking the whole world on alone."

"Maddie . . ."

"Let's drop the subject, Felicity."

Felicity smiled knowingly. Maddie hadn't called her by her first name in days. Her use of it now was a clear indication that she desperately needed a little breathing room. Felicity understood.

"Here we go," she said, handing Timmy to Maddie. "You bathe him and I'll fix him some baby cereal."

Maddie gave her mother an appreciative nod and set to the task, thinking, as Timmy slapped merrily at the water, that she was going to miss him, too.

When Linda arrived arm in arm with her husband, Donald, a little past seven to retrieve Timmy, both Felicity and Maddie relinquished him reluctantly. But they were thrilled that Donald was the one to gather Timmy in his arms and give his son a warm, affectionate kiss. Linda hugged Maddie, thanking her profusely for giving her and Donald a chance to get everything straightened out.

After beaming parents and son departed, the apartment felt sadly empty and disturbingly quiet. Maddie turned on the radio, but the soft rock music only served to heighten the loss.

Felicity watched Maddie pretend to read a magazine as she sat across from her in the living room. Finally Maddie threw the magazine down on the coffee table and folded her arms across her chest. Felicity rose, walked silently over to the couch and sat down at the opposite end, patting her lap. "You look exhausted, baby. Come, stretch out. Rest your head on me."

Maddie hesitated for a moment and then did as her mother suggested. Gently Felicity stroked her daughter's brow and smoothed the hair from her face.

Maddie sighed, her body relaxing even if her mind wouldn't. "Mother?"

"Yes."

"Did you ever sing lullabies to me when I was a baby?"

Felicity didn't answer immediately. "No," she said finally. "But I wish I had."

Maddie nodded and closed her eyes. Before she drifted off to sleep, she turned and looked up at her mother. "I love you," she said in a voice that was barely more than a whisper.

MICHAEL WENT THROUGH the motions of host and "father" of the bride like a robot that night. He barely touched his dinner and kept missing cues during the rehearsal. The whole family knew something was amiss. And that something spelled Maddie. But Michael looked daggers at anyone who so much as mentioned her name.

All that evening Felicity's words echoed in his mind. He couldn't shake them off any more than he could shake off visions of Maddie. Only now he saw her white with rage, then stretched across her bed crying, then staring at him, her beautiful hazel eyes filled with fury and pain. Those visions stabbed through him.

There had to be time to straighten things out, he thought. Race back there tonight, after the rehearsal was over, bang on her door, demand to see her. Take her in his arms. Feel her body respond.

Felicity had said she loved him. Was that her interpretation? Or had Maddie told her that she loved him? She'd never told him. He felt cheated.

"Michael, you keep missing the beat. Slow down. You're walking me to the altar, not rescuing me from a burning building," complained his sister Jessie.

"Sorry," he mumbled.

He tried to concentrate, but his mind seemed determined to rebel. *Do I love Maddie? Is that it? I know I want her. I know I can't push her out of my head. I know I feel so damn good with her that I want to sing. I know when I'm making love to her I feel this exhilarating sense of connection. Is that love?*

He broke out in a sweat. He was trembling.

"Come on, Michael. We're almost there," his sister whispered. "Keep the beat and we'll be home free."

Keep the beat. His heart was beating wildly. *Keep the beat. The beat of my heart.*

12

WHEN FELICITY INSISTED on staying with Maddie on Friday night instead of returning to her suite at the Ritz, Maddie didn't argue. She didn't want to be alone. More than that, her mother's presence was proving to be a great comfort.

The next morning, when Maddie awoke a little after ten, Felicity was already in the kitchen.

"Coffee?"

Maddie nodded groggily. She sat down at the kitchen table. Felicity brought over a steaming hot mug.

"It isn't instant," Maddie marveled after taking a sip.

"I detest instant coffee," Felicity said lightly.

Maddie laughed. "I'm just surprised you know how to make fresh coffee."

"I know." Felicity grinned. "You no doubt think all I'm capable of making are reservations. Or dialing room service."

"Well . . ."

"You're right. But if one puts one's mind to coping with a new situation, one can surprise oneself."

Maddie eyed her mother shrewdly. "Somehow I think we've moved from making fresh coffee to making generalizations, Mother."

"Don't you have a wedding to attend this afternoon?"

"I told you last night that, under the circumstances, I'm not going." She glanced at the kitchen clock. "I should call Mrs. Harrington and tell her. I'll wait a little longer."

Felicity studied her daughter carefully. "You look dreadful, darling."

Maddie laughed dryly. "All the more reason not to go to a wedding."

"You aren't going to feel or look better until you confront this matter."

Maddie's eyes narrowed. "Let's not overdo the motherly advice. Really, I'm a big girl now." Immediately after the words were out, Maddie regretted them. She reached out and touched her mother. "I'm sorry. That was nasty."

Felicity gave Maddie a pensive look. "I suppose I am pushing it a bit. It's funny. All these years that you've been grown up I've never really thought you were ever in need of motherly advice. The truth of it is, I've always felt rather in awe of you."

Maddie stared at her mother, wide-eyed. "In awe of me? For heaven's sake, why?"

"Oh, you always seemed so self-contained, so sure of yourself...so in control of everything. You never seemed to need anything . . . or anyone."

"But . . . that's exactly how I've always seen you. I was simply following your lead. Never all that successfully."

"You put on a good act."

Maddie observed her mother for several moments. "You put on a better one. I kept wishing I'd be as good at it someday as you."

Felicity shook her head sadly. "It isn't a goal to aspire to, darling, believe me. Oh, it's one thing to have confidence in yourself, to go after your dreams, to feel good about your abilities. But we all need someone. It's only that some of us are more lucky than others at finding that someone."

Maddie stared miserably at her mother. "Yes, some of us are very unlucky." And then, with a whisper of a smile, she added, "At least we've found each other."

Felicity smiled, squeezing her daughter's hand. Then she glanced idly around the room. "I wonder how Timmy is doing back home."

"I know," Maddie said with a sigh. "The apartment doesn't feel the same without him." She sipped her coffee for a bit and then rose. "Well, I'll go take a shower and get dressed." She hesitated. "Then I'll phone Mrs. Harrington."

It was nearly eleven when the doorbell rang. Maddie was in her room dressing. Felicity, still in her robe, went to answer the door.

Who is it?"

"Michael. I'm not leaving until I see Maddie, Mrs. Sargent. You can call the police. Hell, you can call the militia. I have to see her."

Felicity sighed and opened the door. "Oh..." she murmured as she saw him standing there dressed to the nines. Some men looked especially good in tuxedos. Michael Harrington put them to shame. He looked absolutely glorious.

His midnight-blue eyes glinted as he stared Felicity down. "In case Maddie forgot to mention it to you, we have a wedding to attend this afternoon. I've come to pick her up." He brushed past her.

"Wait, Michael. Go into the kitchen and have a cup of coffee. Let me have a word with Maddie."

Michael rubbed his jaw. "This whole thing is driving me crazy. Maddie drives me crazy. I can't sleep. I have no appetite. I can't think straight anymore." He paused. "Okay, I'll go get some coffee."

As Michael headed for the kitchen, Felicity proceeded to Maddie's room with determination in her step.

"Who was at the door?" Maddie asked, slipping a sweater over her head.

Instead of answering, Felicity gave her daughter a tip-to-toe inspection. "Really, darling, that won't do at all."

Maddie looked down at her feet, which were covered by wool socks, her dungarees, her favorite gray mohair sweater. "Won't do for what?"

"For a wedding, of course."

Maddie stepped back, tripped over her shoe and landed on the bed.

"Michael was at the door."

Maddie's heart started to pound. "You *did* send him away. Tell me you sent him away."

Felicity smiled airily. "He's in the kitchen having a cup of coffee."

Maddie was horrified. "In the kitchen? In *my* kitchen? Drinking coffee?"

"My fresh brewed coffee. Oh, dear, it's probably stale by now."

"What is the matter with you, Mother? How can you be thinking about stale coffee at a time like this?"

Felicity shrugged. "Really, dear, I'm not thinking about coffee nearly as much as I'm thinking about what you're going to wear to Michael's sister's wedding." She smiled brightly. "The man looks positively smashing in a tux, Maddie. You'll have to come up with an outfit equally wonderful."

Maddie fought back tears. "Why are you doing this? You said you would help me."

Felicity smiled tenderly. "I'm trying my very best, baby. He loves you, Maddie."

"He told you that?" Maddie stared at her mother in disbelief.

"Well . . . not in so many words."

"Oh, Mother, don't do this to me."

"He's got all the symptoms, darling."

"Oh, no, now you sound like Liz. Symptoms! I'll tell you what you can both do with your symptoms!"

"That's better," Felicity said, unperturbed. "Be angry. It's far more becoming than being miserable. There. There's some color in your cheeks." She walked to the closet. "Now what were you planning to wear to the wedding?"

"I am not going to the wedding."

"I'm afraid Michael is bound and determined to take you. I wouldn't put it past him to cart you off dressed just the way you are now. Wouldn't that be rather embarrassing for you?"

"He wouldn't."

"Shall we find out?"

Maddie was silent.

"Ah, here's a lovely red dress. Oh, no, that's the one you need to take back to the cleaners. Dear, dear. It really did shrink, didn't it?"

Maddie rose reluctantly and stood, arms akimbo. "All right, if it will make you happy, I'll put something appropriate on and go to the wedding. But only because I believe you would actually encourage Michael to drag me off like this. Why you've suddenly taken his side, I don't know. Michael Harrington is not in love with me. He's never said a single word about love. He's never given me one hint of wanting anything more than a casual affair."

She strode over to the closet and pulled out a pretty green chiffon dress. "I'll tell you why I'm really going to the wedding. To prove to you, to Michael, to myself, that I can get along without him just fine."

"Yes, dear."

"I mean it."

Felicity smiled. "Do you need any help?"

Maddie glared at her. "Oh, you've done enough already."

"Well, then, I'll leave you to it." She started for the door. "I'll keep Michael company."

"You do that."

Felicity turned the knob. "I've got a lovely gold pin with me in my pocketbook that would look wonderful on that dress."

"I don't want to look wonderful," Maddie said pointedly.

Fired up the way she was, she couldn't look anything but, Felicity thought.

Maddie stayed in her room for several minutes after she was dressed and ready. The problem was, she wasn't ready. She wasn't ready to face Michael. She'd hoped to have more time, more distance. More fortitude.

She silently rehearsed what she would say, what he would say, what she would answer. The rehearsal only added to her agitation. Her palms were sweaty as she opened the bedroom door. Her legs were shaky as she walked down the hall.

Michael must have heard her. He stepped out of the kitchen into the hall.

The sight of him took Maddie's breath away. The contrast between his tanned, hard-edged features and the refined, well-tailored black tux was devastating. The aura of raw masculinity he exuded was so strong that Maddie had to dig her fingernails into the palm of her hand for control.

The space between them, no more than ten feet, crackled with electricity. Michael's dark eyes drifted from her face, took in her soft green chiffon dress, stunning in its simplicity. He returned his gaze to her face. He could see the heightened color in her cheeks. She was very beautiful. Even at this distance he could detect the faint, inviting scent of her floral perfume. It instantly evoked erotic fantasies, much to his dismay.

"Nice day for a wedding," Maddie said, injecting a note of false brightness into her voice that fooled neither one of them.

Suddenly she realized she was frozen to the spot, in a panic about getting another step closer to him. She felt light-headed, as if she might faint.

Felicity popped her head out of the kitchen and smiled at Maddie. "What a beautiful dress, Maddie. You look wonderful. Doesn't she, Michael?"

Michael was as rooted to his spot as Maddie was to hers. He felt equally light-headed. "Wonderful," he murmured.

"Well, you two had better head off. You know that old song, 'Get Me to the Church on Time.'"

Maddie testing herself, took one step, then another. Okay. She was doing okay.

Michael smiled at her concentration. He began to feel a bit more relaxed. He stepped toward her. Pretty steady. Yeah, he'd be okay.

They were two feet apart. Felicity discreetly slipped back into the kitchen and began banging pots and pans.

Maddie smiled at her mother's obviousness, but without realizing it that smile also took in Michael.

He found her smile dazzling. "You really do look wonderful, Maddie."

Her smile deepened. "Thanks. So do you."

He hesitated. "Listen, Maddie . . ."

"No, Michael. Not now. Let's just go to the wedding and . . ." She started to say, "Get through it," but realized that would sound awful.

Michael smiled, and Maddie knew he'd most likely read her thoughts. Oh, well, he had to realize this was going to be an ordeal for her.

An hour later Maddie was distraught to discover that the wedding was proving more of an ordeal than she had expected. As she watched Michael, who was giving the bride away, walking down the aisle with his sister Jessica, Maddie found herself having to fight a crazy sensation that it was her wedding day, not Jessica's. Even her eyes played tricks on her. She could see herself in Jessica's wedding dress, arm in arm with Michael. Only he wasn't giving the bride away. He was marrying her.

The scent of all the flowers decorating the chapel, and the bouquets carried by the bride, flower girl and bridesmaids, had a dizzying effect on Maddie. She fixed her gaze on Michael as he drew nearer her pew. He looked so proud, so regal, so intoxicatingly handsome. He made a perfect . . . groom.

Michael as groom. She shook herself. Was she truly insane? Insanity continued as her eyes locked for a moment with Michael's. He smiled, and Maddie could have sworn his lips had moved, that he had whispered something to her. It looked like . . . "I do." Her heart hammered. Her throat was dry. She gripped the pew with whitened knuckles.

The bride swished by in her full-length satin-and-lace Empire gown. Then the flower girl and the bridesmaids. They all carried gardenias. Maddie's head whirled. The scent, this close, was cloying. Her vision was blurred.

The setting was too perfect, the fantasy too real. The sight of Michael, in his tuxedo, walking up to the altar, was creating havoc within her.

As she listened to the ceremony, she had to fight back the impulse to cry. People always cried at weddings, but Maddie was afraid that if she started she might not stop.

Michael was standing off to the side of the bride and groom. Maddie tried to avoid looking at him, but her eyes seemed to have a will of their own. His gaze was focused on his sister and the groom. He looked very solemn.

The minister's voice droned on. Michael was only half paying attention. While he trained his eyes on Jessie and his soon-to-be brother-in-law, his thoughts were far removed from them. He couldn't fathom the turmoil inside him. It had been building all morning, but it had begun in earnest when he caught Maddie's eye as he was walking down the aisle with Jessica. The crazy thing was, when he looked from Maddie to his sister, suddenly beneath the bride's net veil, smiling warmly, tenderly, erotically at him...was Maddie's face. He'd had to blink several times to dispel the vision. He'd almost missed a step.

Hazily both Michael and Maddie heard the minister pronounce the happy couple husband and wife. Tears filled Maddie's eyes as they kissed. Michael had to squint to keep the tears from rising in his eyes.

And then, as the couple turned up the aisle, Michael's eye once again caught Maddie's. Her breath caught in her throat.

Oh, Michael, I wish this were our wedding. I wish that it were us walking up the aisle, hand in hand, looking radiant as brides and grooms always do on their wedding day. Oh, Michael...

Mustering all her strength, she pasted on a congratulatory smile, praying that for once Michael would not be able to read her mind.

His own smile was enigmatic. What was he thinking? she wondered. What was he feeling?

After the ceremony Maddie stood on the sidelines as family pictures were taken. At one point Mrs. Harrington pulled her into one of the group shots, insisting that Michael, whom she pushed beside her, put his arm around her. And smile.

The reception was in the church basement. The hundred or more guests feasted from a buffet table, took time out for hugs, kisses and congratulations to the bride, groom and family of each. Before the three-piece band began the dance music, Jessica called all the single women in the room to gather behind her for the throwing of the bouquet.

Maddie ducked behind a group of middle-aged men and women. No way was she going to join in that quaint ritual.

Unfortunately Mrs. Harrington spotted her and motioned vigorously for her to join in. There was no way out of it. Maddie flushed scarlet as Michael caught sight of her trying to make herself scarce in the back of the group. She glared at him as he cocked his head in amusement.

Maddie resolutely kept her hands at her sides as Jessica gave everyone in the group a bright smile and then turned her back to them and tossed.

Maddie stared with complete dismay at the bouquet, which was zeroing in on her. Thank heavens for the aggressive and perhaps desperate young woman on her right. Just in the nick of time, the woman's hand darted out and grabbed the bouquet, accidentally knocking Maddie to the side.

The young woman gave Maddie an apologetic smile. "Oh, I'm sorry. I didn't mean to shove. It's just that this is the fifth wedding I've attended this year. And, well . . . I'd really like the sixth to be mine."

Maddie smiled. "I wish you the best of luck."

A minute later Michael was behind her.

"That was a close call."

"I do believe your sister must have eyes in the back of her head," Maddie said, trying to look amused.

He gave her a considered look. "You certainly were determined not to catch it. Are you superstitious?"

Maddie tried her best to play this coolly. "No. I just didn't want to ruin it for someone who really wanted it."

"I see."

He leaned toward her. For one panicked instant Maddie thought he was going to kiss her. What would happen then to her cool control? It would vanish instantly, that's what.

He didn't kiss her. Instead, he merely asked her to dance. He was smiling, but there was a smoldering look in his eyes.

He put his arm around her waist. He felt her stiffen. "It's only a dance, Maddie."

She wanted to refuse. She wasn't at all sure she could handle even a dance with Michael. To feel his arms around her, his warm breath ruffling her hair, to feel his long, muscular, oh-so-familiar body pressed against hers . . . it was too much. But as she started to turn him down, she saw the implacable set of his jaw, the glint of determination in his eyes.

"All right. One dance. And then I'm leaving."

He pulled her close as the band played an old senti-
mental fox-trot. "We've never danced together."

She swallowed. No, they'd certainly skipped the usual
preliminaries. No wining, dining, dancing, courting.
They'd desired each other too much. They hadn't wanted
to waste time, play games. And even now Maddie felt
that same hungry yearning. Even as her mind rebelled.

Had it been as wonderful for him? Had he felt her tenderness as she had felt his? Would it be as hard for him
to forget her as it was going to be for her to forget him?

Maddie broke away as soon as the dance was over. "I
have to go."

"I'll drive you."

"No. No, you shouldn't leave."

"I'll come back. The family will understand."

"No. I'd rather get a cab."

"How about dinner tomorrow night?"

Maddie shook her head.

He gripped her wrist and led her off to a quiet corner.

"I know I should have told you about the L'Amour deal
straightaway," he started to explain.

"Don't, Michael. That's the way it goes in business. I
guess I was naive enough to think…." She stopped. "Well,
this experience has helped me to grow up. I'm a big girl
now, Michael. Sargent Skin Care will survive without
Barrett's. When the next deal comes along, I'll be a lot
shrewder, I assure you."

"I've been trying to talk to you about the next deal,
damn it, but you won't give me a chance to get a word
in. And I really don't want to get into it here. Let's get
together tomorrow. Look, I'm not as big a bastard as you
are casting me. Give me a chance, Maddie."

"Michael, we had a brief fling. And you can go off
knowing you taught me more about passion and busi-

ness than . . ." She pressed her lips together, trying to steady her breath. "More than I wanted to learn." With that she broke free of his grasp and darted through the merry crowd of celebrants.

MICHAEL HAD TO FLY back to New York on Monday. He called Maddie at work and at home every day that week, but all he got was a secretary or an answering machine. He left messages, insisting that she give him a chance to outline a promising new deal for her. He left his office and home numbers, but Maddie didn't call back.

Maddie, determined not to take any crumbs Michael wanted to throw her way, stubbornly ignored his messages.

On Friday, a clear, crisp day, Maddie decided to take a walk during her lunch break. She strolled down Newberry Street, a quaint Boston thoroughfare lined with little gift shops, art galleries and boutiques. Maddie glanced idly at the window displays, uninterested in doing any shopping until she came to a small toy store. She stared at the displays of dolls, trucks, stuffed animals and, on impulse, walked in and purchased a large white cuddly teddy bear.

She left work early that day, ringing Linda up to say she'd like to stop by and visit her and Timmy. Linda was delighted. Once again she told Maddie she'd be forever grateful to her for helping her get her marriage back together.

Maddie arrived at Linda's doorstep just after four. She felt a little silly holding the giant teddy bear, but she knew Timmy would love it.

"Hi," Linda greeted her cheerily and grinned at the sight of the stuffed animal. "This must be Tim's lucky day. Two visitors bearing gifts. And it isn't even Christmas."

"Two . . . ?" Maddie didn't finish her question. As she stepped in the door, she saw Michael Harrington sitting in the living room merrily bouncing Timmy on his knee.

Maddie's first instinct was to bolt. But Michael had already looked up and so had Timmy. At the sight of her Timmy giggled gleefully. Michael's response was less expressive, but his smile, a little awkward, and charmingly boyish, had a devastating effect on Maddie.

She stood there, unable to look into his eyes. Linda stood behind her.

"Go on in. Michael's been singing your praises again. He keeps telling me how great you were with Timmy. Not that I had any doubt you would be."

"Again?" Maddie echoed, her gaze finally directed at Michael. "You've been here before?"

Michael stood with Timmy in his arms. "I stopped by one other time I was in town for the day. Just to see how he was doing. If he got over his ear infection." He smiled crookedly, redness sneaking up over his collar. "I guess I got kind of attached to him."

Maddie nodded. She didn't know what to say. Michael walked over to her with Timmy. "Why don't you hold him? Or are you nervous again now that you're out of practice?"

Maddie laughed softly. "No. I'm sure it's like riding a bike." She showed Timmy his gift. He grabbed for the bear, and then Maddie took them both in her arms. She walked over to the couch, spotting, as she sat down with Tim, another teddy bear that bore a remarkable resemblance to the one she'd just given the baby.

Michael grinned, dropping into the chair across from her. "I guess we have very similar taste."

Linda stood in the entry. "Hey, you two, can I ask a big favor? I just need to run down to the store for some milk. I'll be back in five minutes. Could you keep an eye on Tim for me?" Michael, ignoring the look of discomfort on Maddie's face, said, "Sure, we'd love to."

Once Linda left, Maddie began busily playing with Timmy.

"You never answered any of my calls, Maddie."

She gave Michael the briefest glance. "I thought you'd get the hint. I don't want to do business with you, Michael." She hesitated, and when she spoke again, she kept her eyes on Timmy. "Or anything else. We had our little fling. No strings, no promises, remember? Well . . . it's over."

"It isn't over, Maddie." He walked over to her, took Timmy in his arms and leveled his gaze on her.

For all her anger and hurt, she couldn't help the flash of arousal that shot through her.

"Linda will be right back, Michael. This isn't the time or the place."

"Okay, then let's go over to your apartment when Linda gets back." It was a statement not a question.

Maddie met his gaze. Only now did she see that his features looked a bit ragged. So this last week hadn't been a breeze for him, either, she thought.

"All right," she relented. "We'll talk back at my place."

13

MICHAEL, USUALLY SO SMOOTH when it came to business—and it was business first, he'd firmly decided—could find no easy way to begin as he stood facing Maddie in her living room. So he dug his hand into his pants pocket and pulled out the tube of the Sargent "wonder cream," tossing it on the coffee table.

Maddie stared at it and then looked up at Michael, puzzled.

"Have you ever heard of Childcare? They're the leading manufacturer of infant furnishings in the country. Last year they broke into infant's clothes. They're already in the black. Barrett's carries their full line."

Michael stopped to take a breath and then sat down in an armchair. Maddie, following his lead, sat across from him on the couch.

He leaned forward. "They've decided to break into a new market. Skin care for babies. Hypoallergenic powders, soaps, shampoos, lotions." His face broke into a smile. "An ointment that really works on diaper rash."

Maddie stared at Michael, but she didn't say a word.

"The president of Childcare is Joel Epstein. A terrific guy. He reviewed your portfolio, had his lab have a go at your wonder cream." He hesitated, then rose, crossed over to the couch and sat down. His eyes burned into her. "He wants you, Maddie."

She kept staring at him.

"No punches pulled. No other companies considered. He's ready to work out a deal with you." He smiled crookedly. "Of course, Barrett's would like the opportunity to introduce the new line. But after the products are introduced into the market, Epstein plans a major marketing campaign and full saturation. Supermarkets, drugstores, department stores. Upscale, downscale. In short, he wants to see Sargent Babycare products in the hands of every concerned mother across the country."

Maddie finally found her voice. "I can't believe it. I never really...considered that market."

"Epstein is willing to invest enough money to enable you to branch out. What do you think?"

Maddie's eyes were wide. "What do I think? It's...fantastic. It's...wonderful."

"It will put Sargent on the map, Maddie. It's what you wanted. What you always dreamed of."

She shifted her weight on the couch. Yes, it was what she wanted. What she'd dreamed of. It was the financial coup of a lifetime. So why did she have this funny, let-down feeling?

"This was what you had in mind for me all along?"

"Well...almost all along," he admitted. "I was wrong to hedge my bet, Maddie. I should have told you about L'Amour straight off. But you'd had quite a night and...I didn't have the heart to tell you. And afterward...I was sure you'd toss me out on my ear. I didn't want you to toss me out, Maddie."

"Is that why you thought up the Childcare deal?"

"I guess there was some of that. And part of it was that I did feel I owed you. But the main reason, Maddie, is that I happen to believe in what you have to offer." He guided her chin in his direction. "If Timmy could talk, he'd say the same."

She smiled. "I don't know what to say. You certainly keep on turning my world topsy-turvy."

"Does that mean you forgive me?"

Her eyes held his steadily. "As long as you promise to play it straight with me from here on out."

Michael grinned. "Scout's honor."

After a few moments he rose from the couch and looked down at her. "Now that we've settled that, we can put business aside." As Maddie's breath caught, he pulled her up to him, his mouth on hers before she could protest. He kissed her roughly, his tongue thrusting past her teeth.

His mouth never left hers as he unzipped her dress. Maddie was conscious of nothing but his lips, his tongue, his hands on her skin, the smell of wool and after-shave lotion.

Only when he began to slip her dress off did Maddie pull back. "I don't think this is wise, Michael."

"It's the smartest thing I've done in two weeks," he murmured into her hair.

Maddie's hazel eyes glistened with excitement. "Maybe you're right."

With a wriggle she was out of the dress. In one swift movement Michael pulled off his sweater. She was unbuttoning his shirt as he lifted her in his arms and carried her into the bedroom.

They finished undressing each other before they fell into bed. Michael stroked her body with possessive tenderness. He whispered wonderful things as he caressed her. He told her how much he missed her, how beautiful she was, how good she felt, how in sync they were. He said every wonderful thing in the world except that he loved her and wanted to marry her, have babies with her, grow old with her. That wasn't part of the deal.

He slid on top of her, and she felt him inside her. Even as she let him draw her into that warm, soft, erotic depth, some part of her felt incomplete. Maddie wasn't sure if Michael sensed the change, but his movements slowed, and with sensitive patience he held back until finally all thought eluded her and she arched against him in ecstasy.

In the pearly grayness of dusk they lay in each other's arms. He stroked her back, kissed her damp hair, rested his free hand between the satiny warmth of her thighs. "Let's stay like this all weekend."

Maddie didn't argue as she snuggled against him. "Mmm, I could stay like this forever."

Michael cupped her chin, his eyes sparkling, his smile tender. "That's not a bad idea, Maddie."

She smiled hesitantly. "Are you serious?"

"You changed my life, Maddie. You and Timmy both. I know we have this . . . no-strings deal and all. But what if I wanted to renegotiate? Make a new deal with you?"

Maddie's heart was racing. "What kind of deal?"

He grinned. "You're going to make this hard on me, aren't you?" His eyes glistened. "Remember I told you that old man Barrett wanted me to make Boston my base?"

Maddie nodded. Her whole body was trembling.

"Well," Michael went on, "I decided it wasn't such a bad idea. I make the switch next month."

Maddie smiled. "I bet that will make your family happy."

"Not as happy as they're going to be when they find out they've got another wedding to plan."

He laughed as he saw the incredulous look on Maddie's face.

"I love you, Maddie."

"Oh, Michael, I love you too. I have from the beginning."

His arms enfolded her. "Did I ever tell you, Maddie Sargent, how terrific you look with a baby in your arms?"

"I do?"

"So what do you say, Maddie? Why don't we get married and have one of our own?"

Maddie felt little pinpricks of happiness travel down her spine. "Only one?"

Michael grinned. It was the warmest, most tender, most loving grin Maddie had ever seen. "Maybe two. Think we can handle two careers, marriage, a couple of kids?"

They looked into each other's eyes and laughed. "Nothing to it," she murmured, kissing him.

Some things just come naturally....

NATURAL TOUCH

Cathy Gillen Thacker

Chapter One

"Can you show me where your tummy hurts, Melissa?" Sarah asked gently.

Melissa pointed to the center of her tummy. "Right here, Dr. MacIntosh."

Sarah gave her patient a reassuring smile, palpitated the child's abdomen lightly and became perplexed when she found no tenderness or signs of abdominal abscess. Except for the stomachaches, which were so strong they often had the little girl in tears, Melissa appeared to be in excellent health. Deciding some lab tests were needed before she could make a diagnosis, Sarah explained to the child and her mother' what was to be done, took some samples, then called in her nurse to collect them.

While she waited for the results of the in-office tests, Sarah's thoughts turned to one David Buchanan. He was a puzzle. A Dayton lawyer, he had phoned her earlier in the day saying he needed to see her. Refusing to disclose the reason for the meeting, except that it was a highly personal matter and best handled at the end of the workday, he had arranged to come to her office at five-thirty. That was in half an hour. Since he had called, Sarah hadn't been able to get his low, resonant voice out of her mind, or shake the feeling of impending doom. He hadn't sounded happy; she could bet whatever news he had for her wasn't good.

"The results on Melissa are in," Carol said, looking in on Sarah. A registered nurse, with three children of her own, Carol ran the office with laudable efficiency. She was easy to work with and very good with children, and Sarah considered Carol her right hand. She didn't know what she would do without her.

"The white blood-cell count and urinalysis are both normal."

Sarah sighed, relieved. That was good news, but it didn't begin to explain why Melissa was so miserable. Sarah walked back into the examining room and informed Melissa and her mother that the test results were normal. Then she encouraged the little girl to talk some more about the stomachaches, and it soon became clear that the cramps occurred only during school recess, when Melissa had no one to play with.

"So you're lonely during recess," Sarah concluded, her heart going out to the troubled child.

Melissa nodded, her face crumpling with the admission.

Now knowing the attacks were emotional in origin, Sarah discussed with Melissa and her mother ways to eliminate some of the child's stress—and the butterflies in Melissa's tummy. Then satisfied her patient was on the road to recovery, she bade them goodbye and retreated to her private office.

She looked at the clock as she sat down behind her desk, feeling suddenly anxious again. Fifteen more minutes until David Buchanan's arrival. What did he want with her? she wondered.

DAVID BUCHANAN BATTLED the downtown Dayton rush hour traffic with the ease of an experienced commuter, both hands on the steering wheel, dark blue eyes on the road, his mind on the meeting ahead. Although his Blazer supplied plenty of room for his tall, rangy frame, he felt confined and on edge. Hoping to ease his tension, he flexed his broad shoulders once, and then again. As his muscles relaxed, his mind turned back to the lady doctor with the low, husky voice and the no-nonsense yet unquestionably polite manner.

Although he'd been his charming best on the phone, he'd still had a hard time convincing Sarah MacIntosh to meet with him. Not surprising, though, because he wouldn't give her any details. But how could he? News like that deserved to be delivered in person, and there was no telling what she might say or do upon hearing it. She would be distraught, certainly... maybe even go... beyond that. David didn't know if he would have to offer a shoulder to cry on, some practical words of comfort or advice, or even a way out of what was bound to be a wrenching, demanding situation. Because if she decided to go ahead and meet her obligation, her life would be changed irrevocably.

"YOU'VE BEEN NAMED GUARDIAN of Elizabeth Smith's three children," David finished some twenty minutes later. Probably the roughest twenty minutes of Sarah's life, he thought.

Wordlessly Sarah took the will he handed to her and studied it. "She never said anything to me about becoming a guardian," she murmured in a dazed tone of voice several moments later.

Liz had been under no legal obligation to tell Sarah, although David had urged her to do so when he drew up the will. "The law doesn't require you to assume responsibility for them," he pointed out. He had no desire to push Sarah into a corner she didn't want to be in. "This is just an indication of Liz's wishes."

Sarah flipped through the document again, then asked, "You wrote the will for her?"

"Yes. Eight years ago, when she was still living in Dayton. I'm also her executor." He reached into his briefcase and pulled out an envelope. "She gave me this, to be opened by you at her death."

Turning pale, Sarah took the letter.

David moved to the window and turned his back, giving her privacy. He'd guessed from their phone conversation that she was young; seeing her, he decided she was in her middle thirties, same as he was. He hadn't expected her to be so beautiful, or so unconsciously sexy—he couldn't help note that she made even an austere white lab coat look good. In fact, everything about her was alluring. Her short, red-gold hair, pale brown, almost golden eyes, fair skin and sensual lips. She came up to his chin and, he noted, had great legs.

On the surface, she was handling her friend's death well, with the composure of a physician, a person for whom death was a daily met fact of life. But he could see her grief beneath the facade. It was hard for him not to touch her and offer some comfort.

It had been harder telling her that Liz had been killed some three months ago when a faulty gas water heater had exploded in Liz's home in Cleveland. Although her children had not been hurt—they'd been at school at the time—everything else had been destroyed by the fire caused by the explosion. Her friends from the college where she taught English literature had arranged and paid for the funeral. An older couple—neighbors—had taken the children in. Not until David had become aware of Liz's death through a mutual acquaintance had her will been presented.

Sarah finished reading the letter. Still feeling stunned, she asked, "Why didn't anyone call me when she died?"

David had asked the same question. He turned toward her and leaned one shoulder against the window frame. "First of all, Liz's address book and all her personal papers were burned. Then the kids, who were understandably pretty numb, didn't do anything about notifying people or arranging the funeral. Josh, the oldest—seventeen, I believe—says he doesn't even remember much of it, much less who was there."

"So he had no way of knowing that I wasn't notified."

"Right." David watched the shifting emotions on her face, adding, "I understand there were a lot of people there, friends from the university and neighbors."

"Did Josh know there was a will?"

"When I talked to him, he said he vaguely remembered his mother sitting him down and telling him she had written one. He was about eight or nine at the time. He doesn't remember her mentioning you specifically, but he admits he didn't pay much attention. His dad had just died, and he didn't want to think about his mom dying, too, or what would happen to them if she did."

Sarah slowly folded the letter, holding it in her hand as if it were the most precious of treasures. "So he blocked it."

"I think so."

Sarah nodded and brushed a stray tear from her cheek. "Did you know her well?"

"No, I didn't. I wish I had." He recalled that she had been very nice and also levelheaded in their business dealings. That had made him wonder about her decision not to tell Sarah she was naming her guardian of her children. It was quite a lot to lay on a person unexpectedly, and David knew that Liz had realized that, too.

"Was there some reason you can figure she didn't tell you she had named you guardian?" David asked, filled with curiosity.

Sarah was silent for a few seconds. Finally she shrugged listlessly and said, "She probably knew I would have said no back then. Eight years ago I was still finishing my residency at Miami Valley Hospital. I was single. I didn't know the first thing about raising kids." She sighed and ran both hands through her hair.

"Has that changed?" He was aware it was a rude question, but he had to ask. It was his responsibility to see the children were well taken care of, and he intended to do just that, even if it meant hurting Sarah's feelings. He knew from her reputation in the community that she was a fine physician, but what kind of parent she would make was another matter entirely.

Sarah raised her head and stared at him defiantly. "If you're asking me if I have hands-on experience, Mr. Buchanan..."

"I am." Damn the torpedoes, full speed ahead.

Her eyes glittered resentfully, but didn't waver from his. "The answer is no."

He had to push it. "You've never been a mother?"

She flinched and dropped her eyes. "No," she said after a moment, the hurt look back on her face.

David wondered at her hurt—or was it remorse?—intrigued and sympathetic all at once. He walked toward her and stopped when he was only a foot away. "You're single?"

She nodded, and moved back from him. "Divorced."

"Is this something you want to do?"

She looked away, as if she were struggling with some inner demons and didn't want him to see. "It's what Liz wanted," she said, looking again at the letter in her hand.

"But is it what you want?" he persisted.

"Is there anyone else who might assume guardianship?"

David shook his head, perplexed by her attitude. It was obvious she cared, that she wanted to take the children. Not once had she said she couldn't do it. Yet it was also obvious she had grave doubts about her ability to handle the situation. And that was strange in an otherwise so confident a woman. For God's sake, she was a pediatrician! She ought to know everything about children. "Aside from you," he said, "the only option is to put the children in foster homes, then hope for adoption later."

"Together?"

"Separately is more like it."

"What about the older couple who've been taking care of them?"

"They love the kids, but they're in their early sixties...."

"I understand," she said quietly. "Three school-age children are a lot to take on."

"You don't have to answer right away. I know you need time to think about it." *Anyone would.*

Deep in thought, Sarah seemed to barely hear him. "You said you've seen them?" she asked, turning to him abruptly, a hopeful look in her eyes.

"Yes, yesterday. I drove up there."

"And?"

David shrugged. "Physically they're fine. Emotionally they're still recovering from their mother's death. But they've all had some counseling from Social Services and they're doing okay."

She sat back down in her chair, regarding him all the while. "There's more to this than what you've said, isn't there? And don't put me off. I can tell by the look on your face that there's a problem."

David sighed. "The children have banded together, closed ranks, with Josh in charge. Frankly, I'm not sure anyone can step in as parent figures at this point, unless Josh wants them to."

"What about the older couple they've been living with, the neighbors? How have the children reacted to living with them?"

"They've remained guests. They want no part of joining any other family."

"I see." She was silent, looking down at her clasped hands. "How did they react to the news that I'd been named their guardian?"

"They protested mightily." *And then some.*

"They don't want to live with me?" She looked up, her eyes demanding an honest answer.

"They don't want to live with anyone," he qualified.

"Well, I guess it's reasonable for them to feel that way."

"Tell me about your relationship with the family," he encouraged gently.

Sarah smiled, her face lit by the warmth of fond memories. "I don't know if you can understand this, but Liz and I had the kind of friendship that didn't require daily visits. We could go our separate ways for months at a time, and then get together or talk on the phone, and it was as if we'd never been apart." She looked as if she'd been able to pour her heart out to Elizabeth, and David envied her that.

"So you didn't see her often?"

"Not after she moved to Cleveland. With our schedules, we were lucky to get together once a year, for a day or two at a time." Sarah's voice caught and she turned away from him.

Fighting the yearning to take her in his arms, David waited for her to compose herself, then asked, "How did the children regard you?"

She shrugged, blinking back tears. "I think I was more a benevolent aunt to them than anything else. They knew how close Liz and I were, of course, but I was her friend, not theirs."

Her voice trailed off. She was obviously wishing she had spent more time with the children as well as their mother, thinking no doubt how much easier all this would have been now if she had. Abruptly she pulled herself together and asked, "How soon can we arrange to move the children down here into my custody?"

David was taken aback. She'd come to that decision awfully fast.

"This is what Liz wanted. I'm taking them." Her voice was firm.

He studied her wordlessly.

"They need me now, even if they don't know it," she said more gently. "Fortunately I'm in a position to care for them."

So her finances were fine. She'd said nothing about loving them. "What about emotionally? Are you equipped to give them as much as they're going to need?"

A bead of perspiration broke out on her upper lip, and suddenly, she seemed very vulnerable. "Of course I'm equipped to do that." She held his gaze. "I want to adopt the children. I want to care for them and give them a home."

Maybe so, David thought. Nonetheless he had the unsettling feeling Sarah was withholding every bit as much as she was telling him about herself and her real feelings. The question was why. What was she hiding? What didn't she want him to know?

SARAH SAT IN THE JUDGE'S CHAMBER, her hands clasped loosely in her lap. To the casual observer, she knew she looked relaxed. Inside she was nervous as hell. Part of her said she didn't have the vaguest idea what she was doing, agreeing to take on three orphaned children. The other part said she'd be crazy not to take the children when she knew chances were she would never have a child of her own. Never...

Then there was Liz's letter; she couldn't get it out of her mind: "Should anything happen to me, I want them with you, Sarah," Liz had written, "not just because we share the same values, or the fact that you've always been like a sister to me, but because I trust you to be able to love and nurture and care for them better than anyone else. I know I'm asking a lot, but I have every faith in you. Just love them and take it one day at a time."

Sarah sighed. It had been just like Liz to write a note to make sure Sarah knew she was serious, that she'd thought very carefully before making the decision. Now it was up to Sarah to do one last thing for Liz. And Liz's children.

Moments later, the hearing began. "So, Dr. Mac-Intosh, you're willing to accept guardianship of the children?" The judge, a man in his mid-fifties, was peering at her over the lenses of his bifocals.

"Yes, I am," Sarah said.

"You know what this entails?"

"I think so. I've never been a mother, but—" Never? That wasn't exactly true. She had been a mother in a sense, just not the sense the judge would want to hear about, or she could talk about.

She started again, aware that David was watching her very closely. "I'm a pediatrician. I work around children all the time. I understand them. I know how to get them to talk to me. I know how to treat them with courtesy and respect. I can't promise instant love. But I can promise I'll see they're well taken care of physically, and emotionally, I'll do my best." She couldn't pretend she and the children weren't virtually strangers, or ignore the fact it would take time for them to become a true family, yet she was confident that with love and patience it could be done.

"There's no doubt you're a very respected doctor, with an excellent reputation here in Dayton," the judge said. "It's whether or not you have the time for the children that concerns me."

"I would make time," Sarah said passionately, leaning forward in her chair. "I've already started thinking about how I could rearrange my schedule, cut down a little on my office hours." She hadn't realized until she'd entered the judge's chambers how very much she wanted those children. Now she knew if she didn't get a chance to make a home for them for whatever reason, her heart would break. And it would be one more hurt on a whole stack of personal hurts.

Convinced of her sincerity, the judge asked her and David a few more questions, then said, "I'm ordering a six-month trial run for this arrangement because I want Dr. MacIntosh and the children to be sure this is what they want before we see about making it final. In the meantime, I want Mr. Buchanan to continue an extensive search for blood relatives on the father's side as well as the mother's. I understand he was an Air Force pilot?"

Sarah nodded. "He was killed during a routine training mission."

The judge sighed. "The Smith kids have had a tough time of it."

"Yes, they have," Sarah said softly. "And I intend to see their life is easier from now on."

The judge smiled. "I admire your willingness to try this."

It was obvious, however, that David didn't share the judge's admiration. Sarah called him on it as they walked out of the courthouse into the fresh April air and bright sunshine. "You think I'm behaving recklessly, don't you?"

They headed for the parking lot. "I know you mean well," he said with a troubled voice. "I feel responsible for those kids, Sarah. If either of us puts them through any more hell, even inadvertently..." His voice broke off.

Remembering how she had failed her own children, Sarah gulped and looked away. What happened wasn't her fault—everyone said so. Then why couldn't she believe it? Why did she still have this lingering guilt? Why, even now, couldn't she talk about it?

"Sarah, talk to me. Tell me what's on your mind!"

"I can't."

"Why not?" Anger filled his low voice, and she felt his frustration acutely.

He closed in on her, until she was backed up against a car.

"David, I—" No longer able to block out his commanding presence, she let herself look at him as she'd wanted to when they'd first met.

He was a very virile looking man. His dark hair was being whipped around by the cool, spring breeze. His face was lean, angular, his lips full. He was an attractive man, and she was letting herself concentrate on that instead of his words and what they were implying. The light touch of his hand on her shoulder brought her back to reality.

"I won't hurt the children. Or fail them," she said stubbornly, telling herself it would be so.

"Wishing for something doesn't necessarily make it happen, Sarah," he said with rough impatience.

She stared at him, irritated by his lack of faith in her. A lack of faith that had also been exhibited by her ex-husband. "If this is the way you feel, why did you recommend to the judge that I take those kids?"

"Because it was the only chance for them to stay together, and I felt they deserved to have at least that much."

She knew then, from the careful way he was looking at her, that he had somehow realized her I-can-do-this attitude was all an act for him and for the judge. Because deep inside Sarah had more doubts about the wisdom of her actions than David did. She knew what the judge and David did not, that her motivations were not completely unselfish. She was taking those children, not just because she owed it to Liz, or because they had no place to go, but because she needed them, too. They were her last and only chance of having a family, and she had longed for one for a very long time.

No one had understood that about her. Not her friends, not her mother or father. Her ex-husband, William, had been the worst. He had called her a coward and accused her of deliberately hurting him. But she'd known she couldn't go through that hell again. When their marriage had ended, she'd given up hope of ever having a family and had resigned herself to being a failure as a wife and a mother.

Now she was going to be a mother. Her only worry was, could she really do all she had claimed? Could she really make the three Smith children feel happy, safe and secure? Could she make them a family? And if not, could she cope with another loss? Sarah thought not. So she would just have to find a way to make this work. One way or another, she would have to make this work.

Chapter Two

"Double fudge pie à la mode and coffee with cream. I would've thought a physician would choose something more wholesome," David commented, holding out her chair in the airport coffee shop.

Sarah accepted his help graciously, then watched him slide into the chair across from her. At his suggestion, they had driven to the airport together to pick up the children. She was grateful for the company; this wasn't something she wanted to face alone. And he was proving to be a very pleasant, very masculine distraction, with his bedroom eyes, muscled body and sensuously husky voice. He was a very good-looking man; he obviously knew it and used it to his advantage. "I eat sweets when I'm nervous," she admitted. "For some unexplained reason they calm me down."

He eyed her figure innocently. "You mustn't get nervous very often."

He was right; she didn't. She grinned, feeling a warmth generated by his gaze that was strictly of man-woman origin. "From what I hear attorneys have their share of vices, too. What are yours?" she asked, thinking, probably women.

"The regular vices, or the ones I employ when I get nervous?" David asked, adding dressing to his salad and mustard to his hamburger.

"Both."

His eyes lit up boyishly as if he had a wealth of bad habits to choose from. And was perversely proud of them all. "I drink beer and eat cookies. Together."

"Ugh!" She made a face. "And when you need to get rid of stress?" she prompted, taking a bite of her pie. As she had hoped, it was rich, warm and fudgy.

"When I get edgy I play racquetball."

Sarah nodded and murmured to herself, "I should have guessed." He had the attractively lean physique of someone who played a strenuous sport, and also a way of concentrating one on one that would make him very good at a sport for individual players rather than teams.

"Why?"

"The physique," Sarah replied, meeting David's gaze. Because she was a physician she had no hang-ups about bodies.

The glimmer of a smile reached his eyes. She would've given a hundred dollars for his thoughts. "What do you do for exercise?" he asked.

"Nothing regimented or planned. Mostly I climb stairs at the hospital, park my car way out in the lot and hike into stores, stuff like that. Sometimes I roam the shopping malls when I have a few free hours. And I have a rowing machine and an exercise bike at home. I used to go to a gym, but that got to be too much of a hassle." She took another bite of pie.

"Because of your unpredictable schedule?"

She blushed a little. "Because I got hit on. You know how it is. Gyms and supermarkets have become the singles' bars of the eighties."

He nodded. "It can be hard to get a little privacy."

That was precisely why she exercised—to get some time to herself to clear her mind. Having to deal with some buffoon trying to make small talk and who only wanted . . . well, she found the whole situation trying. Being with David, though, was anything but irritating. Maybe it was because he was a lawyer and used to having people confide in him.

"So what do you do when you're not exercising and not at the hospital?" he asked, sipping his iced tea.

"I'm a patron of the arts. My parents love the symphony and the theater, and I spend most of my free time catching performances and exhibits here and there."

"Sounds cultural." He was teasing her again.

"What do you do in your spare time?" She realized she had done most of the talking.

"Read a lot. And I like to cook."

It was her turn to look at his waistline. "You don't show it."

He grinned, as if to say touché.

Suddenly Sarah found herself wanting to stop time, to keep them there forever in the safety of the coffee shop, away from the real world and its heartaches and complications. But all around were signs of life, people moving on. Crowds surged through the terminal, past the gift shop, toward the baggage claim. Flight announcements were being made over the intercom system. She glanced at her watch and realized how late it was. Once again, without warning, she was very nervous.

"We'd better go," David said, pushing back his chair and helping her out of hers. "Don't want to be late."

Together they walked toward the appointed gate, which was crowded with people. David took a long look at Sarah's face, then a hand on her arm, guided her to an unoccupied corner of the waiting area.

"You're pretty nervous, aren't you?" David asked softly.

Sarah nodded, disappointed she hadn't hidden it better. She noted how calm and self-assured he looked. Reasoning that maybe talking about her fears would make her feel less anxious, she asked, "How *do* you start a conversation with your new dependents?"

"Beats me," he replied. "Saying hi, I guess." And then without warning, he asked, "Is there some reason you doubt your ability to be a mother?"

Unknowingly he'd struck a nerve. She turned away, walked over to the window to watch a jet land.

He followed her and positioned himself where she couldn't ignore him. "Have you had experience as a stepmother?" he continued, studying her face.

"No, I haven't," she answered calmly. She turned to face him and forced a smile. "Listen, could we drop this? Talking about it is making me nervous." Her heart was beating rapidly in her chest, and this time it wasn't just because of his seductive presence.

"Sorry."

But he wasn't sorry, she thought, turning toward the runway again. He knew with an attorney's sixth sense that she was keeping something from him, something vital and private that hurt whenever she thought about it. That didn't mean she had to reveal herself to him, though.

Seconds later, the arrival of the children's plane was announced. Now that the waiting and worrying were finally over, Sarah found her confidence returning. She turned to David, her anxiety taking second place to her excitement at seeing the children again. It had been almost a year. She imagined that they had grown and changed a great deal. "Let's go."

As they headed toward the double doors leading to the exit ramp, she found herself surveying him. Although moments before he'd been concerned, now nothing of his worry showed. His expression was pleasant, hopeful. She knew that he would not let the children see his reservations about her. Relief flowed through her.

Passengers began coming through the exit doorway. Two elderly couples, a family, several college kids.

David touched her arm. "There they are."

Scott emerged first. He was small for his ten years. His dark gold hair, cut very short, was rumpled, and he had the look of a child who was perpetually curious. Sarah smiled at his self-assured gait.

Julie followed. Eight years old, a little on the thin side, but almost as tall as Scott. Clutching a worn, stuffed Garfield to her chest, she looked adorable and very shy.

Then came Josh, who seemed very self-conscious and hesitant.

As Sarah embraced each child, she was reminded of all the times she had seen them. Maybe it wasn't often, but seeing their changes over the years had meant a lot to her. Still, she knew that to them her presence then had had very little impact. She was just their mother's friend, whom they saw once a year. How was she going to take them past that, she wondered, and make them her own? Would they resent her trying to? She thought that Scott and Julie, being so young, would not be entirely opposed to having her as their guardian. But Josh, who was seventeen, was a different story. Already it was clear he wanted no part of living with her.

She stepped back to take a better look at him, noting his grown-up attire—sportscoat and tie—and the faintly paternal air he displayed toward his brother and sister. "I think you've grown," Sarah said awkwardly, amazed to find him nearly as tall as David.

"Maybe." Josh shrugged indifferently.

She had the sense he wanted her and David to keep their distance. She smiled, refusing to be put off so easily. "In fact I'm sure you have. You must be, what, over six feet tall now?"

"Six one," he mumbled, nervously running a hand through his short, dark blond hair.

Suddenly, she realized the sooner they got out of the airport the better. "Maybe the best thing to do is to get you home," she said firmly, taking charge.

Josh nodded, but stayed where he was, his feet planted apart. At that moment he looked about as movable as a mountain. In fact, none of the children looked pleased to be going with her. Sarah's heart started pounding. This was going to be much, much harder than she had anticipated. David had known and had hinted at it, but she hadn't believed it. Until now.

"I'll bring the car around," David offered agreeably. "Josh and Scott can see to the luggage."

Needing to do something, Sarah said, "I'll help them."

"That's not necessary," Josh asserted. "Julie can do it. Right, Julie?"

"Right," she replied, casting an adoring look at him. She put her hand in his.

Taking the rebuff in stride, Sarah told herself not to feel too discouraged.

Minutes later, they'd collected the six brand-new suitcases. The contents were all the children had in the world, and looking at the bags, Sarah was reminded of how much they'd lost. Their parents, their home, everything. She had to be careful not to expect too much from them, she warned herself sternly. Making a new home with her in a new city wouldn't be easy, but if she were patient and kind, they would make it. She had only to believe that, she decided firmly, for it to come true.

"THANKS FOR STAYING AROUND to help the children get settled," Sarah said later that day as she and David finished up the last of the dinner dishes. It was barely nine o'clock, but the children were all upstairs, getting ready for bed.

"I thought you needed the help," David said quietly, turning to face her.

She nodded, careful to keep her expression impassive.

"You're disappointed, aren't you," he said softly, "that they're working so hard to keep you at arm's length?"

Disappointed didn't begin to cover it. She felt a hurt that just wouldn't quit. But she knew that she was being unreasonable hoping for any reaction other than hands-off. "I had no right to expect them to behave otherwise under the circumstances."

"Maybe not, but they could make it easier for you."

Sarah sighed, secretly agreeing with him. Josh's refusal to let her help with the suitcases had been just the beginning. From the time they left the airport, he had kept up his paternal act, letting her know subtly that he was in charge of his brother and sister. She felt like a custodian, an innkeeper, and at that moment she wasn't sure it would ever get any better.

This wasn't what Liz wanted for her children, Sarah knew. She'd wanted them to have a parent, someone who would give them love and guidance, not just pay the bills and see they had a roof over their heads and food to eat. But that was all Josh was prepared to let her do. If he had the means to support his brother and sister, Sarah didn't doubt that he would have made a home for them himself. And she couldn't blame him for feeling that way. If the same thing had happened to her . . .

"How did you and Liz meet anyway?" David asked, changing the subject adeptly.

He had a way of studying her that left her feeling at once vulnerable and cared for. Sarah smiled, relieved to be able to converse about happier times. "We were next-door neighbors, here in Dayton. I sublet the condominium next to hers. I had just started my residency. She was working part-time as a substitute teacher and caring for the two boys. We used to have coffee together every few days and cry on each other's shoulders. I'd tell her how hard my life as a resident was, and she'd tell me how tough it was raising two young boys and being pregnant with a third child when her husband was gone more hours than he was ever home."

"You hit it off right away then?" His voice was low and mesmerizing.

"Yes." Sarah held herself very still, trying not to react to his seductive presence. "She was like the sister I never had and vice versa."

His gaze lowered to her mouth for a moment, then returned to her eyes. She felt the impact of that look, as if he had actually touched her, and a tingling warmth surged through her.

"When did Elizabeth move to Cleveland?" he asked.

Sarah had to fight to keep the breathlessness out of her voice. "About six months after her husband died." The accident had devastated Liz. Only the fact that she still had her children to raise had kept her going. "She got a job teaching English literature at Cleveland State University. I knew she had to go, but I was sad to see her leave."

David nodded and they lapsed into silence. A silence that was anything but comfortable, Sarah mused. She knew he'd been watching her all evening. Almost every time she had looked over at him, she had found him looking at her. Then and now, it was hard to tell what he was thinking. She only knew that he wanted to know more about her, and that she was equally interested in him. But he had a latent sensuality that she found too attractive, too dangerous, for her own good. Wasn't her life complicated enough right now without bringing a man into it, too?

"I'm sorry this afternoon was so tough for you," he said, his deep, honeyed voice breaking into her thoughts.

So was Sarah. But she wasn't thinking about the kids now, or the hardships and adjustments that lay ahead of them. She was thinking about David. He was unmistakably a man who knew what he wanted and didn't have any qualms about going after it. The question was, could she deal with him if he came to desire her? She'd have to. Hadn't she been disappointed enough? Why even give him the opportunity to hurt her? She knew there could be no other outcome. Not if David was the type of man she judged him to be, the kind who wanted hearth and home and family and all the traditional things.

"I hope it will get better, but if it doesn't—"

"Stop it, David." She didn't want to hear the rest. She forced herself to calm down, to take a deep breath. "I won't let myself think that way. This might be the only chance I'll ever get to have a family and—"

His eyebrows went up, and she realized at once she had said too much. "I'm not going to let the children down," she said finally, aware her voice had a slight edge. Her hands were trembling. "I'll find a way to reach them," she finished, shoving her hands into her pockets.

He studied her carefully, and after a moment, he said, "I hope you can. If you need me, or if you just want to talk, call me anytime. At home or at the office." He pressed his card into her hand.

His touch was as warm and soothing and powerful as his look; she had to fight to keep herself immune. Sarah looked down at his business card. "Thanks," she said.

He put both hands on her shoulders and made her face him squarely, his eyes lingering on the pulse beating rapidly in her throat. "You know, it wouldn't surprise me if you wanted to give up."

"After one day?" Sarah tried but couldn't turn away from his searing gaze. His touch inflamed her skin, and it was all she could do not to step into his embrace.

"I'm not questioning your ability."

"Then what are you trying to say?" she asked, moving away, feeling the need to distance herself from him, yet at the same time needing to know how he felt, what he was thinking of her. The spicy scent of his aftershave was filling her senses, beckoning her back.

"That whatever happens, I'll understand. And I'm here to help, so call me anytime day or night."

In his eyes, she saw a sense of caring she hadn't found in an eternity from any man. She thanked him warmly, knowing she wouldn't call him. He was too distracting a presence, and she needed to direct her full attention to the children. David made her want to think only of him. And that, as tempting as it might be to indulge in, just wasn't for her right now.

Chapter Three

David wandered through the various exhibits at the Dayton Art Institute, surveying the collection of Oriental, European, and pre-Columbian paintings. Normally he enjoyed visiting art galleries and museums. He also liked gala affairs, such as this reception for the new collection of seventeenth-century paintings. Tonight, however, his mind was on only one thing—Sarah MacIntosh.

Less than a week had passed since they'd picked up the Smith children at the airport. He'd offered his help, given her his card. She hadn't called. Nor had she returned any of the four brief messages he had left with her service earlier in the day. Of course it was a Friday and doctors were notoriously busy on the last afternoon of the regular workweek. She'd probably call him this weekend.

In the meantime it was hard for him not to think of her. She'd already made quite an impact on his life. He'd never met anyone so capable and so vulnerable at the same time. She was an open book, yet she was also a lady of mystery, with secrets she was determined to keep. Like why she probably would never have children of her own. Was she sterile? Or just sure she would never marry again? One thing was for certain, he hadn't been able to keep her image out of his mind. He wondered if she was beautiful all over. And if there would come a time he would be able to see for himself, to have her in his arms, in his bed, those slim shapely legs tangled up with his....

Slowly threading his way through the well-dressed crowd, David made his way to the next exhibit. From a distance he heard a soft musical laugh. A flirtatious, familiar laugh. David turned. Seeing Sarah standing across the room surrounded by men, all the blood drained from his face.

She looked extraordinarily sexy in an off-the-shoulder, figure-hugging black dress. David frowned, watching her flirt, a glass of champagne in her hand. He realized that he was jealous, and that he was also angry. Dammit, if she was too busy to return his calls that afternoon, then what was she doing at this party?

Before he could think about what he was doing, he strode toward her, his lips set grimly. Her face paled as she saw him approach, but that only made him all the more determined to have his say, to find out what kind of game she was playing. Flirting with him shamelessly one moment, crying on his shoulder the next, then avoiding him completely. Did she just not care?

"David..." She swallowed hard, could barely get out the word.

He saw the guilt on her face and it only enhanced his anger. He'd been a fool to think she was interested in him or would take the children's welfare with the seriousness he deemed necessary. Obviously, they had resisted her, and she, taking that to heart, had all but abandoned them. And she had abandoned him, too, not letting him know one thing that had been going on at her house—in her life—all week! When she must have realized that he cared, not just about the children, but her, too.

This wouldn't do at all. And as executor of Liz's estate, it was up to him to fix the problem. He would make Sarah see she had to do a better job of communicating with him and caring for the children. No matter how long it took or how difficult it was.

"Hello, Sarah." Grimly he stepped in to take her arm. "If you gentlemen will excuse us." He nodded to the circle of admirers, then returned his gaze to Sarah. "We have to talk."

"Can't it wait?" Sarah asked, feeling as if her smile was frozen on her face. She hadn't expected to see David at the benefit at all, and certainly not looking so furious and upset. At first, she couldn't think what she'd done to make him react with such barely leashed anger. Then she remembered. She really should have made more of an effort to return his phone calls. But then hindsight was always better, wasn't it?

"No, Dr. MacIntosh, it can't wait."

She had no choice but to go with him. It was either that or let him scold her in front of her friends. Still smiling, she let him lead the way. Predictably David didn't slow his stride until they disappeared through swinging double doors into the back of a dark, deserted auditorium. He released her arm as they entered and she took up a position against the rear wall. He stood in front of her, so close that only mere inches separated them. Sarah inhaled the tangy scent of his aftershave and felt a peculiar, melting sensation in her lower abdomen. A sensation that seemed to increase in intensity with every shallow breath she took.

"Had enough drama for one evening, David?" Sarah asked, keeping her voice calm and making eye contact with his chest, rather than his mesmerizing gaze. She knew he wanted her to look at him directly, but she wasn't about to. Not when her knees already felt as insubstantial as jelly and she was having difficulty breathing. No, she wouldn't look into his seductive eyes.

"No, not yet," David replied, stepping closer still. Watching her steadily, he planted one hand on the wall behind her. He wasn't touching her, but Sarah was acutely aware of his strength just the same. Furious with her reaction, she lifted her chin to confront him and found herself sinking into the soulful depths of his eyes. What was it about this man that made her think about stolen kisses and moonlit nights, and made her feel like such a lovestruck schoolgirl?

"What about you?" he continued, his gaze drifting to her lips. "Got enough men dancing attendance on you?"

"That's unfair," she said hotly, turning away from him and trying to slip past. She'd just needed to laugh for a few minutes, escape.

"Is it?" He swiftly put his other hand on the wall beside her, effectively trapping her in place.

"Yes!" She stared up at him, temper burning in her eyes.

"You know, I wouldn't have thought you'd want to get away from the kids this soon. But then," he added, his voice lowering another silky notch as he looked at her knowingly, "I figured you for the type who'd return her phone calls, too."

"I returned two of your calls, David." Just not the third and fourth. Anxious to shift the blame away from herself, she said, "That secretary of yours must not be very efficient."

He sighed and swore, then shaking his head, he dropped his hands and admitted, "The young woman you spoke to isn't very efficient. And she's not my secretary. She's a temporary."

"I'm sorry," Sarah sympathized readily. She knew how difficult it was to run an office without adequate help.

"So what's going on with the children?" *Why haven't you called?*

"We've had a rather rocky start," Sarah replied, knowing David wouldn't let her leave until he had gotten some answers. "They're still adjusting to their new home." She hadn't called him because she hadn't wanted him to know how much of a failure she felt. She had hoped every day it would get better and that she would have something positive to report. But it hadn't happened, and before she knew it, almost a week had flown by. But he'd been in her thoughts constantly.

"Just how unhappy are they?" he asked.

She took a deep breath, deciding abruptly he might as well know the whole truth. He probably wouldn't rest until he discovered it anyway. "They're about as unhappy as it's possible to be, I guess. They don't like their new schools. They don't like the way I cook, although they're way too polite to say anything. I don't know, David. They're just so miserable." She ran a hand through her hair, feeling the tears she'd been suppressing all week come to the surface. "And try as I might, I just can't seem to make it any better for them."

"That's why you left them alone tonight?"

She sighed. "I thought maybe some time apart would do us all good. I talked to the mother of one of my patients, and she thinks I may have been smothering them, and that what I need to do is relax, not push so much. Just let them get close to me at their own pace, whatever that may be. She warned me it might be very slow. The truth is this past week I've hardly let them breathe without phoning in to check on them. I was home every night at five o'clock. I didn't go to the office or the hospital until they were all in school. I think they picked up on the fact I'd rearranged my schedule to be with them." She recalled how they had watched and listened to everything she said and did with breathless, uneasy attention.

"I'm sorry. I had no idea you were having such a tough time. I had hoped once they were moved in they'd relax a bit. Is there anything I can do?"

She was suddenly aware that his eyes were on her bare shoulder, that her heart was again pounding at his nearness, and that she wanted very much for him to kiss her.

Looking as if he were struggling with the same thoughts, he stepped back and said, "Look, I know I don't have any experience here, because I've never had kids, either." Sadness appeared on his face but quickly disappeared. "Perhaps if we work together, both spend time with them, we'll be able to help them adjust," David finished hopefully.

Sarah felt herself turn to ice. "No." *That won't do.* She moved away from him, knowing she needed more than physical distance from this man. She needed emotional distance. She needed him to stop trying to break down the barriers she was so painstakingly erecting.

"No?" His brows rose a fraction of an inch. He looked as if he could hardly believe—never mind understand—her objection.

"No," she repeated calmly, taking a deep breath.

"Why not?" He moved toward her slowly.

She was aware her pulse had adopted a machine-gun pace again. With all her remaining self-control, she willed herself to look as relaxed as he seemed to be. "Because it wouldn't be fair to the children, that's why."

"Why not?" he asked again, casually sliding his hands into his pockets.

She swallowed hard. His apparent ease was counter to everything she felt. In a voice that shook slightly, she said, "Because that would give them a false impression of what life with me would be like. I'm a single parent and will continue to be. So was Liz for a while."

He studied her relentlessly and a faint blush crept into her cheeks. "You think they'll adjust easier if there is only a single adult around?"

"Yes. Don't you?"

He shrugged, and her eyes were drawn to his broad shoulders. She couldn't help but notice how strong and powerful they seemed, and how sexy he looked in the black-and-white evening clothes.

"Maybe. And then again, maybe not. There are three of them and one of you. I'd think right now they each need as much attention as they can get. Even with the two of us, it'd be hard. With only you there..." His voice softened. "I just don't want to see the kids deprived of anything we can reasonably give them."

There was that *we* again, she thought. "David, this isn't your problem," she insisted.

"Maybe not." He kept his reasonable tone.

"Maybe?" It was her turn to correct archly.

"Okay, so it's not. It still feels like my problem." He moved toward her appealingly, his hands spread wide.

"Sarah, I'm not going to be able to concentrate on anything else unless I know those kids are all right. And the only way I'll really know they are is if I'm there to see it, not just every couple of months, but once a week. Or more. If that's selfish and self-centered, okay, but I want to be upfront about this, and not come off later as some jerk who's just out to meddle, and put his two cents in where it's not wanted."

What could she say to that? She respected and admired him for being so compassionate. Most lawyers in his shoes wouldn't have been. Worse, she felt like a heel for refusing his offer to help. And why? Because she found him desirable. Surely, she thought irritably, she could get herself under control if she just tried a little harder to ignore his sexiness. Besides, she was behaving selfishly, thinking only of her own comfort and not the children's.

"You're sure you want to get involved in this?" she asked slowly, still not entirely certain that agreeing to his plan was the right thing to do.

"Yes," he assured her. "Besides, it'll be good practice for me when I have children of my own."

At his cheerful revelation, she felt herself freeze up again. "You want a family?" she asked, trying to sound casual, wondering just how important a family was to him.

"Very much. And the sooner the better." He held her glance for a curiously long moment, then unable to understand what was going through her mind, admitted softly, "I was going to ask you the same, but I guess you've already answered that by taking on the Smith children."

She had, Sarah thought. And she hadn't.

But she wasn't going to get into that with him now. Maybe not ever, because his revelation had made him more off limits than ever to her.

As if suddenly mindful of how long they'd been gone, David glanced at his watch. "I guess we better get back to the others," he said, although he looked reluctant to do so. Again his gaze roved from her lips to her bare shoulder, then back to her eyes.

Sarah knew that the way he'd propelled her from the room earlier had raised more than a few eyebrows. Tongues would probably be wagging for weeks. "I guess we'd better," she said dryly, again taking the arm he offered her.

The rest of the evening was uneventful. Sarah talked with many old acquaintances, looked at scores of paintings. Yet through it all her mind was never very far from what David had revealed to her. Of course he wanted his own children. He was the kind of person who deserved to have them, who would devote his life to raising them. Once she had wanted that, too. But two miscarriages and the disappointment that had followed had convinced her it would never happen for her. She would never be able to give the man she loved a child, and that hurt, but she had accepted it. Hence, she was very determined to become a mother to the three orphans, to make them her family.

David knew none of that, of course, nor did she intend to tell him. She'd learned a long time ago that making her private hurts public only intensified them, and that she didn't need. She didn't want anyone's pity.

Several hours later Sarah was sure she had chatted aimlessly with everyone at the reception. Except the person uppermost on her mind. Curious as to where he had drifted off to, and with whom, Sarah looked for

David. She didn't find him. Surprised by the depth of her disappointment—what did it matter to her how David spent his time—she decided to call it a night. Unfortunately, it wasn't nearly as easy to rid herself of David's beguiling image as it was to leave the museum.

WHEN SHE GOT HOME at nine-thirty, the house was quiet. Scott and Julie were fast asleep, but as she'd half expected, Josh was awake. His door was open, his light on. A book lay open on his chest.

"Hi," Sarah said softly, standing in the doorway. "Having trouble sleeping?"

"A little."

"What were you thinking about just now?" Sarah asked, knowing her question was bound to be unappreciated. He'd looked as if he were deep in thought, and she wanted to help with whatever was bothering him. If only he would let her.

To her surprise, Josh answered her diffidently, "Scott's birthday is in another week."

"We'll celebrate it however you think best," Sarah assured him promptly.

Relief was obvious in Josh's face, yet he remained uneasy, rubbing his fingers along the spine of his book. "The thing is," he said without looking at her directly, "I don't have any money. And Julie and I would like to buy him a present."

"I'll be glad to give you whatever you need—"

"I'm not asking for a handout," he corrected, offended.

She swore inwardly. She'd made another mistake. *Okay, go easy now.* "You want to earn the money?"

"If there's something I can do for you," he answered hurriedly.

Sarah didn't know whether to laugh or cry. Josh was already doing far too much around the house; they both knew it. Breakfast dishes, laundry, making sure the bathroom was spotless after the younger children had used it. And she hadn't had to assign him those chores. He seemed to anticipate everything, right down to taking out the trash at night. And yet there was this distance between them, as if an invisible line had been drawn. He didn't want to get close to her. She could understand his reticence. First he lost his father, then some eight years later, his mother. He didn't want to get close to another adult. He didn't want his brother or sister getting close to one, either. The potential for hurt was too great.

And yet Sarah wanted to reach out to him, to ease his burden, to erase the frown lines on his forehead and make him drop his preoccupied overly adult manner. She wanted him to have a chance to be a kid again, to live his life without so many worries.

"Well, the grass needs mowing," she said finally. In the past, she'd always employed a firm to do her landscaping chores, but she supposed that could change. "And my flower beds could use a good weeding."

"I'll get on it first thing in the morning." He hesitated. "You won't tell Scott you're going to pay me, will you? Julie, either? She never could keep a secret, and I'd rather wait until we go to buy the gift before I tell her what we're going to do."

Sarah understood. "I won't tell them. What are you going to get him, by the way?"

Josh shrugged. "A new football or a Frisbee, I guess."

Sarah paused, remembering a conversation she'd overheard. "Didn't Julie say something about getting him a book on dogs at the school library? What was that all about?"

"One of your neighbors has a new puppy. We saw it the other day when we were walking home from school. Scott wanted to know what kind of dog it was, and I told him I thought it was some kind of terrier, but I wasn't sure."

Scott had gone on and on about that dog, Sarah remembered. In fact, they'd all talked excitedly for several minutes. In the whole week they'd been with her, they hadn't gotten worked up about anything else. "Have you ever had a dog?" she asked curiously. Was this something they wanted that she could give them?

"No." He frowned. "Mom . . . she never wanted to fool with pets. Scott knows he'll never own one now, that it's out of the question. I made sure he understood that."

They wouldn't even ask her for anything, Sarah thought, discouraged.

"If he reads a book at least he'll know all about them. Then when he grows up and gets his own place, he can get a pet then. Maybe he can get a job walking someone's dog this summer. It'd be a good way for him to earn money and be around animals at the same time. Or he could give them baths or something. Of course if that's . . ." He had to swallow hard and force himself to ask, "if it's okay with you?"

"That would be fine," Sarah said. "In fact, I think that would be a great project for him this summer."

She lingered in the doorway for several seconds after that, wishing for further conversation, even a simple goodnight, but he didn't look at her again. She knew the territorial lines had been drawn, and for the millionth time, she wished she had a clue how to get

through to him. Because until she won over Josh, she
hadn't a prayer of winning over the other two.

Sarah spent the next hour in her room, ironing some
shirts for the boys, thinking about possible presents for
Scott's birthday. But always it came back to the dog.
She had just about decided to get one when the phone
rang. She expected it to be the hospital or her answering service, and was surprised to hear David's voice.

"Hi. I hope it's not too late to call. I just wanted to
make sure everything was okay. I looked for you at the
reception area when I was ready to leave and heard from
one of your physician friends that you'd left much earlier."

Sarah couldn't help but smile. She didn't want to admit it to herself, but she was pleased at his attentiveness. Wary of it, too. Because he was knocking down
one by one all the barriers she'd set to keep them only
minimally involved with one another. Worse, he was
acting as if he had every right to do so, not just because
of the children, but because of his interest in her. An
interest she returned no matter how much or relentlessly she fought it.

"The kids are fine," she said softly. Suddenly needing to talk to someone, she told him about her recent
conversation with Josh. "So I got to thinking maybe a
dog is the answer," Sarah finished.

"A puppy or an older dog?" David asked.

"Gosh, I don't know. An older dog that's already
trained would be easier to handle, but on the other hand
younger animals are so free spirited." And her house
could use a little laughter.

With a smile in his voice, he said, "You want a
puppy, don't you?"

Sarah marveled at how well David already understood her. "I guess I do. Maybe a few animal-oriented shenanigans would help break the ice between me and the kids."

"If you like I could help you find a puppy."

Sarah paused. She knew she should say no, but with Scott's birthday only a week away, she'd have very little time to find one herself. "Would you mind?" she asked tentatively.

"On the contrary. I'd be delighted. It'd give me a chance to do something for the kids."

"It's a deal then," Sarah said, a little cautious over the arrangement she'd just made. The last thing she wanted right now was to depend on David.

Over the next week she and David talked almost daily as he kept her informed about his search and the possibilities. When her choice was made, Sarah mailed a check to the breeder and David picked up the female beagle pup Friday afternoon after work. By then, both were so excited they could hardly wait to give Scott his gift the following day.

"You're sure you can't sneak out tonight to see her?" David asked late Friday afternoon, chuckling as the puppy climbed onto his lap and tried to lick his face.

"I wish I could." Sarah sighed. This had been her idea, and as yet she hadn't had the chance to even see the dog. The birthday celebration was scheduled for the following afternoon, and there was still so much to do. "I've got to stop by the bakery. Get dinner. And I promised Josh and Julie I'd take them to the mall tonight and keep Scott amused while they run off to buy his presents."

"I understand." David's voice was warm and relaxed. He laughed again and she could hear the puppy's excited yips and pants. "I'll see you tomorrow then."

"Right. And thanks for all you've done."

There was a brief silence during which she could almost see him smile. "My pleasure."

Afraid Josh would think up a reason to refuse her gift, she only mentioned to him that she, too, had gotten Scott a gift that would be delivered the next day. Josh said nothing in response, didn't even question what the gift was, and she let the subject drop.

As planned, David came over promptly at four Saturday, entering as nonchalantly as possible, a wicker basket over his arm. Amazement and delight on his face, Scott ran over to see what was in the basket. Sensing he was in new surroundings, the puppy began to bark. Minutes later, boy and beagle were romping over Sarah's living-room rug.

"What should we call her?" Scott looked up at Sarah, for the first time directly soliciting her advice.

Sarah tried to contain her excitement. This had been a good idea after all. Even Josh was petting the brown, black and white dog with the long, floppy ears, the huge expressive eyes.

"I don't know, Scott. I think that's up to you. And Josh and Julie." Sarah's eyes met David's. Though she had paid for the puppy—David's own presents were a feeding dish and rubber bone—the puppy felt like *their* gift. She knew she couldn't have managed nearly as well without his help, and she smiled at him, expressing her gratitude. He smiled back warmly, clearly pleased at the way everything had worked out. Sarah suddenly realized that the bond between them had deepened.

"I think we should call him Snoopy," Julie said, her eyes glowing as she sat next to Scott.

Scott looked up at the ceiling. "The puppy's a girl, remember?" Scott reminded his sister.

"Oh. Well..."

"Snoopette?" Josh teased, and they all laughed.

Scott scowled thoughtfully. "I know! How about Lady?"

That wasn't the most original name, either, Sarah thought, but it was something they could all remember. "Fine with me," she said.

The others agreed.

David stayed on for dinner, cake and ice cream. The two adults were just starting on the dishes when the phone rang. Sarah answered it. She listened carefully, snapped a few orders, then said, "I'll be right over. Fifteen minutes, max."

"Trouble?" David asked as soon as she'd hung up.

Sarah nodded. "One of my patients is in trouble. Poisoning." She glanced out the back window at the three children playing with Lady and a football in the yard. "Josh is an excellent baby-sitter and normally I wouldn't think twice about leaving him in charge. But with the puppy here, not even settled in yet, I just don't feel comfortable doing it. Would you mind terribly staying a while?"

"Be glad to." He followed her to the front door, his brisk steps matching hers. He promised to explain to the kids why she'd had to leave so abruptly. "Just go to the hospital and do what you have to do," he said in the soft, serious tone she was beginning to know so well. And she knew with him there she truly didn't have to worry.

WHEN SARAH RETURNED hours later, the house was quiet. She walked into the living room and found David on the couch, the Sports section of the paper in hand. "Kids asleep?" she asked.

"Everyone's asleep. Even Josh. I guess Lady tired them all out. She's asleep on the back porch."

Sarah tossed her purse and keys on the coffee table and sat down in a chair next to the couch. "Thanks for hanging around."

When she'd called at shortly after nine to say she'd be home in a little while, she'd told David he could leave then. He'd insisted on staying, and now she was glad he had. It was nice to come home to find a man waiting for her, a man she was—unexpectedly and recklessly—beginning to care about.

"How's your patient?" David asked, putting his paper aside.

Sarah rubbed the back of her neck and stood up. Images of the three-year-old girl rushed through her head. "She's going to make it," she answered. It had been rough, though. Her patient would be in the hospital another few days, and they'd have to wait to see if there would be any permanent damage to the liver or the brain. All because someone had carelessly left a bottle of adult aspirin within a child's reach.

"Tired?" David stood and walked over to her side.

She nodded slowly. Suddenly, she was unable to take her eyes from his face. Her heart was beating fast.

"You look exhausted," he said, and stepping behind her, began to massage the tension out of her shoulders with a steady soothing motion.

Caution warned Sarah not to let down her guard, and she resisted his touch, stiffening her shoulders and pulling them slightly forward. But after a few moments, she found herself relaxing. The pressure of his hands was heavenly. Sarah sighed and closed her eyes, letting herself lean back against him.

It was crazy, letting it go on, but it felt so good. It felt so right somehow to have him here, waiting for her to come home, caring about what happened to her, caring enough to be there.

Without warning, the hands on her shoulders paused, then slowly turned her toward him. One arm moved to circle her waist. His other hand came up to cup the back of her neck. Sarah barely had time to whisper his name before his mouth came down on hers.

Her first thought was that she'd never been kissed like this before. He claimed her mouth with a pressure that was at once possessive and lazy, wild and soft. He didn't ask permission but merely took, and then gave. And gave some more. She responded with unexpected passion, her hands moving first to his shoulders, then to the nape of his neck. At her surrender, he made a low approving sound. No one had ever felt so right to her, and she was lost in the moment, and in him. By the time the kiss ended, her whole body felt hot, shaken by his touch.

He, too, was trembling, so much he had to pull back.

She saw then that this wasn't what he had intended, that they had both been carried away. Struggling to regain her former composure, she asked haltingly, "What was that for?"

"I don't know," he admitted. Ever so gently, his hand cupped her chin and lifted her mouth back to his. He touched his lips to hers, withdrew, then added, "But I'm about to do it again."

Chapter Four

"No, David. I'm sorry, but this can't ever happen again," Sarah said shakily, placing her hands against his chest and putting more distance between them.

"Why not?" he asked with a sexy growl. He twined his fingers with hers.

Heat radiated through her fingers. She tried to extricate her hands from his, but he held on determinedly. "Because my life's too complicated right now. I'm still trying to get the children settled. A romance along with everything else..." She knew it would be courting failure.

He released her fingers, only to enfold her hands between his and gently rub them. "What about after the children are more settled?"

What then? Sarah wondered, aware of the desire still surging through her. When she had no excuses, no reasons to say no? Would she possess the courage to begin again, to try to build a committed relationship with a man? Or would she do as she had in the past, and run like hell from the possibility of intimacy? If only she weren't so drawn to David, she thought. If only he weren't so beguiling, so right in many ways. Except one.

He very much wanted children of his own, and that she couldn't give him. She couldn't give that to anyone.

"Why do I think there's more going on here than just your concern for the children?" he asked, reading more of her feelings than she would have liked.

Panic swept through her—that he would discover her inadequacy and leave. And she'd promised herself she would never feel so helpless again and put herself in a position where she could be abandoned. She looked away.

"David, I had a bad marriage," she said at last.

"And you don't want to try again, is that it?"

"I don't think I could bear another failure." *Especially not with you.*

"Well," he said, sighing. The beginning of a smile tugged at the corners of his mouth. "That's encouraging."

Despite her sadness, she found herself grinning back. "I can't imagine how—"

"You're thinking of me as a serious suitor. That's exactly the way I want you to think of me."

"But—"

"I know, I know." He laid a finger over her lips. "It's too soon. I'm rushing you. You have a lot on your mind."

His hand moved to her shoulder, caressed it for a moment, then dropped down to his side. She had the sudden realization he wasn't going to take no for an answer. And that maybe she didn't want him to. "You do understand?" she said finally, aware her pulse was racing again and her throat was suddenly very dry.

"Sure. And maybe you're right." The roguish grin was back full force. "Maybe we do need to get to know one another a little better before I kiss you again."

That wasn't what she meant at all and he knew it. "David!"

"We better call it a night." He leaned forward to kiss her brow before she could interject further. "I'm always here for you if you need me," he reminded her.

Sarah looked up at him tremulously. Precisely what she was afraid of.

To Sarah's mixed feelings of disappointment and relief David didn't try to kiss her again or further their relationship physically in any other way. But he did phone her often to check up on the kids. On several days he also stopped by briefly after work to check on Lady. All too aware of their mutual attraction, Sarah was wary of his attentiveness. But when a full ten days had passed without David's initiating some intimacy between them, she began to relax. Then on a Tuesday he stopped by her office unexpectedly. "How about lunch?" he greeted her. "Got plans?"

"Lunch?" Sarah stared at him in surprise.

"Yes. Everyone has to eat. Even pretty doctors, or so I'm told."

"I thought we agreed not to see each other socially, one on one." Despite her resolve to be immune to him, her pulse had picked up the second she'd laid eyes on him.

"*You* said you didn't think it was such a good idea," he pointed out. "*I* admitted no such thing."

"Meaning you haven't given up on me?"

"Not a chance, lady. I've just been giving you time to adjust to the idea. Now that you've had it..." His voice trailed off, and his eyes hungrily roamed over her body.

She knew he found her very attractive, and she'd never felt quite so beautiful as she did at that moment, with the sunlight gilding them, the soft spring breeze warmly caressing their bodies. It was a gorgeous day, and he was as full of spring fever as she. "David, David. What am I going to do with you?" she whispered, the warmth of a blush stealing into her face.

"Come to lunch with me, Sarah." He repeated his invitation firmly, his eyes holding hers rapturously.

Was that all he wanted from her? Sarah didn't think so; nonetheless she felt the last of her resistance dissipating. "I don't have a whole lot of time," she warned, knowing that she had given in to his suggestion too easily.

"Neither do I." He must have seen the guarded expression on her face because he tried to tease her out of her reserve. "Think about it, Sarah. What could be safer than a quick meal in a public place?" His touch on her shoulder was all innocence, telling her he wouldn't take this any further than she wanted.

He was right; nothing could possibly happen at lunch. Besides, she had missed seeing him alone, talking to him about matters not related to the children. What could one lunch hurt, anyway? As long as he still knew where they stood, and she'd already made that clear. "All right," she said finally, knowing he'd just scored his biggest victory with her.

"SO WHAT'S BEEN HAPPENING with you?" Sarah asked when they were settled in a cozy restaurant down the street from her office.

"Not much. Work's okay. I have a full-time secretary again."

She grinned. "Congratulations. Now all you have to do is train her."

David fell silent, the look on his face troubled. "I won't have to do that," he said, looking down at the menu. "Georgia's worked for me before."

Clearly he was upset. "Why the frown?" she asked softly, wishing he would confide in her.

He was silent for a long while, then he put his menu aside and looked at her frankly. "Georgia used to have a drinking problem. It was so severe I had to fire her."

A shiver went through Sarah. "She's better now though, I take it?"

He nodded. "She's going to Alcoholics Anonymous, looking better and more in control than she has in years." He fingered the silverware alongside his plate. "The problem is she's disappointed me so many times in the past that, even though everything seems fine, I'm still not sure I can trust her. Yet because she was once a valuable employee, I feel I owe her a second chance. I'm not sure anyone else would give it to her; she's lost three others jobs in the past four years. Word gets around in legal circles. Anyway, I want to help her." His mouth tightened. "But I don't want to jeopardize my practice in the process."

"You think she might drink on the job?"

"She did before." He was silent for a moment. "The problem is I'm a soft touch and a hopeless optimist. I expect things to work out simply because I want them to." He shrugged. "And the more I want something to work, the more blind I am."

Wanting to comfort him, Sarah reached across the table and covered his hand with her own. "None of us is perfect, David."

"I know. It's just..." He frowned unhappily. "I feel so damn guilty for being so suspicious of Georgia, for watching her like a hawk. What's more I know she notices, and she's hurt." He shrugged again.

The waiter appeared to take their orders. After he'd left, David turned the conversation to Sarah's life. "You seem to be getting along better with the kids."

She was and she wasn't, Sarah thought. "It's going very slowly," she admitted. She wished she could make the children her own a little more quickly, but she knew they were still missing their mother very much. She also knew that would get better with time, though they might never call her Mom. In her letter, Liz had advised her to take it one day at a time; and that was what Sarah was trying to do.

"Did Josh remember to sign up for his Scholastic Aptitude Test?" David asked, offering her a breadstick and then taking one for himself.

"Yes, but I had to remind him three times. I'm a little worried about him, David. He shows so little interest in college now. The last time I saw Liz, she told me that she and Josh were planning several trips to colleges this year to see the campuses." She had offered to do the same for him, but he had immediately rejected the idea, refusing even to talk about it.

"It's natural for him not to want to leave Scott or Julie now."

Sarah nodded. "I guess. But sooner or later he's got to have a life of his own."

"I'm sure he'll come to that conclusion, too, given time."

"You're right. Again."

Their smiles met. Sarah found she was glad he had dropped by, and when it was past time for her to return to the office, she realized she didn't want to leave him. "We should do this again sometime," she said, as David pulled up his car in front of her building.

"We should do it again *soon*. And make it dinner, not lunch." He stroked her cheek, tracing its curve. "Saturday night, my place? What could it hurt?"

Talking to him, being with him, had made her feel better, less harried. "No pressure?" she asked, knowing she wouldn't be able to resist his kisses. And his kisses could easily lead to...

"No pressure," he repeated solemnly.

She didn't trust his promise, but she did want to be with him. "Saturday night, eight o'clock," she said finally.

"You won't regret it."

Wrong, thought Sarah. In some ways, she already did.

"YOU WEREN'T KIDDING when you said you liked to cook," Sarah said Saturday evening as she walked into David's kitchen. Located on the middle floor of his spacious tri-level home, the large emerald-green and beige kitchen seemed to contain every culinary appliance and gadget invented and then some. Gleaming copper pots hung from the ceiling. A large butcher block stood in the center of the room, the makings for a salad laid out on it. Soft music played in the background. In the dining room beyond, Sarah could see a bleached oak table set with china, flowers and candles. She was impressed by the cozy atmosphere of his home, and by the trouble he had gone to.

"No, I wasn't kidding," David replied, opening a bottle of red wine to give it time to breathe. "What about you? Do you like cooking?"

Sarah grinned. "I have a short, excellent repertoire of dishes. But to keep up with you, I'm going to need to expand." She looked around. "What smells so wonderful?"

"Beef Stroganoff." Without warning, he was behind her with a chef's apron. "Better put this on to protect your clothes." He slipped it over her neck and knotted it at her waist.

Sarah could feel the warmth of him, and a maelstrom of sensation hit her. She turned to face him, smoothing the apron over her hips. "Thanks," she whispered.

His gaze followed the movement of her hands before returning to her face, and Sarah saw his eyes glisten with arousal. She swallowed hard, trying to control the small flames sparking inside her. "Someday you're going to make some woman a very good husband," she said, hoping the lighthearted comment would ease the sudden tension between them.

"Yeah, well, I hope so." His eyes held hers, telling her of the storm within him. Then he turned away. "I guess we better get started on that salad."

Sarah smiled, relief washing over her. "Just tell me what to do."

He let her slice the tomatoes. Sarah concentrated on her chore, afraid to look at him directly. "I've never done a whole lot of cooking. When I was still living at home, my mom did most of it. I set the table."

"An only child?"

"Yeah. My father is a physician, my mother a nurse. They live in Toledo."

"Are you close to them?"

"Yes. Of course, with all of us working, I don't get to see them as often as I'd like. But they're close enough that I can drive up for a day or so whenever I get the yen to talk, and I like that.''

"How was your childhood?''

"Happy. Normal. I spent a lot of time playing doctor with my dolls.''

"Not nurse?''

"No. I was always too bossy to take direction from a doctor.''

He laughed. "Yeah, I can see that. You're definitely a leader.''

"Of course my mom was disappointed I didn't go into nursing.''

"But she understood.''

"Oh yes. It was just that she figured if I were a doctor I'd never have any kind of personal life.'' And she'd been right, Sarah thought dispiritedly. Her marriage hadn't worked out. Neither had her wish to have a child....

"Did she work when you were little?''

"No, not until I was in high school.''

"She just took care of you, huh?''

"And did a lot of committee work for various charities and the arts.'' They assembled the salad and slid it into the refrigerator to chill. While he washed the utensils, Sarah cleaned the counters. "To tell you the truth, my mother isn't very maternal. She loved me and all that—I never doubted that for a moment. She gives to people, but not in any really personal way. Do you know what I mean?''

"Yeah, I think I do. She's very reserved?''

"Yes.'' Sarah nodded. That was precisely it.

David leaned against the counter. "My mother was just the opposite. Very earthy, very giving. Mothering just came naturally to her.''

"Yeah." Sarah made a rueful sound. "The natural touch. Some of us have it and some of us don't."

"Hey, don't say that." He crossed to her side and slid his arms around her waist. "You'll get the hang of it. It's just going to take time."

She wanted to believe that, that someday Scott, Julie and Josh would really be her family, and not just her legal charges. And she wanted to believe that she could give David everything he needed and wanted. But she couldn't. She had failed in the past, and she was still filled with terror that she wasn't ever going to be good enough.

He looked down at her, and accurately reading her insecurity and guessing the root of it, his expression softened. Determination—and caring—filled his lambent gaze. "Sarah," he whispered tenderly, pulling her closer, "you have so much to give. If only you knew..." And then his lips were on hers, ardently moving over her mouth, telling her just how much he cared. His tongue plunged deep into her willing mouth, and Sarah shivered, her body weakening against him. Holding his head between her hands, she kissed him back, tasting his moist warmth again and again, until they were both trembling and breathless. When at last they drew apart, Sarah saw the unashamed desire in David's eyes, and she had to fight the impulse to touch his still-wet lips. She wanted more but knew it was impossible. What had happened to her resolve? Here she was on their first dinner date, and all her poise disintegrated at a kiss.

An unsteady breath escaped David's lips. Looking as if he was reading her thoughts, he released her ever so slowly and turned toward the open bottle on the windowsill. "I think the wine's breathed enough," he said, suddenly becoming the perfect host. "What do you say we take our glasses into the den, listen to a little music while the Stroganoff simmers."

Sarah nodded. Her pulse was still racing, and her knees were still weak and shaky. Maybe a glass or two of wine would calm her down. "Okay."

She removed her apron while David poured the wine. She mentally reviewed their conversation, hoping to pick up where they had left off, and decided to get him to talk more about himself. "Did you like being married?" she asked quietly, as they made their way into the den.

"Yes. And no," David said, settling next to her on the sofa in front of the fireplace. "Obviously there were problems in my marriage, or we wouldn't have gotten divorced. Ideologically I like the institution. I would like to be married again someday."

The sounds of Genesis floated from the stereo. Sarah looked around at the stacks of books and magazines, the extensive record collection, the plants and mementos and knickknacks from various places around the country. Like the rest of his house, his den was masculine and cozy, the furnishings chosen with care. A blue, red and gold Persian rug, garnet-red sofa and matching wing chairs, light oak paneling... She liked everything she saw; it all suited him perfectly. More, he had really settled in here, really made an effort to make a home that was welcoming and soothing.

Restlessly he got up to stir the fire, then add another log to ward off the chill in the cool, rain-scented night air. He sighed deeply. "But if I do marry again it would have to be to someone who wanted a family as much as I do."

His words hit her like a blow to her midsection, reminding her all over again how wrong she was for him.

"Is that what happened in your first marriage?" Sarah found herself asking, in a tone that sounded remarkably composed. "You wanted children and your wife didn't?"

David nodded, returning to his seat. He took a sip of his wine. "Alanna was president of her own graphic-design firm. We got married when I finished law school. Those first years, with me setting up a practice, were really tough on us financially. We both wanted children, but only when the time was right. Before we knew it, years had passed and Alanna hit her mid-thirties. Time was running out. But by then Alanna had come to like our life and didn't want to change it one iota. She liked her freedom and felt children would be an unnecessary burden. She wanted us to reconsider having children at all."

"But you couldn't do that?" Sarah saw the pain in his face.

"No. Having a child of my own wasn't something I was willing to relinquish. It still isn't."

"I see." Sarah sipped some wine, amazed her hand wasn't shaking. She wished she could give David what he wanted. But she knew she couldn't take the devastation. It would break her heart to have another baby and lose it again.

David sighed. "I felt betrayed," he admitted. "I felt she had made a commitment to me to have a child, and she reneged on it."

A chill went through Sarah, and she hugged her arms to her chest, trying not to think about how much David's anger reminded her of her ex-husband's anger. "If Alanna had been unable to have children, instead of just unwilling, would it have made a difference to you?" She phrased her question with utmost care.

David clearly thought it an odd question, but after a pause, he answered her. "Sure. I would have considered adoption happily. I'd even take on a stepfamily." He looked at her meaningfully. "But if at all possible, I want to have my own natural child. I just want the experience of raising my own child."

"While you're searching for a wife, you could adopt right now, even as a single person," Sarah suggested, wanting to see his reaction.

David nodded. "Like you're doing? I know. I've been thinking about it."

"And?" Sarah waited for his answer with bated breath. She wanted him to find happiness, even if she couldn't contribute to that happiness.

"And I still want to find that special woman first." He paused, searching her eyes. "Can you blame me for wanting everything?"

No, Sarah thought, she couldn't blame him. She just wished that life were less complicated. And like it or not she knew the day was coming when she would have to tell him that she wasn't the woman for him and never would be, that she couldn't give him what he wanted so desperately. With every wonderful moment she spent with him, she dreaded that prospect more. Dammit, why wasn't life ever fair?

Chapter Five

If you tell her now, you'll break her heart, David thought, studying the investigator's report. *And if you don't, you may be letting her in for an even bigger letdown.*

He didn't want to hurt Sarah. His protective instincts toward her and the children were very strong. He knew how hard she was working to make a home for the children and how they were resisting her at every turn. He knew she sometimes felt dispirited and inadequate, because she didn't know what to do when they wouldn't talk to her. She didn't want to push them, but it drove her crazy when she thought they were upset or depressed, and they wouldn't admit it.

He trusted that all of their problems would be solved with tender loving care and a lot of patience. But right now Sarah was having a hard time of it, and to tell her he'd found a lead on a distant male relative of the children—would send her into a tailspin. The relative, Liz's cousin, was young enough and seemed stable enough to be able to care for the children. Sarah would constantly worry about the possibility of losing them. And they would pick up on it, as they picked up on her occasional lack of confidence. Or worse, she might gradually withdraw emotionally from them, for fear of getting hurt herself. That kind of action would only hurt them all.

So what to do next? Because the cousin was in the Army, stationed in Germany and currently out on maneuvers, David would be unable to reach him for several weeks. Better he keep the news to himself, David decided, after wrestling with the matter for more than an hour. She might be angry with him later for saying nothing, especially if the cousin came forward to claim the children, but that was a risk he would just have to take. He had no other choice. His first priority was to protect Sarah and the children, and to help them become a family as Liz had wished.

And it wasn't just a professional obligation driving him. He wanted Sarah MacIntosh. He wanted all of her, body and soul, mysteries and contradictions, red-gold hair and golden eyes. He wanted her in his life. He wanted to understand why she kept pulling away from him, why she was afraid of a few kisses. A very capable woman, she trembled at his slightest touch. That night at his house when she had kissed him back with the ardor of a woman who knew what she wanted, he had seen fear and confusion in her eyes when he had released her. What had her ex-husband done to her and why was she still afraid? he wondered. He knew he would find out—there had never been anything that he'd wanted that he hadn't gotten—and he wanted Sarah more than anything he had ever wanted in his life.

ACROSS TOWN, Sarah was in the midst of a busy day. An outbreak of strep throat had doubled her usual patient load. She'd come in early and worked straight through lunch, but at three o'clock she still had about a dozen patients left to see. She knew she would be late getting home and that Josh would manage admirably in her absence; he'd probably have supper ready for them all when she walked in the door. She smiled. She and the children weren't over the hump yet, but they were making progress, getting a little bit closer, a little more comfortable around one another with every passing day. That was a start. And good starts led to success.

She wished that David would be waiting for her tonight, too. She knew it was crazy and shook her head. He wanted something she couldn't give him, yet she couldn't stop thinking about him. Was it possible with time she would be able to work something out with David? He'd said he'd accept a stepfamily. But she wasn't sure she could ask him to make the sacrifice of foregoing his own child. She did know they shared something, which she wanted with all her heart to continue. But enough ruminating, Sarah thought, it was time to get back to work. She picked up the next chart and frowned when she saw Melissa Anderson's name on it. What was she doing back, and so soon?

Sarah walked into the examining room, an expression of determined cheerfulness on her face, and greeted the girl and her mother. "So how are you feeling, Melissa?" she asked.

The little girl complained of more stomachaches even though she'd already made friends at school. An abdominal palpitation told Sarah the child's liver and spleen were enlarged. She also noted the yellowish cast to Melissa's complexion, and after asking Mrs. Anderson a few more questions, she decided on a blood test. Minutes later, her diagnosis was confirmed.

"Melissa has hepatitis," Sarah said, returning to the examining room.

"Is that why I feel so bad?" Melissa asked.

"Yes." Sarah explained that it would take several weeks for Melissa to feel better, and during that time she needed rest and a lot of fluids.

"Do I get to miss school?"

Sarah grinned, glad she had at last succeeded in cheering her patient up. "Oh, yes."

Melissa smiled back and employed the latest slang for great. "Dude," she said.

"YOU SEEM UNUSUALLY preoccupied," David observed as he and Sarah carried picnic gear from his Jeep the following weekend. A short distance away, all three children romped with the puppy.

Sarah suddenly felt apologetic. They'd been planning and looking forward to this group outing all week, and now all she could think about was complications at work. "I'm sorry. I'm worried about a patient of mine, a little seven-year-old girl. She has hepatitis." Sarah sighed and sat sideways on the picnic bench, her sneaker-clad feet on the bench, her arms hugging her knees.

"You like this little girl a lot, I take it?" David put charcoal in the grill and doused it with lighter fluid.

"She's adorable." She closed her eyes and shook her head. "Maybe I just need to get my mind off my work for a while."

He wiped his hands on a paper towel, struck a match and ignited the charcoal, then came toward her, a mischievous look on his face. "Ah. The lady wants to be entertained."

As always, when confronted with his undivided attention, her senses leaped wildly. Fighting a blush, she bantered, "With a capital *E*."

He drew her slowly to her feet. "I think I can manage that." Sunlight was all around them, and suddenly, the very air burned with expectations. They were so close ... and yet were kept so apart, by circumstances, complications.

His eyes darkened sensuously. "Don't," she said, her voice barely more than a murmur. "Don't kiss me."

His eyes darkened even more. "I want to."

"I know." And she wanted him, too. "But the children—"

"I think they've seen a kiss before."

She was sure they must have, but it wasn't the children she was truly worried about. It was herself. Being in his arms again, feeling the drugging power of his kiss, would make her forget the time and place. And how unsuitable they were for each other.

"All right," he said after a moment. His gentle hand beneath her elbow guided her to sit beside him on the bench. In silence, they watched the children play. She had no idea what he was thinking and wasn't quite sure she wanted to know.

"Amazing how much joy a puppy can bring, isn't it?" David murmured, as Lady ran to fetch the Frisbee.

Seizing a subject they could talk about—anything to keep from thinking about kissing him—Sarah asked casually, "Did you ever have any pets?"

"Oh, yeah." He grinned. "There were seven kids in my family. We had all sorts of cats and dogs, most of them strays we'd convince our parents to let us keep. Since there was no animal shelter for almost fifty miles—we lived in an impoverished area of southeastern Ohio—they usually let us."

"Your childhood sounds as if it was a lot of fun."

"It was, although I did resent having to wear hand-me-down clothes all the time. And we didn't even get a television until I was twelve. Of course I don't know that it was all that bad. I grew up loving to read. Books are very important to me."

"To me, too." She felt pleased they had that in common. "What did your father do?"

"He was a jack of all trades, a handyman who did all sorts of carpentry work and repairs."

"He must be awfully proud of you now."

"He is. I'm the legal expert in the family. I get all the calls for counsel."

"And your mom, what does she do?"

"She was and still is a homemaker. She had her hands full taking care of us. We were always fighting or carrying on over something."

"Did you have chores?" She thought she knew the answer to that.

"You better believe it," he affirmed, leaning his back against the table and stretching his long legs in front of him. "There was always kindling to split, animals to feed—we raised chickens, cattle and hogs—a garden to weed, apple and peach trees to care for. Mom did all her own canning and freezing, and we were all expected to help with that, too."

Hence his love of cooking and his ease in the kitchen, she thought. "And you enjoyed every minute of it."

He nodded, laughing. "Of course you never would have gotten me to admit that at the time. Like all kids, I complained loudly about all the work I had to do."

Hearing about his life made her feel she knew him so much better, and she felt the urge to hold his hand. But hand-holding led to hugging, and hugging led to kissing, and that led to . . .

And she was trying to go slow with David, to decide day by day what to do, how much and when to tell him. "And after chores, then what?" she asked instead.

"Well, we had this bike. My parents picked it up at some rummage sale, or maybe we got it in exchange for some work my dad did, I can't remember. Anyway, it was a bicycle built for two. Gold. Absolutely the neatest thing we ever had." He smiled, remembering. "That bike got years of wear. It was a lot of fun." He sighed, stood and went to poke at the coals. "I always meant to pick up one for myself."

"Why don't you?" Sarah reached into the cooler and pulled out the chicken David had marinated.

He shrugged, then stretched, his shirt pulling across his chest. Her eyes were drawn to the sinewy surface, and she wondered what it would be like to make love to him, with nothing separating the smoothness of his skin from hers.

"Bikes like that are hard to find. Besides, who would I ride it with?" He turned to her. "On second thought, I know who I'd ride one with now." He looked her up and down assessingly, a teasing light in his eyes. "Okay, woman, you're on. The next time I see one. We'll see what you're made of."

She smiled. "Okay."

The children and Lady returned in a group, and they spent the next couple of hours laughing, joking, enjoying the puppy's antics, and eating. Finally, when everyone was replete with David's delicious dinner and sated with sunshine and fresh air, they drove home.

The children were sitting in the back, and Julie had fallen asleep against Josh's arm. Watching them, Sarah couldn't help but wish it was she Julie had turned to, that they would all let her mother them just a little bit more. Despite all the closeness they'd shared earlier she still felt like the children's custodian. She was closer to most of her patients, even little Melissa, than she was to them.

Sarah shook off the self-pity resolutely. The closeness would come, she assured herself firmly. She just had to hang in there.

"Hey, Sarah, did Josh ask you if he could go out with his new friends yet?" Scott asked.

Josh sent him a censuring look.

"Josh?" Sarah prompted softly but received no reply, just a long-suffering sigh and a wary look. "It's all right," she said soothingly. "I want you to make friends." And abandon, she said to herself, the parental responsibility he felt for his siblings.

"Sarah's right. You should have a social life of your own," David said quietly, pulling the car into her driveway.

He switched off the ignition and turned to look at Josh. "Maybe the three of us—" he shot a glance at Sarah, who signaled her approval "—could work out some conditions for your going out."

Because Josh still looked apprehensive, Sarah added, "For instance, I want to meet your friends first before you go anywhere with them."

Josh frowned. "My curfew with Mom was midnight," he said finally. Despite his typically noncommittal expression, Sarah could sense just how elated he was at the thought of being able to go pal around with friends once more.

She looked at David. Because she was so inexperienced at making these types of decisions, she needed his help. "Sounds reasonable," Sarah said, relieved to find that David agreed with her and also found it a laudable time. Although technically David didn't need to be involved in these kinds of family matters, she found she wanted him to be. It helped, having him around and knowing he was there for her and the children when they needed him. And he was slipping so easily into the father role in her new family.

They unloaded the car and Josh woke Julie. Sarah went upstairs with her, helped her into her pajamas, then stayed a while to read her a short bedtime story. After making sure the other two were settled in their rooms, Sarah went down to the kitchen. She found David at the sink washing the picnic dishes. "You didn't have to do that," she said.

David gave her a knowing grin. "How else am I going to get brownie points with the lady of the house?"

"Is that what you want? Brownie points?" She was shocked to hear how throaty and sexy her voice sounded. Shocked to realize how much she wanted him.

"Among other things." He tossed the towel aside, and hooking one hand around her waist, led her out the back door onto the dark, screened-in porch.

All around them was the lingering smell of freshly cut grass and azalea blossoms, all the soft seductiveness of a summer evening. She was suddenly aware she had been yearning to hold him all day. But there were all the reasons in the world why they shouldn't be together—not now, not ever. "David," she whispered tremulously, starting to protest, because of the children's presence upstairs, the early hour, anything that would save her from the shattering, overpowering intimacy of that first touch.

His hand cupped the back of her neck. "Sarah, I want you," he whispered back, "and I know you want me. It's written on your face every time you look at me.

Let me hold you, just for a moment, please." And then
with no further warning, his mouth was on hers. His
lips were tender and demanding, taking, seducing expertly even as they gave. His tongue explored the honeyed cavern of her mouth, over and over, as if he
couldn't get enough of her and never would no matter
how much he tried.

Unable to restrain herself, Sarah returned the slow,
hot caress with every fiber of her being, not caring that
they could be interrupted at any moment, that she was
acting like the worst kind of fool. She ran her palms
across his shoulders, craving to feel his skin beneath the
sweatshirt.

At her response, an earthy gasp left David's throat,
and his hands moved down her spine, lingering at her
waist, pressing her close against him. Then his hands
moved upward until they rested just beneath her
breasts. A warm ache spread through Sarah, and she
sighed his name and kissed him more deeply. He was
everything she had ever wanted; he made her feel more
alive, more a woman than she had ever imagined possible. She knew he cared about her; it showed in every
tender touch of his lips against hers.

When his hands slid higher, she didn't resist. "Oh
God, Sarah," he murmured, claiming the fullness of
her breasts, massaging the sensitive skin with the palms
of his hands. Sarah closed her eyes, succumbing to the
whirlwind of pleasure within her. She could feel her
nipples peaking against the thin cotton of her shirt and
bra, demanding an even more intimate touch.

His lips moved from her mouth to her neck, and his
hands tugged at her shirt. Cool air assaulted the bare
skin of her back, then she felt his palms up and down
her spine. Her body tensed in eager anticipation, and

she became aware of a slow, steady pulsing deep inside her. Both their hearts were pounding.

Knowing how reckless she was behaving, she still wanted them to be as close as it was possible for a man and a woman to be. She wanted to take him deep inside her and discover just how wonderful their loving could be. But when he reached for the catch of her bra, sanity returned, and with it the realization that this wasn't the time or the place.

She put her hand over his. "David, no," she whispered hoarsely, and pushed against his chest.

David released her at once. She saw from the rueful expression on his face that he had been caught as unaware as she. That he'd intended only a kiss and hadn't ever meant to go further. She also saw the love he felt for her reflected in his eyes, and knew she wasn't wrong to care for him. Foolish, but not wrong because he was a good man, a man worth loving.

Then a sexy smile curved the corners of his mouth, and he looked not the least bit sorry things had gotten out of hand. "I guess this is where we say goodnight, hmm?" he drawled huskily. He stepped back a pace and looked at her hungrily.

At his hot-blooded glance Sarah felt a blush steal into her cheeks. She'd met her match all right.

"Before I go, I want you to know I really enjoyed being with you today," he said. "I can't remember when I've had such a good time."

Sarah smiled. Leave it to David to make explanations and apologies completely unnecessary. Never had she appreciated his slow and easy approach to loving more. "Me, either," she said softly, holding his gaze for a long, tender moment, knowing that, like it or not, she had at last found the man of her dreams. "Me, either."

Chapter Six

Beware, here comes the spoiler, David thought, as he made an unscheduled entrance at Sarah's office. He wished he didn't have to tell her about the Smith cousin, but he did, and he had to do it now. All he could hope for was that she was in a good mood and would take it well, that she wouldn't jump to conclusions about what was going to happen before all the facts were in.

Unfortunately, though, it didn't appear to be a good time to talk to her. Sarah was standing at the window, lost in thought. Her complexion was pale, her face drawn. He thought there were tears glistening on her cheeks. What had happened? he wondered, alarmed. "Sarah?"

She wiped her cheeks and after a brief moment turned toward him. "David, hi." She made an effort to sound cheerful and composed.

"Is this a bad time?" he asked gently, searching her face. Right now it was all he could do not to cross the room and take her into his arms. But sensing she would reject him—this was after all her place of business—he settled for simply closing the door behind him, guaranteeing them some privacy.

She offered a shaky smile. "Yes and no. I had a rather rough day." Tears welled up in her eyes at the confession, and she bit her lip.

Casually, he closed the distance between them until he was near enough to touch her. But she still had that slight defiance in her posture that said she didn't want his tenderness or his pity, and that all she wanted was to be left alone. But he couldn't leave her now, knowing she was upset. "Want to tell me about it?" he asked.

She sighed, and said tiredly, "Stephanie Andrews, the mother of several patients of mine, had a miscarriage today. The baby was to have been her fourth child. I heard she'd been admitted, and I went over to the hospital to see her." The words were spoken in a monotone.

"And?" David sat down, his eyes never leaving her face.

She hugged her arms to her chest. "Stephanie is blaming herself for the loss."

And Sarah seemed to understand that, he couldn't help but notice, all too well. "Did she do anything to precipitate it?" He leaned back, his eyes never leaving her face.

"No!" Sarah's response was vehement—and evasive.

David exhaled slowly, knowing that if he were patient enough, steady enough, he'd eventually get the answers he wanted. "But she's blaming herself anyway."

Sarah nodded, first avoiding his eyes, then giving him an imploring glance. "That's why I went over to see her. I thought maybe talking to me would help."

"And it didn't," David said, keeping his voice neutral.

"No." Again, Sarah sighed with a great weariness of soul and turned away from him. She hugged herself tighter. "I don't think anything anyone does or says right now will penetrate. She's too wrapped up in guilt." Tears filled her eyes and fell down her cheeks.

David was on his feet again, suddenly not giving a damn about propriety, or that she might not want him to hold her. She needed to be held. Hands on her shoulders, he turned her to face him. "You're sad because you weren't able to help her?" Somehow it seemed to him there was more to it than that.

Sarah had promised herself she was never going to tell David about her own feelings. She couldn't bear it if he pitied her. But she also knew it was foolish to keep it from him now, when he could see how much she was hurting and wanted to help. Maybe he would understand how she felt, maybe not, but she'd never know unless she confronted him with the truth. Besides, for the first time in ages, she needed to talk to someone.

The decision made, Sarah took a deep breath. "I'm sad because I understand what she's going through only too well," she said, her voice shaking slightly, pain coursing through her. "I had two miscarriages myself."

To her relief there was no pity in his eyes, no revulsion, no morbid curiosity about what was wrong with her. Only pain and sadness. At last, she thought, she'd found someone who understood and sympathized.

"I'm sorry," he murmured, taking her into his arms. "I had no idea." His arms tightened around her possessively, and she relaxed his embrace, no longer trying to shut him out.

"It isn't something I can talk about," she said after a long while, feeling tears begin to fall again. "It just hurts too much."

He leaned back, bewilderment on his face. "Sarah, surely you don't blame yourself?" he asked, his brows furrowing.

She looked up at him, saying yes with world-weary eyes. His attitude changed abruptly. His face took on a harsh expression, and he seemed to want to shake her, to make her wake up and see it wasn't so.

She lifted her hands in a gesture of helplessness, wishing she could do something to erase the terrible burden of guilt she carried around with her, the ceaseless feelings of inadequacy. She took a deep breath, bracing herself for the discussion coming. She could see he was angry with her, as a physician she knew he was right to be so.

Determinedly she brushed the tears from her face and tried to explain how her heart and mind differed in this one area in ways far beyond her control. "Oh, David, it's just all so complicated," she whispered wearily. "Intellectually, of course, I know there was nothing I did to cause the miscarriages." The lump in her throat grew until she could hardly stand it. "Emotionally is a whole other ball game."

"Why did you lose the babies? Do the doctors know?" he asked.

Sarah could see he had many questions. She decided to answer them. She moved away from him, her voice getting stronger. "The first time the miscarriage was due to an infection. The second time there was a problem with the placenta."

He scowled, and Sarah guessed his ignorance about such matters. "Are they liable to recur?"

Sarah sighed. Now that her emotional storm had passed, she felt tired and numb. She wanted nothing more than to go home, climb into bed, pull the covers over her head and hide there for a few days. "There's no reason they should," she said, looking down. She swallowed hard. "But they can't promise me it won't happen again." And that she couldn't bear thinking about.

"Sarah," David said, and she looked up at him, knowing what he was about to say, and not wanting to hear it. Tears in her eyes, she continued implacably, "Medical statistics support the fact some women have a tendency to miscarry repeatedly. I'm one of those women."

David regarded her stoically. "What does your doctor say?" he asked quietly.

"The usual medical tripe," she answered defiantly. But fear began to grow in her. Now that David knew the truth about her, would he walk away from her and all they'd shared?

Ever the lawyer, he wanted more information. "What medical tripe?"

She clenched her fists and wished that he would walk out now and get it over with. With effort, she kept her tone calm and matter-of-fact. "He says there's no reason for it to happen again, that I should try and get pregnant." But Sarah didn't believe her doctor, and she knew she couldn't go through again the hell she'd already suffered twice. To let herself hope, only to have her child die in her womb. No, she just wouldn't do it; it was too cruel, to her and the baby.

David didn't miss the unwilling look on her face. It reminded him of his ex-wife, and he went cold inside. He'd sworn he wouldn't get involved again with a woman who didn't want any part of having his child. "But you don't want to," he said, feeling himself go numb around the heart.

She looked him straight in the eye. "I endured two miscarriages, David, and they're more than enough. Do you have any idea what that's like? To carry a baby around for three months? To wait to feel the child move only to feel a blinding pain instead months and months too early!"

He blanched at her vivid description. But that didn't change the way he felt. "I'm sorry you suffered. I'm sorry you lost the children."

"So am I." She swallowed hard.

"Is that why you got divorced?" he asked gently, already sensing the answer.

After a moment, Sarah nodded. "Yes. William, my husband, wanted me to try again. I just couldn't." She lifted her hands helplessly and then dropped them in front of her.

David closed the distance between them. He felt anger that Sarah had been hurt. And he felt fear that she might not be willing to try to give him a child. Not just any child, but his child and Sarah's child.

"He blamed you for the loss, didn't he?" David said.

She nodded, and tears rolled down her face. David took her in his arms again. She sobbed against his chest, dampening his shirtfront. "He never said so directly, of course, but he hinted that at my age and with the strains of my job..."

David was aghast. "He wanted you to give up medicine?"

"Temporarily, until after the baby was born."

"And you didn't want to do that."

"No. Besides, there was no medical reason for me to go to bed and languish."

David figured the request was merely William's cloaked attempt to control her. Apparently Sarah was wise to that, too. "So you ended the marriage."

"Yes. And I haven't looked back."

Until today, David thought.

"That's why having Liz's children is so important to you, isn't it?" he said slowly.

She looked up at him, an expression of hope on her face. "I know I'll never have my own child. The fact Liz named me their guardian and that she died when she did make me think it was something that was meant to be. Does that sound silly to you?"

He shook his head slowly. "No, I don't think it's silly. I believe there's a reason for everything," he said. *And maybe even a reason I was brought to you. A reason for you to hope for a child and to try again.*

"Anyway," Sarah said, "today when I was with Stephanie, it just brought it all back. I came over to my office for a good cry."

"Feel better now?"

She nodded. "Much. Thanks for helping me work some things out. Talking about everything, having you understand, well, it helped." David held her tightly, the affection he felt for her mingling with a need to protect her.

Abruptly she pulled away from him and asked, "Why did you drop by anyway?" Alarm appeared on her face. "Is something going on with the kids? Nothing's wrong, is it?"

David swallowed hard. How could he tell her now that there was a blood relative who just might be interested in taking the kids? Much as he knew he ought to, he just couldn't. He'd do it later, when she was feeling less vulnerable. Right now, he didn't think she could stand any more hurt. He forced himself to smile. "I was in the neighborhood, and on impulse I decided to drop by and see how you were doing. I thought you might like a hand with dinner."

"Oh, that's sweet. But Josh is cooking tonight." She paused. "You want to come home for potluck?"

He grinned and laced his arm through hers. "Lady, I thought you'd never ask."

"YOU KNOW WHAT you need?" David asked several hours later, as he and Sarah settled down to watch the television news. The children, having done their homework and had their showers, had gone upstairs to read before lights out. It was a custom Liz had started with the kids, and Sarah and David were both pleased it had been continued.

"No, David, what do I need?" Because of David's concerted efforts to cheer her up, Sarah no longer felt the crushing despair and depression she had earlier. She no longer felt so hopelessly inadequate. So she couldn't have a child? So what? She had David, and the kids.

David reached over and twined his fingers with hers. "You need some time off. A reprieve for adults only. And I know just the place to take you."

She looked at him warily, reading the desire in his eyes. Was she ready for this? Was it wise? "David—" She started to protest, even though she knew she would say yes.

"Say yes, Sarah." He bestowed light butterfly kisses on her lips.

Unable to resist him a second longer, she found herself sighing yes into his mouth. Arms wrapping around her, he drew her closer still and gave her a kiss that had her shuddering.

"When?" she asked, long moments later, when they had pulled apart.

"Friday, when the kids are at school. Think you can clear your schedule?" She nodded. "Great. Now all we have to figure out is the where. Ever been canoeing?"

"Uh, no."

"Well, it's about time you learned then. Don't worry," he said confidently, reading the look of alarm on her face. "We won't tackle any whitewater, and I'll teach you everything you need to know. It'll be great, you'll see. And very relaxing."

She suddenly saw unbidden, undeniably sensual images of him sweeping across her mind, and doubted that the outing would be relaxing. David in casual clothes, his tall body stretched out beside hers, radiating masculine energy and purpose. David, his hair tousled, his eyes laughing, looking at her in that very special way that said she was his and his alone. David kissing her, holding her close, making her feel like a woman again....

She realized abruptly that although he hadn't said he still wanted a child, he hadn't reassured her that he didn't. What if her first instincts were right? What if she shouldn't get involved with him? What if despite their companionability, their chemistry, they were still wrong for one another because they wanted such different things in life? And why did the thought of not seeing David again hurt so much?

"Don't frown like that," he whispered sexily in her ear. "Canoeing isn't that hard. I promise. We'll have fun together."

Sarah knew that. But she also knew she shouldn't go out with him, that she wasn't ready to become anyone's lover. Yet whenever she was around David, she wanted to forget everything that stood in their way, including her inability to have a child.

"Friday morning at nine," he repeated firmly, not taking no for an answer. "Rearrange your schedule and be ready." He winked and lowered his voice. "I will be."

WHY IN HEAVEN'S NAME did she ever agree to go out with him again on Friday? Sarah wondered ruefully, climbing into bed later that night. Playing hookey on a deserted river somewhere. Talk about the perfect setting for tomfoolery!

So what should she do? she wondered anxiously. Or should she break off with David now? No. She couldn't. Should she take it one day at a time? Maybe. Should she try to make him give up wanting his own child? It was a long shot, but with time and patience, it might work. Then they could adopt. Or just raise Josh, Julie and Scott.

Her heart filled with hope. All she had to do was go slowly, try to make sure he understood her before they got in too deep. At least that way, they had a chance. And maybe a chance was all it would take.

"I SEE YOU'RE ALL READY to go," David remarked early Friday morning.

"And not just that. I'm really looking forward to our outing," Sarah announced cheerfully, loading the picnic basket into his car. By mutual agreement they had divided up the chores. He'd called ahead and rented the canoe, and arranged for transportation back upriver once their journey was completed. Sarah supplied the food and drink.

"I'm glad to hear that," David said huskily, unexpectedly backing her up against his Jeep, his hands trapping her. "Because I haven't been able to think about anything else since we made the date." Before she could do so much as take a breath, he leaned forward and kissed her, his mouth moving on hers provocatively, possessively.

She felt overwhelmed, because he was so strong and so tall. And because just by touching his lips to hers, he made her feel cherished and beautiful and womanly. She had promised herself she was going to go slow, but she melted into him anyway, savoring every touch and taste, and knowing that if the day went anything like the morning greeting, he was going to be very hard to resist later on. And that her already weak defenses were treacherously splintering every single time he touched her.

When he finally raised his mouth from hers, she reeled slightly. His strong arm was there to steady her. "I've missed you," he whispered. "It's only been a couple of days, but I feel like it's been a couple of years. What about you? Has our date been on your mind, too?" He stroked her cheek.

She'd thought about it dozens of times, been so excited the night before she'd been unable to sleep. "Yes," she managed finally, aware of her pounding pulse.

He grinned, studying the emotions he saw on her face. "You like the idea of playing hookey, hmm?"

"Oh, yes." She liked feeling carefree and high spirited again, if only for a little while.

"Then we'd better get going, hadn't we?"

To Sarah's delight, David was in no hurry to get to the river outside Dayton and drove at a leisurely pace. For the first time in weeks, Sarah had a chance to simply sit back and enjoy the verdant scenery, the dappled sunlight through the trees. It was almost an hour before they reached their launching spot. David loaded their picnic gear into the center of the canoe. Then he held the craft for Sarah. "Okay, step in, but keep your weight right in the center. Canoes are pretty tippy."

Carefully Sarah settled herself in the bow. David handed her a paddle, then climbed into the stern and picked up his. Moments later, they were heading downstream, the water placid and muddy brown.

Sarah could hear birds calling. The scent of morning dew still hung in the air. From far away, she caught the odor of burning wood.

"You do this often?" she asked, finding the experience incredibly tranquil. Paddling wasn't that hard, for the current was pulling them along at a steady pace and David was doing the steering.

"Not as often as I like," David replied. "But I needed some time off this week."

She turned to look at him, and the boat tipped lightly. David grinned.

He had a very sexy grin, she realized, her heartbeat speeding up a little. "Why this week?" she asked casually.

He sighed, and dipped his paddle in the water a bit more forcefully this time. "Lots of things."

Okay, so maybe he didn't want to talk about it. Then again, maybe he just wanted to be asked. "Such as?" she prodded, deciding that she needed to know.

"Georgia, for one thing," David answered.

"How is she working out?"

"Fine, so far."

Detecting a troubled note in his tone, Sarah said slowly, "But you still don't trust her."

"The truth? No, I don't. I guess she disappointed me too many times before."

"Has her work been okay so far?"

"Yeah, it has. In fact it's been damn near perfect."

"Then what are you worrying about?"

His mouth twisted in a wry grin. "I don't know."

There was a long moment of silence. Sarah knew he was still upset about something and that he was no longer thinking about his secretary—if he ever had been. Somehow, the subject of Georgia seemed a dodge. "What else is on your mind?" she asked, wishing they weren't sitting so far apart and that she could see his face without having to turn around.

He studied the rippling surface of the river. "Not much."

Figuring to hell with the paddling—she wasn't being that much help anyway—she shifted her body completely and faced him, laying her paddle across the gunwales. "David, I leveled with you."

He looked up at her then, and it seemed an effort for him, suddenly, to hold her gaze. "It's work," he said finally.

When nothing more was forthcoming, Sarah asked quietly, "You can't talk about it?"

He hesitated. "Not yet."

She understood confidentiality. David was an important attorney in their city. "Okay," she said simply.

He smiled and looked at her wearily. "Just like that? Okay?"

"Just like that," she affirmed.

He grinned. "You're a wonderful woman, you know that?"

The way he looked at her, she was beginning to.

They stopped around noon, hauling their canoe up onto the shore. They spread a plastic-backed cloth under a huge silver maple tree, and sitting side by side, feasted on cold chicken and potato salad. They finished with thick slices of chocolate cake and mugs of hot coffee.

"You pack a mean lunch," he said afterward.

"Yeah, I know. My specialty." She grinned and leaned back on the blanket. She looked contentedly up at the blue sky dotted with fluffy white clouds. "The only thing missing is a little music."

He laughed. "The birds in the tree aren't enough, for you, hmm?"

"Maybe it's being around the kids so much—Josh is constantly playing the radio—but I've started listening to music more since they got here." It was a pleasure she had almost forgotten, strange as it seemed. Was that an indication of how sterile and joyless her life had become?

"Let me guess," he said, eyeing her. "You listen to one of those elevator music stations, the kind you probably play in your office?"

"Nope."

"Hard rock, then."

"Wrong again." She playfully plucked a little clump of grass and tossed it his way.

He ducked the errant green and pretended to study her with comic concentration. "Sing-along recordings of 'Hickory Dickory Dock' and 'Three Blind Mice'?"

She pretended to be highly affronted. "I *am* a pediatrician, David. Not in need of one."

"Oh. Sorry."

"The hell you are."

Looking impossibly mischievous, he guessed again, not bothering to deny the obvious. "Oh, I know." He lifted his hand in excitement and snapped his fingers several times. "One of those stations that plays all orchestral, symphony music."

Sarah shook her head, pleased she had kept at least some mystery in her life. "Wrong again," she announced smugly.

He sighed and stared at her, perplexed. "What else is there?"

"What else is there?" she echoed, sitting up. "How about good old country-and-western?"

"You can't be serious!" He shook his head in utter amazement.

"I listened to it a lot when I was a kid. And I went to Vanderbilt med school in Nashville, Tennessee, which is, as you know, the home of country music."

He looked both impressed and intrigued as he helped her pack up the picnic basket. "Did you ever go to the Grand Ole Opry?"

"Oh yeah, I loved it. Of course I haven't been back since I graduated, but I keep telling myself someday." The cleanup finished, they stretched out on the blanket once more.

"I would've figured you for a rock 'n' roll type," he said.

"I am. In fact, I like all kinds of music. But country-and-western is my favorite."

"How come?"

Sarah had to think about that for a moment. "The unvarnished truths in the songs, I guess. The lyrics are always so concerned with the basics of life. You know, the trials and tribulations of finding a good man or woman, of having a baby, of getting and keeping a job. I guess I wish life were that simple for me, or that happiness was as easily found as some of the songs seem to indicate.''

"Happiness is easy to find," he said rolling toward her, so that they were lying face to face next to each other. "I've found happiness just being with you," he said softly.

And then there was no more chance to talk. His face was suddenly over hers, and her arms came up to wedge distance between them. She felt as if she were trying to keep a hurricane at bay.

When his mouth lowered to hers, she expected strength, the single-mindedness of long-suppressed desire. Instead, he kissed her with tenderness, his mouth moving slowly and softly across hers. So warm and so close, he made her aware of erotic depths she hadn't known existed. She moved her legs, savoring the feel of his hard body against the softness of hers. His weight like a blanket of heat, he moved with her, sliding one leg between hers, kindling hotter fire. Sensation swept up her body, intensifying as his tongue slipped inside her mouth to twine with hers. Over and over he tasted her, drugging her to everything but his need. And her passion.

His hand slid down her body, and she offered no resistance as he opened her blouse and slid a hand beneath the lacy fabric of her bra. She moaned, her rose-colored nipples peaking and hardening against his palm. His lips moved gently down her neck, across the slope of her exposed shoulder, to one pouting crest. He took it into his mouth, suckling her gently, flooding her with waves of tantalizing heat.

"Oh, David," she whispered, shuddering uncontrollably and feeling as if she were drowning in erotic sensation. She'd never felt this way, so cherished and adored. Any more and she would be lost to everything except the need to be with him, to be as one. And not just now, but forever.

His mouth moved up against hers again. This time, he kissed her hungrily, his tongue plunging into her mouth, his hunger tempered only by his tenderness. Her breasts were crushed against his chest, her body supporting his. She felt as if every time he kissed her, he claimed her a little more. And she felt she claimed him. She moved her legs restlessly, needing him to hold her and keep on holding her, knowing the love she had found with him was almost too good to be true. His hand slipped between them to the catch on her jeans, and that simple act rocked Sarah back to reality. She became aware that they were lying on a deserted riverbank, completely out in the open. Anyone could come along and discover them. She hadn't even thought about that while she was kissing him. Nor apparently had he. Suddenly she was scared of all she was beginning to feel for David, and he for her, the fact that her feelings were out of control, that with much more kissing they could easily find themselves making love here and now, holding nothing back.

She put a hand over his and held it still.

Realizing she wanted to stop, he withdrew his hand and held her tightly instead. They stayed like that for several moments, catching their breaths. Sarah felt safe again.

"Oh, Sarah," he whispered, threading his hands through her hair, drawing back so he could look at her. All the affection he felt for her was reflected in the blue of his eyes. "I've wanted to hold you like this all week. You're all I've been able to think about, dream about." His lips brushed her brow, dropped to the curve of her cheek. "I want to be with you all the time," he whispered. "I get so frustrated knowing I can't see you whenever, wherever I want."

"I feel that way, too," she whispered back, her thoughts becoming faintly troubled. Because of their responsibilities, it just wasn't possible for them to be together a lot. Not now. Maybe not for a long time. Slowly the problems they faced penetrated her passion-clogged brain. There was so much they hadn't even discussed, so much he had to understand before they could take this any further.

And David was looking very much as if he wanted to start kissing her again.

"David," Sarah said firmly, pushing him away and struggling to sit up before she could lose her nerve. "We have to talk."

Chapter Seven

David heard the panic in her voice, the force behind the command. He knew she meant business, that she was already feeling regret. She was about to hit him with a list of all the why-nots in their relationship, and he didn't want to hear or think about any of them. He sighed. Why couldn't anything ever be easy?

Why did everything always have to be so... planned, so ordained? Though knowing Sarah the way he was beginning to, he supposed he should have expected at least this much. She never walked into anything blindly.

"Okay," he said slowly, with a great deal more patience than he felt, sitting up and a little bit away from her. He took in her tousled, sexy appearance—her hair all disheveled, her lips still red from kissing, her blouse still open—and felt a familiar stirring within him.

He forced himself to look into her eyes. "What's on your mind?"

She stared at him incredulously. "You sound as if you expected this to happen!"

He shrugged. "Didn't you?" It wasn't as if he'd hidden his intentions. He'd kissed her when he picked her up, and she had responded. Besides, it wasn't as if they were hurting anyone.

Color creeping high into her cheeks, she looked away. "I think we should look at this realistically."

The brushoff, here it comes. "Realistically, or cold-bloodedly?" he interrupted, feeling very angry. They were getting so close to each other; now she was pushing him away. He could see her fear, yet he'd done nothing to make her so hesitant, so sick at heart. But he knew he was getting blamed just the same.

"You and I don't want the same things, David," she continued stubbornly.

She was talking about his desire for a child, he knew, which neither of them really wanted to get into now. "You'll be the judge of that?" he said cooly.

She shot him a look and stood up. "I think I'm qualified."

The problem was, so did he. He also got to his feet, being careful to give her the distance she so desperately wanted. At least a bit of it, anyway. He watched as, her back to him, she did up her blouse. "So tell me what else's wrong."

She whirled to face him, her hands in the back pockets of her snug-fitting jeans. He could see she was angry. Her chin lifted defiantly as she answered him, "I thought I made it clear from the beginning I wasn't interested in a relationship, not at this point in my life."

"You came with me today," he pointed out calmly.

"Because I needed a little time away from the office and the kids. I didn't intend for you to seduce me."

David hadn't, either. "So we got carried away," he said softly, seeing nothing wrong with that. He knew she wasn't shy, but emotions were another matter. Apparently Sarah couldn't handle those, and he had to admit both of them had gotten a little out of control today.

"This isn't like me, David. I don't rush into bed with someone!"

He couldn't deny it was happening fast. "Maybe you haven't ever been with the right guy."

She glared at him. "I suppose this is par for the course with you, hmm?" Not waiting for an answer, she stalked off down the bank.

He caught up with her in two long steps and spun her around. "No, it's not par for the course with me," he said angrily. "I don't seduce women, Sarah. When and if they make love with me it's because they want it, too. We're not talking about force here." Maybe she wished there had been, he thought, because then she could've hung on to that for an excuse. She wouldn't have had to face the fact she desired him.

"I know that." She swallowed hard.

"But you're angry with me."

"You almost made me forget who I was, where I was." Her voice became almost inaudible. "All the reasons we can't be together."

"Because I want children."

"I can't give you a baby. I don't want to be hurt."

"I would never hurt you," he said softly.

She shrugged off his hands. "Not deliberately, no. But our situation—"

"—is not permanent. You're not sterile, Sarah."

Her face turned pale. "I told you—"

"And I listened. So you're not ready to try to have another child now. I accept that."

She went even whiter. "Not ever, David. I'm not ever going to let myself get pregnant again."

He studied her, wondering if she'd had herself sterilized and was afraid to tell him. "You're taking measures to that end?" he asked.

She looked surprised. Blushing a little, she admitted, "No. Not at the moment. I didn't expect—"

David gave a sigh of relief. "So today—"

"I could've become pregnant, yes, and had to go through that again."

He was silent, understanding now why she was so angry and acted so trapped. "I'm sorry this caught you unawares today. I didn't realize." He'd just assumed because she was a physician she would be protected.

"Well, now you know," she said waspishly.

He also knew how deep her aversion to pregnancy went, and he disagreed with it. Knowing he should be honest with her about his feelings, he said, "About your feelings about getting pregnant—"

"David, there's nothing to be gained by discussing this."

"I think there is." He took her in his arms. "I think given time and the love of a man you really care about, you'll change your mind."

She shook her head, her body stiff and resisting his embrace. "I won't, David." She pulled away from him entirely, a stubborn tilt to her chin. "And I don't want to be hurt."

Wearily, David rubbed a hand across the back of his neck. "Sarah, I told you earlier that I wanted a family. I don't care if I have to adopt. I still want my own biological child, I won't lie to you about that. But it wouldn't be the end of the world for me if I don't get one."

She studied him closely. "You say that now," she said quietly, hurt obvious in her eyes. "But I don't think I could take it if you made that sacrifice now and blamed me later."

"I wouldn't do that," he murmured.

"How can you be so sure?" Her voice was a broken whisper.

He gently pulled her against him, hoping his tenderness would win her trust, hoping his embrace would show her that he wouldn't let her run from him. "Because I take responsibility, here and now, forever after."

She was silent. He could see in her eyes that she wanted to trust him, but in the end her cynicism won out. "I still don't think it's wise for us to become intimately involved. Especially now that everything is out in the open."

He stared at her, frustrated and angry that she was being so stubborn and cowardly. He released her and walked a short distance away. "What are you trying to tell me? That by keeping our relationship platonic you'll be able to avoid getting hurt?" That she'd be able, he wanted to add, to avoid facing up to what she saw as a glaring inadequacy in her life?

"Maybe," she answered.

He wouldn't let her fool herself. "Don't you know it's too late for that?" he asked quietly. "What we've started to feel for each other, Sarah, can't be stopped."

"It could if you wanted it to."

He shook his head. "Some things you can't control," he said simply, walking toward her. "This is one of them. Sarah, I care about you." He wanted to say he loved her, but he knew it would only frighten her more. "I care more each day, and I don't want to hurt you. I think if we're careful, if we continue to go slowly, we can avoid that."

A glint of humor was suddenly back in her eyes. She stuffed her hands in the back pockets of her jeans. "You call what just happened 'going slowly'?"

He grinned, hooking his fingers in his belt loops. Considering that he had wanted to do that for weeks, yeah, he'd been going at a snail's pace. But knowing she'd been stunned enough for one day, he merely shrugged and said, "How about we continue our ride downstream?"

To David's relief, Sarah agreed, and once they were en route again, she seemed to relax. He used the quiet time to reflect on what had just happened, and realized he had pushed it with her. Tried to guide her into intimacy too soon. She'd almost given in to him, and they both knew that once intimacy entered their relationship there would be no turning back.

Her anger then made sense and shouldn't have been unexpected. That she'd calmed down now was a relief. He had to be more careful; he couldn't risk scaring her away and losing her. As for what she'd said about not being able to have children, that didn't make sense. She wasn't thinking like a physician—more like an emotionally overwrought woman. He had no doubt she could have a child. He'd like it to be his.

Getting her to see that, however, might take a lot of work. But it would be done. One way or another he'd see to it, because if anybody on this earth had ever deserved to have a child, he thought, it was Sarah.

DAVID AND SARAH were silent as he pulled his truck into her driveway. He clicked off the country-and-western station he'd had on and turned to face her, one hand sliding along the back of the seat. "Still mad at me?" he asked.

Sarah wished she could be, or that things were that simple. "No," she said softly. "I realize that what happened this afternoon was as much my fault as it was yours.''

It had been too long since she'd been with anyone, that was all. And David made her feel very desirable. Just thinking about the way he'd kissed and caressed her sent shivers down her spine.

His hand traced the curve of her shoulder. "Does it have to be anyone's fault?" he asked.

No, but it made it easier for her to deal with if she could believe it wouldn't happen again. Because she was beginning to see that she needed David in her life, yet she couldn't give him what he needed in return. She knew what he had said about adopting, but she'd also seen the look in his eyes when she had told him she couldn't bear a child. He hadn't believed her incapable of carrying a baby to term, just like William hadn't. And until he did believe, until he understood, how could she trust herself to love him or be loved by him in return?

"I can see this is still going to bear some thinking," he said softly.

"I guess it is," Sarah confessed, echoing his gentle tone. She wanted things to work out with David, because if nothing else, she wanted him as her friend.

"Maybe we should just take it easy for another day or so. Then after the weekend, I could give you a call?"

He was promising a much-needed respite. Though Sarah knew she'd rest easier if she simply said no to romance ever, she couldn't bring herself to do so. Instead, she took what he offered, hoping the lull would help her to come up with some solution. "I'll talk to you Monday, then?" she asked.

He nodded. "Monday it is."

Pulling out of the driveway, David went straight to his office, still dressed in his jeans. In late afternoon, the four-room office looked deserted. A printer was cranking out a contract, and David paused briefly to inspect a page. Seeing no errors in spelling or typing, he then headed for his private office. He ran into Georgia just as she was coming out of the washroom. "Oh, hello, Mr. Buchanan. I didn't think you were coming in today."

"I wasn't. But I had a few things I wanted to check on." And he'd needed to get his mind off Sarah.

"Oh, well." Georgia looked at him, a smile on her face. "Is there anything I can get for you?"

David shook his head. Was it his imagination or did Georgia seem unusually flushed? Lately she'd been grumpy in the morning, complaining of a headache, then as the day wore on she'd get increasingly ebullient, almost giddy at times. If she were drinking on the job again... Dammit, she'd promised him she was through with alcohol, that she was going to AA. And he'd believed that; that is, until now.

Returning his perplexed look, she pointed to his desk and said, "You've got about thirteen phone messages to return." Her voice was quiet and professional, disabusing his notion that she'd been drinking.

David felt immediately guilty for suspecting the worst. She did seem fine now, although she looked a little flushed. "Thanks, Georgia." He went into his office. Maybe he'd been overreacting, he decided, sighing.

For the next half an hour all was calm and uneventful. David caught up on some briefs he'd been meaning to finish. Georgia worked steadily, stapling contract pages together. Only when she appeared unexpectedly in his doorway did he again have the nagging sensation something was wrong.

"I know you have another client coming in today, but would you mind if I went home about half an hour early?" Beads of perspiration were dotting her upper lip. She looked as if she were about to be ill.

"Are you all right?" David got up and guided her to a nearby chair.

"No, actually, I'm not feeling well. One of the other secretaries in the building said something about a virus going around. I think I may have caught it."

She did look shaky and ill, David thought, abruptly deciding that she was indeed sick, not inebriated, as he had first suspected. He felt like a heel. "Of course it's okay if you leave early. Do you want me to call you a cab?"

"No, I can have my daughter come and get me. She had the afternoon off today."

"Okay. Well, if you're sure there's nothing I can do."

"There isn't. Just muddle through without me." Her attempt at lightheartedness only half succeeded. It was obvious she'd known all along what he'd been thinking and hadn't said a word, merely continued working to prove her innocence. That made him feel all the worse.

He decided to make it up to her and said, "Georgia, don't worry about anything here. I'll take care of everything." Thanks to his rift with Sarah, he had nothing to do that weekend but work anyway.

"You're sure?" Georgia asked, pushing a hand through her gray hair.

"Of course. Just go home and get some rest," David said. "We need you at your best."

"I'm sure with the weekend coming up I'll feel much better Monday," she said gratefully.

David nodded, advising with a grin, "Two aspirin, lots of liquids..."

Georgia smiled back. "And call my doctor in the morning. I know." She stood up and went to phone her daughter.

Now if only, David thought, he could get hold of Sarah that easily. But he had promised her he wouldn't call her until Monday. And he had to keep that promise, difficult as it would be.

TELLING DAVID NOT TO CALL was the stupidest thing she'd ever done, Sarah thought irritably. It was late Saturday afternoon, and she was stuck home with nothing to do except think about him, all she was missing by not being out with him, or letting him come over.

Well, this wouldn't do at all. She got out the Entertainment section of the newspaper. "Does anyone want to go to a movie?" Sarah called upstairs to the children.

Scott was the first down the stairs, screaming, "Sure!" Julie was last to deliver her opinion. "I can't," she said morosely.

"Why not?" Sarah asked, perplexed.

"'Cause I've got to do my project for school."

This was news to Sarah. "What project?"

"We have to make a pillow the way the pioneers made them."

"You mean sewn by hand?"

Julie shrugged. "I guess."

"Did you get an instruction sheet on it?"

After a moment, Julie nodded, and Sarah told her to get it so they could study it. "You don't have to do that for her," Josh said quietly. "I can help her."

Sarah smiled. "I don't mind." It was the first time Julie had come to her with anything. She was thrilled to be able to help. And yet at the same time she didn't want to make too much of it for fear of scaring the children away. She had to be careful not to overreact.

"Here it is, Sarah." Julie sat down beside her on the sofa. Quickly, they scanned the sheet.

"Well, it looks like we're going to have to go to the fabric store," Sarah said. "Josh, Scott, do you want to go?"

Scott jumped at the chance to go anywhere. "Yes," he said, then ran to get his jacket.

Josh shook his head. "I think I'll stay home." He paused, then added diffidently, "That is, if it's all right with you."

Was he upset with her? Sarah couldn't tell. "Of course," she said lightly. "We'll bring pizza home for supper." The kids were fond of pizza, so she made a point of serving it once a week. Anything to make them feel more at home with her. And she sensed too many home-cooked meals or too much tender loving care made them feel uncomfortable. Still it was hard for her not to smother them. She wanted so much sometimes to be able to just take them in her arms and hold them all close, to tell them everything would be all right. But she also knew that, for them, everything never really would be, because they had lost both their parents. They might grow to love her with time, but she could never take Liz's place in their hearts. Nor would she try to. The best she could do was supply them with concern and support, some sort of structure. The rest would come with time. She was sure of it.

Minutes later, they were on their way. With both children's help, Sarah managed to locate everything they needed for the pioneer project. Then they picked up dinner. But when they arrived back at the house, it was dark and silent. Lady was on the back porch, asleep.

A note from Josh was on the kitchen table. "Sarah, my friends called. I'm going out to see a movie with them. Back later. Josh."

Sarah stared at the note, hardly able to believe what she'd read. Josh had just broken every single rule they'd agreed on. Why? What was she going to do?

"What's up?" Scott asked. "Where's Josh?"

Julie put her shopping bag on the counter.

"Josh won't be joining us for supper," Sarah said calmly, taking off her jacket. She would call Josh on this, but she'd do it privately. She didn't want the other children upset, especially when they were just starting to be comfortable with her.

Although she'd lost her appetite, Sarah forced herself to eat with the children. When they had finished their milk and cleared the table, she sent them upstairs for their showers. Then she went to the phone in her den and dialed David's number. She was thankful he was home.

"I know we agreed to take a break for a few days," she began.

"I'm glad to hear from you." His voice was warm, caressing.

Sarah swallowed hard. It was important David think her competent to handle the children, and yet he had to know about the crisis she had on her hands. "David, I've got a problem with Josh." Briefly she explained.

"You mean he just took off?" David asked incredulously when she had finished.

"Yes." Sarah held the receiver closer to her ear. "David, what if he's testing me?"

"Do you want me to come over and be with you?"

Yes. "Better not," Sarah said after a moment. "If we're both here, Josh might feel we're ganging up on him."

"You're probably right."

"I think I can handle it."

"Don't let him push you around, Sarah."

"I won't."

"And I'm here if you need me."

"Thank you." She felt better just knowing he was there.

"You'll call me? Let me know what happens?" he pressed.

"First chance I get," Sarah promised.

"I am glad you called," David said softly.

So was Sarah. Maybe more than she should be.

JOSH SLIPPED IN at twelve-fifteen. Sarah was sitting up watching for him. The other children had long since gone to bed. Shoes off, house key in hand, he was starting toward the stairs when Sarah called out, "You're pretty late."

He stopped. His shoulders went up. Ever so slowly, he turned toward her. An insolent look was in his eyes. "It's only fifteen minutes past midnight," he said carelessly.

Sarah felt her temper rise. Deliberately, she kept her tone even and firm, showing none of her inner turmoil. "You also forgot to ask permission to go out with your friends."

He regarded her steadily, not moving. "How could I ask you? You weren't here."

"You could have waited until I got home," she pointed out gently.

He shrugged again, even more indifferently, as if he were perfectly justified in what he had done. "They wanted to go for a burger first, then see a movie, pal around."

"And so you just left."

"No. I wrote you a note, and then I left." A bit of insolence had crept into his voice. But at her disapproving look, he started over, "Look, Sarah, I'm sorry. Next time I'll ask first."

Sarah was tempted to tell him there wouldn't be a next time, and let him stew about that possibility for a few days. But alienating Josh would also alienate his younger brother and sister, so Sarah forced herself to remain steady. "What would your mother have done if this had happened?" she asked instead.

"It wouldn't have happened with my mother," he countered, matching her even tone for even tone.

Sarah sighed, thinking how hard it was to deal with a child who was so much an adult.

The defiant look was back on Josh's face. "I didn't have to ask permission."

So that was the problem—he thought she was babying him! Sarah relaxed. "Josh, I just need to know where you are," she said simply. Maybe later, they would be able to drop some of the restrictions on him, but until they became a real family, and knew one another well enough to second-guess, this was all very necessary. "I also wanted to meet your friends."

"Yeah, well..."

"Is there some reason you don't want me to meet them?"

"No."

But there was; she could tell. "Josh?"

"You're not my mother. I—" He bit off what he'd been about to say and took a deep breath. "Look, I know you gotta do what you think is right. So if you want to ground me..."

Strangely, Sarah didn't. She instinctively felt he was expecting her to do just that, and that maybe he even wanted that as an excuse to be angry at her, to maintain the distance between them. She wasn't going to give him that excuse, she decided rashly. She was not going to be that predictable. "No, Josh, I'm not going to ground you."

He stared at her disbelievingly, as she went on, "I do want to meet your friends. Have them come over tomorrow. You can play football or baseball outside. But I want to meet them all. Every single one of them."

"You're sure?"

Sarah smiled. "Positive. The sooner I meet your friends, the sooner we'll all get along."

Josh nodded his assent, still looking confused, and disappeared up the stairs.

Oh, who was she kidding? Sarah thought, the moment Josh disappeared up the stairs. The way things were going now, she didn't know if they'd ever work this out. It couldn't be clearer that Josh didn't want another parent. Truth be told, he didn't want to be there at all.

But it *was* what Liz had wanted. Sarah had only to get out the letter her friend had written, to know how important it was she keep trying. For Liz's sake, for the children's, maybe even for hers.

Her spirits bolstered, Sarah started for the stairs when she heard a car pull up out front. Looking out the living-room window, she recognized David's car.

She slipped quickly out of the front door and walked down the driveway. Seeing her, David waited in his car. He opened the door on the passenger side, and said, "I hope it's not too late to come by. I was worried."

"You could have called," she pointed out, smiling and getting in beside him. She was glad to see him.

"Yeah, I know. But I wanted to see for myself that everything was all right."

She filled him in, and when she was finished, he said, "It's not surprising he'd resent being told what to do, where to go, whom to see. Seventeen-year-old kids are notoriously independent."

"I know." She shivered from the cold. He put his arm around her, and Sarah rested her cheek on his shoulder.

"Your instincts were probably right."

Even in the darkness, Sarah could see the uncertain set of his mouth. "You don't really think that," she said, realizing it was very important to her what David thought.

"No, I don't," he admitted reluctantly. "I would've grounded him." He sounded very sure of that.

Sarah couldn't agree less. "And I probably wouldn't have even if he had been really insolent."

"How come?" David pulled her closer.

"I don't know." Sarah stroked his thigh absently, then realizing what she was doing, she quickly folded her hand on her lap. "I guess because I think he needs love right now more than he needs discipline. I don't want anything to get in the way of that."

David covered her hand with his. "You have a lot of heart."

She smiled, glowing from his praise. Feeling a need to inject some lightness into the conversation, she teased, "And you're crazy, coming out in the middle of the night like this. Just to see if I'm, we're, all right."

He stroked her cheek. "I care about you, Sarah."

"I know that," she said softly, looking up at him. The truth was she was falling in love with him. But she still wasn't sure this was the right time for her to let love happen. Her life was so complicated. She couldn't bear it if anything went wrong with her friendship with David, too, and with her life with the children so shaky right now... No, she couldn't risk it.

Because David was looking very much like he wanted to kiss her, she slid away from him. "Well, I better go back in," she said hastily.

"I'll walk you to the door." He had jumped out of his side, and opened her door before she could stop him. Their steps echoing in the silence of the night, they walked, side by side, to the house. Sarah thought that although they weren't touching, they looked very much a couple.

"I've got to work tomorrow," he said, "on account of taking Friday off."

She smiled. "So do I." She had rounds at the hospital and some insurance paperwork that had to be filled out by Monday.

"Otherwise I'd come by."

She shrugged, glad the problem with Josh had been, if not forgotten, at least temporarily put aside. "I have to help Julie with her sewing project anyway."

"Maybe I could see you Monday." Hope underscored his voice.

Sarah's spirits rose. "Lunch?" she suggested, looking in his eyes.

"I'd like that a lot."

He still wants to kiss me. "Well, goodnight." Sarah leaned forward to give him a quick kiss on the cheek, but he turned slightly at the very last second, so that her mouth came in contact with his. When she didn't pull back, his mouth closed over hers completely. Sarah drew in her breath, called upon every bit of inner strength she possessed and moved away from him. Even though the kiss had lasted only a couple of seconds, she was trembling from head to foot, filled with a wanting that electrified and stunned her. Damn him for making her want him even more.

He reached up and smoothed her hair away from her face. There wasn't a shred of apology on his face, only lingering tenderness and a look of satisfaction. "Goodnight, Sarah," he said softly after a moment, and then languidly retraced the steps to his car.

Sarah stared after him, with a mixture of amusement and bewilderment. She might continue to say no, but he would always insist on yes, and heaven only knew where a combination like that might lead.

Chapter Eight

David called early Monday morning, his low voice every bit as beguiling over the telephone as it was in person. "About that lunch I promised you, no can do. I'm going to be stuck here in the office all day."

"Why? What's up?"

"Georgia's out with the flu." He sighed deeply, making no effort to hide his chagrin.

"Oh, David, I'm sorry." She knew how frustrated he got when his office was out of kilter. "Is there anything I can do?"

"Well, that all depends," he drawled. "Can you find me a temporary who can type and spell and doesn't file her nails and chew three wads of gum at the same time?"

Sarah laughed. "Sorry, can't help you there. You're swamped, hmm?" Even though she knew it was unwise to let herself count on him emotionally, she had been looking forward to their time together, to furthering their friendship. There was still so much she wanted to know about him.

"Yeah, I really am but, uh, there is something I need to talk to you about."

His tone had turned abruptly serious. Sarah straightened. "David, what is it?"

There was a brief silence before he replied, "I'd rather not talk to you about it until I see you. What would you say to dropping by my office sometime today, if not at noon then later?"

Sarah checked her schedule. That would mean a cross-town drive during lunchtime, and she had to be at the hospital no later than one-thirty.

"I'd rather it didn't wait," David pressed.

Puzzled, Sarah decided to do as he asked. "I'll come by at noon then."

"All right. See you then."

He hung up and Sarah sat staring at the phone. She had no idea what was going on. Several questions ran through her mind, and she could hardly wait for noon to arrive, so she could clear up the mystery.

When the time finally came, she hurried to David's office, and to her surprise, found him as somber in person as he had been on the phone. "I called ahead and sent for a couple of sandwiches and salads. They should be here in a few minutes," he said, closing the door behind her and returning to his desk.

"Thanks." Sarah sat in a chair in front of his desk. It wasn't like David to be so formal with her and look so grim. A feeling of unease descended on her. "What did you want to talk to me about?" *Please don't let it be bad news,* she prayed.

David didn't answer right away. Instead he played with a pencil on his desk. "It's about the children actually," he said finally. He put the pencil down and looked at her, regret in his eyes, his voice soft. "You remember the search for relatives the judge wanted me to conduct?"

No, she hadn't remembered; she'd put it out of her mind—deliberately, she guessed. Her heart slamming against her ribs, Sarah nodded. "Yes, I remember." Oh God, she thought, please don't let him tell me they're going to take them away from me. Don't let him tell me they've found someone else.

David's mouth tightened. He looked as if he were bracing himself for something unpleasant, something he didn't want to do. "I've located a second cousin of theirs. He's in the Army, stationed in Germany. He's married. From what I know so far, he has no children."

For a moment she couldn't move or speak. She felt an ache in her throat, and beyond that, a dulled sense of shock and dread. "I see," Sarah managed to reply, her voice low. She stared at David, angry at fate for dealing her this blow just when she'd finally started to feel comfortable in her role as mother to the children. And she felt full of despair because she didn't know what she was going to do, what she *could* do. She was almost afraid to ask for fear the answer would be that she couldn't do anything. "Is this relative young?" she asked, hoping desperately that he was too young to be made guardian, yet knowing that if this were true, David wouldn't be looking so glum.

"He's twenty-six," David said neutrally.

"Oh." Maybe not old enough to want three children, but certainly old enough to handle them. And he was married. Sarah knew how the court favored blood ties and married couples when it came to placing minors. Without warning, her hands began to tremble. Sarah clenched them tightly together until they stopped. She had to get hold of herself.

His gaze still on her face, David continued, "There's no guarantee of course he and his wife would even be interested in taking the children, and I haven't contacted them yet, but—"

"They might," she interrupted, feeling her stomach surge.

David nodded slowly, his look one of shared pain and compassion. "It's a possibility, one we both need to face."

"The children?"

"I don't think they should be told yet."

"I agree." For a long while, Sarah sat quietly. She was numb with pain and helplessness. The feeling of impending doom surrounded her, and the thought of losing her family—for that was how she thought of the children now—was too much to bear. She swallowed hard against the continuing tightness in her throat. "How long have you known about this?" she asked finally, tears burning her eyes.

"A couple of weeks."

Sarah's head jerked up. They'd been together countless times, yet he'd never said a word! "Why didn't you tell me?" she demanded furiously, feeling her resentment and anger grow. It felt good to focus on something concrete, and he was a handy target.

David squared his shoulders, as if he were about to go into battle. "I intended to," he said stiffly.

His self-righteous attitude irked her. Had the situation been reversed she would've told him! In fact, she would've cautioned him every step of the way. Instead he'd chosen not to mention it at all, and as a consequence she'd forgotten all about the search for relatives of Liz's, and hence, had developed a false sense of security.

"Well, you certainly didn't try very hard!" Sarah snapped, getting up to pace. "Or did you think you needed to protect me?" As her ex-husband had needed to protect her! Dammit, she wanted to be treated like an adult! She'd thought David did, but apparently she had been wrong about him, too. Or maybe she just hadn't wanted to see.

"I did try to tell you. Remember when I came over to your clinic and you were crying? I intended to tell you then."

Sarah calmed down, remembering the afternoon. "But you didn't tell me," she said slowly, recalling how she had cried in his arms. And revealed her most private pain.

David's expression became as tortured as she felt. "You were so upset. After I learned about the miscarriages, what could I say? 'I'm sorry, Sarah, but these children might be taken away from you, too?' I couldn't do it, not then." He ran both hands through his hair. "If that makes me some kind of a monster..."

It did and it didn't. "That explains that day," she admitted, "but later, when we went canoeing..."

He lifted both hands in a supplicating gesture, his eyes beseeching, and reflecting love. "I was selfish," he said. "I didn't want to spoil the moment. I felt us getting closer and I didn't want anything to interfere with that. Telling you, well—"

"It certainly would've spoiled the mood," she said, turning away. She didn't want him to love her, not then. And she certainly didn't want to be protected. Had she had a clue earlier maybe she could have coped better today. Now all she felt was an incapacitating ache.

"Exactly what are you accusing me of, Sarah?"

She stared at him coldly. "By not telling me the truth when you first knew it, you treated me like a child." She couldn't begin to tell him how much that hurt her, that more than anything she needed his respect; otherwise, anything else just wasn't possible. Especially a relationship! The fact he thought her capable of handling so little stung badly. She moved away from him, not caring how churlishly she was acting. "I don't need your protection, David. I don't need your advice on how to run my life, or handle Josh, or anything else! I had that in my marriage. I won't live with it again!" She picked up her purse and started for the door.

David strode after her. "Sarah!" She heard him calling her but she didn't stop. "Dammit, Sarah, come back here! We're not finished with this conversation!"

But they were. As far as Sarah was concerned, they'd said everything that had to be said.

She got as far as the reception area before he caught up with her, then matched her step for step to the outer door. She turned toward him furiously. "Just what do you think you're doing?"

"I'm going with you." David had had one woman walk out on him every time they encountered a problem. He wasn't going to stand for it again.

"Like hell you are!" Head down, she charged through the door and started for the elevators. He charged along with her. He could see her fury mounting, but he kept on going.

Abruptly she stopped. Her chin up, she tucked her clutch purse tightly under her arm, and said, "David, enough is enough."

His eyes narrowed. "You're not walking out on me."

"We have nothing more to say!"

"I think we do!"

"Well, I think we don't!"

He shrugged, not the least impressed.

"If you want to stay my friend—" Her tone was menacing.

"Oh, is that what we are? Friends? Funny, I thought friends talked things out instead of walking out."

She swallowed, and he pressed on, speaking more softly. "Sarah, I care about you, you know that. I am human. I make errors in judgment just like anybody else. If you're angry, fine, then we'll hash it out. But we will not walk out on each other."

"Is that what you think?" Her chin was raised defiantly, but her eyes were shimmering with unshed tears.

"That's what I *know*," David replied. It was all he could do not to take her and hold her in his arms. "Sarah, please, let's go back to my office. Let's work this out."

She remained still.

"I care about you, Sarah. That's all it is. I'm not trying to control you or tell you what to do. And I'm sorry. It won't happen again."

Her posture relaxed and she fingered the clasp on her purse. Slowly he put an arm around her shoulders, and when she didn't resist, he led her back to his office. Their lunch arrived, and David tried to eat, although he had lost his appetite. From the way Sarah was nibbling at her sandwich, it was obvious she wasn't hungry, either.

"I'm sorry if I was over-emotional," Sarah said.

"Look, I can understand your being upset. What counts is you're not still mad at me."

"You'll tell me if anything new comes up now on the Smith cousin?"

"The moment I'm able to get hold of Sgt. Smith. Right now he's out on maneuvers."

Sarah lapsed into silence. She tried to imagine a life without the children and couldn't. She'd come to count on them being a part of her life. She'd come to count on David, too.

"What are you thinking?" he asked.

She stood and walked over to the window, coffee cup in hand. "What it would be like to go it alone now." After the days and nights of almost having a family. Not everything was working, not yet, but she'd had hopes it would get better. Now she would probably never know if it would have.

Her voice cracked slightly as she impulsively told him what was in her heart. "David, I don't know what I'd do if I lost those kids now." She'd gotten used to planning for four instead of one, to having the sounds of children in her house. She liked having a reason to hurry home at night and finding out about their days. It was fulfilling to help them solve their problems, even if it was only giving Scott a yearned-for puppy, or helping Julie sew a pioneer pillow, or helping Josh sort out some of the confusion in his life. She enjoyed the challenges of parenting, and especially the affection she was beginning to get from the three children. "Being a mother is very fulfilling for me," she said. "I don't know if I could ever go back to living the way I did before, to coming home every night to an empty house, of having hours to fill every weekend."

He walked over and took her into his arms. "I know how you feel. That's why I've found it so hard to tell you about this relative. I want you to know I'll do everything I can to help you keep the children."

"Oh, David," she whispered, the fear of loss like a hard, tight knot inside her.

"It's going to be all right," he said. "If it should come to it, the judge will see you've made a home for the kids."

"What if he doesn't?" Sarah asked, feeling as if her heart was going to break. What if he thought blood was thicker than water? That a married relative was better than a childless friend any day?

"He will, but I'll be there for you no matter what happens." He continued to soothe her, stroking her hair.

She leaned into him, accepting his warmth and his tenderness, needing his strength as never before. She knew his reassurance was spoken from the heart, and it was enough for her for now. Because until David got in touch with Sgt. Smith, or there was an adoption hearing with the judge, there was nothing more either of them could do.

HAPPILY FOR SARAH, the rest of the week went smoothly. Julie finished her pillow. Scott had a performance at school—his class was to sing three songs—and he wanted David to come. Because of continuing problems at the office, David had to meet them there.

"Hi. Glad you could make it," Sarah whispered as David slipped into the seat beside her in the crowded auditorium. Josh had taken Julie off to the water fountain to get a drink. Sarah had stayed behind to save their seats.

"I'm sorry I couldn't meet you at the house," David whispered back, taking the program Sarah handed him. "I had to be in court today and the proceedings ran late."

"I understand." She reached over and briefly clasped his hand in greeting. "Georgia still sick?"

"No, she's back today, thank goodness."

He didn't look very happy, though. "Is everything okay?" Sarah asked.

David nodded, though he wasn't so sure. Georgia had looked so washed-out and shaky today. But then, that was to be expected after a five-day bout with the flu. There was no reason for him to be worried. "This ought to be cute." He inclined his head at the stage, feeling as proud as any parent.

"It will be. Scott has been practicing his music all week."

David gazed at her. Even after a full day at the hospital, she still looked provocative. Her red-gold hair curled attractively, framing her oval face. Her pale, creamy skin never looked smoother. And he had never seen anyone look better in a simple long-sleeved dress. With difficulty, David focused on their conversation. "How was your day?"

"Fine. Busy." She smiled, and then the smile faded into a frown.

"What's the frown for?"

"I was just thinking about a patient of mine who's coming in tomorrow," Sarah explained. Melissa still wasn't feeling well, and Sarah was frustrated that she hadn't been able yet to render a definitive diagnosis. She felt for both the child and mother; knowing how much Melissa had been sick lately, it couldn't be easy for either of them.

However, there was nothing to be gained from worrying tonight, Sarah decided firmly, putting the case from her mind. She would take things one day at a time.

That's what she had to do in her personal life, and that's what she had to do in her practice.

Josh and Julie returned. They smiled and said hello to David. Sarah slid her knees toward David to let the children pass, and the touch of her legs against his thighs sent spirals of warmth through her veins. Even after she had turned back, her skin still tingled. When David reached over and took her hand in his, she knew he needed her touch as much as she needed his.

The three of them talked for a few minutes, then fell silent when the curtain rose. All eyes focused on the children's choir as they sang "America the Beautiful," "My Country 'tis of Thee," and "Yankee Doodle Dandy." All were wearing star-spangled vests, red-and-white striped pants, white shirts and top hats.

Listening and watching, Sarah felt tears of pride come to her eyes. For the first time in her life she knew what parents felt when they talked about getting a lump in their throat every time they saw their child perform, or watched them compete athletically. It was a very moving experience, and Sarah realized how much she had come to love the three children in the short time they'd stayed with her.

When the curtain came down, the crowd gave the children a standing ovation. David squeezed her hand, then nudged her shoulder, and directed her attention to Josh. He was every bit as choked up as David and Sarah. Sarah had to swallow again. The lump in her throat was never going to go away at this rate.

Soon pandemonium broke loose as the children were dismissed. Julie tugged on Sarah's hand. "Can we go see my pillow now? I want to show David what we made!"

"Sure, Julie. I'd love to see what the two of you made," David said. Sarah felt a blush spread across her cheeks.

"I'll stay here and wait for Scott," Josh murmured protectively, watching the stage. "He'll never find us in this crowd."

Sarah was torn, wanting to stay with Josh and go with David. "Why don't we all wait and go together to see the pioneer display?" David suggested.

Josh looked at David, then after a moment, he smiled. "Okay," he relented.

Not "I'd like that," Sarah thought, or "What a good idea," but "okay." Still, it was a start.

Scott came running up. "David! Sarah! Did you see me?" He had taken off the costume supplied by the school and was dressed now in dark trousers and a white shirt. He looked excited and happy, happier than Sarah could remember seeing him since he had arrived. It was happening, she thought, just as David had promised her and she had hoped. Slowly but surely the children were settling in. Even Josh, as unwilling as he was, was adapting slowly. Maybe not willingly, but he was adapting just the same.

"Yes, we saw you." David ruffled Scott's hair, and clamped him affectionately on the shoulder. "You were great! You were all great!"

Scott's eyes twinkled.

"Great job, Scott," Josh said. He, too, clapped his brother on the shoulder.

Sarah bent to give Scott a hug. "Honey, you were marvelous. I loved your performance, every single minute of it!"

Scott beamed. Together, they went to see Julie's pillow, which her teacher had put on display. Julie gave

David a blow-by-blow description of how it was put together. Then they went into the cafeteria for punch and cookies before heading home.

Back at Sarah's, Scott and Julie immediately went up to bed. Josh hung around in the living room where Sarah and David sat on the sofa. "Is there something you want to ask me?" Sarah asked softly. Josh was so hard to read, so hard to help. He didn't want to be loved, and yet she knew he needed affection badly, maybe more than the other two, because of his steadfast refusal to let himself get close to anyone since his mother's death.

"Yeah. Here's the deal. Some of my friends and their dads are going up to Michigan on the July fourth weekend for a backpacking trip. I was invited to go but, uh, everybody else is taking their dads and..."

"You feel awkward about going, is that it?" Sarah prompted gently, when Josh didn't finish. It must be hard for him, having to explain to everyone that he didn't have parents anymore. Living with two losses was bad enough, without constantly having to talk about them. And then there was the fact of her guardianship.

Josh nodded, not quite meeting Sarah's eyes.

"I could go with you," David offered casually, leaning forward on the sofa. He waited for Josh's reaction. "That is, if you'd want me to," he finished quietly.

Josh studied David, emotion shimmering in his eyes. For the first time in months he looked hopeful. "You'd do that?"

"Sure," David said. "In fact I'd love to. I've always enjoyed backpacking. It's been a while since I've done anything like that, though."

"Well, don't worry. Most of the other dads are getting ol—Uh, they're going for the first time in a while, too."

David grinned, then looked at Sarah. "That is, of course, if it's all right with your guardian here."

Josh tensed, but he forced a smile as he shifted his gaze to her.

"Of course. I think it's great. Just keep David and me apprised of the details," she said.

"I will." Josh's smile became a grin that bounced from ear to ear. When he reached the stairs he took them two at a time. "I think I'll call Ronnie now."

"You like his friends?" David asked, after Josh had disappeared.

Sarah nodded. "Most of them are, like Josh, very responsible. They're also pretty shy, none of them involved with girls, but I figure that'll come in time. Josh has enough to deal with right now without having to worry about a girlfriend, too."

"I hope you don't mind my offering to take him camping. It seemed like the thing to do."

"Yeah, I saw that look on your face when you realized you should've asked me first," she teased, taking the hand he offered her and moving over to sit next to him on the sofa.

"Then you're not angry with me, for jumping the gun?"

Sarah shook her head. "No. I want you to get close to him." She wanted them to be a single happy unit.

Silence fell between them. "I felt like we were a family there tonight," David said finally. "Like I was the dad and you were the mom and we had these three kids."

From the emotional yet casual way he spoke, Sarah knew it was a dream come true for him. Unbidden, tears of happiness came to her eyes. The knot was back in her throat. "I felt like we were a real family, too," she whispered. And maybe they were a family now, not perfect yet—far from it—but definitely a unit.

Liz would have been pleased.

Absently, Sarah stroked the back of David's hand, her fingertips light and caressing on his skin. She looked into his eyes, and seeing all the love reflected in them, she knew it was inevitable they would become lovers. The bond between them was growing stronger every day. Could she wait until all the children were completely settled in before pursuing her romance with David? Suddenly even a week or two seemed an impossible amount of time to wait. "You've done a lot for us. I'm very grateful," she murmured, wishing there were some way short of making love with him that she could let him know all that was in her heart.

"Oh, Sarah." He caressed her face. "If you only knew how much you've already given me, just by letting me be a part of your life."

Mesmerized by the way he was touching her, the sensations flowing through her, she was motionless, waiting, her breath suspended in her throat. Yet all too aware the children were just upstairs and might come down at any moment....

He bent to kiss her gently, his lips moving softly and tenderly across hers. "Tonight I had an idea of what it could be like for us, for them, if we do get together," he said softly. "I felt like I had everything."

That meant he didn't need a baby after all, she thought, relieved and overjoyed. Her feelings of inadequacy fluttered and slipped away. She knew now he could love her completely, without always hungering for the baby she was unable to give him.

He pulled back finally, his blue eyes holding hers. "I think I had better get out of here while it's still possible for me to do so."

Sarah knew exactly what he meant. And for the first time the prospect of becoming closer, more intimate didn't alarm her. She and David would have it all someday, she was certain.

Chapter Nine

The two weeks that followed were the best in Sarah's life. David called her every day. They had lunch together, occasionally dinner—sometimes with the kids, sometimes without. They went to a garden show and a new art exhibit that Sarah wanted to see. At David's request, they went to the new James Bond movie, and a Cincinnati Reds' game. Never much of a baseball fan, Sarah was surprised at her enjoyment of the baseball game; they decided to take the kids for a doubleheader the next day. As expected, they all had a wonderful time and acted just like a family.

Sarah loved every minute she spent with David, but she felt he had given her much more than she had ever given him, and she decided to remedy that right away. So the following Saturday morning, after calling on a ruse to be sure he was home, she drove over to his house, a gift for him in the back of her hatchback.

"Surprise!" Sarah shouted the moment he opened his front door.

David stared at the beribboned present in front of him. "A bicycle built for two," he murmured, amazed. "Where did you find it?"

"I got it at a bicycle shop downtown," she said. They had specially ordered it for her.

David circled the garnet-red bike, with its elongated frame and two sets of pedals and handlebars. Too overcome for a moment to speak, he looked at her in wonderment. "This is great," he said at last, nodding approvingly. "It's just right."

Happiness flowed through her. "You're sure?"

"Positive. Although I can't believe you remembered that I—"

A soft blush spread across her cheeks. "I remember everything you say," she said quietly. She remembered his every word and gesture, the way he looked, the way he acted, even the way he drove a car or the exact way he looked the first day they'd met. Even when she hadn't wanted to think about him, she had remembered. And today... today was for making memories, she thought.

"I felt I owed you something," she said, smiling, "for all you've done for me and the children."

"You didn't have to do this."

"I know."

"Thank you. Thank you very much." He pulled her near for a heartfelt kiss, and when they drew apart, long moments later, she felt as if she had stars in her eyes. She knew she had jelly in her knees. And David in her heart.

Looking as if he needed distracting, he said, "What do you say we try out the bike?"

Sarah grinned, warming to his mischievous gaze. "You're on. I feel I ought to warn you, though, I have never been on one of these things."

"Well, they're a little bit tricky. What do you say I take the back?"

"You must like the rear view," Sarah said, remembering he'd insisted on the back of the canoe, too.

David cast a teasing glance at her derriere. "As a matter of fact—"

Sarah felt herself blush crimson. "That's not what I meant."

"Seriously, it'll be easier if I'm in the back. That way I can steer."

"If you say so," she replied.

They walked the bike to the sidewalk, and Sarah climbed on. She rolled up the sleeves of her shirt so that her upper arms could get some sun.

"Where are the kids this morning?" David asked, climbing on behind her.

"They're all on school field trips. Josh went to Kings Island Amusement Park. Scott went to the Center of Science and Industry in Columbus. And Julie is on a day picnic with the Brownies."

"I didn't know she belonged."

"She just joined." Sarah looked back at him, noting how ruggedly fit he was. "I was a Girl Scout."

He looked her up and down. "I should've figured," he said dryly.

"Nothing derogatory in that remark, I hope?"

"No, there isn't, cross my heart." He made the appropriate gesture, once more drawing her attention to his muscular chest. "I bet you didn't know I was a Cub Scout and a Boy Scout."

Sarah laughed, picturing him in a little Cub Scout uniform. "Did you behave yourself?" she asked.

"Except on camp-outs." He gave her a devilish grin. "Then it was frogs in the tents and fake spiders in the soup."

"You must have been hell on your scoutmaster."

"To tell you the truth, I think he enjoyed the shenanigans more than we did, although he tried never to let us know that."

Sarah was willing to bet so, too, if David had been anything near as engaging a child as he was a man. "Then we really ought to be able to handle this bike," she said.

Unfortunately, riding the tandem bike turned out to be anything but easy. Five minutes, half a block and three near collisions later, Sarah was drenched in sweat and feeling more clumsy and inept than she ever had in her life. "I thought you said this was fun!" She shot him a mock angry glance.

"It is!" He gave her a wink. "Once you get the hang of it."

Sarah used the back of her wrist to wipe the perspiration from her brow. "The way we're going, that'll be the day."

He planted both feet on the ground, and brought the bike to a halt. "Okay, woman." His tone was playfully gruff. "Stop your muttering and get back here."

"I beg your pardon!" Sarah said, glad of any excuse to step off the bike.

"We're going to switch places. Maybe we'll do better if you're in back."

They switched places, and Sarah found herself eyeing David's broad back. Suddenly she thought of how it had been ages since she'd really kissed him. Images of David caressing and undressing her filled her mind.

"Ready?" she heard him ask, interrupting her thoughts and bringing her back to reality.

With such an attractive view directly in front of her, she'd have to work very hard just to concentrate on what she was doing. "As ready as I'll ever be. Let's go."

It was easier with David riding in the front, and they moved forward. Down one block, then another. On the next street Sarah thought there was loose gravel glinting in the distance. "David, I don't—"

"We're doing fine," he said confidently, picking up speed.

"David, there's—" Her words died in her throat as she got a little off balance, making the bike tilt to the right. Then the rear wheel went left and the front wheel went right. The next thing Sarah knew gravel was spitting up in her face and she tumbled forward, landing on top of David. The bike was on top of them both.

"Ouch," David said, cautiously lifting his head.

Sarah wasn't sure if she'd broken any bones. Some gift this had turned out to be.

"Are you all right?" David sat up, and helped her do the same.

"I don't know," Sarah mumbled, watching the trees spin. "Are the trees supposed to be going round?"

"Lie back down," David ordered.

A minute and a half later, the vertigo had passed. "I think I should call an ambulance," David said, starting to get to his feet.

"Don't be ridiculous," Sarah said, grabbing his arm, feeling the tense strong muscles beneath her fingers. "I'm fine. I'm just too lazy and embarrassed to get up. Do we have to ride the bike all the way back to your house?"

He grinned. "It's either that or walk it back."

Sarah chose the former. Fifteen minutes later, dusty and exhausted, they walked into his house and parked the bike on the back porch. "You know, maybe on second thought that wasn't such a great idea."

"Are you kidding me?" he said. "It was a great idea. I loved it."

"Did you?"

"Yes. Almost as much as I love being with you."

Without thinking she lifted her fingertips to his cheek and tenderly rubbed a smudge of dirt from it. His eyes holding hers, he turned his lips into her palm and brushed his mouth so tenderly across her palm that her breath caught.

Silence fell between them, rife with unspoken thoughts and the passion they were no longer able to fight. A pulse hammered at the base of her throat—at his nearness, the intimacy, the early morning hour. Suddenly, she yearned to know again the heat and texture of his kiss, to feel his tongue sliding over hers.

The light pressure of his thumb on her chin tipped her head back. Blood thundered in her ears and she couldn't find enough air to satisfy her lungs. She stared at him, driven by some magnetic force as mysterious and ungovernable as the seasons. This had been coming for a very long time and she wanted it as badly as he.

"I love you, Sarah," he said softly, the emotion clear in his eyes.

"And I love you," she said, knowing it was true. Their being together had been inevitable from the start. From the way David was looking at her, he apparently knew it, too.

He bent to kiss her, with his tongue tracing the shape of her mouth. Her breath shuddered out and he nipped her lower lip and drew it between his teeth. "I don't care if it's old-fashioned. I don't want to let you go," he murmured. "Not now, not ever."

"Oh, David, I don't want to leave you, either."

He wrapped her in his arms and pulled her into the haven of his body. She went gladly, willingly, sinking against him with a sigh of pure delight. "I want you," he muttered, holding her tight. "I want you so much I ache."

At that, the last of her reservations fled. All that mattered was that they be together intimately. David curved his hand on her hip and pulled her against him. Their bodies pulsated together and her breasts began to tighten, sending currents of fire racing through her. The pretensions between them vanquished, he slowly reached a hand down to release the zipper on her shorts. The snowy white fabric pooled around her ankles, trapping her in place. Liking the delicious feel of being his captive, she made no move to free herself from his arms. She opened her mouth to the hungry fierceness of his kiss, returning all that he gave, letting him know that she needed him, too, as much as if not more than he needed her.

The outside world fell away until there was only the two of them, only their rapidly beating hearts, only the feelings of love and tenderness and yearning between them.

His mouth brushed hers, softly, evocatively. Pausing long enough to get a breath, he held her against him fiercely. "I want you every way possible," he confessed lovingly, his blue eyes a sexy counterpoint to her golden ones. "I want you beneath me, all limp and ac-quiescent. I want you over me, arched and in control."

A slow sultry smile curved her lips at the images he was conjuring up. She smoothed a hand from his chest to his shoulder. Her words came out a whisper, her mouth just inches from his. "I want that, too," she murmured, feeling as if she would drown in the depths of his hot-blooded gaze.

Sarah shifted against him, returning kiss for ungovernable kiss. He trailed his fingers down the naked skin of her abdomen until he encountered the lacy sheath of her panties, and all that was hidden beneath. His touch was all the more hypnotic for its feather lightness as he stroked her repeatedly, lingering between the softness of her thighs. He knew instinctively where to touch, how to arouse and tantalize until she felt her body quicken and then surrender.

Sarah kissed him back repeatedly, showing with actions rather than words just how much she wanted him, too, that he was all she could think of, all she wanted. All she had ever wanted.

Suddenly she felt impatient, needing to touch him as he had touched her. She undid his belt, and without removing his shorts, slipped her hands across the flat of his stomach, then lower still. She felt pleasure flood her at his reaction, that she could make him feel as he did.

He groaned as she tightened her hand around him. "You make me crazy with wanting," he murmured, his low voice warm and rough against her neck.

She smiled, her lips curving into his skin, then was held spellbound by his hypnotic eyes as his fingers released the buttons on her shirt. She'd never felt any shyness about her body; she didn't feel it now. And yet she'd never felt so beautiful, so revered as she did at the moment.

His hands tightened on her hips and he drew her up to him. "Come to bed with me."

"Yes," she whispered, knowing she'd never wanted anyone in her life as much as she wanted him at that moment. She was his now, and he hers—they were making a commitment with what they were about to do. Slowly, shedding their clothing and kissing intermittently, they moved toward his bedroom.

His bed was unmade, his covers still rumpled from sleep. He followed her down onto the sheets, his body covering hers. She welcomed the hard pressure of his weight. Impatient to know all of him, she shifted her body to accommodate his. One hand sliding beneath her back, he arched her up against him. The moment of joining was blissfully sweet and slow. He eased into her, making them one, then held her tight, stopping only long enough to fold her legs around him. His arms around her, he moved within her, until they were as close as it was possible for two people to be, until their lives and bodies, their hearts and minds, were helplessly intertwined. The rhythm was slow, his lovemaking both tender and fierce, as stroke by stroke he made her his and discovered her wanton core. He made her feel gloriously weak and clinging and impossibly alive. He demanded everything . . . and gave everything in return. When the moment of surrender came, he held her close and hugged her tight. She'd never been happier in her life.

THE NEXT TWO WEEKS were sheer heaven for Sarah. David loved her fiercely and never missed an opportunity to show her how deep his feelings went. More importantly, he seemed to understand her completely. He accepted her flaws as readily as her good qualities, and didn't try to change her. He was kind and thoughtful, always there when she needed him.

In return she gave more of herself than she ever had to any man. She did small things, like picking up a new bestseller for him she knew he wanted but hadn't had time to go out and buy. She learned to prepare spaghetti sauce exactly the way he liked it. She developed an affectionate tolerance for John Wayne and Jimmy Stewart movies, and he in turn began to like Doris Day and Katherine Hepburn movies. She made time to talk to him every morning, lunch hour and night. Their exchanges were often brief, but they were always meaningful and brought them closer. She cherished the moments and began to depend on them to brighten her day.

The only problem was that she and David never seemed to have enough time together by themselves. His moving in with her was out of the question under the circumstances. It would be confusing to the children, and it might count against her in the adoption proceedings they planned. So, for the time being they would continue as they were. But she had to admit that all things considered, they were doing great. David never even brought up the subject of babies or her getting pregnant. As for their lovemaking it just seemed to get better and better. Indeed the only problems looming on her horizon were the question of whether the Smith cousin would want Liz's children—he and his wife were still unavailable—and the medical conference she had to attend. She had engaged a baby-sitter to take care of the children while she was gone, but she still hadn't summoned up the nerve to tell them. She knew she had to do it soon.

So one afternoon she gathered them around her. "I need to talk to all of you about something," she said calmly, trying to hide her uneasiness. "I have to go to Nashville the first week of June to present a paper at Vanderbilt University."

"Do we get to go with you?" Julie asked.

Sarah frowned. Now came the hard part. "Well, that's during the final week of school. Josh has his exams, and I don't think you should miss class, either," Sarah said.

"So?" Josh asked, not seeing the problem.

"So, I wanted to let you know that I've arranged for a sitter."

Josh paled. "You've got to be kidding. You got a sitter for us?" he repeated incredulously.

Trying hard not to let Josh see she was also beginning to get upset, Sarah nodded slowly. She'd known that Josh would resent her action, but she couldn't possibly leave the three children alone for the three days she was going to be gone. "Yes, Josh, I did. Her name is Mrs. Franklin. She's a nurse at the hospital, and has three grown children of her own and several grandchildren." Sarah trusted the woman implicitly, and she knew Mrs. Franklin got along well with children, even the most uncooperative.

"I don't care who she is," Josh said, pushing back his chair. "I don't need a sitter."

Julie looked frightened. Scott seemed upset. Too late, Sarah realized she should have talked to Josh first, alone. She swore inwardly. "Josh—"

"I don't suppose you'll change your mind on this."
He looked at her questioningly.

Sarah had the feeling she was being put to another
test. She shook her head. "No, I can't. For my own
peace of mind, I want someone else here. And then, too,
you need someone to keep house. You can't do that and
watch the children and study for your final exams."

Josh started to speak but bit off his words. "All
right," he finally said, looking surly. "If that's what
you want, we'll have a sitter." His tone was brusque and
angry.

"Can we go up to our room to play?" Scott asked
quietly.

Julie edged closer to her brother.

Sarah nodded, and watched them depart. She felt as
if she'd lost a battle, that maybe she'd just lost all the
ground she'd gained.

THE NEXT DAY Sarah brooded over Josh's behavior. He
was still angry and withdrawn when she left for the
clinic in the morning. Perhaps she should have comforted him, but she was a parent now and it was up to
her to make such decisions. Josh had to accept them.
Besides, he had a couple of weeks to adjust to the idea
of a sitter. It wasn't as if she had sprung it on him one
minute and then taken off the next.

During the afternoon a problem with a patient took
precedence over her family problems. Melissa came in
again, this time with a cut on her hand that required
several stitches.

"So how did this happen?" Sarah asked the seven-
year-old.

Melissa looked sullen. "I broke a bottle."

"What she means is she smashed a bottle she found by the playground at school," her mother said, frowning.

Perplexed, Sarah looked at Melissa. Then she called in her nurse, Carol, who took the girl off to get a toy from the For Especially Good Patients box.

"What's been going on?" Sarah asked Mrs. Anderson. "Has Melissa been having problems at school again?"

"It never stops. Sometimes I just don't know what to do. She's so moody, Doctor! Up one minute, down the next."

Sarah frowned. "Does she appear unusually frustrated?"

"No."

"She's been tested for learning disabilities?"

"Twice. They haven't found anything. They did—" She stopped and bit her lip.

"What?" Sarah prompted.

"Well, when I went to the school to get Melissa, the guidance counselor pulled me aside. She said she thought Melissa might need to start seeing a psychologist." She sighed, then went on. "She's so moody. She just... I swear sometimes she's like a stranger to me. I look at her, I look into her eyes, and I don't even know who she is."

Sarah had treated children who had emotional problems, and one or two who were mentally ill, but she didn't think Melissa fell into the latter category. There must still be something they were overlooking. "It could be a food allergy," she said. "Sometimes— rarely—a child will present the symptoms you've described as part of an allergic reaction."

When Sarah got Mrs. Anderson's permission to have Melissa tested by an allergist, she set up an appointment with one right away. Although it would be several weeks before all the results were in, she already felt better, knowing something was being done to help the little girl.

She stopped by David's office on the way home. Georgia greeted her and buzzed David's office. Dressed in a vivid red dress and a paisley scarf, the older woman was perfectly coiffed and made-up, looking completely recovered from the flu. She straightened a stack of papers on her desk and said, "So, how are things at the hospital?"

"Busy. Here?"

"The same." Georgia smiled.

"Georgia." David appeared, a grim look on his face. "Citibank just called. They said they haven't received the papers on the Marlin deal. Those were supposed to have gone out last Friday. What's happened?"

"I don't know." Georgia shrugged. "I sent them by courier."

David sighed. "All right. I'm sorry if I snapped at you. Just follow it up or send over another copy by messenger. The loan officer there is livid."

"I don't blame him," Georgia said. "I know how important those papers were." She frowned, looking as upset as David.

Satisfied the mix-up was being handled, David turned to Sarah. "Hi." He leaned forward to give her a kiss on the cheek. "I'm sorry for ignoring you. It's been a rough day." He ushered her into his office and shut the door.

"I know. I tried to get you on the phone three times."

"Yeah, well, it's been one screw-up after another." He ran both hands through his hair.

"Why?" Sarah watched him loosen his tie, realizing that something extraordinary had to be going on, or he wouldn't be near this upset.

"I don't know." He lowered his voice. "Lately it seems a lot of the paperwork leaving this office hasn't been arriving where it's supposed to, or there're missing pages if it does. Or the wrong contracts are being sent to the wrong places. And—"

"Have you talked to Georgia?"

"Yeah. She has an explanation for everything."

"You don't believe her?" Sarah asked.

"I think she may be drinking again. I could shoot myself for even thinking such a thing, but Sarah, this is exactly what happened before, and the reason I fired her."

Sarah thought back to what she'd seen in the reception room. "She looked fine to me."

"I know. And yet..." His voice trailed off and he swallowed hard.

Sarah hoped for David's sake the problem wasn't serious. "Maybe she is screwing up a little. Maybe she just needs time to get back into the routine. A few wrong papers sent here or there doesn't necessarily mean she's been drinking."

"Maybe you're right. Maybe this is all a fluke." He paused and shook his head. "And maybe it's just been too long since I've had a break."

Sarah smiled, glad to see the return of his usual optimism. "Maybe," she said slowly.

He picked up on the faintly suggestive note in her voice, and his gaze darkened seductively. "So, why did you stop by to see me?"

Sarah sobered. "A couple of things actually. I wanted to ask if you'd heard from the Smith cousin yet."

"No. He's not due back from his leave until June the tenth. I'll call him then to follow up on my letter explaining the situation."

Sarah nodded.

"Nervous about it?"

"Yes."

"Well, remember that Liz's letter counts for a lot. She wanted you to have the children. And things are working out. There's no reason for the judge to place them elsewhere."

"I know." At least intellectually. In her heart was another matter. But there were other things on her mind, which she wanted to discuss with David when there was no chance of the children overhearing or walking in mid-conversation.

"Why the worried look?" he asked.

She told him about the new problem with Josh.

"Sounds perfectly normal to me," David said, putting his feet up on his desk. "Surely you don't expect a seventeen-year-old boy to be overjoyed at the prospect of getting a sitter?"

"Well, no." Sarah blushed.

"There you have it then." David smiled encouragingly. "He'll adjust, I guarantee it. Now me—" he got up to walk over to her side "—that's another matter entirely." He wrapped his arms around her. "I don't want to be away from you at all."

Sarah hugged him back tightly. "I don't want to be away from you, either," she murmured contentedly against his chest.

"How would you feel about having company when you're not attending seminars?"

"You want to go with me?"

"If you'll have me."

She broke into a wide smile that came straight from her heart. She realized they had never spent an entire night together, never had any time that was really theirs and theirs alone. This could be that chance. "Oh, David," she said softly, "nothing could make me happier."

Chapter Ten

"There've been very few moments in my life that I've wanted to go on for eternity. This is one of them," David said on their first night in Nashville.

"I know what you mean. I don't want tonight to ever end, either," Sarah said, turning toward him. They were lying together, limbs entwined, on a real feather bed. They'd elected to stay in a bed-and-breakfast inn instead of a hotel. Now, surrounded by lace curtains, flowered carpet, fresh flowers and antiques, Sarah was blissful. She traced a pattern in the hair on his chest, sighed contentedly and cuddled even closer. "Right now I feel my life is as perfect as it's ever going to get."

"Oh, I don't know about that." His arms tightened around her possessively. "In fact, I think we're just beginning." His lips descended on hers. Hot and persuasive, his kiss stole into her heart and filled her body with fire. She was breathless and tingling when they finally broke apart. She felt delicate and feminine and loved. His hand stroked her breasts and on up her arm, the expression on his face, the sound of his voice, as warm and soothing as sunlight. "Do you realize this is the first time we've ever been completely alone for more than three or four hours?'' he asked softly.

Sarah nodded, all the love she felt for him welling up in her heart. "And the first whole night we've ever been able to spend together." She rolled toward him and pressed tiny kisses into the curve of his shoulder.

He threaded his fingers through the silk of her hair, idly separating the short, curly strands. Steady and stroking, his touch was as comforting as a lullaby. "I've been dreaming about sleeping with you for weeks now."

"We haven't been together nearly enough."

"Not ever enough." He kissed her again, lightly, tenderly this time, then with effort drew back and smiled. Without warning, he slipped out of her arms and left the bed. "Stay right there," he cautioned brightly.

Sarah propped herself up on her elbows, the sheet falling down to her waist. "Where are you going?"

"To get your surprise," David replied mysteriously.

Seconds later, he jumped back into bed, one hand behind his back. "Now, close your eyes and hold out your hand."

Sarah did as she was told and felt something like cardboard placed in her hand. "Okay, you can look now," he said.

She opened her eyes. "Tickets to the Grand Ole Opry! David, how did you manage that?" She had tried to get tickets, but was told the shows were sold out.

David grinned, looking pleased with himself. "It wasn't easy, but I knew how much you wanted to see Rosanne Cash."

"Oh, David, thank you. This is wonderful." She threw her arms around his neck and hugged him.

"I know. But it's not the only wonderful thing I have planned for us." He rolled over suddenly, so she was on her back beneath him. "Tomorrow night we're going on a riverboat cruise of the Cumberland River. And the next night we're going to go to Opryland complex, to hear the jazz I like."

She smiled, lifting her mouth to his. "Sounds good so far."

"And in between there will be meetings for you and historic places for me to visit." His lips trailed kisses down her neck.

"And one cocktail party at the university, don't forget." Sarah spoke in a husky whisper, groaning at what he was doing to her.

"I haven't," he said. "I'm looking forward to meeting people you went to school with."

Sarah threw an arm dramatically across her brow. "I hope they don't start telling stories."

David's eyes lit up. "Like what?"

She blushed. "I was the only one to faint during the first surgery."

"You?" He chuckled.

"Yeah. It was something about the smell of antiseptic, I guess."

"Obviously you've gotten over it."

She nodded, abruptly becoming more serious. "I've gotten over a lot of fears." Like the fear of becoming involved again, the fear of being hurt. She was willing to risk loving David now, because she felt she had everything to gain.

"Have I told you recently how much I love you?" David asked hoarsely.

Sarah smiled, happiness welling up inside her. "Only about ten times a day."

"Hmm. I can see I've been derelict in my duty." He slipped a little lower and kissed her shoulder. "I guess I'll have to say it with flowers then." He moved to the edge of the bed, reached underneath and pulled out a tissue-wrapped bouquet of white and yellow freesias. "These are for you."

"David." She stared at him, overcome by his tenderness.

"I want you to know how much I love you, Sarah," he said softly, squeezing her hand.

"I love you, too," Sarah whispered, "very, very much." She twined her arms around his neck and showed him how she felt. They didn't have much time, true, but they would make the absolute most of it.

SARAH WAS AS BUSY AS EVER when she was back in Ohio several days later. She had three patients in the hospital, and Melissa was back, this time looking very pale. Slightly breathless, she was too fatigued to even sit up during the exam. The results of her allergy tests had all been negative, so clearly her symptoms were caused by something else. Suspecting anemia, Sarah had a blood test done, which confirmed her diagnosis.

She explained her findings to the girl's mother. "Melissa has hemolytic anemia. There are several different reasons for this to occur, so I want to run more tests to figure out what exactly is causing Melissa's. Then I'll be able to prescribe a specific method of treatment. It would be easiest if we admitted her to the hospital for a few days. And you'll be able to stay with her if you like."

Sarah accompanied Melissa and Mrs. Anderson to the hospital, and after seeing them comfortably settled, she headed for a phone. She called home and told Josh she would be late and would probably miss supper. Then she went to the hospital library to read the latest articles on anemia and hepatitis. She had an idea, finally, just what might be causing Melissa's problems, but she needed to be sure.

It was nearly eight-thirty when Sarah arrived home. Josh approached her the moment she walked in the door.

"The guys called. They want to see a movie at nine o'clock. Can I go?" he asked.

Sarah looked around. The house was as neat as a pin. As usual, Josh had lived up to his responsibilities and done a lot more besides. "Where are your brother and sister?"

"In watching television."

"What movie are you going to?" she asked pleasantly.

"The new Stephen Spielberg flick."

"Sounds fine." Now that school was out, she didn't mind his going out occasionally on weeknights. "Be home by midnight, though, okay?"

Josh nodded and headed for the door. "I left you some dinner in the fridge," he called over his shoulder, slamming the door behind him.

Well, that was something, Sarah thought, exhausted. She heated her dinner in the microwave, carried it into the family room and watched a Disney movie with Julie and Scott.

Around ten, Julie said, "Oh yeah, David called you a couple of times."

Scott yawned. "I said we should write it down so we'd remember to tell you, but Josh said no, it wasn't necessary."

"In the future, write it down," Sarah said. Josh knew how much David's phone calls meant to her. Had he done that on purpose, or was it typical of a boy his age not to address much importance to a personal call? And yet Josh had always before been reliable with any message for her, whether it be from the hospital, or a patient, or David.

Sarah walked the children upstairs. She visited with each of them a while, tucked them in, then returned downstairs to call David. They talked for some time, then agreed to meet the next day for lunch. It was almost midnight by the time Sarah hung up, but there was no sign of Josh.

He'll be home any minute now, she thought.

I don't want to ground him.

He knew I said midnight.

The show he went to was over at eleven.

Where is he? Has something happened? Panic welled up inside her, and Sarah found herself pacing the floor. She had visions of him in a car accident, visions of him being mugged, or getting drunk.

By the time he sauntered in around one she was livid. Nonetheless, she told herself to calm down, to approach Josh with great tact. "So how was the movie?" she asked, working to control her temper.

"The movie was fine." He shot her a bored look.

Easy now, Sarah told herself sternly. "Any trouble getting home?" Maybe there was an explanation. Liz would have given him the benefit of the doubt. "A flat tire or something?"

"No." Josh seemed to be daring her to challenge him. "Why?"

Sarah paused, feeling tempted to let it go. She really didn't want to get into this with him. It was late, she was exhausted; and she had a heavy schedule the following day. She was already upset by this, and talking about it was likely to upset her further. Yet she also knew, if ever a gauntlet had just been thrown down, if ever Josh had tried to test her, this was it.

"You're an hour past curfew," she pointed out calmly.

"You were late getting home, too, tonight." His tone was polite, but his eyes were insolent, ready to do battle.

"Josh, I was at work. This is different."

He sat down on the sofa, flinging one leg over the end, and stared up at her. "Tell me something, Sarah." He slouched down a little lower. "How come I'm old enough to stay home and baby-sit Scott and Julie the nights you can't get home for dinner—"

"Those have been very few," she interrupted heatedly.

"They still exist," he said bluntly, then continued, "How come I'm old enough to cook dinner and run the washer and clean up the stupid house, but I'm *not* old enough to go out with my friends and come in without you waiting up for me like some... housemother." He uttered the word as if it were filthy.

Was that how he saw her? Sarah had to blink back tears. She knew he had never completely accepted her as a guardian, but to be thought of as a jailer—for obviously that's how he saw a housemother—especially when she'd been trying so hard to make him feel loved... It hurt a lot. And it made her feel more inadequate than she ever had before. The thought pressed into her brain: *Maybe I'm not cut out to be a mother after all, if after the past couple of months, this is still how he feels.*

Remembering her decision to honor Liz's request to care for her children, Sarah bit down on her frustration and decided to address only the issue that immediately needed solving. "Josh, we have rules here. You deliberately disobeyed me."

He looked at her, waiting, saying nothing.

"You're grounded."

"Fine." He got up and started to walk off.

"For one month."

He abruptly stopped, and slowly turned around. The teenage surliness had fled; in its place was an unexpected, faintly pleading expression. He wet his lips. "A month?" He repeated, staring at her in shock.

Already regretting the impetuousness of her decision—maybe a week would have been better—Sarah nodded. She couldn't back down now, when he seemed to have accepted her authority over him as a parent. "Until July the tenth." *Liz, forgive me,* she thought, *next time I'll know better.*

He tried to weasel out of it. "Look, I'm sorry—"

"Fine. Maybe next time you won't be late," she said unsympathetically, turning away. She knew he was sorry he'd been grounded, not that he'd blown curfew again. Suddenly she felt as if she were doing fine. She'd gotten his attention; that was something.

"Sarah, July fourth is the camping trip to Michigan. David already said he'd go."

Sarah swore mentally, realizing she'd forgotten, and turned back to him. "I'm sorry," she said with difficulty.

Josh was furious again. "You can't mean I can't go?"

"I mean you can't go," Sarah repeated firmly, holding his gaze.

"Dammit, Sarah, that's not fair!" He threw up both arms in protest, then flung them back down.

If I back down now, he'll never accept my authority again. And if he didn't, Scott and Julie wouldn't. Like it or not, she had to stick by her decision. Echoing words her own mother had said to her, Sarah said firmly, "I'm sorry, Josh. You should have thought of this before you broke curfew. No camping trip. That's final."

"I FEEL SO GUILTY," Sarah told David on the phone the next day.

"It sounds to me that you did exactly the right thing. And as far as the camping trip goes, I'll make it up to him later. We can go to Michigan alone, later in the summer."

Misery engulfed Sarah. She'd never felt quite so mean in her life. She didn't like being the disciplinarian, even when she knew damn well it was for the children's own good, and that she owed it to all of them to be firm. "He's so angry with me."

"Kids get angry with their parents."

"I know, but..." She thought of the cold, unforgiving way Josh had looked at her that morning. A shudder went through her. What if he never forgave her for this? She knew how much that camping trip meant to him.

"Give him time, Sarah," David soothed. "He'll settle down. He settled down about having a sitter while you were in Tennessee, didn't he?"

"I don't know, David. He was really upset."

"I imagine so, but maybe that's what he needed to shake him up. Look at it this way. Last night was the first time you and Josh reacted to one another as mother and son. I think Liz would've been proud of you, and I'm sure she would have done the same."

Her spirits lifted at the optimism in his voice. "You're probably right." Sarah sighed.

"So in the meantime, how about dinner out?"

"I don't know. I'd better be home tonight." And probably until Josh cooled off.

"How about Saturday night, then? I'll take you some place special?"

Sarah agreed. "I've missed you," she said softly. It seemed years, instead of a few days, since Nashville.

"THE TEST RESULTS are all in on Melissa." Carol handed her a thick file.

"Great." Sarah sat down to look at them. Minutes later, she was smiling. Not because the news was all good—Melissa wasn't out of the woods yet—but because she knew what they were dealing with now.

She met with Melissa and both her parents, and explained that the girl had an inherited disorder—Wilson's Disease. "It's caused by a buildup of a copper protein in the body. That's why she had hepatitis, anemia, the abdominal pains, and why her behavior has been a little erratic lately. The good news is the condition is completely reversible. Melissa will have to take a medicine called penicillamine, and you'll have to watch her diet to make sure it's low in copper, but she's going to be fine."

"Thank goodness." Melissa's mother was filled with relief. "I was so afraid."

"I know." Sarah spent some more time with the family detailing the treatment, comforting them, reassuring them. She was exhilarated; she had helped the little girl, maybe even saved her life. She only wished she could be as successful with her own situation.

Why was it so easy for her to be a physician, constantly making difficult decisions, never losing faith in herself and her abilities? When with one blowup with Josh, she felt like a total failure as a woman and a mother. He was still angry at her, and now she was completely unsure of herself.

Was it like this for every parent? she wondered, walking out to her car. Did all parents suffer the same doubts and insecurities, and have second thoughts after doling out a punishment? Or was it just her?

Chapter Eleven

"I have some terrific news," David announced over dinner the following Saturday night. They were seated at a table before the fireplace in a country inn twenty miles north of Dayton. The music was soft and soothing, the lighting dim and romantic, the service unhurried and personal. All in all, David couldn't have picked a better place, Sarah thought.

"So tell me," she prodded. Good news she could always use.

David grinned. "I heard from Sgt. Smith this morning. He and his wife talked it over, and neither of them feel able to take on the responsibility of the children at this time or in the future. So they're legally giving up all claims to them."

"David, that's wonderful!" Sarah sat back in her chair, sighing her relief. Suddenly, a dreadful thought flashed in her mind. "There's no one else, no other possible guardian?" She hoped not. Maybe it was selfish of her, but she wanted to keep the children. She wanted to continue trying to make them as happy and content as they deserved to be.

There were still problems with Josh. He had recovered from his disappointment over missing the backpacking trip, but there were times he didn't accept her authority. And she knew that living with her was difficult for him. Josh had been hardest hit by his mother's death. Maybe because he'd taken on so much of the responsibility for his siblings, maybe because he'd had the most time to love his mother. For whatever reason, she knew it was still very hard on him. But he was trying to fit in—at least as much as he was able—and he was also going through a tough time in his life. Being a teenager wasn't easy under any circumstances. Still, he was a good kid. In time he'd come to accept her, she was certain of it.

"No. Sgt. Smith confirmed that he, too, is the last of the line," David replied. "So it looks like you have a free and clear path to the finalization of the adoption."

Without warning, Sarah felt overwhelmed with emotion. A lump formed in her throat, and tears stung her eyes. She hadn't realized until that moment—she hadn't even let herself think—about how empty her life would be if the children were to leave. "That's such a relief," Sarah said shakily, realizing with joy she was just that much closer now to getting everything she wanted.

"To me, too." He took her hand.

Sarah thought he had never looked more handsome. Wearing a dark suit and tie, with the heady scent of his aftershave clinging to him, he was tantalizing. She had much to be grateful for, she realized, as a wave of contentment swept over her.

David's eyes brightened at her loving look. He reached for his fork and knife, and carefully cut into his chicken. "Don't look at me that way," he murmured teasingly, "if you ever want us to finish dinner."

Sarah couldn't resist teasing him. "What way?" she asked coyly, rubbing her knee against his.

His breath caught, and he shot her a look that told her she would pay for that. Then he lowered his eyes again, saying gruffly, "You're distracting me. Eat."

"I know I'm distracting you." She smiled, and began eating. As the aroma had indicated, the food was heavenly.

"So," David said after a few moments, "back to the kids, how are they?"

"They're much better actually. I guess you were right, David. Josh did get over my grounding him. Or he seems to have anyway."

"Do you think he's going to try to get you to back down?"

"I don't know. I don't think that's where he's heading with all his newfound cooperativeness." Still, it was hard to reconcile his anger then with his pleasant attitude now.

"Maybe he really didn't want to go," David offered optimistically. "Maybe his misbehavior was a deliberate attempt to have you ground him. Because that way he wouldn't lose face with his friends for not wanting to go."

Sarah thought that over and shook her head. She still remembered how excited Josh had been when he'd broached the subject. "I don't think so, David. The look on his face when I told him he couldn't go... Well, he was really disappointed."

"Hmm . . . whatever the reason, I still think you did the right thing, grounding him."

Sarah hoped so.

"Don't look so unhappy," he said gently, reaching out to take her hand again. He stroked her palm. "It's all going to work out. Josh will have his chance to go camping later in the summer. Maybe you could go, too. We could take all the kids and make a real outing of it."

"I'd like that very much," she replied, thinking it would make Josh happy, too. She knew how much he respected David, and how he needed a strong male influence in his life. She only wished the two could spend more time together, perhaps on a daily basis, so they'd be more like father and son.

After they'd finished eating, David took Sarah out onto the small dance floor. He held her close, not caring they were the only couple on the floor, or that there was more than one set of eyes on them. "I've missed you since we've been back from Tennessee," he murmured, closing his arms around her even more possessively, leaning his chin against the top of her head.

"And I've missed you," Sarah whispered back, loving the feel of his arms around her, his body so close to hers. She missed his warmth, his tenderness. She missed being able to kiss and touch him whenever, however she wanted.

David danced her around, until his back was to the other diners in the room. He touched his lips to the top of her head gently, and looked down at her with hot, hungry eyes. "My bed isn't the same without you. Neither is my breakfast table or my dinner table. I get lonely even riding in the car."

She laughed playfully, her voice as soft and yet as serious as his. "I hope you don't get over that."

"I've been thinking a lot about the two of us lately," he said, as they swayed together to the music. "I don't want to be away from you as much as I have been."

His words were a balm to her soul. It helped, knowing he was as dissatisfied with their limited time together as she. "I don't want to be away from you, either, but you know my situation."

"The adoption will be final in another couple of months," he pointed out calmly.

I want to marry him, she thought. *I want to spend the rest of my life with this man.*

He paused when the song ended, but kept her in his arms. Another song started. David still didn't move. "I've always wanted a family, you know that."

"Yes," she said softly. She swallowed hard, not sure what was coming next, only knowing she was nervous.

His arms tightened around her, and his voice grew more serious. "But more important than anything else to me right now is building a life with you."

"I know that, too."

"Marry me, Sarah," he said softly, persuasively holding her as if he never intended to let her go. "Build a life with me."

She had hoped to hear those words for longer than she wanted to admit. A long sigh of contentment swept through her and she slumped against him. "Oh, David," she whispered, tears of happiness flooding her eyes. "You're sure?"

He nodded slowly. "Very sure."

He waited, needing an answer as much as she needed to give one.

For Sarah there was nothing to even think over. She knew she loved him, and he loved her. They were good together, and would be good parents to the three children. She'd already had a taste of what it would be like to be David's wife, his partner. That he would be a very giving, gentle husband, optimistic, never bullying. Standing on tiptoe, oblivious to the others around them, she reached up to give him a kiss. "Yes, David," she said, "yes."

The rest of the evening passed like a dream. But by the time they approached Sarah's house, she was coasting back down to reality. She wanted to tell the world her news right away, but because of the children, she realized that was foolish.

"I think we'd better wait until after the adoption before we tell the kids and make a general announcement," Sarah said.

David nodded as he parked his car in front of her house and turned the engine off. "I agree. They have enough to handle right now, and you want to—" He stopped and blinked. "Where's your car?"

Sarah looked at the empty driveway, alarm flooding her senses. She'd left her car in the driveway, she was sure of it. "I don't know," she said slowly, making an effort to stay calm. "Maybe Josh put it in the garage." Although there had been no reason for him to do so. She almost never kept it in the garage.

David looked grim, and together they walked briskly toward the house. A peek through the garage windows showed it to be empty.

"The kids didn't have permission to go anywhere?" he asked.

"No." Sarah closed her eyes, horrified. Either there'd been an emergency and Josh had rushed someone to the hospital and forgotten to call her service, who in turn would have notified her at the restaurant, or he'd ignored his being grounded and taken off—in her car. Finding both possibilities equally unpalatable, Sarah started for the front door. Thank God she and David had decided to come home early, she thought.

"Maybe there's a good explanation for this. Maybe they left a note," David suggested. "Hell, maybe the car was even stolen."

"Somehow I doubt that," Sarah said dryly, entering the house.

Downstairs, there were no kids, no note, no indication of where they'd gone. Upstairs was a different story. Sarah reeled at what she discovered, and sank down on Julie's bed. "David, their clothes are gone," she whispered, feeling tears well up in her eyes. Every single item they had brought with them to her home.

Too late, she understood why Josh had been so obedient the past three days. He'd merely been biding his time, falsely earning her trust, so he could take off like this. And she had been completely fooled, had never even seen a hint of his intentions. What kind of mother was she? She didn't think the same thing could have happened to Liz.

David sat down beside her and took her into his arms. "It's going to be all right," he reassured her. "We'll call the police and they'll find them. Tonight. You'll see."

For once his touch didn't help. Sarah pulled back slowly, her head full of images of the children running away from her. "What if they don't?"

"They will," David said firmly, and walked out into the hallway where the telephone was.

Too shaken up to be coherent, Sarah gratefully let him take charge.

THE NEXT TWENTY-FOUR HOURS were the hardest Sarah had ever spent. Sick with worry, she couldn't sleep or eat. She couldn't seem to do much of anything except stay by the phone and wait for it to ring. David stayed by her side. He tried his best to comfort her by saying that Josh would take care of the other children, that he'd come to his senses sooner or later and bring them all home. Or at least call and let her know they were all okay.

Sarah knew David meant well, but try as she might she couldn't share his optimism. Instead she dwelled on the worst, imagining the worst possible scenarios. The three of them in a car wreck, miles from help, hurt and bleeding. Had Josh remembered to tell them to put on their seatbelts? Was he driving carefully or was he speeding carelessly, taking crazy risks to avoid capture by the police? She pictured the three of them being robbed by malicious thugs, being lost, hungry or simply scared.

And worse than that, was her guilt. Shouldn't she have seen this coming? Why hadn't she done something that could have prevented this from happening? Instead of trusting time and patience to iron out their difficulties, she should have tried harder to work things out with Josh, even if it meant quarreling nonstop for a while.

Unable to work, and knowing she'd be foolish to try, she had canceled her appointments and asked another pediatrician to cover for her at the hospital. She tried watching television to no avail; everything—from the commercials to the actors to the settings—reminded her of the children. She thought she would go out of her mind with worry, and she finally broke down and cried for what seemed an eternity, with David holding her in his arms.

Late Sunday evening, the police found the children and Sarah's car at a seedy motel outside of Columbus. They called Sarah to let her know the children were all right, if a bit angry at being caught, and Sarah and David both wept with relief.

David quickly made a few phone calls, and by pulling some strings, managed to have the children brought directly back to the Dayton police headquarters, instead of being held in the Columbus juvenile-detention center. He also arranged for Sarah's car to be driven back.

"What do you think is going to happen now?" she asked David as they prepared to go to police headquarters to get the children. She no longer trusted her judgment in regard to the children.

David shrugged. "I don't know. I guess we take it one step at a time. I know you're upset—and you've got every right to be—but try to stay calm."

It was good advice, and Sarah decided to follow it.

Later, she was never sure what she expected when she first saw the children again. Maybe that they would be bedraggled. Instead, they were as well groomed as usual, their clothes clean. They weren't hungry; Josh made sure they had a dinner of hamburgers and milk shakes. So they were fine physically. But they did look emotionally drained, and tired, and as scared as she felt.

Sarah knew from the way they watched her that they expected an angry explosion. But she wasn't angry, just hurt. And it took all she could do to hold back the tears, not to break down in front of them.

Josh had a surly, insolent look on his face. The other two clung to him. Their continued emotional distance, their banding together against her, stabbed Sarah even more.

"If you're going to yell, just do it and get it over with," Josh mumbled finally, when it was clear no scolding was immediately forthcoming.

"Oh, we're not going to yell, but we're going to talk all right," David said. He put an arm around Sarah's shoulder, his hug telling her to stay strong.

"But just not here," Sarah said, not wavering as she looked at Josh. Liz would never have tolerated back talk from him, she knew. And Sarah had to put her foot down on it, too. But not here. This wasn't the time or place.

They were silent as Sarah signed them out, and David saw that the car-theft charges were formally dropped. The silence continued as they walked out to David's car and during the ride home.

Sarah stared straight ahead. She felt like crying again. And she was beginning to be very angry, too, at Josh, for all he had put his younger brother and sister through. Maybe he had needed to run away to prove something, to make a point, whatever. But he hadn't needed to drag the other two through the ordeal, too. And she would make very sure he knew that.

It took all her strength to remain quiet until they were not just home again, but Scott and Julie were bathed, and tucked in for the night. Then she began what she knew was going to be a very rocky confrontation.

"Why, Josh?" Sarah asked.

"Why do you think?" Josh shot back angrily. "Because I don't want to live here anymore, that's why!"

"That's enough rudeness, Josh." David stepped forward to intervene.

Josh immediately lapsed into silence, not because of David's remonstration, Sarah knew, but because Liz had raised him to behave better. "I want out of here," he said finally. "Scott and Julie want out of here, too."

David sighed, and Sarah saw he was equally frustrated and infuriated. "There's no place else for you to go," he pointed out quietly. "This is where your mother wanted you to be."

At the mention of Liz, Josh exploded. "Don't you think I know that?" he shouted. "What do you think—that I'm stupid?"

He stared at Sarah steadily, and with an effort, lowered his tone. "I knew about the will. I knew she wanted us to be with Sarah. I also thought she was wrong. We don't belong here."

Sarah stared at him shakily, thinking that he'd been under a tremendous strain and probably didn't mean half of what he was saying. He was just a scared kid putting on a brave front. She took a deep breath, fighting for calm, but nonetheless feeling all the blood drain from her face. "You knew all along?" she whispered.

"Yes, I knew," Josh admitted, not dropping his gaze, tears running down his face.

Sarah swallowed hard, aware she was crying, too, and that she had no idea what to say or do next. She only knew she was hurt beyond measure, that she'd never felt so rejected or inadequate.

"Why didn't you tell us?" David asked, the only one of them retaining any outward composure.

Josh shrugged. He swallowed so hard his Adam's apple moved up and down. "I thought the only copy of the will had burned." He paused, searching for words, and began to pace. "Mom wrote that will years ago. We hadn't talked about it in a real long time. At first I didn't even remember there had been a will. By the time I did, we were already living with the older couple down the street. But I was taking care of Scott and Julie, and I knew I could keep doing it. I was going to be eighteen in another year."

Sarah could see how proud he was of his manhood, how grown-up he felt. Some of the hurt left her. She knew now she'd never really understood him, never looked at this from his point of view, never really even tried. She'd thought a lot about them as a family, about what was good for the whole, but not a lot about what was good for Josh. She was at fault here, too.

"And you'd been the man of the house for a very long time already," Sarah added, remembering how much help he had been to Liz. And later to her. Josh was right. Most of the time he did behave like an adult.

Josh looked at her and nodded. "I'm sorry," he said softly. Sarah saw that he meant it.

Josh continued with difficulty. "I know how much Mom liked you, but she was wrong about giving us to you to raise. We don't need you, Sarah. And you sure as hell don't need us."

His words cut through her like a knife. How could he have gotten that impression? Was it because she hadn't said she loved them outright? But she'd thought that would pressure them to say it in return, even if they didn't mean it. Had it been because she had tried to give them the time and space to adjust emotionally? "Josh, that's not true."

"Isn't it?" he demanded. "All you care about is what goes on at the hospital—and him!" He pointed to David.

David stepped forward. "It's been a rough few days," he said quietly. "Josh, I think you need to go up and get some sleep. I think you'll feel differently in the morning."

For a moment Josh looked like he would argue, then bolted for the stairs.

David turned to Sarah. "You look like you could use some rest, too."

She swallowed hard and ran a hand through her tousled hair. "I don't know if I'd be able to even shut my eyes." She'd probably just lie there, worrying that Josh would try to run away again. Then they'd have to go through this again.

David walked over to stand beside her. "I'm staying. I'll sleep on the sofa down here. No one will run away again, Sarah. I'll see to it."

At his reassuring words, Sarah turned to David, tears running down her face. And then she was in his arms, sobbing as if her heart would break.

SARAH CANCELED her appointments and arranged to take the rest of the week off. Although the children were home again, Sarah knew that as a family unit they were still far from out of the woods. Especially judging by the scared, somber looks on the children's faces. "How many pancakes? Scott? Julie?'' Sarah asked, injecting cheerfulness into her voice.

"One," the two younger children answered in unison, their tones subdued but relieved.

"You're sure that's all?" Sarah asked, serving their favorite breakfast. Both children nodded but avoided looking directly at Sarah. They're taking sides, and they were against her, she thought, dismayed but not all that surprised. Would things continue that way? she wondered.

"Josh?" Sarah tried to sound pleasant. They would have to talk soon and at length, but it could wait a few more days, until he'd had a chance to calm down, to see everything wasn't as bad or inflexible as he had claimed. She was sure, as was David, that Josh would settle in again, given half a chance and very little pressure.

"One," Josh said laconically, also avoiding looking at her directly.

"Okay. Here you go." Sarah smiled and made no comment about his lack of appetite. She was surprised he was even eating anything. She'd heard him tossing and turning throughout the night, and didn't think he'd slept a wink. He'd never looked more miserable. She knew how he felt; she'd had exactly the same kind of night. And she could guess that applied to David, also, although he didn't show it.

David held out his plate. "Those look good, Sarah. I'll have several." Sarah smiled at him, grateful for his cheerfulness.

Unhappily, the rest of the day—and the next three— passed in much the same desultory fashion. Sarah tried to interact with the children, but they refused her every overture, politely tuning her out. David, who continued to sleep on her sofa, was rebuffed, too. As hard as they both tried, they couldn't break through the children's barriers.

By the fifth day they knew they couldn't continue to drop everything in hopes of effecting a speedy reconciliation, and David was more than happy to return to his office, Sarah to her clinic. Ever optimistic, he was sure things would eventually improve. She wasn't so sure, but she also knew a return to routine was bound to help even just a little.

When David arrived at his office, he found all was not going as smoothly as he hoped. Instead, everything seemed to be in turmoil there, too, judging from the stack of unopened mail and unfinished paperwork piled upon Georgia's desk. She was deep in conversation with another woman, and sensing something important was up, David merely said hello and went into his office. If Georgia had been drinking again, and she looked as though she had been, he wasn't sure he wanted to know about it. Not then.

A few minutes later, she came in. This time he couldn't ignore her condition. She looked terrible. Her skin was blotchy, her eyes bloodshot, her hands shaking slightly. In truth, she looked hungover, David admitted to himself. His spirits, already low, fell lower. Why was he so naive? he asked himself. And what was he going to do now, when he could no longer deny his employee's drinking problem and the fact it was interfering with her work—and his livelihood?

"Don't you want to know who that was?" Georgia asked, sitting in a chair in front of his desk.

He met her eyes directly and thought that if he had any sense, he would fire her on the spot and be done with it. But the two of them went way back. David remembered how Georgia, already an experienced legal secretary, had shown him the ropes when he, fresh out of law school, had started his practice. She had helped make him a success and supported him whenever the going had been rough. Now it was his turn to support her, to give her another chance. "Not unless you want to tell me," he said quietly.

"Sandra is from Alcoholics Anonymous. I'm going to a meeting there with her tonight." She paused. "It's my first."

David sat in stunned silence as Georgia continued wearily, "I lied to you when I told you I had been going earlier. I had been thinking about going. I wanted to go, but I couldn't. I thought I could get off the bottle cold turkey without any help from anyone else." She rubbed her face with both hands.

"And did you?"

"For a few days. It didn't last." She looked up at him. "You knew all along I'd been tippling a little here at the office, didn't you?"

He nodded. It embarrassed him to have this out in the open, but it also made him feel better, because they weren't lying to one another anymore. "Yes."

"But you didn't fire me," she said softly, shaking her head in wonderment, tears falling down her face. "Why not?"

"Because I believed in you," he answered. "Because I know how good a secretary you are when you're sober." He paused. "What happened to make you call AA?"

She forced a weak smile. "I didn't wreck my car or anything. Didn't even black out. But when I got up this

morning and looked at myself in the mirror, I didn't like
what I saw very much. I went to the kitchen to get my
morning shot of vodka, and then... I don't know, it just
hit me how far I've sunk. I'm a drunk, David. Right
now I don't even know if I can get sober." Her hands
were shaking badly.

David walked around his desk and patted her awkwardly on the shoulder. "Well, you can sure as hell
try," he said, knowing at last he was doing the right
thing. "And I'll be here to help you every step of the
way."

Chapter Twelve

The crisis with the children precipitated a meeting with the judge in charge of the case. On the scheduled morning, Sarah made sure the children were dressed in their Sunday best, with shoes shined and hair neatly combed. They had never looked nicer, yet they exhibited all the gaiety and life of a funeral party.

"Is everybody ready to go?" Sarah asked.

The children nodded, not speaking.

Feeling grim and less than hopeful herself, Sarah led the way out to the car. They were quiet and depressed on the ride to the courthouse. She turned on their favorite radio station, but that didn't seem to help, so she switched it off and finished the drive in silence.

As she'd expected, the judge didn't mince any words when he met with Sarah and David in the privacy of his chambers. He read the report by the caseworker assigned to them, and then frowned as he set it aside. "I understand there have been a few problems the past week," he said, looking at Sarah.

Sarah nodded, then expanded on what had happened, filling in the details—especially Josh's and her continuing quarrel over his curfew—leading up to the incident. She'd decided earlier that rather than pretend the children's running away was no big deal, she would be honest and open. The situation had been tough recently, and she felt it was right that the judge know that. And that he also understand how much she and David had been trying to patch up the differences. But the question was, was that good enough? "David and I both spent the next four days with them, attempting to work things out," she finished.

"And did you?" the judge asked.

David spoke up before Sarah could reply. "As much as it was possible to do so in a short period of time, Your Honor."

"They're all right now, I take it?" The judge raised his brows and he slid his glasses further down his nose.

"Physically they're fine," Sarah said, but even as she spoke, in her heart she knew that it wasn't working. Maybe it was time she faced that fact. Depression swamped her.

"Emotionally they're still coming around," David added cheerfully. He shot Sarah a meaningful glance. She knew he wanted her to downplay the problems, but she couldn't do that, not about something this important.

"What exactly does that mean? Coming around?" the judge asked. He looked straight at Sarah.

"It means," Sarah said slowly, "that none of them is eating very much at all. They aren't talking to me. They don't even want to be in the same room with me." Although never completely free with her, they had relaxed the past couple of months—enough to tell her a few hopes or fears, and laugh in her presence. Now all that had stopped. They were more withdrawn than when they had first arrived. Their continued silence was painful to her and, perhaps, equally painful to them.

"I see. And do you think this will change?"

The fifty-million-dollar question. Sarah lifted her shoulders, not knowing what to say. "I wish I could say for certain this is temporary," she began carefully.

"But you can't," the judge finished for her.

"No," Sarah admitted sadly. "I have every hope, of course, that we will work things out, but..." She couldn't give any promises.

"I think it *is* temporary, Your Honor," David said firmly.

The judge raised a brow. "You're not doing the adopting, Counsel."

But he would've been, Sarah thought, and looked at David. He was angry; she could tell by the subtle shift in his jaw, the reserve in his eyes when he looked at her.

"Bring the children in," the judge instructed the bailiff. When the children were settled in front of him, he asked Josh, "What concerns me now is not that you ran away, although I think we all agree that was a foolish thing for you to do, but how you feel about it now. If you had it to do over, would you still take off?"

Josh looked at David, then the floor. "No," he said finally.

David breathed a sigh of relief.

Sarah wasn't convinced. She had been around Josh enough to know when he was just doing what had to be done, and she could see that was what he was doing now. Trying to keep them all out of trouble. His words were little comfort to her.

"Do you want to stay with Sarah?"

There was a silence. Josh looked at Scott, then Julie. Rather than answer, he shrugged indifferently, as if it barely mattered to him one way or another.

The judge gave him a moment longer, then asked gently in a tone that inspired confidences, "If you had someplace else to go—maybe a relative—would you go there?"

Josh nodded immediately. "Probably. The truth is we really don't want to be adopted," he said, looking straight at the judge.

Sarah felt something in her go cold and numb. Dimly she remembered she'd felt that way after her miscarriages, but realized that this hurt much worse. Because she hadn't known her babies, and she did know—and love—Josh, Julie and Scott.

"We just want to stay somewhere until I'm old enough legally to take care of Scott and Julie," Josh continued, leaning forward. "I'll be eighteen in another nine months."

The judge sighed. "Yes, well, that's another matter."

"He can do it," Scott piped up in his brother's defense. "He can take care of us. We know he can. And we'll be good, too, we promise."

The judge nodded, not commenting, then excused the children. He looked over at Sarah. "Not exactly a glowing recommendation, is it?"

To her horror, Sarah started to cry. Her throat ached unbearably with the effort it took to contain her sobs. Her life was such an incredible mess now, and all she'd wanted to do was love them. But she hadn't been able to do that, just like she hadn't been able to bear a child.

"They've been through a lot the past couple of months," David pointed out, not giving up hope. "It's going to take time."

"I agree," the judge said, removing his glasses. He rubbed the bridge of his nose, then looked at David and Sarah. "It may not be possible for the children to be adopted together. They're obviously a tightly knit little group. They'd probably have to be split up—"

"No." David and Sarah said in unison.

The judge's expression softened. "I can see you both care about them. How they feel isn't as evident. So I can't approve an adoption at this time, not when there are so many problems."

Sarah's shoulders slumped. She had expected this, but now that the decision was made, she suddenly realized she wasn't prepared for it.

"And I would understand if you wanted to call it quits," the judge continued gently, permitting no interruption from David. "You're a single woman, childless. You've no experience in parenting at all. Taking on these children under the circumstances was a difficult task at best. It hasn't worked out well. I know you feel a certain obligation to your friend, but I would understand if you wanted to call it quits." He put his glasses back on and peered at her closely. "Do you want to continue on as their guardian?"

"Yes," Sarah said, "I do." She thought of Julie, cuddling up to her as she read her a bedtime story. She thought of Scott, playing with his puppy, and Josh, shyly yet proudly introducing her to his friends. And then she thought of Josh telling her he had never wanted to live with her, that he'd known about the will all along, and deliberately concealed his mother's wishes.

She thought of the way he had looked when he'd been returned to her by the police, and the silent way the children had banded together since. She thought of the coldness and silence in her house, of the emptiness and pain she felt in her heart, and of how awful it would be to be a child and feel unloved.

She thought of Josh's telling the judge he would be willing to live anywhere else, as long as the kids stayed together, as long as Sarah wasn't part of his life.

She'd ignored the signs of her lack of parenting abilities for a long time, but she couldn't do that any longer. Some people had a natural touch. Some, like her mother, and now Sarah, didn't. David was wrong; mothering wasn't something that could be learned. You could either do it or not. And you couldn't make people love you. The children didn't love her, probably never would.

It didn't matter that Sarah loved them.

What mattered was what Liz had wanted for her children. And a loveless existence wasn't it.

Sarah took a deep breath, knowing she had to be braver and more selfless now than she had ever been in her life. "The problem is I'm not sure if I should." Ignoring David's incredulous glance, she said all that was in her heart. "I've been over it and over it all week. I've tried everything I can think of to get through to them, to get them over this anger they feel toward me, and nothing's worked." Her voice broke. "I wanted it to work. I still do. But I also know they need a parent in their lives, someone they can count on and confide in, someone they can love. Maybe I'm not that person."

David stared at her, speechless.

"I've tried my hardest," Sarah said, the tears rolling down her cheeks, doing her best to keep her voice from breaking. "I just don't know what else to do."

The judge called the children back into his chambers. David was furious and upset, but at a warning look from the judge, also very silent. Sarah watched the children carefully, hoping for some sign she'd been wrong about what they wanted. She would have welcomed them back in an instant and would have fought to make the judge give them all a second chance. But they didn't even blink when the judge told them his decision. They simply stared at him, and then went willingly with the bailiff.

Sarah wanted to take them home with her one last time, to say goodbye in private, but the judge saw no reason to delay the inevitable. He ordered the children be taken right away to a county facility for displaced children, until suitable foster home or homes could be found, and their belongings sent to them there.

As soon as they were out of the judge's chambers, David lashed out at her as if she'd turned into the world's most villainous criminal. "Sarah, you can't let the children be put in a foster home. It's not too late to change your mind."

"Isn't it?" She whirled on him, feeling suddenly furious and hurt that he wasn't more supportive. She'd just lost her only chance to have a family, and not because she'd wanted to but because she had to. Liz had counted on her, and Sarah had failed her—everybody—miserably. Why did David persist in prolonging her misery by rehashing what could never be changed, no matter how much they both wished for it?

"Dammit, Sarah, you're hurt and you're not thinking straight." David grabbed her shoulders and shook her. "For God's sake, please, please don't do something you're going to regret the rest of your life!"

Tears streamed down her face and her voice broke. She was startled to realize the low moan she heard came from her own throat. "Do you think I want to do this?" she asked, blinking hard.

David stared at her a few seconds and then flung her away from him disgustedly. "I'll tell you what I think! I think you gave up on those kids long before you ever got into this courtroom today."

Had she? She kept her eyes on the wall beside him and listened to the little breath she took, which was the only mask for her swallowed gasp of pain. "Maybe you're right," Sarah said remotely, after a moment. As she continued to stare at the wall she lapsed into a peculiarly unfeeling state. She'd known since the children had been returned to her, after trying to run away, that everything had changed. All the good they'd felt toward one another had vanished, and nothing would ever be the same again, no matter how hard any of them tried.

David closed his eyes, and when he finally opened them again, Sarah had seen resignation there. Wordlessly, they drove to her house and packed the children's things. He volunteered to take the bags over to the county home.

Alone, Sarah replayed the awful events of the day—it had all been a nightmare. Tears blurred her eyes. She had to think about what was best for the kids, she thought for the millionth time. As much as she wanted to lie to herself, she knew she could never be a mother to them, or any other child.

AFTER THREE DAYS of calling Sarah and being told she was too busy with work to see him, David decided to just come by her house on the weekend. Fortunately she was home.

He'd expected her to look exhausted and drained, her eyes to be red and swollen from hours of crying. Instead, she looked the way she did when they'd first met—calm, in control. And untouchable. He'd decided after some thought that maybe that was just her way of coping. He knew she prided herself on her cool, and that she still needed time to adjust to the loss of the children.

He himself conceded to her decision. During the drive to the country facility the day of the hearing to drop off the children's things, he had turned the situation over and over in his mind. And when he had been unable to see the children, he'd decided at that point that it was all for the best.

David sat beside Sarah on the couch and took her hand in his. Her fingers were limp, cold. She was staring straight ahead at the television set. He knew she wasn't listening to a word. Now she gave him a remote, disinterested look, as if she had all her barriers up again and was never going to let them down. He had to reach her soon; otherwise he'd lose her forever. And that scared the hell out of him. He would make her see it wasn't over between them, even if it hadn't worked out with the children. They could still have a life together, a home, a family. Because despite everything, and he had to admit to himself that he was very disappointed with her, he still loved her. And he knew she still loved him. She had to. What they'd shared couldn't be erased—it had been deep and everlasting. They'd been planning to get married.

"I went by a jewelry store today," he said softly, trying to recreate their mood on that night he had proposed to her and she had accepted. He could still remember the way she looked, the way she had felt in his arms, all warm and soft. She could be that way again. But right now it was his turn to give to her, to help her snap out of this bone-deep depression she was suffering. And the only way to do that was to go on with their lives. "I saw some rings in the window," he continued, stroking the back of her hand. "I know we never talked about stones." He paused, a smile in his voice. "I don't know whether you like diamonds or sapphires or emeralds—"

She pushed his hand away. "David, I can't think about engagement rings right now."

Take it easy on her, he cautioned himself. *She's been through a lot.* "When?" he asked gently. He didn't want to push her, and yet he also knew he couldn't take much more of this mourning.

She looked at him blankly, as if her mind were a thousand miles away.

"When do you want to get a ring then?" David repeated, trying not to show how hurt he was at her continued disinterest. It was enough she'd abandoned the children, without turning her back on him, too.

Without warning, she became stiff and tense. "David, when I agreed to marry you, I still had the kids. I thought everything was going to work out, that I could give you a family, even if the children weren't your own."

"And now?" he asked slowly.

"Now everything's changed. I blew it with the kids. I'm not cut out to be a mother."

She was overreacting again. "Sarah, that's nonsense," he said more gruffly than he intended.

"Is it? Then why do I feel like such a failure?" she snapped back angrily. He tried to embrace her; she wouldn't let him. Moving away deliberately, she continued, "David, I'm not like this in any other area of my life. I'm not inept and stupid and bumbling."

She wasn't inept and stupid and bumbling now, he thought, but he sensed it would be pointless to argue the point with her. Instead he chose another tack. "So mothering takes longer to learn."

"No, it doesn't," she countered, her eyes filling with tears. "I'm a pediatrician. I see brand-new mothers every day. I see women carry babies to full term and deliver them one hundred percent healthy against all odds. I see miracles of spirit and loving all the time. Some people are able to do this, and to them it's as easy as breathing."

He'd never hated her stubborn streak more than at that moment. "You're telling me because it isn't a cinch for you that you're ready to just quit, give it all up?"

"Give what up, David?" she asked tiredly, her deep depression evident once again. "I've already lost everything."

He was overwhelmed with frustration, but he fought to contain it. He would make her see reason if it was the last thing he did. "Okay, so things didn't work out with the kids. We can still have a family."

Her face suddenly paled. "I told you how I felt about trying to have a baby."

"We can adopt," he said quietly. "I know the lists for infants are long, but given time—"

"David, I don't want to do that, either." She swallowed hard, growing even paler. "Don't you see? I've failed enough children in one lifetime!" She clenched her hands tightly, looking even more miserable.

"I want a family, Sarah," he said firmly. Her giving up on the Smith children was hard enough; denying him a family, too, was past the limit of his tolerance. He wasn't willing to give up the experience of raising children. She knew that; he'd made it perfectly clear. To have her suddenly renege on him reminded him of his ex-wife. The broken promise, the subtle way he'd been led on to believe ... Bitterness swept through him. He couldn't believe he'd gotten trapped in exactly the same situation again.

"I can't give it to you, David. I'm sorry. I thought I could, but when the kids left, when the judge took them away from me, I knew I could never try being a parent again." She looked at him beseechingly, begging him to understand. "I can't. I just can't."

"You mean you *won't* give me children," he corrected, feeling his anger, his sense of betrayal increase. "You won't adopt. You won't help me have a family." He paused, watching the color drain from her face. "You know what I think? I think you're afraid to put yourself on the line, to really make and stand by a commitment." He knew she was looking for an easy way out now—a man who'd make no demands on her, ask nothing of her. And the sound of that was very familiar. Dammit, he'd had one wife who had promised him everything and never delivered. He wasn't going to have another.

She pulled away from him and stumbled blindly to her feet, the tears streaming down her face. "That's not true, David. You know it's not. I'm not doing this deliberately to hurt you."

"You're right. You haven't thought about me at all!" She flinched and he continued moving to the far side of the room, feeling even that wasn't far enough for him to go. Before he could stop himself, the angry words spilled out and he was telling her all that he felt but hadn't dared say. "You know why you don't have a personal life, Sarah? I'll tell you why! Because you never stick around long enough to have one. Well, you can't run forever, Sarah," he said gruffly, and walked out.

Chapter Thirteen

Sarah parked her car in front of the county home for children several days later, feeling very nervous and scared. She'd forced herself to accept the breakup with David, that his loss of faith in her was irreparable. At first she couldn't believe he'd really walked away from her, without a backward glance. But as the hours, then days passed, and she had no word from him, she knew it was true.

She had never loved anyone the way she loved him, but she knew it was impossible for their relationship to continue. It was selfish of her to want to be a part of his life when she wouldn't—couldn't—give him the things he wanted. But it hurt, cutting that tie with him. And she sensed it would hurt for a very long time.

His accusation that she didn't stand by her commitments stung her to the quick. He'd thought she'd given up on the children long before the meeting with the judge, and after reading Liz's letter countless times, she'd decided he was right. She'd also decided now to give it one more try. Not that it was going to be easy. Part of her was afraid to even go to the home, the other part of her knew she had to. She still loved those children, and she had to tell them how she felt. She had to stop running.

They met in the small visiting room. Josh leaned against the wall, Scott and Julie huddled together on the sofa. They were dressed well, their hair neatly combed, but they had all lost weight and there was a new wariness in their eyes. Sarah knew then how much she had hurt them by giving up on them.

"I've missed you," she said simply, not knowing how else to start. When the children didn't respond, she rushed on. "I want us to try again. I know I made a lot of mistakes. We all did."

"Josh said you never wanted to adopt us, that you never cared about us at all. You were only doing it 'cause you had to," Julie said suddenly. She looked at Sarah challengingly, as if daring her to deny it.

The words hurt. "That was true at the beginning," Sarah said, taking great pains to be honest with them. She walked over to sit next to Julie. She took the little girl's hand, trying to tell her with her touch how much she really did love her. "When I first agreed to be your guardian, I didn't really know what all that would entail, but I was determined to do what was best for you just the same. I really wanted you to be happy with me."

"But we weren't," Josh said quietly, giving her a dagger-filled look.

She knew that was only a half-truth, that Josh was deceiving himself now the way she had been deceiving herself. Trying to find reasons not to try again. "Maybe that was because you wouldn't let yourself be happy, Josh," she said quietly.

Josh's expression became a little contrite and he shifted restlessly.

"The bottom line is I love you all very much." She'd never told them that before, and maybe she should have.

Tears were welling up in Scott's and Julie's eyes. "If you loved us so much how come you gave us back to the judge?" Scott asked accusingly. "How come you let them put us in this place?"

Sarah swallowed hard around the knot of emotion in her throat. David was right; she never should have allowed that. "I thought I was doing the right thing," Sarah said. "I thought maybe you'd be better off with someone else."

"I don't want to be with anyone else!" Julie said.

"I know that," Sarah said. She also knew she was a poor substitute for Liz. And maybe they should have discussed that fact more openly, too. Tears streaming down her face, at the thought of the woman they had all loved and lost, she said, "I know you only want to be with your real mother. I understand that. Believe me, I do. And it was never my intention to try to take her place or to make you forget her." Sarah swallowed hard, knowing she had to talk about that next. "But your mother isn't here now. And she isn't ever coming back." Sarah lost her voice; it was several moments before she could continue. "Your mother wanted you to be with me. She wrote me a letter before she died and she told me she knew I could do it, that it would be hard, but that it could work out." She looked up at Josh. "I guess the problem was I didn't believe it. Because I didn't know anything about being a mother and you guys had had a very rough time... I don't know. Maybe I expected everything to be too perfect.

"I know I made mistakes," she continued, before Josh could interrupt. "I know if you agree to come back and try again that I'll probably make more mistakes. But it can still work for us if we just talk to each other more. You'll have to tell me when you're upset or angry. We probably won't always agree, but we can try to understand each other."

Josh crossed his arms over his chest, trying hard to look surly despite the moistness in his eyes. Like David, he probably would never forgive her for giving up on them. With a sinking heart, she feared nothing she said was going to make a difference to him.

"We don't need a mother," he said succinctly, making each word a hard staccato.

"That's where you're wrong," Sarah said firmly, dashing her tears away. "Josh, you do need a mother as much now as you did when your mother was alive. And Julie and Scott need a mother, too." Whether he realized it or not, he needed to be a kid again. "You need to go to college and have a life of your own. I can take care of Scott and Julie while you do that, if you'll let me. And you need to have a home to come to, and I can give that to you, to you all, if you'll just let me."

Josh was silent for long moments, refusing to look at Sarah. "The judge already made his decision," he said at last.

"It can be changed." Sarah leaned forward earnestly. "If we all go to him and tell him we're willing to try again."

Scott and Julie looked up at their brother. Seeing he still didn't trust Sarah, they moved away from her.

Sarah tried for several more minutes, using every approach she could think of. To no avail. The interview ended with the three children standing together, not speaking to her, not even looking at her. Once again, they had banded together against her. Once again, she had lost.

DAVID WALKED THROUGH the museum, remembering the first night he had seen Sarah there. She had looked so lovely in that black dress. And he'd been so jealous. Later, all he'd wanted to do was hold her. And that feeling had never stopped. Even now, he still loved her. He still wanted a family, also, but he was beginning to see that life without Sarah was no picnic.

If only he could forget how she walked out on those children. He'd never thought she could be so cold or so heartless. He knew her reasons had been noble, but misguided. And she had hurt those children terribly. She had made promises to them, and to him, and she had broken them all.

The rational half of him said he couldn't trust her, that he would be a fool to go anywhere near her again. Oh, he knew Sarah hadn't done any of it deliberately—but then neither had David's ex-wife. The end result in both situations had been the same.

David sighed, and wandered to another exhibit, not really seeing any of it, not really caring. He had only come there to feel close to Sarah, to bask in the memories. He remembered when Scott had sung in the school choir. David had felt so proud of him. When Josh had asked him to go camping with him, well, that had been one of the happiest moments of David's life. Later, of course, it hadn't worked out.

Nothing had worked out, and here he was alone, childless, when all he'd ever wanted was a family. Children like Josh, Scott and Julie....

SARAH SAT IN HER OFFICE, the early evening gloom around her. It was six-thirty, but she was in no hurry to go home. These days she had no reason to rush off. There was no one waiting for her at home. No sounds of laughter or television in her house. No music, no feet running up and down the stairs. There was only Lady to feed, and Sarah could hardly look at her without breaking into tears.

And now there was no more David, no more phone calls, no more impromptu visits from him at work, no more romantic interludes in his bed. There was no joy in her life, no intimacy, no love. She missed David every minute of the day. She wanted him back. And she also knew, no matter how much she hoped, that it wasn't going to happen. David was a strong man, with perfectly reasonable needs, which she couldn't meet. And she loved him too much to expect him to settle for anything less, because she knew if he did he would never really be happy. And most of all, she wanted happiness for David. He deserved it, more than any other person she knew.

Restlessly, she got up, fatigue pulling at every muscle. She walked to the bulletin board behind her desk. It was filled with pictures of patients, artwork from some of them. There were letters from parents of patients, too. The one from Melissa's mother caught her eye. She smiled. Melissa was doing so well now. Her mother had written a letter thanking Sarah for her part in her daughter's recovery. " ...you were always there for us, you always listened to Melissa and believed in her, even when her father and I and the school counselor didn't know what to think...."

Sarah moved listlessly away from the bulletin board, the words from the thank-you note still going around in her head. Melissa's mother was right, Sarah realized bleakly. Sarah had been there throughout the ordeal, had instinctively done and said the right thing. It had taken months to make a correct diagnosis, but never once had Sarah given up or turned Melissa over to another pediatrician. All along, she had known she could help the little girl.

And now she knew she could help the Smith children, but it was too late. Too much time had passed; they wouldn't listen to her. And if she were to go to David now to tell him she had changed her mind, that she wanted a family, with all her heart, would he believe her? Would he trust her to raise his child? Or would he think she was handing him a line, like his wife had done for ten years, in order to hang on to him?

"Sarah?" Carol appeared in the doorway. "Got time for one more visitor before you head to the hospital?"

"Sure," she said, "send them in." What did she have to hurry anywhere for? It was probably some pharmaceutical company salesman.

She turned and saw David in the doorway. Her heart stopped.

"Hi," he said simply, looking very glad to see her.

Sarah's hands started to tremble. She clasped them together, willing them to be still. "Hi." How was it possible her voice could sound so cool and composed?

He shut the door behind him. "How have you been?" He walked toward her casually, greeting her with the affection of an old friend. And yet he couldn't seem to tear his eyes from her face.

"Uh, fine," she answered vaguely, looking at him nonstop, too. "You?"

"Okay." He stopped and shook his head. "No, that's not the way it is. The truth is I haven't been fine. I've been lousy."

Tears burned Sarah's eyes. "I've been lousy, too," she whispered, taking a small step toward him.

He quickly covered the distance between them, his arms held open wide. "Think you can find it in your heart to forgive me?" he asked.

She nodded, burying her face in his chest. She knew compromise was a part of life, and she would work with David to make their relationship work. "Oh, David, I'm sorry," she said, her voice breaking. "I have so many regrets."

"So do I." He leaned away from her. "Sarah, I love you. Despite everything, that has never changed."

"I love you, too." Her voice was soft and full of the longing she felt.

"Then you'll marry me?" he said, searching her face.

She nodded, and her being brightened with hope. "If you'll still have me."

They sealed the promise with a kiss. When they finally broke apart, they were both trembling and breathless.

He took a deep breath and said, "There's one more thing that has to be said. If you don't want to have a baby or adopt, I understand. I won't push it."

It touched her he was ready to make that sacrifice for her, but he was all wrong about what she wanted and needed. Already she was thinking about the children, and that if she and David went to talk to them together, maybe something could be worked out. It was worth a try anyway. "I do want a family," she said, meaning every word.

"You're sure?"

"Yes. Having you and the children around gave me a chance to see what it would be like. I miss it, David, and I miss them almost as much as I missed you."

"You don't know how glad I am to hear you say that." He hugged her fiercely, and then released her. "Wait right here. I have a surprise for you."

He returned seconds later, Josh, Scott and Julie in tow. Sarah stared at them, speechless, almost afraid to hope.

"We wanted to say we're sorry," Josh began. "We know we made a lot of mistakes. You said you expected everything to be perfect. Well, we kind of expected that, too." He shot a grateful look at David. "David made me see that I didn't always get along with my mother, either. In fact I think we fought more than you and I ever did. She would have grounded me for missing curfew—the first time."

Sarah laughed, tears sparkling in her eyes, feeling at last as if she just might have acquired that natural touch. "It's hard enough being a teenager without having to cope with an instant mother, too," she said, more than willing to meet them all halfway.

"Yeah, well, maybe I could've been a little nicer. I—" Josh choked up briefly "—I knew how hard you were trying. Getting that puppy for Scott. Helping Julie with her schoolwork. I want you to know it wasn't all bad. And I...I'm sorry I tried to act like it was."

"Thank you for saying so. It helps me to know that," she said. She knew it had been very difficult for him to tell her that, and that his doing so was a sign of how much he wanted this to work.

Maybe the time apart hadn't been all bad. It had given them all time to realize what they'd had, and to consider what they wanted in the future.

"So, gang, do we go to the judge and tell him we want to try it again?" David asked.

Julie nodded, running over to give Sarah a hug. Scott and Josh followed. "You bet," Sarah said. This time, they really would have it all.

Epilogue

"Ready to go?" David asked, coming into the bedroom. In jacket and tie, he looked handsome, self-assured.

"Almost," Sarah said, fastening a golden hoop earring. She turned slightly, so David could zip up her dark blue dress. "Are the kids ready?"

"Mmm. Josh is wearing his cap and gown. Julie's got on her shiny black shoes and her best dress. Scott's wearing a tie."

Sarah smiled, feeling as if her life was absolutely perfect. "Can you believe Josh is graduating tonight and that in a few short months he'll be going off to college?"

"I know. It seems incredible." David shook his head in disbelief. He put his hands around her and pulled her closer. Sarah laced her hands around his neck and looked up into his eyes. "Glad you married me?" he murmured.

"More so every day," Sarah replied. In the six months they had been married, the five of them had become a true family. She and David had adopted the three children and were both beginning to feel like old pros at parenting. Sarah knew now that it was a combination of a natural touch—that intuitive sense of what to do or say in any situation with a child—common sense, and a lot of plain, old-fashioned work. She'd done her share of struggling to see the kids had everything they needed from her emotionally, and in turn, they'd worked hard to please her. Give and take, that was what parenting and marriage really were all about.

And David had been a rock throughout everything, always there with a kind word and soothing presence. He'd added a strong male presence to the family, a more complete sense of togetherness and harmony. And he'd given her so much love and tenderness in the bargain. Sometimes she felt like the luckiest woman on earth.

"I've been thinking," Sarah said, "now that Josh is going off to college and we're more confident in what we're doing, maybe it's time we thought about expanding our family."

David was absolutely motionless, his expression calm but hopeful. "You mean adopting a child?"

"I'd like to try having our own first." At his look of stunned surprise, she added, "I know it might not work out." But she felt now that it would. She didn't know why; she just did. And the power of positive thinking, as David had taught her, could go an awfully long way.

"But then again it might," he said softly, all the love he felt for her reflected in his eyes.

"I'm willing to try if you are." Her newfound courage flowed through her. The possibility of having another miscarriage still frightened her, but whatever happened, she knew David and the children would be there for her. She had to take the chance, because she wanted a child with David more than anything in the world. He hadn't pressured her, but she knew he felt the same way.

David hugged her fiercely. "Oh, Sarah. Nothing could please me more."

Sarah smiled. David turned her around and kissed her, his lips tenderly moving across hers.

Seconds later, there was a knock on their bedroom door, and they moved apart reluctantly. "Mom! Dad!" Josh called out from the other side. "Hurry up, will you, or we're going to be late!"

"Well, we can't have that," David said, his grin promising that he and Sarah would pick up where they had left off later. "We'll be right with you, kids!" they called in unison, and hand in hand, they went to join their children.

He'd hired a mother—
and acquired a wife.

TO LOVE THEM ALL

Eva Rutland

CHAPTER ONE

MARCY HELD THE PHONE a little distance away. Still the harsh voice boomed in her ear and thundered over the crackling wire.

"Three weeks ago! It happened three weeks ago and you're just telling me now?"

"I'm sorry, Mr. Prescott. But it was difficult to—"

His tirade cut her off. "Surely I should've been informed before now. My own sister..." He raged on, bitter, accusing. She shouldn't have been surprised. Diane had said he was explosive. For a moment, the thought of Diane shut out the voice.

Diane. Happy, laughing Diane and David. Dead.

"What the hell is going on out there in California that it takes three weeks to get a simple message to a man!" The storm of his fury swept across the miles, lashing out at her and shocking her into retaliation.

"Really, Mr. Prescott, you're acting like—" She stopped, gained control of herself. "We're wasting time. There's been enough delay as it is." She remembered the long telephone trail through faraway unfamiliar places. Ecuador, Bolivia, Colombia. Finally, in a remote corner of Peru, some distance from Cuzco, a crisp impersonal voice had informed her that Mr. Prescott was out in the field, but could be reached by radio. Was there a message?

No. No message. Marcy had left her number, explaining that it was urgent Mr. Prescott return her call as quickly as possible....

"Do you know how hard you are to reach? We've been trying to find you for days, and—"

"Well, you should have tried harder!" He was shouting now and Marcy shouted back.

"You're being unreasonable!"

"Unreasonable! For God's sake! You're telling me that my sister drowned three weeks ago and you expect me to be...be..." He broke off with a choking sound and Marcy was instantly contrite. Of course he'd be upset, hearing it for the first time.

"I'm so sorry," she said. "And I'm sorry to have to tell you like this. I apologize for the delay, but it really has been difficult to reach you."

"I see. I see. Look, I didn't mean to be rude. I—I just—"

"I understand. I know this has been a shock. I wish—"

"Are you sure? Both of them?" He spoke so quietly now that she had to strain to hear him. "How did it happen?"

As briefly as she could, she told him about the boating accident on the Sacramento River and the rescue attempts that had failed. Her own tears started again, and she was glad her office door was closed. How many times had she been told, "Marcy, try to be more professional. Don't get personally involved."? But how could she be impersonal about the Nelsons? They were like family. The same week Marcy had moved into her condominium, the Nelsons had moved into the one next door—almost two years ago. Marcy had just been transferred from the Los Angeles office, and the Nelsons, Diane said, had decided that Auburn was the perfect town for them. Small and quiet, a good place for the children to grow up and for David to write his detective novels. Marcy had become close to the family, and now she felt as bereft as Diane's brother did.

"I should have been there." He sounded lost and kept repeating the same thing. "I should have been there." Was he regretting his six-year absence?

She found herself trying to comfort him. "These things happen. There is nothing you could have done." She hesitated. He hadn't mentioned the children. "Our concern now must be for the children."

"Children?" He sounded surprised, as if he had forgotten they existed.

"Davey and little Ginger." A sob caught in her throat and she needed a minute to steady her voice. "Some... some decision has to be made."

"Oh." Now it hit him. "My God! The kids! They must be... Are they all right?"

"They're being well cared for. We—"

"Where are they? Are they with you?"

"No." She'd wanted to keep them, but it wasn't allowed. "We've placed them temporarily with Mr. and Mrs.—"

"We?"

"Placer County Child Welfare." At his startled exclamation, she hastened on. "We were given jurisdiction until we could locate you—or some other relative. *Is* there someone else we should contact?"

"No."

"You are the only living relative?"

"Yes."

"Then in that case..." She hesitated. So much to burden him with, all at once. But she had to ask. "Do you wish . . . that is, are you willing to assume responsibility for these children?''

"Of course." His answer was firm and that in itself made her apprehensive. He hadn't even had a chance to think it over yet. Surely he wouldn't want the responsibility of two young children, especially if he knew there was an alternative. . . .

"I'll be there as soon as I can get a plane out. Where do I pick them up?''

Pick them up? Did he think he could just walk in and pick them up as if they were a package waiting at the post office?

"Mr. Prescott, there are certain procedures."

"Procedures?''

"Papers to be filled out. Steps to be taken to establish legal guardianship."

"I see. Have the papers ready, would you? I should be there within the next few days. Now, where will I find the children?''

"Contact me at this office when you get into town." She gave him the address. "I'm Marcy Wilson, in Placement."

"Thank you, Miss Wilson. I'll be in touch."

Marcy hung up, but her hand remained on the phone, one polished nail beating a rapid tattoo against it. She was more than a little perturbed, and it was some time before she picked up a pencil to make a notation on the pad in front of her.

September 18. Contacted by Stephen Prescott, natural brother of deceased mother. Only living relative. Indicates willingness to assume resp . . .

She stopped writing. He didn't *really* want the children, did he? He had never seen them. And how could he take care of them, moving about as he obviously did? She thought of his quick answer. "Of course.... Where do I pick them up?" But that was a spur-of-the-moment decision—the shock of hearing about his sister's death. He probably felt a sense of obligation.

Ha! From what she'd heard of Stephen Prescott, he wouldn't feel obliged to do anything. If she had an alternative plan—one that was actually better for the children—surely he would not object.

Marcy scratched out the last sentence and wrote instead, *Indicates that he will arrive in a few days to discuss legal guardianship.*

There! It wasn't exactly a lie. Prescott would have to be evaluated before he could obtain custody and... Marcy paused in her reflections. Next of kin had priority. If he were willing and financially capable...

That check! They might never have known of his existence if it hadn't been for that check. Marcy sat upright in her chair, vividly recalling the day Diane had shown it to her.

It had been one of those late-summer evenings, still light out, and still warm. Diane and Marcy were sitting on Diane's patio sharing cheese and wine, and watching the children at play on the lawn below them. Marcy remembered the check because the amount had been so inconceivable.

"Five thousand dollars for your birthday?"

"That's my big brother. Always willing to give me anything—except himself!" Diane's laugh held a tinge of bitterness. "I think he expects Dave to dump me at any minute. So he tries to keep me fortified with these little handouts.''

"Some handout!" Marcy sputtered.

"Yes. Steve was always generous with money, even when he didn't have much to give. Once he gave me the money for a red coat." Marcy watched Diane's face take on a dreamy expression as she explained that there hadn't been much money when she and Steve were young. Their mother had died when she was two, and their father, a traveling salesman, had to spend much of the little he earned paying for their care. "It was September, and school was about to start. I was twelve—you know how clothes-conscious girls are at that age. I'd seen this red coat and I wanted it with a passion. Steve was fifteen. He'd been caddying all summer at the golf course and was saving to buy a car. He gave me the money for that coat.''

Diane's voice faded, and for a moment, there was only the clatter of David's typewriter inside and the cries of the children below.

"He sounds like a good brother," Marcy ventured, feeling a little anxious as she watched Diane's eyes fill with tears.

"The very next day, he left home. Just walked out. I couldn't find him anywhere. Dad...nobody could. And...oh, Marcy, you don't know. You can't imagine what it was like." She choked on a sob. "I never knew my mother, and Dad was away all the time. And he kept changing baby-sitters. Steve was all I had, Marcy. And when he left... I hated that red coat. I had to wear it for two winters and I hated it every single minute of that time. I hated Steve, too.''

"But this check... You must have seen him again—"

"Ten years later. Oh, after about two years, I guess, the postcards began. And after a while, money and presents. Every now and then he'd telephone. Always from a different place. Then, when Dad died, Steve came back. Suggested I go live with him."

"And did you?"

Diane shook her head. "I didn't need Steve then. I had Dave. And would you believe it?" Diane put down her wineglass and looked earnestly at Marcy. "I hadn't seen my brother in ten years. And we had our biggest—no, erase that. Our only fight—but it was a big one. Just because I said I was going to marry Dave. Would you believe it?"

"He didn't like Dave?"

"He didn't even know Dave. He said it was stupid to tie myself down to some jerk who'd probably walk out on me within six months. I told him he'd know all about that—leaving was something he'd been doing himself for years." Diane took a swallow of wine and sighed. "Steve looked stunned at that, and I suppose he was a little hurt. He kept telling me I was too young, that I didn't understand. But I was too mad to listen to anything he had to say. We just kept sniping at each other until he finally yelled, 'Go ahead—marry him! Get your heart broken! Ruin your life! Have a couple of kids and really mess things up!'"

"Well, I told him I hoped he'd never marry because I'd really feel sorry for his wife and kids. He said I'd never have to worry about that because he sure as hell wasn't going to."

Marcy stared at Diane. Her brother sounded completely irrational.

"I should think he would have been glad for you." Marcy thought of her sister, Jennifer. Everything had seemed so right when Jennifer and Al got married. And Marcy had been genuinely pleased for her. But in their last telephone conversation, Jennifer had sounded listless . . . almost unhappy.

"Well, he wasn't glad for me," Diane went on. "But later he did calm down and apologize. And I suppose we made it up. At least we got back to the postcard-and-check routine. As you can see, he's very generous." Diane held up the check. "But I haven't seen him in six years. And you know something, Marcy? I still miss him." Her eyes misted again. "I really miss the brother I had before . . . before the red coat."

Now, sitting alone in her office, Marcy remembered the loneliness in Diane's voice, the hunger for the brother who hadn't been there for her. Except with money. But money wasn't enough. She thought of Davey and Ginger, who, more than anything now, needed love and total commitment—a need she was sure Stephen Prescott couldn't fill.

If only I'd been home the day of the accident, Marcy thought, as she put down her pencil. But she knew it wouldn't have made any difference. Since she wasn't a relative, the sheriff would not have released the children to her.

Anyway, she hadn't been home. She'd been in Reno with Tom Jenkins for the opening of the new show at the MGM. She'd got home long after midnight. It wasn't until the next morning that she heard about the accident from a neighbor. How an officer from the highway patrol had come with the dreadful news and had tried to find someone in charge. Kim, the teenage baby-sitter, had been frightened and at a loss. Other neighbors were just as helpless. The officer had called Protective Services to pick up the children and padlocked the Nelsons' condo.

Immediately after hearing the news, Marcy had rushed to the office to confront Jo Stanford, her supervisor and close friend.

"Sit down and get control of yourself," Jo ordered, bringing her a glass of water. Marcy was crying hysterically, and it was some time before she'd calmed down enough for Jo to reason with her. "You know I can't let you have them, Marcy. I realize that you're a friend and that you've often looked after them—yes, even overnight when their parents were away. But you know this is different. You're not a relative...."

"Then if I can't have them, I want the case."

"I can't do that, either," said Jo, who ran her department as efficiently as she did her two rough-and-tumble boys. "You're too close."

"For goodness sake, Jo! These kids have just lost both their parents. They need *me*—not a stranger. I've got to see them through this. I have to, Jo."

"All right," Jo conceded reluctantly, "I'm short-staffed this week, anyway. And it's just a matter of locating the next of kin."

Later that morning, Marcy had gone to see the children. They'd been placed with Sarah and Henry Jones, a warm, loving couple who at the time had only two other children in foster care, a small baby and a boy, Troy, about Davey's age. When Marcy arrived at the house, Ginger ran straight into her arms.

"Marcy, where's my mommy?"

Marcy held her close and glanced at Davey, who was sitting quietly. Too quietly. Her heart ached for both of them. She took them to the park, and there, by the duck pond, she tried to explain. She told them that Mommy and Daddy had gone to a place called heaven, where all good people go.

She found it very painful. Davey said nothing, but the faraway look in his sensitive dark eyes made him seem much older than his five years. Ginger, who was not quite three, started to cry. She didn't want her mommy to go anywhere, she whimpered. Who would take care of her?

Marcy's heart almost broke when Davey said, "Don't cry, Ginger. I'm going to take care of you." It was the first time he'd spoken.

Marcy wrapped her arms protectively around both children, assuring them over and over that everything was going to be all right. But was it? She thought of Diane's absent brother. Would he really want them? And if he did, would it be the best arrangement for the children? Anyway, the first procedure was to find him.

Marcy and a lawyer from the department searched through the Nelsons' papers. It was hard for Marcy to enter that familiar apartment, so reminiscent of life. And now, of death. The fuzzy bear they'd won at the county fair, just a few weeks earlier, stared at her from one corner of the beige sofa. Davey's train lay on the living-room floor, and the bowl of roses on the coffee table gave off a sweet musty scent that permeated the whole room. Marcy wanted to tidy up, smooth the rumpled beds, throw out the dead roses. But they were to touch nothing except papers that might yield information about the next of kin.

Most of the letters were from David's agent in New York. When they called him, he confirmed what Diane had already told Marcy. David had grown up in an orphanage, and had no family. All the agent could supply was David's social security number and his listed next of kin—Diane, his wife.

Marcy kept insisting that Diane had a brother. She had seen the check. Finally they found a postcard from him, mailed from Hong Kong. No address. Then they found a short note on letterhead of the Semco Oil Company, based in New York. They called the office and spoke to Stephen Prescott's secretary, who informed them that he was somewhere in South America.

So the calls began.

Meanwhile, Marcy spent as much time as she could with the children. Just loving them, trying to bring happiness back into their faces. She often took them on little excursions and was delighted when people thought they were her own.

"Because they look so much like you—at least Ginger does," Jo Stanford said. "She's got your dimples and the same wide blue-green eyes. Different coloring, though."

That was true. Ginger's curls, which tumbled freely to her shoulders, were definitely blond, while Marcy's short stylishly cut hair was the color of burnt copper.

"She's delicate and small-boned, too—like you," said Jo. "And that frail look is probably just as deceptive. I bet she's as stubborn as you are."

"I am not stubborn," Marcy protested. But she had been unaccountably pleased by the comparison. She'd always been close to these children. And now, with their parents gone, she began to wish that they could really be hers. It might just be possible, she thought, and even mentioned the idea to Jo, who looked astounded.

"You're absolutely crazy, Marcy. They're not up for adoption."

"I know. But suppose their uncle doesn't want them. Don't look at me like that. From what Diane told me about him, he—"

"Marcy, I know what you think of this uncle. But we're taking it one step at a time. He *is* the next of kin, and..." She held up a conciliatory hand. "When we get in touch with him, we'll talk about willingness and suitability. Until then..." Jo paused to look hard at Marcy. "Let's be realistic. You know the agency frowns on single-parent adoptions. Besides, how could you afford two children? You can hardly afford yourself." She didn't say it unkindly, but they both knew it was a reference not only to Marcy's modest salary, but to her extravagance. Twice during the past six months she'd had to ask for a salary advance.

"Why don't you get married and have your own children?" Jo suggested. "There's Gerald.... No. Not Gerald. But there's that banker, Tom Jenkins. Now, he could afford you. Let's see, I think Jenkins is your best bet. Why don't you go after him?"

Marcy just smiled. She didn't tell Jo that Tom was already hinting at marriage, and that she was having a hard time fending him off. She'd always been fond of Tom, but she didn't feel special about him—or about anyone else for that matter. And she certainly couldn't get married just to take care of Ginger and Davey!

Then she thought of Jennifer. Her sister, who lived in nearby Shingle Springs, was married and financially comfortable and had recently said she wanted to adopt a child. Marcy was sure she'd be happy to have Ginger and Davey. The children would be family then....

The moment Jo went back to her own office, Marcy called Jennifer. But her sister no longer seemed as enthusiastic as she'd been when they had previously discussed adoption. Marcy hung up the phone with the same sense of vague uneasiness she'd felt after their past few conversations. It wasn't like Jennifer to be so evasive, so...so apathetic. Why had she changed her mind? Was something wrong? Marcy vowed to visit her sister and find out. Soon.

After that, she had resolved to follow Jo's advice. To take things one step at a time. She knew she'd been very unprofessional about this case. And that was exactly what Ginger and Davey had become, she reminded herself—another one of her cases. She would just have to wait until she heard from Stephen Prescott.

And now she had. Marcy picked up the folder and got to her feet, still deep in thought. He'd said he would come. To take the children?

There was a light tap at her door, and without waiting for an answer, Gerald Sims walked in. He was robust and sandy-haired, with a sprinkle of freckles across his nose. He wore a brown tweed suit and his thank-goodness-it's-Friday smile.

"Day's end. Let's hit the road, toad!"

Marcy repressed a wince and made herself return his smile.

"How about dinner in Folsom?" Gerald asked. "The Gaslight's got a new show going. I hear it's pretty good."

"Sorry, Gerald. Not tonight. I promised to take the Nelson kids—"

"Again!"

Marcy just nodded. She went into the larger office and placed the folder in Anita's basket, which was already over-flowing.

"All work and no play—that's Dullsville, kid."

"It's not dull. We're going to the circus. Would you like to come along?"

"No, thank you." Gerald walked her to the car, declaring that after working with kids all week, he'd had enough of them. He meant to enjoy his weekend—in adult company.

Marcy wondered about his remarks as she drove home. If Gerald didn't really like children, why hadn't he transferred to another department? Marcy loved them and if she had her way... Well, she wouldn't think about that now.

She turned into the Woodside complex and parked her Volkswagen. Living in a Woodside condo, with a fireplace and a loft bedroom, was one of her extravagances. The apartment buildings, which had been designed to take advantage of their natural setting, were surrounded by the massive trees of the Auburn woods. Now the landscape was aglow with red, green and gold beauty, as the late-afternoon sun glistened on the colorful leaves of early autumn.

Marcy's feet crunched along the gravel path, and she scooped up a handful of walnuts before climbing the steps to her apartment door. She'd have to hurry and change; she still had to stop by her bank's automatic teller before she picked up the children. She tried to figure out how much money she would need. Three tickets—no, four. On impulse, she'd also invited Troy, the other boy in the home; he got out so seldom. Okay then, for the tickets and other extras—would forty dollars do it? Would that leave enough for her car payment and the rest of the month? Oh well, she'd think about that tomorrow.

MONDAY AND TUESDAY were hectic. The Braxton boy wasn't working out with the Emorys and might have to be moved again. Poor little ten-year-old. Too many problems. Too many parents. She made an appointment to discuss the case with Dr. Jackson; perhaps they could arrange for counseling. Tuesday afternoon, two abused children were brought in and had to be placed immediately. The cases piled one on top of the other, and Marcy found herself working late, after Jo and everyone else had already left.

She went into the central office for the Braxton boy's file so she could take it to her six o'clock meeting with Dr. Jackson. But the folder wasn't in the filing cabinet nor in Anita's basket. Someone should speak to her about the filing, Marcy thought irritably. Then she noticed a stack of folders on top of the cabinet. Perhaps . . . Yes, there it was, right in the middle. She tried to ease it out.

"Excuse me, please."

Marcy jumped, jerked the folder, and the whole pile came tumbling down, scattering folders and papers over the floor.

That did it! The perfect disastrous end for a perfectly disastrous day! Exasperated, she turned to face the intruder.

"My fault! Sorry." The man had bent down toward the fallen papers.

"No! Don't touch those!"

At her sharp cry, he straightened, suddenly towering over her. He had black hair and very dark eyes, she noticed, and a face so deeply tanned, so vibrantly alive, that it was as if he'd brought the whole outdoors in with him. He gestured toward the papers.

"I'd like to help, but..."

Marcy caught the hint of puzzled amusement and felt flustered. "It—it's just that they have to be sorted," she explained, "and they're...well...confidential."

"Oh. Okay, in that case, I won't look." He flashed her a warm, conspiratorial smile. Then he bent down again, resting easily on his heels, like an athlete. "I'll pick them up and you can sort."

Mechanically, Marcy sank to her knees to replace the papers he handed her. Brown...Jones...Johnson... No, that went in the Thomas file. The names floated before her, and she felt clumsy and confused.

Darn Anita and her stupid filing! Then Marcy flushed. She knew it wasn't the scattered folders that had disconcerted her. It was something about his smile, a smile that made her feel strangely excited and a little giddy. The way that lock of hair kept falling across his forehead reminded her of...someone. Who was he? Could he be the new lawyer they were expecting? He looked so...outdoorsy. Even in that well-cut business suit. His hands looked so brown against the papers...

strong and work-roughened. Not the hands of a man who sat behind a desk all day.

Marcy finally put the folders back on the filing cabinet, hoping everything was in order. She turned to him, a little breathless.

"Thank you. Now, how can I help you?"

He fumbled in his pocket and produced a piece of paper.

"I'm looking for Placement."

"You're in the right office." Maybe he *was* the new lawyer, she thought hopefully.

"Good." The smile reappeared, and she watched, fascinated by the way his eyes lit up and crinkled at the corners. "I'm to see a Marcy Wilson."

"I'm Marcy Wilson."

He held out his hand. "Steve Prescott. I'm here to pick up the Nelson children."

CHAPTER TWO

FOR A MOMENT, Marcy could only stare. This was Stephen Prescott? She had expected...what? Well, certainly not this handsome sun-bronzed man with such friendly good-humored eyes that...Davey! Davey's eyes! No wonder he looked familiar.

"Miss Wilson—it is *Miss*? I want to thank you. I really appreciated your call, and I came as soon as I could. Now, I'll need some directions. Where do I pick up the children?"

Marcy pulled herself out of her daze.

"You can't!" She caught herself and gave him an apologetic smile. "That is, not just yet. But I'm glad you're here, Mr. Prescott. We've been waiting for you to arrive. Won't you come this way, please, and we can talk."

She led the way into her office, the high heels of her tiny boots clicking on the hardwood floor. His footsteps echoed behind hers, and she was ridiculously glad that she had worn her black boots with the stylish ankle cuffs. Glad that her black gabardine skirt made her look trim and smart—then was annoyed with herself. Why on earth should she care how she appeared to Stephen Prescott? And what was making her feel so flustered? She took several deep breaths and was almost composed by the time she reached her desk. He sat down when she gestured toward a chair, but Marcy was acutely aware of his steady gaze, even as she lifted the wide cuff of her turquoise silk blouse to glance at her watch.

Almost six.

"I'll be with you in a moment," she said. "I just have to make one quick call." She dialed Dr. Jackson's extension and informed his secretary that she had an emergency. Would it be convenient to see him in the morning instead?

"Thank you," she finished, then turned to the man in front of her. "You got here in good time."

"Yes," he answered. "I arrived in Sacramento this afternoon, and rented a car. There was no connecting flight."

"No. We're rather isolated here in Auburn," she said automatically, her mind racing, trying to focus on the real issue. Ginger and Davey. Their future, their happiness. With this man? Marcy tried to brace herself against the strange effect he was having on her. She remembered what Diane had said: *I really miss the brother I had before the red coat.* Diane... "I'm extremely sorry about your sister and her husband. I know this is very difficult for you."

"Thank you." He shifted in his chair. "More difficult for the kids, I think. That's why I came right away."

"How long do you plan to stay?"

"Let's see. I have a meeting in New York the day after tomorrow...."

Marcy felt herself grow hot. He really did think he could just barge in and snatch up the kids!

"That doesn't give us much time," she said, more curtly than she'd intended.

"Well, I'll be here all day tomorrow. I do have to see a Sheriff Olsey, though. He sent me a cable."

"May I see it?"

"The cable?"

"Yes. And perhaps a passport or driver's license." He frowned and she opened her hands in a gesture that was helpless as well as explanatory. "Agency regulations. I don't doubt that you are who you say you are, but I'm required to have positive proof before I can proceed."

"Of course." He handed her the crumpled cable and a worn driver's license, an international one that had been issued in England.

"You live in England?" she asked, noting the license number on a pad and wondering if that was where he planned to take the children.

"No. I—er..." He started to add something but changed his mind. "Satisfied?" he asked, when she handed the identifying articles back to him.

"Yes."

"So it's okay for me to get the kids?"

She looked again at her watch.

"It's rather late. Perhaps—"

"Yes, I know it's late, but I don't have much time. Look..." He stood up abruptly, running a distracted hand through his hair. His voice was heavy with impatience. "Look, Miss Wilson. It was already three weeks after the accident when you contacted me. But when you called and asked me to come and pick up the kids—"

"I did not ask you to come and pick up the kids."

He stared at her. "You certainly did. You told me—"

"I asked if you were willing to assume responsibility."

"Same thing."

"Not quite." Marcy folded her hands and looked up at him, forcing herself to speak calmly. "If you remember, when we talked on the phone I told you that there were certain procedures."

"So give me the papers. I'll sign them."

She shook her head. "It's not quite that simple." She paused. This was not the time to discuss references or proof of stability. "Mr. Prescott, it's late. Ordinarily, this office would have been closed by the time you arrived."

"I'm sorry." There was that smile again, touching some chord inside her that leaped in response. "I do appreciate your taking this time. It's just that I'm anxious about the kids. I don't want them to think they're abandoned."

"The children are being well cared for. Mr. and Mrs. Jones are warm, experienced foster parents and they've been wonderful for Ginger and Davey."

"Well, okay. Yes. But..." He was no longer smiling, and Marcy noticed that his face looked strained and anxious. "Couldn't I... Look, I want them to know that I'm here for them, that they don't have to live with strangers."

How ironic, Marcy thought. Who was more of a stranger than he?

"I understand. I know how anxious you are to see them." She hesitated. "I gather you've never met the children."

"Well, no." He shook his head. "You see, I travel quite a bit and—"

"Then perhaps it would be best if you give them a chance to get acquainted with you first. If you like, I could take you out there in the morning and introduce you." Again she hesitated. "They've known me for some time. I live next door to their place and I became very close to the family."

He looked at her with new interest.

"You knew them? Diane?" She nodded and he leaned forward. "You've been with them? Talked? Were you there that Sunday?"

"No. But later."

"Tell me." He sat back in his chair, as if he were suddenly very tired, and regarded her earnestly.

So she had to tell it again. More detailed this time—how the river was dragged, though the bodies weren't recovered. How they'd placed the children. How they'd searched the apartment for clues to his whereabouts. When she finished, he sat quietly, a faraway look in his eyes. Like Davey.

"Did you get settled? Find a hotel room?" she asked gently.

He came to with a start. "Yes. The Auburn Inn."

"Then you could meet me here tomorrow. At ten?" Then she remembered her appointment at nine with Dr. Jackson. "No. Perhaps we should say ten-thirty. We could go out to see the children."

"Yes. All right." He was still not looking at her and he sounded a little subdued.

"Then we can come back here and discuss legal guardianship."

"Legal guardianship? Discuss it? What are you talking about?" Now he looked directly at her, his eyes wary and alert. She could have kicked herself.

"The procedure I mentioned." She kept her tone light, and stood up, her signal that the conference was over. "We'll talk about it tomorrow."

He, too, stood. "Wait a minute. You keep talking about this procedure. What do you mean, 'legal guardianship'?"

Oh, Lord! she thought. Now I've got his hackles up. Establishing legal guardianship was such a routine procedure for agency employees that they tended to forget it wasn't something lay people ever thought about. Well, he ought to be forewarned. It was only fair to explain.

"You see, Mr. Prescott, because of the very tragic circumstances—with no will and no relative to take charge—the children were made wards of the court. Just temporarily," she added hurriedly, as she saw his brow crease. "It's a legal requirement. Their case has been assigned to me."

"Case?"

She nodded. "It's fairly routine. But before you can be granted custody, you have to satisfy the court that—"

"Look, lady, don't give me all that legal hogwash." He leaned across the desk, a dangerous glint in his eyes. "We're talking about my sister's children. God knows, I wish she were here to take care of them herself. But she isn't. So I'm taking them! And I don't intend to let a lot of red tape stop me!"

"We're not here to stop you. In fact..." She swallowed. "I'm here to help you. But you may wish to secure the services of an attorney."

"What the hell do I need with an attorney?" He threw up his hands in exasperation. "Look, you know I'm the kids' uncle. You sent for me yourself and—"

"You're absolutely right, Mr. Prescott. You do have priority," she said, hoping to placate him. "But, in the absence of a will, the law is for your protection as well as for the children's."

He seemed calmer but still looked dubious. Marcy spread her hands.

"I just wanted you to know that you have the option of retaining an attorney. But it's not necessary. I'm very familiar with the procedures. And, as I said, I'm here to help you work things out." She smiled, but he did not smile back. "Now, it really is late and all this will take some time. So I'll see you here tomorrow at ten-thirty."

He shrugged, as if acceding to the note of dismissal in her voice.

"Okay. Ten-thirty."

When the door closed behind him, Marcy sank back in her chair, engrossed in thought. She'd told Steve Prescott she was there to help him.

But that wasn't quite true. Because helping Steve Prescott was the last thing on her mind. She had been deep in plans for Ginger and Davey, plans that definitely excluded their uncle.

The door opened, and she looked up to see him again.

"I wanted to ask you something."

"Yes?"

"Diane. You said you were her friend. Do you know... Could you tell me..." His face was sober and very intent. "Was Diane happy?"

"Very happy," she said. "I've never known a happier family."

"I'm glad," he said simply, and she sensed the relief in his voice. "Thank you, Miss Wilson." Then he was gone.

Marcy sat staring at the closed door. He cared! He really did care about Diane. Even if he hadn't seen her for six years. Maybe he cared about the children, too. But was caring enough? If he was going to be away for weeks at a stretch...

One step at a time, she reminded herself. When the children met him the next day, she would watch their reaction. She'd watch his just as carefully. As when he filled out the evaluation papers, she'd find out a lot more about him.

I can be professional. I can be fair. And I will do what is best.

SHE DECIDED to treat herself to dinner at Sutton's that night. Cooking was not a favorite pastime, especially when it was just for herself. She usually ate at Sutton's once or twice a week. On weekends it was always crowded with tourists, but weekdays were quiet, and the food was consistently good.

On the way in, she met Gerald Sims. Marcy liked Gerald in spite of his silly rhymes. *Hit the road, toad,* indeed. But he was fun and they shared an easy, bantering friendship.

His broad face broke into a grin when he saw her. "Well, well, here's little Marcy Sunshine herself. Tonight's my lucky night. How about sharing a Chateaubriand?''

"Only if we go dutch," she said. Gerald's salary was no larger than her own, and he was supporting an ailing father.

"No argument from me on that score, kid. My bankroll's on the skids."

Laughing together, they entered the big dining room with the high-beamed oak ceilings and the roaring circular fireplace. That was another reason Marcy liked Sutton's—the cozy, homey atmosphere.

Ma Sutton greeted them, and Gerald joked with her as she led them to their table. Glancing across the room, Marcy was surprised to see Stephen Prescott. He was seated at a table by the window.

"That's the Nelson children's uncle," she told Gerald. "He arrived this afternoon."

"Good. That means you'll have more time for me."

Marcy wasn't listening. She was staring at Prescott. He hadn't been served yet, and was gazing out the window. He looked forlorn, even a little bewildered. Marcy felt a tug of guilt. She realized that she hadn't considered his position at all. Here was a man who had just lost his only sister, whom he had obviously loved. She remembered the way he'd asked, *"was Diane happy?"*

And now he was about to have two small children thrust upon him. He was obviously unequipped to look after them, yet he hadn't hesitated. "I'll be there," he'd promised. "I'll pick them up." And he'd been as good as his word.

Impulsively Marcy stood up. "Come on, Gerald. I think we should ask Mr. Prescott to join us."

The surprised Gerald followed her to Prescott's table. He rose to his feet at their approach.

"Hello, again," Marcy said. "I'd like you to meet my friend, Gerald Sims. Gerald, Stephen Prescott." The two men shook hands and exchanged greetings.

"I see you haven't been served yet. Why don't you join us?" Marcy urged.

He looked at Gerald. "I don't like to intrude."

"You won't be intruding. Anyway, it's no fun to eat alone."

Gerald seconded her invitation, and soon the three of them were seated together. The conversation was rather stilted at first. Gerald mentioned the boating accident and offered his condolences. Marcy, seeing the look of sadness on Prescott's face, felt compelled to change the subject.

"We found Mr. Prescott in South America—in Peru, as a matter of fact."

"Oh." Gerald was immediately diverted. "What were you doing there?"

"Wildcatting."

"Huh?"

Prescott grinned. "Speculating for oil. We do some soil testing, maybe a little sporadic drilling."

"In South America?"

"Everywhere. Anywhere. I was in Saudi Arabia last week." He said it so casually, a man accustomed to traveling swiftly from one end of the earth to the other. How, Marcy wondered, could two small children fit into this type of life?

"That must be exciting," she heard Gerald say.

"I guess." Prescott looked up to smile at the waitress, who was setting a plate of salad before him. The woman positively beamed in response.

Foolish girl. He bestows that smile on everyone—like sunshine. Appalled at herself, Marcy dug into her own salad, trying to block out the thought. It was of little concern to her how Stephen Prescott smiled. Or at whom. She turned her attention to the conversation.

Prescott was explaining that Semco Oil was a relatively new company, speculating in new areas. "Where the big companies have not yet dared to go," he said. "Remote places. Unsettled and untamed."

"Must be rough," Gerald commented. "Can't be easy living."

"Well, yeah, you don't find any Hiltons out there."

Or schools either, Marcy thought, her mind on the children. "But you like it?" she asked.

"Yes, I do," he admitted, as he cut into a piece of steak. "I guess I like the freedom—the space. The feeling of being unencumbered by buildings and people."

Marcy thought of her first impression—a man who brought the whole outdoors in with him.

"Don't think I'd like it," Gerald was saying. "Give me lights and action."

"Oh, it has its compensations." Steve hesitated. "I guess you feel close to nature.... It's as though you've never seen a sunset until you've watched the sun go down behind the Andes, all red and gold and purple. Beautiful." He broke off, looking a little sheepish. "Yeah, I like it," he said with a slight laugh, "except for the snakes."

"Snakes!" Marcy almost choked on her wine.

"Yeah." He gestured with his fork. "Do you know, one morning last week I started to put on my boot and darned if there wasn't a purple viper crawling out of it."

"Damn! What did you do?" asked Gerald.

"Do? I kicked the boot across the tent and hopped up on my bed. Acted like a fool." Marcy shuddered, surprised to see Gerald laughing.

Prescott nodded at him. "Go ahead, laugh! That's what all the guys do. They know I'm scared to death of the bloody things."

"And for good reason," Marcy said. "A lot of snakes are deadly!" Goodness, would he be taking the children where there were poisonous snakes? "Do you see many of them?"

"Snakes? Yes, I do." He leaned toward her. "Do you know there are men who've been in this business for twenty years and have never seen a snake? And I've seen nine—this year. Last month in Kenya, I picked up a pile of firewood and right on top was a puff adder." He told how he had scattered the firewood and abandoned the area.

"I can stand up to two-legged or four-legged creatures," he concluded. "But I hate snakes. You can't trust 'em...." He shook his head. "Just like women."

Just like women? The words had been muttered under his breath and Marcy couldn't be certain of what she'd heard. But it sure sounded... *Can't trust women.* Did he mean...

"Well, I think I've bored you enough." Prescott stood up. "It was kind of you to let me join you. But it's been a long day, and I think I'll turn in. Glad to have met you, Mr. Sims. Tomorrow at ten-thirty, Miss Wilson."

"Good night." Marcy stared after him, trying to deal with a mixture of confused emotions. There was something about him, something appealing. A man brave enough to admit fear. *Snakes...just like women...can't trust 'em.* Was that what he'd said? She must have misunderstood. He couldn't have....

"Seems like an all-right guy."

"Oh! Oh, yes." Reluctantly Marcy turned back to face Gerald.

"Eat up," he said. "You're only halfway through that steak."

But for some reason, Marcy didn't feel hungry anymore.

"All taken care of," Ma Sutton said when they stopped at the counter to pay their bill. "That nice gentleman paid for everything."

He *is* nice, Marcy thought. Charming. But I have to think of Ginger and Davey, of their needs. A single man—always away, often in dangerous places. Is he right for them?

CHAPTER THREE

MARCY WAS AT DR. JACKSON'S OFFICE before nine the next morning. But he didn't get there himself until nine-thirty and then had to leave immediately to be in court at ten. So she had no chance to tell him that Jimmy's hostility and belligerence were just the brittle exterior of a lonely, frightened child who...

"For Pete's sake, Marcy, the man's a psychiatrist. Don't you think he can spot a facade?" Jo shook her head. "You can't smooth all the paths, you know. Sometimes a kid has to stumble along on his own. Anyway, you'd better run along. Stephen Prescott's been waiting for an hour."

"He wasn't due until ten-thirty! I guess he didn't know I had another appointment. But I told him ten-thirty and he barges in here at nine."

"He seemed put out when I told him you weren't here. I sat him in your office."

But Stephen Prescott wasn't sitting. He was impatiently pacing the narrow confines of Marcy's office and silently berating her for not being there.

Just where was this Miss Efficiency Wilson now? She seemed mighty anxious to close the office last night. To go and meet her boyfriend. So they couldn't get anything done then. But he hadn't tried to push. Instead, he'd come in early this morning to get the legal details out of the way, so he could fetch the kids and leave. He'd postponed the New York meeting until three o'clock tomorrow. He'd be on time if he could catch that early flight out of Sacramento in the morning.

Where on earth was she? He picked up a paperweight, looked at it, set it back on the desk.

Lord, it was hot! Didn't they have any air-conditioning in this place?

He took off his jacket and threw it on the chair, then loosened his tie. He stood with his hands in his pockets, studying the pictures on the wall. A finger painting of the three bears done in black and blue. A crayon sketch of a lopsided house with smoke coming out of the chimney. An indefinable yellow blob—could it be a cat? Kid's pictures. He thought of Diane's kids and a lump rose in his throat. What did they look like? Did they draw such pictures?

Diane...I'm sorry this happened. I'm glad you were happy. I'm sorry about leaving you back then, but...Mrs. Mason liked you and I thought you'd be all right. Anyway, I had to get out of there. I had to. I know you never understood, but I'll make it up to you. I promise. The kids will never want for a thing. They won't be shoved around like we were. I promise. I'll make it up to you, Diane.

"Good morning. Are you admiring my gallery?"

Trying to swallow the lump in his throat, he turned to face Marcy's bright smile. She looked fresh and serene, and absolutely stunning in that soft, green coatdress. It made those big blue eyes look almost green. Her thick, vibrant copper hair was smooth, curling gently around her piquant, dimpling face.

He stiffened. He knew the type! Probably spent the whole morning primping. And now here she was, wasting time with small talk when he was in a hurry.

"They're originals, you know."

"What?"

"The pictures. Budding young artists whose paths have crossed mine." Gifts of love, from children she loved, Marcy thought. Why on earth was he looking at her like that? "I'm sorry to keep you waiting. But I thought you understood that I had another appointment this morning."

"No, I didn't. I got here early so we could finish up and the children and I could leave on the early plane tomorrow."

She stared at him. "That's impossible."

"Why?"

"You can't get the children today." Marcy took off her shoulder bag and placed it on the desk.

"Why not?"

She spoke in slow, careful tones, fighting to curb her impatience. "I thought I explained to you. There are certain procedures—"

"Okay, fine." He gestured toward her desk. "Will you get those papers and do whatever you have to do so I can leave?"

"I'm not stopping you from leaving today. But you can't take the children."

"Why can't I?" His glare was so menacing that Marcy felt weak.

She leaned against the desk to support herself but her voice remained firm. "I already explained to you that there are certain things that have to be done first."

"Well, do them!" He threw up his hands in exasperation. "Look, I came as soon as you phoned me. Now that I'm here, you want me to sit around for ten days or so—"

"Might I remind you that you only arrived last night—*after* office hours."

"Might I remind *you* that I've been here one full hour cooling my heels waiting for you!"

"Your appointment was for ten-thirty." She glanced at her watch. "It's just that now." He was completely impossible! How could she ever have considered him nice? "I've arranged for you to go out and visit the children and—"

"I don't want to visit the children. I want to take them with me."

Marcy gripped the edge of the desk and tried to keep her voice calm. "I thought we decided last night that we would give them a chance to know you."

"*You* decided." Impatiently he jingled the change in his pocket. "They'll get to know me. They're going to live with me."

"Maybe," she couldn't help saying.

He frowned. "What do you mean, maybe?"

She drew a deep breath. "You will have to file a petition requesting that you be named legal guardian. But first, there are some questions you have to answer, and you'll need to give us references."

"All right. But let's make sure we have one thing straight. I will get the children."

"Probably."

"No. Not probably. Certainly. I'm their only living relative. That must give me some rights."

"I don't deny that. Of course you have priority."

"Okay. So get whatever it is you want me to sign, and I'll sign it. Then I'll take the children and be out of your way."

Marcy threw up her hands.

"You may sign it, but you won't take the children today."

"We'll see about that."

"Indeed we will." Marcy stormed around her desk, jerked open a drawer and plucked out a petition form. She carefully restrained herself from slamming it down in front of him. "If you will complete this form, sir."

He gave her a sharp look before he pulled over a chair and took a pen from his jacket. On one corner of her desk he began to fill out the form. Marcy waited quietly, her hands folded.

When he'd apparently finished, she reached for a guardianship referral form, skipping down to the pertinent questions concerning the proposed guardian.

"Name?" she asked.

He looked up. "What?"

"I have to have your full name."

"Stephen Alan Prescott."

"Age?"

"Thirty-two."

"Occupation?"

"I'm in oil."

In oil?

"Please be more specific, sir."

"Vice president, Semco Oil Company."

Marcy continued the routine questions and when she came to the end, she leaned slowly back in her chair. For a moment they looked at each other; then he abruptly averted his eyes.

"Okay, here's my petition." He pushed the completed form toward her.

She picked it up, glancing at *Reason For Request*. In bold black printing he had written: "I am the only living relative. I want the children. I am willing and able to take care of them."

"Now, is that everything?" he asked, rather crossly.

"Yes, but I have to—"

"You've got the names there to check about references." He pointed to the paper. "I've put down phone numbers. Now, would you get busy calling them so they can okay me?"

"Mr. Prescott, that isn't how we do things. It takes more than a phone call. I'll be sending a questionnaire to each of these people. It has to be completely filled out and signed, then returned to us before we can make a recommendation to the judge."

He slapped a hand to his forehead. "I don't believe this. You give me the third degree. Then you have to write all over the country to confirm what I've already told you?"

"Those are the rules, Mr. Prescott. I don't make them, but I have to abide by them. It's my job."

"Rules! You can't do this; you can't do that. I don't believe you want me to have the children!" In a sudden burst of temper he stood up, shoving back his chair.

Marcy looked at him, conscious of a little tremor of guilt. Could he read her mind? Well, all right, she did have reservations about delivering Ginger and Davey into the hands of this ill-tempered man, who talked as if they were a package to be collected. But she was going strictly by the rules.

"That is not my decision to make," she said crisply.

"Well, you seem to have a hell of a lot to do with it." He ran a distracted hand through his hair. "I rush halfway across the world to see about these kids, and what happens? I'm bogged down in legal hogwash."

"I'm very sorry you feel that way, Mr. Prescott." Marcy called upon every vestige of her training to keep her voice professional. "Now, I have to clarify a few of your answers to these questions. First, a post office box is not a legal domicile."

"Oh. Well, I maintain a suite at the Waldorf, but I'm in New York so seldom, it's better to have my mail go to the post office."

"I see... Then the Waldorf is your legal residence?"

He nodded.

"How many bedrooms in your suite?" she asked.

"How many bedrooms? Why do you want to know that?"

"If this is where you're planning to take the children, we need to know whether or not the accommodation conforms to agency requirements," she said crisply. "Someone in New York must inspect the premises before you're approved."

"I don't believe this! I don't believe it!" He looked so frustrated that some of Marcy's anger dissolved. She remembered that this whole situation had been thrust on him less than a week before.

"Listen," she said. "I know this all sounds unnecessary to you, but we do have to be careful. We have to proceed slowly."

"You're right about being slow." He leaned across the desk, tapping his finger on it. "If I ran my business like you run this office, I'd stay in the hole!"

Marcy sat up straight and glared at him. "This is not a business! We deal with lives. At this particular moment we are discussing and planning for three lives."

"Three?"

"Ginger's, Davey's . . . and yours."

"Mine?" His brow creased and he gave her a puzzled look.

She nodded emphatically. "Have you considered how the care of two small children is going to affect your current life-style?"

"Don't give me that." He shook his head impatiently. "I know children!"

"Have you considered that children have to stay put? That they have to be near schools and—"

"I'll take care of all that."

"How will you take care of it?"

He looked down at her, his face tight. "That, dear lady, comes under the heading of my own concern."

"No, sir. That's my concern." Marcy gripped the pencil so hard that it broke in her hand and she stared at it in surprise. Then, gazing earnestly up at him, she struggled to organize her thoughts. She knew that as an able and willing uncle he would almost certainly receive custody. But he had to be made aware of the children's special needs and he had to prove that he could meet them. She would see to that, and thank heaven she had the rules to back her up! "Mr. Prescott, what I'm trying to explain is that the agency has to be satisfied with your arrangements for the children—where you're going to take them and who's going to look after them."

"*I'm* going to look after them! Why else would I have come here?"

"Who's going to look after them when you're in Peru?"

"Do you suppose there aren't any children in Peru?"

"Are you saying you'd take them with you?"

"I don't know."

"Well, these are the kinds of things we have to know before we can recommend custody."

"Damn it, why are we talking about Peru?" He flung up his hands and took several exasperated steps, before turning to face her again. "I don't know when I'll be back there—maybe not for years. Look, all this adds up to one thing. You're not letting me take the kids today."

"That's right."

"Couldn't I have them on a temporary basis until you get all this thrashed out?"

"No," she said forcefully. "You can visit them. But you cannot take them with you—especially not out of state."

"There must be someone else I could talk to. Don't you have a supervisor?"

"Yes. Mrs. Stanford."

"Will you kindly direct me to her? Maybe she'll listen to reason."

Without a word Marcy picked up the phone.

There was utter silence in the room while they waited.

When the supervisor at last appeared, Steve looked toward Marcy, who had swiveled her chair around to face the window, as if to divorce herself from the whole proceeding.

He turned to the woman who had come in. He felt ill at ease and strangely intimidated by the five-foot-tall lady who stared up at him through her bifocals.

"I'm Mrs. Stanford. You wanted to see me?" she asked.

"I'm Steve Prescott, the Nelson children's uncle. I've been talking with Miss Wilson," he said hesitantly. He glanced at Marcy, who still had not turned around. "And I can't seem to get anywhere with her. She chased me down and I suppose I...well, I'm grateful to her for that." He glanced again at the back of Marcy's chair. "But now that I'm here, she's got me involved in a lot of paperwork that I really don't have time for. I'm willing to do whatever is necessary, give you whatever you need, but I'd like to get on with it and take the children. And I'd like to do it, now, while I'm here."

"I understand how you feel, Mr. Prescott, but...let's sit down and go over this one step at a time." When they were seated, she looked briefly in Marcy's direction, then back at him. "Didn't Miss Wilson explain to you that there are certain procedures? That we have to check references and—"

"I gave her the names of people she can call for references, and I asked her to hurry it up, get in touch with them by phone, but she refuses. Anyway, the main reference you need is that I'm their uncle. Isn't that enough?"

"Not really. There are other considerations we have to take into account."

He stirred in his chair. "I don't understand this. I really don't. When she called me, I came immediately. I thought you'd already decided I was the logical person to take custody of the children."

He listened impatiently as the supervisor painstakingly went over the same points Marcy had already covered. He sat there, stubbornly silent, occasionally shaking his head until, finally, she sighed in frustration.

"Look, Mr. Prescott, we are legally obligated by the state of California to fulfill these requirements." She spoke in a slow, deliberate voice, enunciating every word. "It is not our choice. It is for the protection of the children."

He jumped up then, shoving back his chair. "State of California, huh? Well, there must be some way the rules can be stretched. There must be someone who can put the pressure on. I'll call my lawyer. He knows the governor."

Marcy's chair swung around suddenly and she got quickly to her feet. Both of them turned startled faces to her as she spoke.

"Mr. Prescott, I gather that you loved your sister very much."

"Yes," he answered, feeling a little stunned. "Of course I did."

"Therefore you love—are determined to love—her children."

"Yes." He was subdued now, staring wide-eyed at Marcy.

"I love them, too, Mr. Prescott. I've known them for more than two years and I love them very much." Marcy's voice broke and he was startled to see tears in her eyes. "And I will not—do you understand me?—I will *not* have them hurt anymore. I will not have them further traumatized by you!"

He was obviously taken aback, and said almost imploringly, "But I have no intention ... I would never hurt them. I just want—"

"—to get the kids out of here!" Marcy snapped. "All I hear from you is *get*! 'I want to get the kids.... I want to get out of here!' Get! Get! Get! You want to get the kids and get out of here and go about your business! You want to drag them off with you to some meeting in New York and Lord knows where else after that. You don't want to disturb yourself one little bit to see that these kids have a pleasant transition."

"But I—" He started to speak, but Marcy gave him no chance.

"Do you know what it was like for them? Can you possibly understand how they felt when a policeman came to tell them that their mother and father were both dead? And poor little Ginger still doesn't understand what that means. She still thinks somebody's going to take her to her mother." The tears were almost spilling over now. Prescott took a handkerchief and offered it to her. She brushed his hand away, plucked a tissue from the box on her desk and blew her nose.

"Of course, I realize how they must have felt. That's why I came here as quickly as I could."

Marcy seemed not to hear him. "And how do you suppose they felt when a woman they didn't even know put them in a car and took them to another house to some other people they didn't know, either?" Her words came out fast and jumbled. "And now that they're beginning—just beginning, mind you—to adjust to these people, here you come! To carry them away to some other place! They've never seen you before in their lives. How do you think they'll feel when you... oh, if you really cared, you'd know...you'd know...." Her voice trailed off.

CHAPTER FOUR

HE COULDN'T BELIEVE THIS. She was actually crying—
or about to cry, anyway. As though he were some kind
of devil all set to pounce upon the children and drag
them off to the gates of hell! Instead of an uncle who
really cared, who was just as concerned as she was
about the very things she mentioned. Didn't she realize
that? Didn't she realize he'd come here because he
thought those children needed him?

"Now just you listen to me," he started to say. Then
stopped.

It wouldn't be so bad if she cried. Really cried. He
could stand that. But she was fighting so valiantly for
control. Trying to hold back the tears that shimmered
in her eyes, turning them into iridescent pools of green.

"I'm sorry. I shouldn't have spoken to you like that."

She swallowed, and he saw her neck muscles tense,
watched the rapid throb of the pulse in her throat. "I—
I just want to make it easier for Ginger and Davey. I
wish…" She turned away from him, hiding a grief that
was as stark and real as his own.

He had a crazy impulse to hold her in his arms and
comfort her, to cradle that tousled head against his chest
and tell her everything was going to be all right. Damn
it, everything *was* going to be all right!

"Mr. Prescott, I do think it's best for you to go out and see the children first." The supervisor's voice startled him. He had forgotten she was there.

"Yes," he said. "I suppose so."

"They really should have an opportunity to get to know you. That would make things easier for everyone. Then we can work from there. We really appreciate your coming and we'll speed things up as much as we can." She spoke quickly, with hardly a pause; he knew she was trying to give Marcy Wilson time to compose herself.

"Now..." She slipped off her glasses and smiled brightly up at him. "I know how anxious you are to see the children. I think Miss Wilson was planning to take you out there this morning."

"Yes." But he had the oddest feeling that Marcy no longer wanted to take him out to meet the children, that she didn't want him anywhere near them.

"If we're going, we'd better get started," she said. Without looking at him, she picked up her purse and walked briskly toward the door. He followed her, pausing briefly to thank the supervisor, though he wasn't sure just what he was thanking her for.

Marcy was strangely silent as they drove away, speaking only when she had to give him directions. He'd suggested they travel in his car when he saw her stop by a battered blue Volkswagen. He couldn't have stood the torture of being squeezed up in it. His nerves were stretched tight enough as it was. He'd been getting the third degree since he arrived, and after that scene this morning—damn it, what was he supposed to do to prove he was okay?

He glanced at her. The tears were gone, but she looked so subdued. Not at all like the sophisticated woman who had come into the office an hour ago, talking and smiling.... He found himself wishing he could bring the gaiety back.

"Miss Wilson, you needn't worry about the children," he said, keeping his eyes on the road. "I'll be good to them. I loved Diane, too, you know. I—"

"Yes, I know." She sounded detached.

"I know I'm not the world's best candidate for a father."

She said nothing and her silence irritated him.

"I'm sorry that I tried to rush you, but I do have to be in New York tomorrow. I can't put this meeting off any longer."

"I understand."

The hell you do! You've made up your mind against me. You think I'm a hard-nosed businessman who's trying to squeeze the children in between appointments. I put this meeting off twice. Dropped everything when I heard about Diane. There's six million riding on this merger and they're waiting for my decision. I can't leave them hanging any longer.

"Well," he said aloud, "since there seems no way around all this red tape, I can see I'm not going to get the kids tonight." He was aware that he was conceding, and it made him feel angry with himself. Still, he didn't have much choice. "I guess I'll just have to go to New York and come back here when I'm through."

"It's a shame you have to be so inconvenienced."

Was she being sarcastic? He shot her a quick glance, but he couldn't tell. She was looking out the window.

"I have to go," he said. "It's my job."

"Take the next exit."

He switched to the right lane and drove down the ramp.

"Now follow this avenue to the next corner," she directed. "Then turn right."

He found himself driving through a small community of modest tract houses. Some were freshly painted with neat, well-kept lawns. Others looked neglected—peeling paint, sagging screen doors and lawns that were more weeds than grass.

"Why did you pick this neighborhood?" he asked, when he noticed a couple of broken-down cars in one front yard.

"I choose people, not neighborhoods," she said quietly. "Turn here. It's toward the end of this block."

Suddenly he felt nervous. Diane's children. *They don't know me. They've never seen me before in their lives.* He wished now that they did know him. He wished he'd come to visit them when Diane was alive and happy. He wished he could believe they'd be glad to see him.

"Park here. That's the place."

It was one of the neater houses. But the signs of poverty were there. Well, what did he expect? People who kept other people's children too often did it because they needed the money. Nobody knew that better than he. Feverishly, he reached up to loosen his tie as the painful memory surfaced, almost choking him.

The year his father couldn't find anyone to live in and had boarded him and Diane with the Cooksons... He was eight years old at the time, and even now he could hear Mrs. Cookson's shrill voice, could feel her scrawny fingers biting into his shoulder while she looked sternly down at him.

"You keep your mouth shut, do you hear? Don't you tell Mr. Cookson that your pa was here today!"

Because that was the day Dad had brought the money. The Cooksons were always fighting about money and it scared him. He would grab Diane and run to the back of the yard until all the shouting was over. They were never really mean to him or Diane, but once his dad had left money for new tennis shoes and—

"Good afternoon, Miss Wilson. Why, I'd almost given up on you." A harried-looking woman holding a baby was opening the screen door. It led into a small, neatly furnished living room. Clean and cared for. Steve looked around but saw no sign of the children.

"Hello, Tina. How's my girl?" Marcy touched the baby on the chin and kissed a dimpled hand. "How's the teething?"

"Fine, since we got the teething gel." The woman glanced over at him as she spoke.

"Mrs. Jones," Marcy said, "this is Mr. Prescott, the Nelson children's uncle."

Mrs. Jones stretched out a work-worn hand to Steve. "Oh, those poor little tykes. They really need you. I'm so glad you've come."

"Thank you," he said, smiling. "It's nice that someone's glad," he added, avoiding Marcy's eyes.

Mrs. Jones looked a little puzzled. "Well, you folks just sit down," she said. "I'll go fetch the children. I had them all cleaned up before lunch, but . . . well, you know kids." She disappeared toward the back of the house and Steve turned to meet Marcy's scorching gaze.

"Don't be ridiculous," she snapped. "Of course I'm glad you came. I wouldn't want Diane's children shuffled around in the system for anything in the world. It's just that I want you to be more...more..."

"Sensitive?" he suggested.

"Oh, I suppose...well, yes."

"You don't give me much credit, do you? You think—"

"Marcy!" A tiny girl ran into the room and hurled herself into Marcy's arms, so quickly that he got only a glimpse of her—tangled yellow curls, soiled red coveralls.

He stared at the small figure huddled against Marcy and felt a rush of apprehension. She was so little.

The boy came more slowly, dragging his feet. Cautiously he seated himself on the edge of a chair against the opposite wall. He was holding something—a board?—grasping it firmly, as if for support. He said nothing but looked warily from Marcy to Steve and back again.

Steve's eyes misted and his chest throbbed. This was Diane's boy. Oh, yes! The dark hair and eyes, the set of his mouth. That penetrating look. Yes, even his jeans were slipping down and one scuffed sneaker was untied. Like Diane.

"Marcy," came the little girl's plaintive treble. "Davey and Troy won't let me play."

"She can't climb up to our tree house." Davey looked defensively at Marcy. "She's too little."

"I am *not* too little." She turned to face her brother, one hand brushing back the tumbled hair, and Steve could see that her face was smudged. And very pretty. But not at all like Diane's.

"I told you, Ginger. We're putting up steps. See?" Davey raised his board. "When we get done, then you can climb up. Okay?"

"'Kay." She dismissed him and turned back to Marcy. "Did you bring Lilli Ann?"

"And my dump truck?" asked Davey. "Me and Troy are digging a tunnel and we could—"

"Wait. Wait just a minute," Marcy said. "I told you that I can't get into your house yet. But your uncle can. Davey, Ginger, this is your uncle Stephen. Remember? I told you he was coming to see you."

Both children stared at him. Ginger's look was searching, Davey's still wary. *I must be careful,* Steve thought. He didn't want to overwhelm or frighten them. So he stayed, unmoving, in his chair.

"Hello," he said. And smiled.

Marcy had forgotten that smile, warm, unreserved, yet somehow vulnerable. She sensed his anxiety and found herself hoping that the children, too, would be touched.

"What's an uncle?" Ginger asked.

"That means he's your mommy's brother," Marcy explained, "like Davey is your brother."

"And I love you and want to take care of you." Steve slid from the chair and bent down, resting on his heels in front of Ginger. "Would you like to come and live with me?"

"Will you take me where my mommy is?"

Steve shot Marcy a look of such sheer panic that she answered for him. "No, sweetheart, he can't do that," she said, running her hand through Ginger's hair and trying to keep her own voice steady. "But he loves you very much—just like your mommy and daddy."

For an instant his expression revealed relief and gratitude, then he returned his attention to Ginger.

"I...we could go places and—" He gestured toward Davey, including him in the plans. "We could do things, the three of us. We'll have lots of fun, and..."

"Could I have a pony?" The question startled him, but before he could answer, Ginger prattled on. "Marcy took us to the park. And I rode on one, all by myself. I wasn't ascared. I didn't cry, did I, Marcy?"

"No, you didn't," Marcy answered.

"See?" Ginger appealed to Steve. "I'm not ascared. I like ponies."

Steve laughed. "Well, then, I guess a pony is something we definitely have to think about."

This obviously interested Davey. He climbed off his chair, walked over to Steve and looked directly at him. "Do you have any horses in your yard?"

"Well, no, but—"

"Then I think I'll stay here. We better stay here, Ginger."

Marcy was watching Steve's face. He looked absolutely crushed.

"But I'm your uncle. And I want you to—" He broke off when Marcy touched his arm.

"You kids think about it, and we'll talk later," she said quickly. "Your uncle and I will be back to see you soon. Say goodbye to him now."

"Can't we go home with you, Marcy?" Ginger asked.

"I'm sorry, sweetheart. Not now. Perhaps this weekend. Come and give me a goodbye kiss."

The little girl flung her arms around Marcy and kissed her warmly. Then she turned to bestow the same favor on Steve. Her action took him so completely by surprise that he toppled over, causing Ginger to giggle in delight.

"You should always give fair warning," he said, getting to his feet and smiling down at her.

Davey's goodbye was less exuberant. Still awkwardly holding his board, he offered his cheek for Marcy's kiss, then gravely shook Steve's hand.

Marcy said she had to speak with Troy for a minute, and followed the children out of the room.

Steve stared after them. Until now he had thought of them as, well, as "the kids"...Diane's kids, who'd suddenly become his responsibility. But he had been presented with two distinct and very different individuals. An effervescent, outgoing, talkative golden-haired girl who, tiny as she was, knew what she wanted and said so without hesitation. A lump rose in his throat. How could he make her understand about her mother? And Davey—a quiet thoughtful little boy who was as solemn as a man. But still a child, playing in tree houses, digging a tunnel. *We better stay here, Ginger.* He felt a surge of panic. Suppose they refused to come with him?

Marcy's voice broke into his thoughts. "All right. I'm ready." She slipped her bag over her shoulder and started for the door.

"Thank you for coming, Mr. Prescott." Mrs. Jones, still holding the baby, nodded to him. "I'll expect you back soon."

"Yes, thank you," said Steve. And then they were outside, walking toward the car.

"Marcy," Ginger called from the doorway, "don't forget to bring Lilli Ann."

"I won't forget," Marcy promised.

"Who's Lilli Ann?" asked Steve, as they got into the car.

"It's the Cabbage Patch doll she was given last Christmas. We haven't been able to enter the apartment to get any of their toys. But if you... You are going to the condo this afternoon?"

"Yes, I'm to see Sheriff Olsey at two to pick up the key."

Marcy thought of the abandoned Nelson apartment. That was going to be hard for him. She thought momentarily of accompanying him to make it easier.

Marcy, you get too involved. It was no business of hers.

"Well, I wish you'd look. You might find the doll in Ginger's room, under the bed, or almost anywhere. It's a big cloth doll with a plaid dress and floppy arms and legs, and a head full of yellow yarn."

"All right. A doll. I'll look for it." His mind seemed somewhere else. She saw his brow crease and his hands tighten on the steering wheel. "Look, Miss Wilson. The children. Do they have anything to do with this decision-making?"

"What do you mean?"

"I mean... Suppose they don't... Well, that is, could they refuse to come and live with me?"

"Oh. I see. Well, actually they have little to do with the decision." Her tone became mockingly professional. "It is our considered opinion that children under five are not capable of making such a long-term decision."

"Well, thank God for that!"

She laughed. "You mean you're afraid you can't compete? Don't you have a tree in that suite of yours?"

His smile was rueful. "No, and no pony, either. Maybe I could manage a pony in Central Park. And that might lure Ginger. But I get the feeling she always listens to her brother, and he—"

"Hey, listen. You have to give them a chance to know you. You only spent about five minutes with them. I had planned that we'd take them out for lunch today, but there wasn't time." She hesitated, then grinned. "Since you spent the whole morning being obnoxious."

He turned anxiously toward her, but chuckled when he saw her face. "Well, yes, I did get a little out of hand, didn't I?"

"You did."

"And I'm afraid I made both of us miss lunch. I'm sorry."

"Well, you can remedy that. There's a deli right next to the office. Quick service. You could still make it to your appointment."

As they took their place in line at the deli, Marcy wondered why she felt so relaxed and friendly toward him now. This morning she could have slugged him and never looked back. But now he seemed . . . likable. Perhaps it had something to do with the way he'd responded to the children. He'd been so reticent and anxious and . . . well, he acted as though he really cared. And now he was afraid they wouldn't like him.

"I'm sorry I was so obnoxious this morning," he said as they seated themselves with their sandwiches and drinks. "It's just that I rushed here expecting to find two desperate kids. I thought they'd be frightened and crying. I didn't expect to find them so contented."

"Children have a way of coping," she said. "Sometimes even better than grown-ups."

"It looks that way. They seemed ... almost happy."

Marcy swallowed a bit of pastrami sandwich before she spoke. "You can thank Sarah Jones for that. She has a knack for making children immediately feel comfortable. That's why she's in emergency care."

"Emergency?"

"An emergency placement is when a child has to be removed from his home quickly and suddenly, usually in a traumatic situation. Like Ginger and Davey." She took a sip of her Coke. "Mrs. Jones has another boy whom you didn't see. His mother was hospitalized and there was no one to care for him. But thank goodness, she's recovering nicely, so he can go home soon."

Steve seemed to be studying Marcy, gazing intently at her as she spoke. "You really care, don't you?" It was more a statement than a question, and she felt a little embarrassed.

"It's my job, sir," she quipped. *Someone has to care.*

"And the baby?" he asked.

"Tina? Well ..." Slowly Marcy stirred the ice in her drink with a straw. She felt a little sick as she remembered the day Tina had been brought in to the agency. The big eyes and thin little face, the bloated belly, the scars of abuse. Fortunately, a neighbor had called Protective Services. "Tina had been neglected," she told him, "but now her mother has released her for adoption." Marcy brightened at the thought. Sometimes it took a crisis to bring about a better situation for the child. "Adoption already has a family that wants her.

Just as soon as we can find the father and get his release. So in a little while she'll be out of the system."

"The system? You mentioned that before."

"The foster parent system."

"I see. Well, if you screen your foster parents as carefully as you do a prospective guardian uncle, every placement must be perfect."

She looked up to see if he was joking, but his face was unreadable. "We try. We really do try," she repeated with emphasis. "But it's not always perfect." So many children. So few good homes. If she had her way, she'd make some really big changes. But there was no need to foist the problems of a frustrated social worker on this man. "It's almost two. You'd better go and meet the sheriff." She put down her napkin and stood up to leave. "Thanks for lunch."

"Wait." He caught her hand and she felt an odd quickening in her pulse. "Do you think I'll have a problem?" He looked earnestly up at her. "I mean if my references are okay, am I going to have any trouble getting my kids?"

His kids. He was already thinking of them as his. She liked that. And she might as well be honest. Ginger and Davey did not belong in the system—not when there was a relative who was willing and financially able to assume responsibility.

"Well, no, I don't expect that you'll have any real problem." She looked down at the hand that enveloped hers, giving her a strange feeling of intimacy. "But—now, don't misunderstand me—but I think it would really help your situation if you came up with some plans. That way, when you go before the judge, you'll have some answers. You'll know where you're

going to take the children and how you'll arrange for
their daily care."

"Thanks. I'll do that." He hesitated. "I really do
appreciate the advice. And I'm sorry I was so difficult
this morning." He smiled, gripping her hand tighter.
"Friends?"

"Friends," she said.

IT WAS MORE than just a matter of picking up the key
from Sheriff Olsey. It involved a call to his New York
lawyer, who then called a local lawyer, followed by a
trip to the courthouse where he was officially made
"temporary administrator (pending investigation)."
Only then was he given the key to his sister's apartment.

Sheriff Olsey furnished him with clear directions to
the Woodside complex, so Steve found it without difficulty. He was immediately struck by the country atmosphere and the beauty of the natural surroundings.
It's well-planned—doesn't look crowded, he thought,
as he drove through the winding grounds looking for the
designated parking area. When he got out of the car, a
man who was getting into a blue station wagon gave him
a friendly nod. Steve returned the salute, locked his car
and started up the path. The sounds of the station
wagon had faded, and except for the chirping of the
birds and the crunch of his footsteps on the gravel path,
all was quiet. Funny, that silence in the middle of an
apartment complex. But he liked the feeling. He remembered something in one of Diane's letters. "It's so
quiet and serene here," she'd written. "Good for the
children..." *Diane.*

He walked up the five steps and along the wooden ledge to number 212. He took a deep breath, braced himself, then unlocked the door and opened it cautiously.

Once inside, he leaned against the door, his heart pounding, and looked slowly around. He was in a living room, quite spacious and very bright. A large comfortable sofa lined one wall. It was occupied by a fuzzy brown bear whose glass eyes stared at him. There was a magazine lying open on the coffee table and a white bowl containing dead roses. He breathed in the sweet musty smell of the decaying roses, and imagined Diane arranging them, humming a little tune as she did so, never knowing....

It was so still. He moved, wanting to break the silence, but his feet made no sound on the thick carpet. His foot struck something—a tiny train lying on its side. He picked it up, laid it carefully on the coffee table.

The room was bright, he realized, because the back wall was solid glass and there were no draperies. Sliding doors opened onto a patio where he could see a glass-topped wrought-iron table and four chairs. Almost in a trance, he walked through the apartment. It was exceptionally large, with four bedrooms.

One of the smaller bedrooms had evidently been David's office. There was a well-filled bookcase, the top shelf of which held several books—*Dead Summer*, *Killjoy*, *Death On A Ramp* and others—all by David Nelson. The guy was prolific, Steve thought. And successful. Diane and the children had not been in need. In fact, from the look of the place, they'd been well-cared-for. Steve was glad about that.

On the desk was a typewriter with a half-typed page
in it, an empty coffee cup and a picture of Diane. She
was leaning against a boat, laughing. Steve picked up
the picture and stared at it for a long time, before carefully and tenderly replacing it. Then he walked slowly
out of the room, taking care to step over a half-finished
jigsaw puzzle of Donald Duck. A child had lain on the
floor, fitting in the pieces while her father typed.

*I like you, David Nelson. I never knew you, but I like
you. Because you made Diane happy. Because this is a
happy home.*

He remembered that he was to look for a doll called
Lilli Ann and went back into what was obviously Ginger's room to find it. He looked everywhere—in the toy
box, on the shelves, even under the bed. There were
several dolls, but none like the one Miss Wilson—
Marcy—had described. He wondered if he should take
any of the others. Well, when he came back from New
York, he'd make a more thorough search.

He wandered back into the master bedroom, wanting to capture the essence of Diane that seemed to linger there. He inhaled the sweet feminine scent of
powder and perfume, saw the pale pink robe thrown
across the rumpled bed, the red and white sandal lying
askew on the floor. He found himself staring at the
sandal. It awakened a memory, vague and sweet, a long-
ago memory buried deep inside him. His mother,
laughing gaily as she tossed one shoe after another
across the room. Trying to find just the right pair, because one of the uncles was coming. There had been
several uncles.

"Stevie, honey, you be a good boy, and help Mary take care of your little sister. I'll be back soon. Now, give me a big hug and a kiss."

He would hug her, savoring the special fragrance that was hers. Then he'd count the minutes until her return. She would come in, smiling and happy, ready to play some game or sing a silly song. She never once told him not to tell his dad about the uncles. But he never did. Not even that last time when she went off with one of the uncles and didn't come back.

He didn't say anything when his dad told them that their mother was dead. But he knew she wasn't dead. For a long time he kept waiting for her to come back. But she never did.

And now this room of Diane's reminded him. His mother would have worn such a robe. He reached across to pick up the flimsy material, and as he did, he uncovered something else—a floppy cotton leg, a scrap of red plaid. He straightened up and removed the pillow. He'd found Lilli Ann.

He could almost visualize that last morning. Ginger had probably come into her parents' room, dragging her doll. She'd climbed into bed with her mother just as, long ago, he'd sometimes climbed into bed with his mother. Diane had pulled her daughter close. And Ginger had been happy, basking in the warmth and the love, and the sweet delicate scent. And she had thought that it would last forever. That people who loved you would not go away.

Ginger's mother did not have a choice. He knew that his own mother did, and the knowledge was a pain that had haunted him all of his life.

Suddenly he could hold back the tears no longer, and he broke down. The great racking sobs almost tore him apart, but he wasn't sure whether he cried for the loss of Ginger's mother or his own.

. . . .

CHAPTER FIVE

MARCY STOPPED by the grocery store on her way home
from work. A careful survey of her bank account had
warned her that if she wanted to eat regularly between
now and her next paycheck, she'd better start fixing her
own meals. She could live for a week on the cost of two
dinners at Sutton's. She wheeled her cart toward the
vegetable bins, trying to figure out where the money had
gone. She'd thought she was in pretty good shape.

Well, there were the shoes she didn't need but hadn't
been able to resist. And the two or three long-distance
telephone calls to Jennifer. What else? The tickets for
the circus. But that wasn't too much. And . . . oh, yes,
the calculator for Jimmy Braxton. Odd birthday present to be giving a ten-year-old, she supposed. But that
was what he wanted, and she knew there was no money
in the Emory budget for such a trinket. Mrs. Emory had
mentioned that she planned to bake a birthday cake on
Thursday and Marcy hoped to get the pocket calculator to him by then.

"Marcy Wilson, if you're going to survive in this
business, you'd better learn to leave your work at the
office!" Marcy could almost hear Jo Stanford's voice.
"Get your mind off these children and their problems.
Think about something pleasant for a change."

Something pleasant... Like Steve Prescott, for example. She liked him. She really did. Marcy smiled as she selected three firm tomatoes and placed them in her cart. If anybody had asked her at ten o'clock that morning for her opinion of Stephen Prescott, her response would hardly have been complimentary. But when she'd seen him with the children, so awkward and uncertain, so anxious to please, her heart had gone out to him.

Anxiety. That's what had made him so irritable this morning. He'd turned out to be quite different from what she'd expected. What was it she'd told herself? Steve Prescott "wouldn't feel obliged to do anything!" But obviously, he did. And it was more than a sense of duty. He seemed to really care. He wanted the children, never mind that he didn't have the slightest idea what he was going to do with them when he got them!

She would have laughed had she not been so worried about it herself. Ginger and Davey had had such a good home, such loving parents. And now, even though they seemed to be coping, Davey had that wary look, and Ginger was still waiting for her mommy to come back. Marcy sighed. Now they were to be transferred to an entirely new environment with an uncle who had absolutely no experience in dealing with children.

None of that would be a problem if she could adopt the children herself. Or if Jennifer... Marcy's thoughts reverted to the last time she and Jennifer had discussed the question. She remembered how disturbed she'd been by her sister's apathy that day. *We need to talk,* she decided. *I'll drive out there this Sunday—and I'll take the kids with me.*

After that, she concentrated on her shopping. Salad fixings and lots of fruit. She bought a pound of ground beef that she planned to separate into patties and freeze. She hesitated over a package of four lamb chops. Expensive. But she could freeze those, too; that meant four meals. And since she wasn't going to be eating out... She tossed the package into her cart and wheeled it toward the register, then headed home.

When she reached her apartment, she set the two bags on the floor and rummaged through her purse for the key. She was just inserting it in the lock when she saw Steve Prescott emerge from the apartment next door.

"Hello, again," she said.

He didn't seem to hear her.

"Hello," she repeated, more loudly this time.

"Oh. Hello." His voice sounded bleak, and he looked...lost. She had the feeling he was seeing not her but something else. She was startled by the naked pain in his face; she wanted to reach out, to ward off whatever was hurting him. He was walking past her now, and she tugged impulsively at his sleeve.

"Wait," she said. "Give me a hand, will you?"

"What?"

"With these groceries." She picked up one of the bags and handed it to him so purposefully that he was forced to take it. "I had a heck of a time lugging these from the car. Come on in."

For a moment she thought he wasn't going to move.

"Come in," she said again, and this time he followed her.

"Just put it here," she directed, setting her own bag on the dinette table. But he just stood there, holding the bag, looking dazed. She took it from him and put it next to hers. Something was dreadfully wrong.

"Sit down," she urged, pulling out a chair. "You look . . . tired."

He said nothing, but he did sit down. She wondered what to do now. Offer him a drink, perhaps? Did she have any brandy in the house? She hurried into the little kitchenette and searched through the cabinets. A few weeks before, Tom had brought over a bottle of brandy. Oh yes, here it was. She filled a small brandy glass almost to the brim, then brought it over to him.

"Oh, thanks," he said, looking surprised.

"Just relax while I put these groceries away." She carried the bags into the kitchen and started to unload them, glancing at him from time to time through the opening above the breakfast bar. He sat quite still, staring out the window, only occasionally remembering to take a sip of the brandy.

Something had hit him hard! She'd known that going through the apartment would be difficult for him. But there was more to this, more even than grief. Guilt? Possibly, Marcy thought. Guilt for not having come more often when Diane was alive.

Marcy took out the pound of hamburger and put it in the refrigerator. She'd separate it later. She took out the package of lamb chops, then she looked across at him. If he intended to drive to Sacramento tonight, he'd need some time to settle down and compose himself.

"I think I'll treat you to dinner," she called. He didn't answer and she wasn't sure he'd even heard her.

Well, Marcy decided, she certainly wasn't going to cook dinner in her Liz Claiborne coatdress. He didn't even look up when she passed him on her way to the stairs. In her loft bedroom, she changed into jeans and a rose-colored pullover.

Back in the kitchen, she prepared two potatoes, put them in the microwave and set the timer. She sprinkled all four lamb chops with seasoned salt and slid them under the broiler, then began to wash the lettuce.

THE MICROWAVE BUZZER went off, startling Stephen, and he sat up. Where was he? He looked around and his gaze fastened on Marcy, busy in the kitchen. Gradually it came back to him. He'd helped her in with her groceries. But how long had he been sitting here? He stared down at the empty glass. Brandy. Yes, she'd given it to him, he remembered that now. His mind had been years away. Because of Diane's room . . .

Well, he couldn't sit here thinking about it. He'd better leave—right now. He picked up the glass, hesitated a moment, then walked quickly to the kitchen. She was putting ice into two tall glasses, and he noticed that she'd changed her clothes. She looked like a teenager in those jeans and that pink pullover.

"Thanks," he said, giving her the empty glass. "I really needed that. I'll check with you when I get back. I remember what you suggested, and I'll get back here as soon as I can."

"You're not going?" she asked. "I've almost got your dinner ready."

"Dinner? You're fixing dinner for me?"

She nodded as she poured iced tea into the glasses.

"I invited and you accepted. So you can't leave yet."

He frowned. "I don't remember anything about dinner." He hadn't been that out of it, had he?

"You accepted and I cooked. So, be a good sport and make yourself useful." She was handing him place mats and napkins, but he backed away. For some reason, he was irritated by her coaxing tone.

"Look, I don't have time for dinner," he insisted. "I have a plane to catch."

She stood there, holding the napkins, looking puzzled.

"But it doesn't leave until tomorrow morning. You have plenty of time."

He realized that he'd shouted at her, and felt a little ashamed.

"I don't understand. What's the problem?" she asked. "You said you were hungry. It's just dinner."

"Right." He took the things from her. Why *was* he making such a big fuss? Mats here. And here. Napkins. It was just that he found this whole setup a little too cozy and intimate. No, intimate wasn't the word. He'd been intimate with women before. But never close. And he meant to keep it that way. That was it. There was something about this woman, a concern, a caring quality that touched him, and—

"Silver's in the side drawer!" she called.

Officious, he thought, jerking the drawer open. *She's too damned officious!* Had he said he was hungry?

Well, he hadn't actually said he was hungry and he didn't agree to stay for dinner, Marcy thought, as she took the chops out of the oven. But he does need time, and this will give him a couple of hours to come to grips with whatever is troubling him.

Not bad, Marcy, not bad, she told herself when she'd put the food on the plates. The lamb chops looked and smelled delicious, the butter was melting in the steaming potatoes, and the salad was crisp and colorful.

"Dinner's ready," she announced as she carried the plates into the dining nook and set them on the table. "Why not take off your coat and tie? Make yourself comfortable."

He did as she suggested, but she wondered at the guarded look he gave her and was tempted to call out, "Hey, I'm on your side." But she didn't.

Instead, during dinner, she launched into small talk—the weather, the book she'd just read, the play she'd seen the week before. Anything to distract him from whatever had troubled him so deeply. He answered in monosyllables and she was aware that he was only half listening. It wasn't until she paused, searching her mind for another safe topic, that he finally spoke.

"This is a very good dinner," he said, as if he'd suddenly remembered his manners, "and very kind of you, Miss Wilson."

"It's Marcy, please. Outside the office I'm Marcy."

"Yes, I suppose it should be Marcy and Steve by this time. Do you realize every meal I've had in this town has been with you? I can't help feeling that's an imposition."

"Nonsense," she said, glad to see even a trace of that smile reappear. "Turnabout is fair play. You paid for the other two, remember?" Then she frowned. "Do you mean to say you didn't eat breakfast this morning? No wonder you were so grouchy."

"Well . . ." This time the smile was rueful. "I was in a hurry. I wanted to—"

"Get the children and get out of here," she teased.

"Well, yes. I didn't realize it was going to be so complicated." Now he looked worried, and she was instantly contrite, sorry she'd brought up the very subject that was obviously weighing on his mind.

"Not so complicated," she said. "All you have to do is—"

"Figure out where I'm going to take them and who'll look after them," he broke in rather sharply. "That's not easy. I think my hotel suite would give them claustrophobia. And it's going to take time to find the right person and the right schools. I have a friend who lives in Scarsdale, and I thought I could ask her about all this. But I hate to impose on her."

Of course, he would have a "friend." Marcy wondered why the thought depressed her.

"She'd probably be glad to help you. That's what friends are for, isn't it?"

"Well, I don't know if she... Actually, it's Brick who's my friend. My partner. He's president of Semco. When he called me about tomorrow's meeting, he told me that he and Stell, his wife, had split up and he'd moved out. Moved *in* actually." Steve grinned. "He told me he was at my place."

"I see." Marcy felt ridiculously lighthearted. Strangely glad that Brick was the friend, and that he'd felt free to move into Steve's suite...which meant there was no one else living there, didn't it? She felt herself flush. *Detachment, Marcy, detachment. So what if he has a special smile? In a few weeks he'll be nothing but a fond memory.*

"You shouldn't worry," she said, getting up to clear the table. "Things will work out. You've only had ... let's see ... not even a week. Hardly long enough to think, much less plan. Give yourself time. No, don't bother with the dishes. I'll do that. You go on into the living room. We'll have our coffee there. Coffee and some old-fashioned tea cakes. I bought them at the bakery next to the deli." She realized she was talking too much. It was a relief to escape to the kitchen where she could concentrate on making coffee. Instead of thinking about Steve Prescott.

"'Give yourself time,' she says. But time is just what I don't have," Steve muttered, as he stood in Marcy's living room. Her apartment was smaller than the one next door and was done in muted tones of mauve and slate blue. He watched her come in to set a percolator on the hearth and plug it into the wall socket. There was a certain confidence about her, a quiet poise in everything she did. She seemed, somehow, to be at total peace with herself. She looked as right in those jeans as she had in the sophisticated garb of the morning. He got the impression that she would be no less relaxed before a camp fire in Peru than she was at this moment in her comfortable living room.

"While that perks, I'll get the tea cakes." She straightened up and went back into the kitchen.

When she returned, he was studying one of the pictures on the wall by the fireplace. He thought it looked like a crude charcoal sketch of...well, he couldn't quite decide. What was it supposed to be? A man riding a bicycle upside down? A horse lying on its back? A knight in armor falling off his horse—upside down? He bent his head to examine it the other way around, but he still couldn't make sense of it.

"Another original from some kid whose path has crossed yours?" he asked.

She smiled as she set her tray on the coffee table. "Why, my good sir," she said, "I'll have you know that drawing is an original Picasso!"

"Picasso?" He stared at her in amused amazement. Then he turned back to view the picture, tightening his lips and assuming a pose of mock appreciation. "I see. It's looking better all the time."

Her peal of laughter delighted him.

"It only proves," she said, "that you can get away with anything if you're famous enough."

Over the coffee and cakes, she explained that all the pictures were from her parents' home. When her father died, her mother had sold the house and divided all the treasures among her three children—Bill, an air force officer currently stationed with his family in Japan, Jennifer, who lived with her husband in Shingle Springs, and Marcy. She'd then moved into a retirement community in Phoenix. Yes, Marcy said, the family was from Phoenix; she'd lived there all her life until she'd finished college and gone away to work.

"Goodness," she said finally, "I don't know why I'm doing all this talking about myself."

But Steve knew why. He had prompted her, and deliberately drawn her out, just as he was accustomed to drawing out a prospective investor, looking into his background before accepting his check. There was no reason to be curious about Marcy. But her serene self-confidence intrigued him. And now he knew how it had been acquired. A happy, stable middle-class home, a direct contrast to his own confused and impoverished childhood. Hers had obviously been secure, sheltered . . . loving. And that's what he wanted for Ginger and Davey.

I promise you they will have it, Diane. But how? Where do I start?

Abruptly he rose to his feet. "I've got to get the children. I want to get Ginger and Davey as quickly as possible."

Marcy sat up, startled by the urgency in his voice.

"What's the matter? I thought we'd agreed—"

"Oh, I don't mean today. I've given up on that. I'm going along with all this legal rigmarole, but I want to get them as soon as possible." He shoved his hands in his pockets, jingling his change in nervous frustration as he looked down at her. "Don't you understand? They don't know me. And the longer they stay at this Jones woman's house, the harder it's going to be for them to get close to me. Don't you see?"

She nodded, setting her mug on the tray. Her calmness suddenly irritated him and he moved restlessly about.

"Of course I understand how you feel," she was saying. "But can't you see that careful preparation facilitates a smoother transition?"

Facilitates a smoother transition! Damn all that bureaucratic jargon when he was thinking about the children!

"But I don't have time!" he almost shouted as he ran a distracted hand through his hair. "Sure, I can buy a house in Scarsdale or somewhere. And sure, I can interview housekeepers. But all of this takes a lot of time. Don't you see?" He walked to the fireplace and back, then said in a resigned voice, "Guess I'll just have to move them into my suite temporarily."

"Two bedrooms, did you say?" She wasn't looking at him, but seemed to be intently studying her nails. "I presume your friend will be leaving. Even so, you'd hardly have room for a live-in, a necessity in your case."

He glared at her, annoyed by her logic and, even more, by the fact that she was right.

"What about a larger apartment?" she suggested. "Some temporary place until you buy?"

"Well, yes, I suppose." He clenched and unclenched his fists, feeling at a loss. Where did people with children live in New York? Brick was the only person he knew who had a child and—

"Steve!" she cried. She jumped to her feet, staring at him, her eyes wide. "How often did you say you were in New York?"

"Oh, I don't know. Maybe a month or two out of the year. Off and on."

"Then you could make your home almost anywhere, couldn't you?" She sounded eager. "I mean on a temporary basis."

"Well, yes, I suppose I could, but—"

"So why don't you live here?"

"Here?"

"I mean next door, in David and Diane's place. It would be..." She touched a finger to her temple. "Oh, why didn't I think of this before? It would be so good for the children. They'd be coming home. They'd be in familiar surroundings and have all their own toys, be in their own rooms. It would make things so much easier for them."

He stood with his thumbs hooked into his belt, gazing down at the floor. Moving into Diane's place was certainly a possibility, but...why did he feel he was being manipulated?

"Don't you see?" she burst out. "They could go back to the same schools—Davey's kindergarten, Ginger's nursery school. The same teachers and friends."

And you, he thought. You'd be right next door, holding on to them. And checking up on me.

"You don't trust me to take them away from your watchful eye?" he asked.

"Don't be ridiculous! It's not a watchful eye but a helping hand that you need. And," she added, with a little gurgle of laughter, "helping is my business."

"Your business is to shuffle papers and stretch red tape!" he snapped. "Diane's children are my business."

She put her hands on her hips and glared up at him. "Stephen Prescott, that's unfair. I care about those children."

"And it would be very convenient, wouldn't it, to have them right next door to you!"

"And very convenient for you as well."

He stepped back. "And just what is that supposed to mean?"

"It means—" she began, counting on her fingers "—one, that you have satisfactorily solved the problem of a proper domicile. Two, that the children will not be uprooted. And three, that your pressing need for time has been solved. Here's a place, ready and waiting, that will give you time to establish a relationship with the children, while you search for a permanent residence."

For a moment he stood perfectly still, thinking. It did make sense. But who the hell did she think she was—dishing out all the answers as if he couldn't manage his own affairs! He walked briskly over to the couch and picked up his jacket.

"I'll have to think about that," he said. "Anyway, I plan to look around for a place while I'm in New York."

"Do that. You might find something much more suitable." As sweet as she sounded, he thought he detected a note of sarcasm in her voice. He turned quickly, but she was smiling.

"I'm planning to see the children this weekend," she said. "Did you find Lilli Ann?"

Lilli Ann. He stiffened, feeling it all come back to him. The robe. The sandal on the floor.

"Yes," he said, fingering the key in his jacket pocket. "I found her—on the bed in Diane's bedroom." He didn't want to go back in there.

"Do you mind?" he asked, handing her the key.

"Of course not," she said. "I'll pick up the doll and I'll look for Davey's dump truck too."

"Thanks." He started for the door, then turned around again. "Listen, would you..." He hesitated. Was this too much to ask? But he didn't want to go back into that room until there was no trace of Diane. Of anyone.

"Yes?" she prompted.

"Diane's clothes. And David's too. You're in welfare. Do you know someone who could use them? Or some place to take them?"

"Well, maybe. I could certainly ask."

"If you would and if you could get rid of them, I'd appreciate it. Get someone to help you. I'll pay for it. I just don't want...the truth is, I found those personal things upsetting. And I think it would be upsetting for the children if I do decide—and mind you, I haven't made a decision yet. But if I do decide to bring them here, I'd prefer there was nothing to remind us."

She was looking at him very hard. "Sure," she said. "I understand. I'll take care of it."

"Thank you. I'll be in touch."

CHAPTER SIX

IDIOT, MARCY THOUGHT, as she carefully refrained from slamming the door behind Steve. What was wrong with the man? He admitted that he didn't have a place for the kids to live. And he certainly didn't know the first thing about taking care of them. Yet, when presented with an intelligent and practical plan, he instantly rejected it! Possibly only because it was *her* suggestion.

But you'd better be careful, Stephen Prescott! She who shuffles the papers controls the world... well, at least that part of the world that concerns you. And you'd just better come up with a good plan for those two children!

It *was* true that she liked the idea of Ginger and Davey staying next door, where she could continue to see them and... *Detachment, Marcy.* But she did love the children, and Diane and David had been her friends, and she somehow felt she owed them something.

But it's their idiot uncle's decision, not yours. So forget it, Marcy Wilson.

However, she couldn't forget it, and she spent a very restless night. So, early the next morning, she phoned Gerald to arrange a prework game of tennis. Whacking a tennis ball around always cleared her head, and it was so easy to be able to call on Gerald.

"I don't know how you do it," Jo Stanford had once commented.

"Do what?" Marcy asked.

"Maintain good relationships with several men at the same time, while holding them all at arm's length."

"Oh, it's easy," Marcy had said breezily. "You just establish the ground rules right at the beginning."

But it wasn't always easy. Not when one of the parties became serious. Like Tom... Tom was showing signs of possessiveness. But with Gerald, there was never that worry. He had all he could do for the present, supporting himself and his ailing father, and he was as anxious as Marcy to maintain a "just friends" relationship.

The rest of the week passed in a flurry of interviews, meetings and reports. On Thursday, Marcy picked up Jimmy Braxton at school, took him out for hamburgers and gave him his birthday gift. Maybe, she thought, looking at his worn jeans and the way his arms extended beyond his jacket sleeves, she should have given him clothes instead. But... no. She was glad she'd chosen the calculator when she saw how elated he was. And she would speak to Mrs. Emory about his clothes. The Emorys had several foster children as well as their own large brood, and Marcy suspected that the entire check went toward basic household necessities, since she knew Mr. Emory had been out of work for some time now. She'd try to request a special clothing allowance for Jimmy, she decided.

Still, Marcy felt a little sad when she dropped Jimmy off at the house. She realized that the Emorys simply couldn't give him the loving attention he needed so badly. She would have preferred to move him, but it was difficult to find just the right place.

Anyway, she comforted herself as she drove away, Robert and Joyce Emory weren't undesirable foster parents. It was just that their own circumstances were difficult, and they simply didn't have the time or the training to respond to the emotional problems of such an active and demanding little boy.

Marcy knew that Jimmy yearned for the mother from whom he'd been taken two years before. Though shamefully lacking in the food and shelter department, Jimmy's mother, even through her drunken stupors, had managed to maintain a loving relationship with her son. But when Mrs. Braxton had disappeared for a week during one of her binges, leaving the boy to fend for himself, Protective Services had stepped in. Jimmy had been placed in the first of a series of foster homes; since then, he'd always been adequately cared for—but not with a parent's love. This was what Jimmy missed. And this was not easy to find.

On Saturday, Tom Jenkins took Marcy to dinner and to the symphony and told her more than she wanted to know about stocks and bonds.

On Sunday, Marcy drove to Shingle Springs to visit her sister, taking Ginger and Davey with her, as she'd planned. This turned out not to have been such a good idea. It rained steadily all day and the children couldn't play outside. Jennifer was worried about the damage they might do to her house. Ginger spilled punch on the linen tablecloth, and when Davey said the spaghetti was yukky, she wouldn't eat it either. Jenny had no peanut butter, so Marcy made toasted cheese sandwiches for the children.

After lunch, Jennifer spent half her time nagging the children to sit still and watch television, and the other half complaining to Marcy about Al, who'd left for the golf course early that morning. "How can he be playing golf when it's raining cats and dogs?" she whined.

If I were Al, Marcy thought ruefully, as she loaded the children into the Volkswagen, I think I'd spend my Sundays on the golf course, too. Rain or not. What on earth had given her the idea that Jennifer could adopt *any* child? Marcy's vague unease about her sister was rapidly becoming a full-blown anxiety. What was changing Jennifer from the warm, fun-loving girl who, three years before, had captured the heart of handsome Alfred R. Baker, one of the area's most successful real-estate developers? She'd had a spectacular wedding and then moved to that spacious home in Shingle Springs. Personally, Marcy had always considered Al a little too cocky, but Jennifer couldn't see the faults for the stars in her eyes. Had the romance faded? Perhaps Jennifer was growing bored with her comfortable life; perhaps she and Al had quarreled. Marcy worried about the sister who had always been so close. In fact, Marcy had transferred to the Auburn office mainly to be near Jennifer.

Her sister was just bored, Marcy decided, and that was what made her so irritable. She needed some activity of her own. Well, she and Al belonged to that exclusive racket club with the indoor courts. She would call Jennifer and arrange to play with her next Sunday. Then they could have lunch and a long, long talk—the talk they somehow hadn't got around to having that afternoon.

On Wednesday, she received a call from New York. She recognized the husky voice, and there was a little catch in her throat as she answered. "Yes, this is Marcy Wilson."

"Steve Prescott here. I've been thinking over what you said. Do you think it would speed things up if I changed my address to 212 Woodside?"

Was he bargaining with her?

"Possibly," she answered, unable to stem the tide of joy that was sweeping through her. She told herself it was because the children would still be living next door.

"Then please go ahead and change my address on the petition. I'll be there sometime this weekend. Do you think we might get things settled by the first of next week?"

"That depends on how soon your references get here. But otherwise there would be no problem. Though you'll still have to hire someone. . . ." She paused, remembering that Mrs. Fisher, the office cleaning woman, had mentioned a sister who might be interested. "Would you like me to look around for a housekeeper?" she asked, then wanted to bite her tongue when he answered.

"Thank you, no. My attorney has already contacted an agency in the area. They'll send someone out when I arrive."

Well, la-de-da. I hope your attorney knows what he's doing. She must remember to keep hands off.

"Very well then," she said. "That's taken care of. I'll concentrate on the paperwork." She emphasized the last word, but he didn't seem to notice.

"Er. . . there is one other thing. Did you find someone who could use the clothes?"

"Yes, as a matter of fact, I did. Someone who works here. Mrs. Fisher. She's coming out this afternoon."

"Good." She could hear the relief in his voice. "Thanks. I appreciate your taking care of it. I know it's a bit of trouble."

"I'm glad to do it," she said.

STEVE ARRIVED at the Sacramento airport late Saturday evening. It was raining, a drizzling, melancholy sort of rain, and there was a noticeable chill in the air. He picked up a rental car and drove to Auburn.

Actually it wasn't only Marcy's suggestion that had prompted him to take up residence at Woodside. While he was in New York, he'd had a chance to look at Diane and David's mail, which had been released to him from the Auburn post office. There was business he'd have to take care of. Bank statements indicated large sums of money in three accounts, as well as a safety deposit box. They had not had the good sense to make a will, but Dave did have mortgage insurance on the condo. Steve wanted to convert all the assets into trust funds for the children. Since there was no will, the state would have to get involved and...well, it was better for him to remain in California until things were settled. It wasn't because *she* had suggested he move into Woodside.

Still, as he neared Auburn, he found himself looking forward to seeing her. He wanted to ask her about the robot, which converted into a truck, that he'd bought for Davey. And the stuffed leopard for Ginger. The man at the store had said those were right for their age groups, but Marcy knew the kids. He was a little uncertain about the leopard. He thought Ginger might prefer a pony, but the stuffed ponies hadn't seemed very soft or cuddly. Anyway, it was a *real* pony that she'd set her heart on. And he wanted to ask Marcy if he should take the toys to the children immediately, or save them for a surprise when they came home.

When he reached Woodside, he left the toys in the car and bounded through the rain with his suitcase and garment bag. Since he had to get his key from Marcy first, he could ask her about the toys right away.

When he reached her apartment, he saw that the lights were on and he could hear laughter inside. He hesitated before he pressed the bell. A moment later, the door was opened by a man almost as tall as he, wearing a dark blue suit and thick horn-rimmed glasses.

"Yes?" said the man.

"I'm Steve Prescott. I wanted to see Miss Wilson."

"Who is it, Tom?" Marcy called.

The man stepped back and opened the door a little wider. Steve could see Marcy now. She was wearing something soft in a deep rose color and she was sitting on the floor before a blazing fire. There were things scattered about—a chessboard, wineglasses, a tray with food on it.

"Someone named Steve." There was a question in the man's voice as he turned back to Marcy.

"Oh, Steve! You're here already. Good." Marcy stood up and he could see the rose-colored thing was a sort of pants outfit, all in one piece. The pants were baggy and cinched at the ankle and she was barefoot.

"Come on in and close the door, for goodness' sake."

He came in, still holding his bags, and the man shut the door.

"This is Steve Prescott, Tom. He's moving in next door. Steve—Tom Jenkins. Sit down," she said to Steve. "Wouldn't you like a glass of wine? Or maybe something hot. It's pretty chilly outside."

But pretty damn cozy in here, Steve thought. And she had introduced him to some other man the first day he met her, hadn't she?

"Yes…no, I mean—no, I don't want anything, thank you. I just wanted to pick up the key."

The men stood looking at each other while she fetched the key from the buffet. Steve had the definite feeling that this horn-rimmed character was sizing him up.

"Here you are," she said, as she handed him the key. "I think everything's going to work out just fine. Some of your references have already arrived."

"That's good," he said.

"Sure you won't stay and have a drink or something to eat? There's plenty of cheese and salami."

"No. No, thank you. I'd better go on in. Good night." He nodded to both of them, turned abruptly and went out.

He felt very much alone when the door closed behind him. He wondered why that bothered him; he usually liked being alone. It was just that he'd wanted to ask her about the toys, he told himself. And yes, he hated to go back into that apartment. He hoped she'd managed to get rid of those reminders.

He opened the door and fumbled for the light switch, then stared in surprise. It looked different. Tidy. No bear standing on the sofa. No toys lying around. No dead flowers. The bowl on the coffee table contained a large bunch of colorful fall leaves. In the bedroom the

bed was neatly made, the closets bare. No toiletries.
Nothing. The essence of Diane was almost gone, but he
felt almost as sad as he had the week before, when the
room was full of her presence. He walked through the
apartment and found a certain comfort in little mementos—family photographs, plants Diane had tended,
signs of the happiness that had once existed there.

The next morning when he went into the bathroom to
shower and shave, he looked again at the freshly laun-
dered towels hanging on the rack, the bar of still-
wrapped soap on the basin. Someone had done a very
thorough job. *She* had seen to that. Today was Sunday.
He'd take her out for brunch and thank her. Later, they
could go to visit the children. He whistled as he quickly
showered and dressed—tan slacks, beige-and-brown
striped sport shirt, dark brown cashmere pullover. Then
he hurried over to knock on her door.

She wasn't at home. He checked the lobby and the
laundry room. Maybe she'd just gone out on an errand. He hung around for a while, but when she still
wasn't back at ten, he drove into Auburn, ate breakfast at Sutton's and walked around the little town.

He returned to Woodside at two, but she hadn't come
home yet. Not that he particularly wanted to see her, he
told himself. It was just that Marcy Wilson happened to
be the only person he knew in this town. And he'd
hoped she could accompany him when he went to see
the children.

Well, he decided, she must be spending the day with
one of her men friends, either that Gerald guy or Horn
Rims. A thought jolted him. Horn Rims had probably
spent the night, and they'd gone out together this

morning, and... Oh, hell! He didn't need her to take him to see his own niece and nephew.

When he arrived at the Jones house, he found the children reluctant to come too close. A little shy—he could understand that. He pulled the leopard from the box and held it out to Ginger. She moved forward tentatively and took it, then backed away.

"It's nice," she said, stroking the soft, cuddly form.

"Say 'thank you,'" Davey prompted.

"Thank you," repeated Ginger. Then, "Where's Marcy? Why didn't she come?"

"Ah...she's busy today." He held the other box out to Davey. "Here's something for you, Davey."

Davey cautiously took the box and thanked him politely. And unenthusiastically.

"Well, open it," Steve said. "Let's see how it works."

Davey warmed up a bit as they played with the toy but wanted to go show it to Troy almost immediately.

Neither child seemed interested in going out to dinner with him. Mrs. Jones said she couldn't allow it anyway, without an okay from the agency. As Steve returned to the apartment, he wondered why he'd felt it necessary to rush back from New York.

MONDAY MORNING when Marcy left for work, she noticed that a sealed envelope had been slipped under her door. As she was late, she didn't open it until she got to the office. In the envelope were two fifty-dollar bills and a note:

Miss Wilson,
Whoever cleaned the apartment did an outstanding job. Please see that they are properly compen-

sated. Thank you for disposing of the personal
items.

S.P.

When Marcy got home that afternoon, she went first
to Steve's door. He wasn't there, so she wrote on the
back of the envelope:

> Mrs. Fisher and I cleaned. She was glad to do it for
> the clothes, and I was glad to do it for Diane.
>
> M.W.

She put the two bills back in the envelope and slipped
it under his door.

As MARCY HAD PREDICTED, everything went smoothly.
Steve's references were excellent, Marcy sent in a Recommend Approval form, and without further delay, the
judge declared Stephen Prescott legal guardian of the
Nelson children.

Throughout the proceedings, however, Steve's attitude had been strangely cool and formal. Marcy was
puzzled by this. Of course, they hadn't hit it off too well
in the beginning, but she had since been very helpful to
him and he *was* getting the children. Not that she cared
what Stephen Prescott said or did, she told herself. But
still, it seemed odd. She usually got on well with men.

"Too well," her mother had often said. "You treat
them just like you do your brother." And when Marcy
asked what was wrong with that, her mother had replied that if Mr. Right ever did come along, he just
might be put off by being treated like a big brother.

Well, she certainly didn't intend to worry about Steve's attitude. She would just take her cues from him and stay out of his affairs. Except where it concerned the children, of course. She did think he was making a mistake, hiring that woman from the Alston Child Care Agency, and she was going to tell him so. Right now, in fact. She threw on a sweater, marched resolutely to his apartment and firmly rang the bell.

"Don't stop what you're doing," she told him when he opened the door. "I know you're getting things ready for the children. But I wanted to talk about something."

"Okay," he said. "Come on in. I'm just packing up David's manuscripts to send to his agent."

"All of them?" she asked, watching him take papers from the filing cabinet and stack them into cartons.

"Yep. He says he has someone who can finish or revise all the unsold material, and he thinks it will sell. If so, that would add to the children's legacy." He paused, then looked at her anxiously, as if seeking confirmation. "I think this is what David would want, don't you?"

"Yes," she agreed. "I'm sure that's what he'd want."

"I'm glad to have somewhere to send it," he said, returning to his task, "because, for one thing, I'll have to use this office while I'm here."

"Oh?"

"I plan to stick around until the kids get adjusted. Keep my trips to a minimum."

"Well, that's what I..." She paused, taking a deep breath. He hadn't asked for her advice, but she had to say this. "I don't think it's a good idea to hire anyone from the Alston Agency."

"Oh?" She heard the none-of-your-business intonation in his voice and stiffened.

"They're just baby-sitters," she pressed on. "You need more of an all-around person. Now, Mrs. Fisher has a sister who, so she says, is very good with children, and a hard worker as well."

"Thank you." He kicked aside a box and turned to face her. "I have already hired Mrs. Johnson, whom the agency recommended very highly. I'd credit the word of a reputable agency against the word of somebody's sister anytime."

"Excuse me. It was just a suggestion." She held her back very erect as she walked out.

Officious! Too damned officious. When she can spare the time, that is, from her "gentlemen callers." The guy from the office—Gerald, wasn't it?—and now Horn Rims, and Lord knew how many others.

That bother you?

Hell, no! Just don't like her meddling. I knew it was a mistake moving here.

Proved to be convenient, didn't it?

Too damned convenient—for her!

But she did work fast. You get the kids tomorrow.

That's her job.

Not her job to clean up the place and dispose of all those things.

Doesn't give her the right to run my life.

Does it give you the right to act like a jerk?

Oh, hell!

There was no answer when he rang. But he knew she was in. He could hear a racket, a creaking, almost rhythmic sound. He pounded on the door.

"Come in," she called. "It's unlocked."

She had one of those minitrampolines in the middle of the floor and was rapidly jumping up and down on it. She didn't stop. Only gave him an "Oh, it's you" look.

"You shouldn't leave your door unlocked," he said. "Anybody could walk in."

"You're absolutely right about that." He could hardly mistake her meaning.

"Listen," he said. "I didn't mean to snap at you. I've just been a little uptight. Getting ready for the kids and all."

She didn't answer, just kept bouncing like a jumping jack.

"Damn it! Will you keep still! I'm trying to apologize."

"Unnecessary." She executed a swift half turn and increased her speed. He walked around to face her.

"Hey, cut out these crazy gymnastics and listen to me!"

"I suppose," she gasped, panting a little from her exercise, "that people only jump when you tell them to."

"You're absolutely right about that!" he mimicked, catching her in midair, and setting her down with her feet firmly planted on the solid floor. "Now just keep still a blasted minute! I'm trying to ask you out to dinner. Tonight. To celebrate the kids' coming home tomorrow."

"My, my! Such a gracious invitation!" Her eyes were blue thunderclouds and he was quite mesmerized by them, until he heard her next words. "It really pains me to decline. But I have another engagement tonight."

"That doesn't surprise me. I rather suspected you would."

"Now just what do you mean by that?" she snapped.

"Oh, never mind!" He strode out rapidly, slamming the door behind him.

CHAPTER SEVEN

SHE WAS NOT, Marcy decided, going to let Steve's ani-
mosity come between herself and the children. The adjustment they were making was crucial, and the main
reason she'd wanted them near her was to help them
through it.

"Your uncle Steve loves you," she told them. "That's
why he wants you to live with him. So he can take care
of you. And isn't it nice of him to bring you back to
your own home, so you can go back to your old school
and see your friends?"

The week he'd brought the children home, Steve arranged a memorial service for David and Diane, whose
bodies had never been recovered after the accident. It
was a short ceremony, a simple and moving tribute that
brought Marcy to the brink of tears. Besides Steve and
the children, only she and a few other friends and
neighbors were present. The children sat quietly
throughout the service, their faces solemn.

Afterward, Marcy felt that the memorial service had
been a wise and necessary step, one that allowed all of
them to come to terms with what had happened and to
say a final goodbye to David and Diane.

The children were settling into a routine now, a routine that in many ways was a continuation of the past.
Marcy kept her door open to them as she always had,

with jigsaw puzzles and coloring books in the usual place at the bottom of her buffet. She also continued to take them out for little excursions. Steve did not object to this. In fact, he did not object to anything that made the children happy. He was too anxious to please them, Marcy thought; he couldn't deny them anything. If, once in a while, he did manage a not-too-firm "no," all Ginger had to do was cloud up and wail that she wanted her mommy and Steve would instantly succumb.

His attitude toward the children was so out-of-character, she thought. Once when she'd gone in to pick up the children she heard Steve in his office, evidently on the phone to someone in New York. He was barking out orders in a manner that left no doubt that whoever was on the other end of the line would hop to his bidding. Why didn't he just once bark at the kids? Didn't he know that children needed discipline? He was spoiling them rotten. But, of course, he'd never listen to her; he had to do everything his own way.

If he weren't so bullheaded, she would have felt sorry for him. Not only was he desperately trying to please two small children, he was also forced to cope with a household that revolved around their needs. Each evening when Marcy arrived home, she noticed Mrs. Johnson leaving. So, evidently, the housekeeper was not spending the night, and Marcy suspected she wasn't much help even while she was there.

Her suspicions were confirmed one Saturday in the laundry room. Marcy was just taking her towels out of the dryer when Steve came in carrying two pillowcases full of dirty clothes. He looked a bit harried, but he was whistling a tune under his breath, and when he saw her he smiled and nodded. Davey and Ginger, who were with him, immediately dashed over to her.

"Marcy!" Davey cried, "can we go to Funland tomorrow, or has the bank still got no money?"

"Well, er, we'll see." Marcy shot a quick glance at Steve, hoping he hadn't heard—or had, at least, misunderstood—Davey's reference to the day the automatic teller had registered Overdrawn. He was sorting clothes and putting them into two machines and gave no indication that he'd heard. She quickly drew Davey's attention to another subject. "Here, come help me fold the towels."

"No, Ginger, you get your own," Davey admonished as he began to fold one. "I'm doing this by myself!"

"But I want to help," Ginger whined.

"All right, kids," Marcy broke in before Davey could refuse, "you take one end and let Ginger take the other. Then you'll get it done twice as fast." She was relieved that she'd been able to divert them from the automatic teller incident. Their romp in the park had turned out to be just as enjoyable as the rides at Funland would have been. Besides, her overdrawn bank account was certainly no business of the arrogant Mr. Prescott.

Ho! Ho! Ho! So Miss Efficiency Wilson has areas of inefficiency, Steve gloated as he stuffed a pair of Davey's jeans in with the dark clothes. Can't keep her bank account straight, huh? He wondered why the thought pleased him so much.

"Why are you smiling?" Marcy asked. "You like doing the laundry?"

"Oh! Er, I don't mind. I've done it before."

"Not for a long time, I bet," Marcy said, as she placed the last of her towels in the basket and thanked the children for their help.

"Well," he answered, "it's like riding a bicycle. You don't forget."

Davey ran up to them. "Can I have—?"

"Excuse me, please," Marcy said gently.

"'Scuse, please. I need money for a Popsicle, Steve."

Steve started to reach into his pocket, but Marcy intervened. "May I please have money for a Popsicle?" she prompted.

"May I, please?" asked Davey.

"Please," said Ginger. "Me too."

"Have you had your dinner?" Marcy asked, and when both children shook their heads, said, "Then the answer is *no*. Stay away from the vending machines and count the washing machines. Can you count them for me?"

Davey nodded and went off, counting loudly, with Ginger following.

Steve scowled at Marcy. "I thought they asked *me* for Popsicles."

"Somebody has to say no," she answered, unperturbed. "You spoil them. You must be spoiling Mrs. Johnson, too. Doesn't she do the wash?"

"Alston Agency rules." Steve's mouth tightened as he poured the soap in and started the machines. "She doesn't do wash. She doesn't do cleaning. She doesn't do cooking. She baby-sits."

"From what I can see, she doesn't do much of that," Marcy said. "The kids are in school half the day, and I see her leaving at five. Doesn't she stay overnight?"

"If I pay her overtime." Steve frowned as he dusted soap powder from his hands. "Which I don't mind, but it galls the hell out of me to cook her breakfast the next morning."

"Oh. I see." Marcy's eyes twinkled, and he could tell it was all she could do to keep from laughing. The return of the children, just then, served as a momentary distraction.

"Ten, Marcy. I counted ten machines," Davey burst out.

"Me too," said Ginger.

"Ten! Aren't you smart? Listen, can you hop on one foot like this?" She demonstrated.

"Oh, sure," Davey said.

"Me too," came the echo.

"All right. Try it. Count how many times on one foot." She turned back to Steve as the children went off, happily counting. "Watch out! You might be in the breadline soon. Because if you run your business the way you run your household—"

"Okay. Okay. I've already given the woman notice. But I never had to do all this before. I lived in a hotel and went out for my meals or—"

"Change of life-style, huh?" Marcy teased, as she began to retrieve her lingerie from the gentle-dry cycle.

"All right. Your point has been made. You don't have to rub my nose in it."

"Why, Steve Prescott, I never once said 'I told you so.'"

"No. That's right. You didn't." He watched her shaking out a frilly piece of nightwear that looked as if it belonged to a very seductive woman, though in those jeans she seemed as young and slender as a child. There was obviously more to Marcy Wilson than met the eye....

"Well, happy laundering," Marcy said as she picked up her basket.

"Hey, wait!" His mind had wandered so far afield that he'd almost forgotten to ask, "Look, will you kindly lead me to somebody's sister who does do wash?"

"Fifteen times, Marcy," Davey chimed in, "I hopped fifteen times."

"Me too," said Ginger.

"She did not," Davey scoffed. "She just hopped nine."

"That's great." Marcy put down her basket and bent to hug both children. "Now try it on the other foot." As they began to hop and count, she again picked up her basket of clothes. "I'll see if she's still available," she told Steve as she went out.

"Thanks. I'd appreciate that," he called, hating to see her go. She sure knows how to handle the kids, he thought. They never minded when she said no. They just went off hopping and counting and laughing. He smiled to himself. Laughing. That was it, she made them laugh. Marcy was so lively and yet there was a warmth about her. Yes, he admitted, there was something special about Marcy Wilson, something alluring and... Oh Lord, he'd better keep his distance.

Marcy did manage to engage the cleaning woman's sister for him. Sally Chisholm was buxom and cheerful—"a real jewel," as he described her to Marcy. Beds got made, meals cooked, and the children were brought under control.

"You're too soft with them," Mrs. Chisholm had immediately told Steve. "You've got to let them know you're the boss, Mr. Prescott."

Steve appreciated the order she brought to his household and he was grateful to Marcy for finding her. However, he did not renew his invitation to take her out to dinner. Instead, he brought her a gift the next time he returned from New York. A Rolex watch. It seemed that was what all the ladies wanted.

When he gave it to her, she stared at it, then looked up at him, her eyes expressing a strange combination of surprise, pleasure and denial.

"Oh, you shouldn't! This is too much!"

"Just a little token to say thanks for all the help." He could hardly speak. Her eyes were casting a strange spell over him, and her lips were parted, an invitation he found hard to resist.

"But I didn't . . . I mean, I only helped because I wanted to."

"I know. You did it for Diane." He tore his gaze from that provocative face and concentrated on extracting the watch from the box. "Here. Let's see how it looks on your wrist." He slipped the watch over her hand, but was so moved by the feel of her soft smooth skin against his fingers that he quickly withdrew. "Wear it for Diane. We both thank you." He hurried out before she could make any more protest. And before he was tempted to do more than he should.

MRS. CHISHOLM was never able to stay overnight. "Not when you have half-grown children like I have, Mr. P. I don't mind being away during the day while they're in school. But at night I have to be there to check on their comings and goings. Now, there's my oldest, Nance. She'll be eighteen next month, and she's pretty reliable. I could bring her to stay overnight whenever you're away."

He did make one two-day trip to New York, accepting this arrangement. Everything went well. Anyway, the current situation was only temporary. He had a real-estate agent searching for a small country place in either Connecticut or upstate New York. The kids could have their ponies, and commuting would certainly be easier than from California. If he bought such a place he'd have to hire an adequate staff, of course, but his main worry was to find a woman who could take care of the children and manage the household, as well. His secretary had suggested a nanny for the children and a butler for the household. Steve couldn't help grinning when she said it. A butler? Such a grandiose arrangement had never occurred to him. But, what the hell! He had the money. Whatever the children needed, the children would get.

Meanwhile he struggled with the situation as it was. The children seemed happy with Mrs. Chisholm and their school. He was straightening out their financial and legal affairs, and he didn't plan to make any long trips until the family was permanently settled.

One morning at six, his partner phoned. "Steve, we've got problems."

"Oh?" Steve stifled a yawn and tried to concentrate.

"Peru. There's a hitch about the claims. Holding up everything. You'd better get down there."

"I thought Stan was handling it."

"Oh, hell!" Brick shouted. "You know Stan and the way he fumbles. Anyway, it's your baby."

"Don't see how I can make it, Brick. I don't like to leave the kids. I don't want to leave them until—"

"You think you've got troubles!" Brick bellowed. "All hell's breaking loose up here. Stell's on the rampage. Trying to take me to the cleaners—wants my money and her new guy too! And somebody's got to be here to handle those options on the Saudi Arabia claims, which, I'd like to remind you, is also your baby. Anyway, it'd only take you a week to get things going again. Stan could carry on after that."

A week. Only a week.

"Okay. I guess I can arrange it." Mrs. Chisholm was running the household anyway, and her daughter could stay nights. He would ask Marcy to keep an eye on things.

But when he went next door to talk to Marcy, he saw her going down the steps with Horn Rims. They were holding hands. He felt a sudden sense of loneliness—as if he'd somehow been abandoned. Oh, hell! he thought with sudden anger. What was he thinking of? He didn't need her to look after anything!

ON THURSDAY AFTERNOON, Marcy was able to return Troy to his mother, who had completely recovered from her surgery and was back at work. She was so pleased with the excellent care Troy had received and so grateful for Marcy's help that she invited her to stay for tea and cookies. Marcy didn't get home until almost seven and when she entered the apartment, the phone was ringing. It was Gerald.

"Marcy, would you please come to the hospital? I'm in Emergency."

"Emergency!" Marcy exclaimed. "What's wrong?
Are you—?"

"It's not me. It's Pop. And I don't know what's
wrong. He'd passed out and was lying on the floor when
I got home. I was late because I stopped for a beer. I
should have come straight home. Marcy, I'm scared!"

"I'll be right there," she said. When she arrived at
the hospital, Mr. Sims had already been taken to inten-
sive care. Gerald was waiting for Marcy, and the two of
them went up together.

"They think it's his heart," Gerald said. He was vis-
ibly distressed, and Marcy sat with him in the waiting
area for several hours, until the doctor came out to an-
nounce that Mr. Sims's condition had stabilized. They
were running tests to determine the extent of the damage. There would almost certainly be no change until
morning, he told them, suggesting they go home and
wait.

Marcy could see that Gerald needed food and rest and
urged him to come back to her place. When they got
there, however, he said he wasn't hungry.

"Well, I am," Marcy told him emphatically. "I'll fix
us something light. One good thing about being extrav-
agant is that you're always prepared." As she spoke, she
took a carton of fresh oysters from the refrigerator.

After a bowl of hot oyster stew and a glass of wine,
Gerald said he felt much refreshed and would go back
to the hospital.

"You'll do no such thing," she insisted. "You left my
number and they'll call if you're needed. Why don't you
sleep here on the couch, and if they do call, I'll go back
to the hospital with you." She set out sheets and blan-
kets for him and placed the phone close by. When he

declared he was "as snug as a bug in a rug," she got into her own bed and fell instantly asleep.

STEVE DIDN'T LIKE being away from the children a whole week. He had called as soon as he arrived in Peru, and things at home seemed to be going reasonably well. However, he'd been out in the field for two days because they'd had helicopter problems. It was almost three in the morning when he got back to the station, which meant that it was around midnight in California. But he had to leave for the site at six, when it would be three a.m., their time. Better call now, he decided.

The phone rang and rang. Nancy must be a heavy sleeper, he thought. He gripped the phone hard as he waited. Finally, it was picked up at the other end.

"Hello," said a sleepy little voice.

"Davey! Is that you, Davey?"

"Uh-huh," Davey said with a yawn.

"Why did you answer the phone?"

"It rang."

"Where's Nancy?" Steve felt a growing panic.

"Don't know. Sleeping, I guess."

"Davey, listen to me. You go wake her up and tell her to come to the phone."

"Okay."

Steve held the phone so tightly his knuckles whitened. Why the hell hadn't the Chisholm girl answered? The phone was right next to the bed. No, he thought, the tension easing a bit. She would probably be in the extra bed in Ginger's room, and maybe she hadn't—

"Hello," came Davey's voice.

"Where's Nancy?"

"She's not there."

"Not there! What do you mean? Did you look? Everywhere?"

"Yes. And I called her. I called and called. And Ginger woke up, and she's crying. And Nancy's not here."

Cold terror seized him. The girl wasn't there. The children were alone in the apartment. Now he had awakened them and ...

"Listen, Davey, listen to me." He made an effort to speak calmly and clearly. "This is what I want you to do. You go ... No. You and Ginger stay right there. Understand? I'm going to call Marcy. You wait."

Marcy's phone was answered on the first ring.

"Hello." A man's voice.

"Is this Miss Wilson's residence?"

"Yes, it is. Sims here. Did you want me?"

"What! Oh, no. No. I'd like to speak with Miss Wilson. Please."

"Oh. Sure. Just a minute."

Steve waited, fuming. Damn! He might have known she'd have some joker—

"Hello." Her voice sounded muffled, as if she'd just woken up. Under his panic lurked a disquieting thought. Something he'd have to deal with later. Now his concern was for the children.

"Marcy, this is Steve. I'm in Peru, and the children are alone in the apartment."

"What!"

"That girl—Nancy, Mrs. Chisholm's daughter. She's supposed to be staying with them, but Davey says she's not there, and I ... Marcy, would you—?"

"All right, Steve. I'll go right over."

"I'll give you ten minutes, then I'll call back."

"All right. I'm off," she said.

When he called his apartment again Marcy answered.

"The kids are fine. And don't worry. I'll stay with them. Tonight, and every night until you get back."

"Thank you," Steve said. The relief that flooded through him was overwhelming. With Marcy he knew the children would be safe.

Then the disquieting thought he had earlier shrugged aside returned. Marcy's phone had been answered by a man, a man who assumed the call was for him. And obviously, both the man and Marcy had been asleep.

That bother you?

Hell, no! Why should it?

NANCY TOLD MARCY that she'd just gone out for a few minutes with her boyfriend to get a hamburger. The children were asleep, and anyway, they'd come right back, and would Marcy please not tell her mother what had happened. So Marcy simply told Mrs. Chisholm that Steve had asked her to stay at night, so Nancy would not be needed.

Mrs. Chisholm said that was fine, as she really wanted Nancy at home where she could keep her eye on her "comings and goings."

"Poor Mr. Prescott," Mrs. Chisholm continued. "He just doesn't know what to do with these children. They lead him around by the nose. He needs to get married, and I don't doubt he will soon, the way these women are after him. All the letters he gets. Of course, I never open them, but I can smell the perfume right through the envelopes. Like they just poured it on, so he wouldn't forget. And some woman keeps calling him on the phone. I think she's the one in the photograph I set up on his dresser. Isn't she a beauty?''

She was a beauty. Long blond hair and a wide mouth curved in a provocative smile. And a scribbled autograph, ''To my darling Steve, with all my love, Tricia.''

Yes, Marcy told Mrs. Chisholm, he probably would marry soon. And yes, it would be a good thing. And the only reason she was upset, she told herself, was that someone else would be a mother to Ginger and Davey.

Although Mrs. Chisholm's position had been a temporary arrangement, Steve gave her a sizable bonus when his secretary found a Mrs. Evans, who had good references and no encumbrances. He turned the office into a bedroom and had Mrs. Evans flown out to occupy it. Although she lacked Mrs. Chisholm's warmth, she was efficient, reliable and . . . well, almost suitable.

"ROB PETER . . . pay Paul. Rob Peter . . . pay Paul,'' Ginger sang from her seat on the floor while she tried unsuccessfully to braid the yellow yarn that was Lilli Ann's hair.

"A new nursery song?'' Steve asked, looking up from his newspaper.

Ginger shook her head and Davey replied. "It's not a song. It's what Marcy says—'Can't play now. I got to rob Peter to pay Paul,''' he mimicked, then looked seriously at Steve. "She's not really robbing. She's not a bad guy.''

"Oh?''

"Marcy told me. She's not robbing. She's just making her money go round and round.'' Davey waved his arms dramatically before returning to his book. But Steve could not return to his newspaper.

Making her money go round and round? He knew Marcy worked hard. How much were they paying her? He stirred in his chair, not amused as he'd been earlier, when he heard about the overdrawn bank account. Somehow he didn't like to think of Marcy being pinched to make ends meet. She didn't give that impression; she dressed well, glowed with health, always looked cheerful. Wouldn't even take the cleaning money he'd given her.

Because she was a *giver*. Not a *taker*. Whenever he needed her, Marcy had come through. And not only had he not reciprocated, he'd avoided her like the plague. He'd never even taken her out to dinner. Well... that was because he didn't want to get involved.

Taking a lady out to dinner has never involved you yet.

Right!

He put down his newspaper and stood up to go next door.

CHAPTER EIGHT

HER DINING TABLE was littered with bills, so she must have been busy trying to make her money go "round and round." Evidently she was ready to give up the effort, for she said she'd be delighted to go to dinner with him. He took her to The Captain's Table.

"I'm glad you chose this place. I love it." She looked up from her salad at the hurricane lamps set in sconces in the wall and the antique map of the New World. "Don't you feel you're on board an old ship sailing off to some unknown faraway place?"

"Not really," he said. "I get the impression I'm on an old paddle wheeler that's been converted into a rather luxurious restaurant and docked on the banks of the Sacramento River."

"Oh." She gave him a pitying look. "Must you be so realistic? All right. Try this. Just let yourself go. Feel the gentle rocking of the boat. It *is* rocking—don't you feel it?" He nodded, smiling, and she went on. "Hear the waves lapping against the hull and watch the lights of the other craft as they sail by. Look!"

Their table was by the window, and he could see the lights of a couple of boats that were sailing by.

"Now, just relax," she told him in a coaxing tone. "You're sailing down the Mississippi on a brand-new paddle wheeler—a freshly painted, well-appointed showboat. You've just come from the gaming table after a big win, and you're having dinner with—"

"Then why," he asked, laughing, "do I still feel I'm in a restaurant on an old paddle wheeler that's been—"

"That's only because you have no imagination!" She leaned toward him, her eyes dancing with mischief. "Would you believe you were on a showboat if I sat on top of that piano and sang 'Can't Help Lovin' That Man of Mine'?"

"I dare you," he said with a chuckle, rather enjoying this silly game she was playing. Come to think of it, she was always playing games. She turned disciplining the children into fun. And, yes, even her money problems. What did she call it...robbing Peter to pay Paul? She makes a game of life, he thought, and smiled.

"You needn't smile like that. I'm not going to take you up on your dare. It wouldn't spur your imagination, and I'd just be making a spectacle of myself."

"Not you. You could never be a spectacle. You'd be a vision—a beautiful vision." The words came out almost involuntarily, for that was exactly what he was thinking. She *was* a vision, in a simple shirtwaist dress of lavender silk that gave her blue eyes a violet cast. Her peal of laughter delighted him, as it always did.

Marcy's eyes widened. "Your imagination is operative after all! If you can picture me as a beautiful vision, you might even acquire the visualization technique."

"Visualization? You mean seeing what's before you?"

"No. It's seeing what's *not* before you," she said, as she took a sip of wine. "I read this book—can't remember the title—it describes a technique for getting what you want or bringing about what you wish would happen. You just pretend it's already happened, and you keep seeing it in your mind and it comes true. Do you believe that?''

"No," he said. "I do not believe that." How many times with childlike faith had he envisioned his mother coming home? All the nights he'd lulled himself to sleep feeling in his mind her hugs and kisses as he imagined her return. It had never happened.

"No," he repeated. "I definitely do not believe that."

"I'm not convinced myself," she agreed, as the waiter removed their salad plates and placed the entrées before them. When he had departed, she began to eat with relish, and smiled across at Steve.

"I'm glad I'm with you."

"Oh?" He felt strangely pleased.

"Because—" she paused with a dainty morsel halfway to her mouth "—I love lobster, and you can afford it."

"And I thought it was my manly charm." He chuckled, amused by her frankness. "Tell me, do you make your selection from the menu with a view to your escort's pocketbook?"

"Yes, indeed. My brother, Bill, says it's definitely the polite thing to do." Then she added teasingly, "I'm not sure about your charm, but you have a very nice smile."

"Thank you," he said, rather absently. He was thinking of Horn Rims, who drove a Mercedes. "Then do you choose..." He broke off. He couldn't ask that.

"The answer to your unspoken question," she said calmly, "is no. I do not choose my escorts according to what's in their pockets. I like hamburgers, too. In other words—'' she gave a dramatic wave of her hand ''—king or commoner, it's all the same to me.''

"No preferences?" he asked. *In food or men?*

"Variety is the spice of life. This lobster is delicious." She speared a piece and held it toward him. "Would you like a taste?"

"No!" he snapped, angry that he could not stop looking at her. He wanted to kiss her. He wanted to shake her. He wanted to ask her what the hell Gerald Sims was doing asleep at her place in the middle of the night. No! He didn't want to know.

"My goodness, don't look like that! You don't have to taste the lobster if you don't want to. I'm not forcing it on you. But you've hardly touched your steak. Aren't you hungry?"

"Er..." He tore his gaze from her, and looked down at his wineglass, turning it slowly. "I was thinking of something else."

"Yes," she said. "I suppose you must have a lot on your mind. Is the new housekeeper working out all right?"

"Huh? Oh, yeah, so far so good." At that moment, Mrs. Evans was the farthest thing from his mind. "I—I want to thank you again for coming to my rescue that night."

"Oh, I'm just glad I was there. I was as concerned as you."

"I know. But it was a bad time for you. I hated to disturb you so late."

She shrugged. "No problem."

"I know you had company. The, er, man who answered the phone seemed a little put out." He watched for her reaction.

"Gerald? Oh, no," she said, as she lifted her glass. "It was just that he was waiting for a call."

"He's in the habit of getting calls at your place in the middle of the night?" He could not help blurting it out any more than he could stop the hot blood rushing to his face.

She put down her fork and looked at him. "You're asking if Gerald is in the habit of spending the night at my place?"

"Oh, no. That's not my business."

"It certainly isn't. However, to satisfy your obvious curiosity, on that particular night Gerald had just taken his father to Emergency. I realized he was extremely upset, and in case anything happened, I wanted to be able to go back to the hospital with him. So I suggested he spend the night at my place. On my sofa! When the phone rang at such a late hour, he naturally thought it was the hospital and—"

"All right. All right. I get the picture." His shame was coupled with overwhelming relief.

Why? What's it to you?

Nothing! It meant nothing to him.

"I . . . I'm sorry I asked. I didn't mean to give the impression that—"

"That you thought I was shacking up with any Tom, Dick or Harry that came along?"

"No, I didn't think that. I . . . look, don't be angry with me. Come on, finish your dinner."

She blinked several times. "I'm not angry. And I'm not hungry."

"Would you like a doggie bag?"

"No."

"Dessert? Coffee?"

"No, thanks. Oh, well, I'll have a cup of coffee while you finish your steak."

"Never mind." He pushed back his plate. "I'm not hungry, either. Let's go."

On the drive home, neither tried to engage the other in conversation. They were still silent when they left the car and walked toward the apartments.

"Thank you for a very nice evening," she said politely, as she reached into her purse for the key. He took it from her, opened the door and followed her in.

"I had a nice evening," he said. "I'm sorry it had to end this way. Sorry that what I said made you angry. And don't tell me again that you're not angry."

"But I'm not—" She broke off, then tossed her coat and purse on the sofa and turned to face him. "It wasn't what you said. It was what you implied."

"I didn't imply anything," he argued, aware that this was not exactly the truth. Aware of how desirable she looked in that simple little dress.

"Yes, you did. You have a one-track mind. You think the only thing that can exist between a man and a woman is sex. And that really bugs me. Haven't you ever heard of good old-fashioned friendship?"

"Of course."

"But you don't think of it between a man and a woman, do you? Like most men, you look at a woman in terms of her sexual attractiveness."

"You find that offensive? As lovely as you are?"

"I don't find it offensive, but I just think—"

"Then you shouldn't find this offensive, either." He did what he'd been wanting to do all evening. He took her in his arms. For a moment he just held her cradled against his chest, his face buried in her hair, savoring the sweet fresh fragrance.

"I'm sorry I said something to hurt you," he whispered. "I...I thought... I was so..." He broke off. He couldn't say he was jealous. He wasn't jealous! Lord, she was sweet. He traced light kisses over her temple and closed eyelids. Then his lips brushed hers, slowly, tentatively. Her mouth felt soft and warm against his, and the kiss deepened as she wound her arms around him and pressed closer.

Wild desire churned within him. He wanted this woman. He wanted to hold her. To love her. But somewhere deep in his consciousness an alarm had sounded. This was more than passion. Instinctively he felt that her warm and trusting response was answering more than the urgency of the moment. She was drawing him into the future.

Abruptly he released her, backing away from his own desire and the puzzled question in her eyes.

"I'm sorry," he said. "I shouldn't have done that."

She started to protest, and he turned quickly away. "I'd better end the evening before I find myself having to make more apologies. Good night."

Back in his own place, he took a cold shower, muttering, cursing to himself. He should never have taken her out, never have kissed her. He had sensed from the first that Marcy was a woman from whom he could not easily walk away. And he wanted no woman he couldn't walk away from. His mother's desertion had turned his father into a bitter angry man. Steve had hated him; he hadn't realized until it was too late that his father was hurting, too.

You couldn't trust a woman. Any woman. He thought of that guy he'd worked with down in Mexico—Scully, Sam Scully. Tough guy. You'd never have believed he'd go off the deep end the way he did. They were out in the field, and someone brought in the mail. And Sam got that "Dear John" letter from his wife. And he'd just walked out and shot himself.... And Stell and Brick—crazy in love last year, and now she'd dumped him for another guy and they were fighting like cats and dogs over the kid and the money.

He shook his head as he toweled himself dry. This was a love 'em and leave 'em world, and he wanted no part of it. He'd vowed a long time ago that he'd never fall in love, never marry. He knew that if he were to keep his vow, he'd better stay away from Marcy. Stick to a woman like Trish, who warmed his bed, but not his heart.

CHAPTER NINE

SHE'D BEEN KISSED before. But never had anyone apologized for kissing her. Marcy leaned against the closed door, feeling the humiliation of his rejection. He had practically pushed her away!

Face it, Marcy! He *had* to push you away. You were clinging to him like crazy, virtually inviting him to...

Oh, no! It wasn't like that. It wasn't! Marcy pressed her burning face against the cool panel of the door. It had seemed so natural. The warmth of his arms had been so male, so confident, that she had melted against him. She had sensed a gentle tenderness in him and sensed, too, a passion, an urgency that shattered her every reserve. She had pressed closer, yielding to some primitive desire that clamored to be fulfilled. And he had pushed her away.

She felt a hot flush of anger. You initiated that kiss, Mr. Prescott! And if you think I'm going to spend half the night mooning over it, you're crazy! I'm not Jennifer.

Marcy snatched her coat from the sofa and marched resolutely upstairs. Jennifer. Lord, how she had mooned over Al. Jennifer had practically cried in her soup last week, when they'd played tennis and had lunch together. The whole conversation had centered on Al. His frequent business trips, his golf and how little time he spent with her. Jennifer had sounded so unhappy and unsure, almost as she had in the days before her marriage, when she used to wonder if Al really loved her. Now Marcy was beginning to understand the reason for her sister's depression. It was more than boredom, she realized. Jennifer had become dependent on Al and that dependency made her vulnerable.

Well, it won't happen to me, Marcy promised herself as she vigorously brushed her hair. I'm not going to moon over anyone. So you can spread your smiles and your kisses around just as you please, Mr. Prescott. It won't bother me.

Suddenly she stopped, the brush held in midair. *He* had pulled away. He wasn't spreading his kisses around. Saving them for his true love? The blonde in the silver frame? Well, that didn't bother her, either. She ignored the little ache in the pit of her stomach and eventually fell asleep dreaming of a man whose eyes crinkled when he smiled.

"DON'T YOU LOVE US anymore, Marcy?"

"Of course I love you," Marcy answered, as she scooped Ginger up into her arms.

"How much? How much?" The little girl giggled. It was an old game.

"A bushel and a peck, and a hug around the neck." Marcy gave her a hug, then put her down and sank to her knees beside Davey. She felt a little breathless. The day was mild for early November, and Marcy had jogged through the park, approaching the complex from the rear and coming upon the children playing outside. She pulled gently at Davey's ear and gave him a kiss on the cheek.

"I love you, too," she said. "What are you doing?"

"Making a mountain," he answered, never pausing as he raked leaves into a pile with his hands. "Where have you been, Marcy?"

"I've been visiting a friend who's just come home from the hospital. I'm teaching him to play chess." Gerald's father had had a coronary bypass, and was recuperating at home.

"Why don't you play with us anymore?" asked Ginger.

"Well . . . you've been busy at school, and I've been busy at work." She couldn't tell the children that she had to avoid them in order to avoid their uncle. "And I'm playing with you now," she said, adding a few leaves to Davey's pile.

"My teacher says it's almost Thanksgiving. Is it, Marcy?" Davey asked.

"It will be in a week or so."

"And that's when we're going?" Davey's eyes were eager.

"Going?"

"You know. To 'silomar."

"Oh." That conference at Asilomar. She'd forgotten about it. But Lord, kids never forgot anything.

"You said you were going to take us. You promised," said Davey.

"Me too," echoed Ginger.

"Well, now, I don't know. You see, I'd have to ask your Uncle Steve."

"Well, there he is." Davey pointed excitedly. "Ask him now, Marcy."

Steve had been standing on the balcony observing the little group for some time. Mrs. Evans had asked him to call the children to dinner, and he'd stepped out, looking over the railing.

He'd noticed her immediately. She was wearing a vivid green running suit with a hood. The hood had fallen back, and her hair was blowing in the breeze as she sat in the middle of those leaves, laughing. It was as if the day had brightened as he watched her. She looked so alive as she played with the children. And they accepted her so easily and naturally.

He felt a wave of envy. With him, the children were still awkward and ill at ease. He had tried so hard... "How was school today, Davey?" And Davey would answer in a monosyllable and retreat to his own room or as far from Steve as he could. Ginger would trail after her brother. He felt as though he were walking on eggs, trying to please them, trying to get close to them. But he hadn't managed to make even a dent in their affections. He wanted them to love him, more for their sake than for his own. How could they be happy, living with a stranger? He kept telling himself it would take time, but—

"Ask him! Ask him!" he heard Davey shout.

"Ask me what?" he called good-naturedly, smiling as he gazed down at them, desperately wanting to be a part of their easy camaraderie.

Marcy looked up reluctantly. And she was immediately arrested by that smile and reminded of that kiss. She flushed, remembering his rejection, and felt too confused to respond to Davey's request. When she didn't speak, Davey supplied the question himself.

"Marcy was going to take us to 'silomar. She already promised and everything. Only now she says she has to ask you. Can we? Can we go?"

Steve frowned, and Marcy sensed his irritation.

"I've never stopped you from going anywhere with Marcy. She can take you wherever she wants."

His answer satisfied the children, who began to jump up and down with glee. Marcy felt compelled to explain that they were talking about a five-day trip, which had been planned several months before.

"So come in and tell me about it," Steve said. "Mrs. Evans has chili waiting. There's plenty. Join us, Marcy, and we can talk about it."

Marcy joined them because . . . well, because she'd promised the children and she'd have to clear it with him first. And, she told herself, you don't have to avoid a man just to keep from falling in love with him! Anyway, she was hungry.

Over a really delicious bowl of hot chili, she explained the plans she'd made with David and Diane. During Thanksgiving week, Marcy was to take the children with her to Asilomar, where she'd be conducting a couple of workshops at a parenting conference. There would be other children, too, and programs had been arranged for them, as well as for the parents.

"It might be good for Ginger and Davey to get away for a while," she said, "and it would be a break for you."

Steve seemed very interested in the conference and plied her with questions. She described the various sessions that were designed to help foster parents in the care and guidance of children.

"This conference. Can anybody go?" he asked.

"Why, yes," she said, surprised at the eagerness in his voice. "They're primarily for foster parents, but they are open to the general public."

"Have they found it helpful? I mean these people who attend—do they really get something out of it?"

She hesitated. "Well, those who come intending to get something out of it usually do. So I guess the answer is yes. Otherwise, we would have discontinued it altogether."

"Then I think it's a good idea for the kids. And for me, too. Where do I register?"

"You?" Marcy asked, feeling a little stunned.

"Why are you looking at me like that? I thought you'd be the first to say I need a few lessons in parenting."

SHE HAD NOT BELIEVED he'd follow through, but he did. He even suggested they take his car, since they were all going and surely couldn't fit into her Volkswagen.

"What kind of car do you have in New York?" she asked, as they started out in the modest Chevrolet, the rental car he had driven since arriving in California.

"I don't own a car," he said. "Matter of fact, I've never owned one."

"Oh?"

"Well, by the time I got so I could afford one, I was either in some godforsaken place where we travel by helicopter or in New York where it's easier to take a cab."

"I see." She looked at his hands, firm on the wheel, and noted his relaxed manner as he drove onto the freeway. "You drive as if you've been doing it for a long time."

"I did a lot of driving when I was in the navy. They stuck me in the motor pool right away. Good thing I did a driver's ed course in high school that last year I was

home." He took a deep breath. "Funny. I wanted a car
like crazy then. I thought for sure that by the time I was
sixteen, I... Well, it didn't work out."

"Most kids want a car at that age, but very few get
it," she said, wanting to chase that bitter look from his
face.

"Right." The single word was like the sound of a
door shutting, closing off the past. Marcy realized how
little she knew about this man. How much she wanted
to know.

"When did you join the navy?" she prompted.

"A few months past my sixteenth birthday."

"Sixteen!"

He grinned. "Well, I lied a little. I was on my own
and jobs were scarce, so I joined the navy to see the
world." He chuckled. "Never got off the base."

Marcy was eager to hear more about his stint in the
navy and what he'd done after that. But they were interrupted by a minor squabble in the back seat. Ginger
had torn Davey's comic book. Marcy pulled out the
coloring books and crayons she'd brought, and when
the children were quiet again, she turned back to Steve.

"Did you get anything out of the navy besides a special aptitude for driving a car?"

"Well, yes." He smiled as he gave her a sidelong
glance. "I had to take the G.E.D.—you know, that
high-school equivalency test, so I guess I got my high-
school diploma. And I met Brick." He said that Brick's
father had always worked in the oil fields, and Brick
had plenty of ideas. So when they got their discharge
papers, the two of them teamed up. They started off
doing drudge work in the fields, eventually turned to
speculation, then formed a partnership and...

"Well, we've been pretty lucky," he concluded.

"You must have worked really hard. And you made it on your own. I think you can be pretty proud of yourself." She touched his hand and flashed him a brilliant smile. She didn't add that she thought there was something pretty special about a man who could afford any kind of car he wanted, yet felt comfortable and content driving a modest rental Chevy. Her brother, Bill, who couldn't afford it, and Tom Jenkins, who could, drove only what was flashy, foreign and very expensive.

Marcy watched Steve as he calmly negotiated the heavy Sunday afternoon traffic, and imagined a skinny underage kid deftly handling the trucks and jeeps in a navy motor pool. She saw a man in dingy overalls digging or doing whatever they did in oil fields. She heard a stranger say, "I'll be there to pick them up." She saw a man with a sweet smile stuffing kids' clothes into a washing machine. This was a man who did whatever he had to do, no matter how unfamiliar or difficult. Marcy felt an overwhelming rush of tenderness toward him. She wanted to put her arms around him, lean her head against his shoulder and say, "I think you're great!" Then she remembered. This was a man who did not want to be touched.

"You know," he said, startling her out of her reverie, "I've traveled practically all over the world, but very little in the United States, and not at all in California."

"You're going to love this place. Someone—I think it was Hemingway—called the Pacific Grove area the most beautiful spot in the world."

When they arrived, she could tell he was impressed by
the conference grounds at Asilomar, where much of the
rustic beauty had been retained. The main buildings and
guest cottages, with names like Crescent View, Fireside
and Seaside, were scattered among towering trees. At
the end of the grounds, sandy dunes led to a pictur-
esque and very rocky beach. Marcy and Steve were
housed in adjoining cottages, Marcy sharing her room
with Ginger, and Davey staying with Steve.

Because the other conference participants weren't
scheduled to arrive until three, the next afternoon,
Marcy said the four of them would spend the whole day
together and take the grand tour. They set out Monday
after breakfast in a lighthearted holiday mood. First,
they followed the famous seventeen-mile drive with its
beautiful views: the great Pacific Ocean with the waves
rushing in, breaking upon the rocks and the windswept
beach, the gnarled and twisted cypress trees that bent
inland, as if losing the battle against the wind and sea.
From time to time, they caught glimpses of luxurious
houses, nestled in the hills.

They drove into Monterey and ate at the Carousel,
where the children consumed hot dogs and milk shakes
and took several rides on the indoor carousel, and
where Steve, between mouthfuls of homemade peach
cobbler and mounds of ice cream, remarked that it was
a shame to place a honky-tonk town in the midst of such
natural beauty.

However, he was impressed by the aquarium with its
magnificent man-made fish tanks, tanks so huge one
could walk around them and observe the different spe-
cies of sea life that dwelt in Monterey Bay. They all
agreed that they were lucky to arrive at feeding time.

The children had enormous fun watching the sea otters swim up to catch their portions of fish. Ginger particularly enjoyed the touch tank, lifting out one and then another of the rubbery-looking starfish, which neither Marcy nor Davey would touch. Davey's favorite attraction was the simulated surf. He stood, watching the water gently recede, laughing each time the big wave formed and then surged out with such force that light sprays would come shooting out at him.

They returned to Asilomar contentedly weary, had dinner in the community dining hall and retired early.

The next two days were filled with the real work of the conference. Marcy conducted two workshops, both of which Steve attended. She was surprised by his conscientiousness and active participation. He also attended several other workshops. He's serious about parenting, Marcy thought—determined to be good at whatever he has to do. Again, she felt that rush of tenderness toward him.

Thanksgiving was a day for relaxing and having fun, with excursions in the morning, an early turkey dinner with all the trimmings and, in the afternoon, a social for the adults and supervised play for the children.

"I don't feel social," Steve said to Marcy. "Let's take a walk on the beach."

"I don't know," she said. "Maybe I should be around in case someone wants to talk to me or ask any questions."

"You've been answering questions for two days, teacher. It's time you took a rest. Come on." His hand firmly grasped hers and she had no choice but to follow.

The day was overcast and a little chilly, so they went back to the cottages and changed into warm running suits and sturdy shoes. A few minutes later, they were climbing through the sand dunes toward the beach.

"I feel like I'm playing hooky," she said, laughing. She did feel as carefree as a child let out of school. Climbing through the dunes was difficult, though. She kept slipping backward and would have fallen except for his supporting hand.

"I can see you're not used to roughing it," he said, and in one surprising movement, lifted her in his arms. Her own arms went automatically around his neck, and she felt the light stubble on his chin as it rested against her cheek. Her heart thumped wildly. She told herself it was from the effort of the climb, told herself that the heady exhilaration she felt was purely from the fresh sea air that was filling her lungs.

"Here we are," he said, as they reached level ground. He turned his face toward her as he spoke, and his lips almost brushed hers. She held her breath as his eyes searched hers for a long moment. She thought—hoped—that he was going to kiss her. She felt a wave of keen disappointment when he set her firmly on her feet.

"I'll race you to that rock," he said, pointing to a spot a good distance away from them.

She was glad to run, to let go, to feel the tension flow out of her. For a time they kept pace, but at the last minute he swiftly passed her. When she reached him, he was already standing on the rock, and he stretched down his hand to help her up.

It was a large flat rock, half on land, half in the water. Marcy sat, exhausted but composed, feeling a certain peace as she absorbed her surroundings. Except for the two of them, the beach was deserted. There were only the rocks, the wet sand and the rhythmic gray sea, rolling in, receding and rolling out again. Steve sat down beside her, and she felt as if they existed in a world apart.

"Now, isn't this better than standing around saying 'how do you do,' and 'how do you like the conference'?" he asked, as he tossed a stone into the water.

"Definitely," she answered. "And how *do* you like the conference, sir?"

"It's great! What I like most about it is listening to the foster parents themselves talk about how they handled this situation or that. They're a good group. This foster-parent system of yours is terrific."

"Not really. There are...many imperfections." When he looked at her in surprise, she added, "These people here are just the tip of the iceberg, or maybe I should say the cream of the crop. They're sincere, like you," she said, smiling. Then she frowned, and one slender hand made circles on the rock as she looked out to sea. "For every good one, there are ten others who are barely adequate."

"But you—the agency, I mean—is so thorough about selection and supervision. I should think—"

She turned a serious face toward him. "The average social worker has a caseload of between fifty and sixty children. When you consider that he or she has to counsel the children, the natural parents, if they're still around, as well as the foster parents, you can imagine how little time there is for each. And how hard it is to spot the bad ones."

He shook his head. "You surprise me, Marcy. The way you do your job, anyone would think you were all for the system."

"I told you. I just work there. I don't make the rules."

"And if you did?"

"I'd try to change things." It seemed a time for sharing, and she told him of her dreams. Children's homes, supported by state and county. They'd have clinics and playgrounds, supervised programs and counselors, well-trained and loving house parents. There would be good care and a securely established routine, the kind of stability that could never be attained when children were shunted from one home to another. She talked eagerly and earnestly about the ideas she had been formulating ever since she'd begun to work with children.

He listened to her and was impressed with her sincerity. More than once he had called her *officious*. But this was a woman who cared. He looked at the blue-green eyes, so alive with love, and with hope for her children. He watched the dimples that disappeared and reappeared in her cheeks, the soft, full mouth. Then, because he couldn't help himself, he kissed her.

She felt the warmth of his encircling arms, the pressure of his mouth against hers. He kissed her again and again, and hot waves of pleasure flowed through her, mounting with the intensity of the incoming tide that beat against the rocks, setting free an erotic yearning deep inside her that clamored to be fulfilled. Her fingers tangled compulsively in his hair and she pressed closer. The sharp cry of a gull echoed her heart's own cry of ecstasy and she wanted him to never let go.

She was unprepared when he gently released her. "I think we'd better check on the children," he said. He was breathing hard, and his voice was hoarse.

He's running away again, she thought in puzzled frustration, as he took her hand and they walked back the way they had come.

CHAPTER TEN

THE RECREATION ROOM was full of children. Some were clustered at big tables, playing dominoes or checkers. In one corner, two games of Ping-Pong were in progress. Other children were gathered in groups, talking and laughing. Ginger detached herself from one group and ran over to them.

"Marcy, I learned a new song!"

"You did? That's great. You'll have to sing it to me when we get to the cottage." But Marcy's eyes were scanning the room. Where was Davey? Steve, too, was searching.

"Davey? Where's Davey?" he asked. "Ginger, where's your brother?"

"Don't know."

Marcy's heart lurched and she felt a tiny ball of fear settling in the pit of her stomach. The fear grew as they toured the building and still didn't find him. Steve approached one of the play leaders.

"He was here a few minutes ago, with that group." She pointed to several boys stationed around a video game, boys a little older than Davey. Marcy thought it was just like Davey to join them—always trying to act older.

When questioned, one of the boys said yes, Davey had been there but he'd gone out.

"That way," he added, indicating the rear door.

When they didn't find him outside, or receive an answer to their calls, Marcy was really frightened. Had he ventured out too far, become lost? Been lured away? She tried to stifle her fears, telling herself she was being ridiculous. He'd probably just returned to the cottage.

"I'll go check the cottages while you look around here," she told Steve. He nodded, already starting toward a wooded area.

She went back into the hall and left Ginger in the care of Amy, a member of the Placer County staff. When she didn't find Davey at either cottage, she ran to meet Steve halfway. He looked just as strained and anxious as she felt.

"I didn't find him, either," she cried. "Oh, Steve what can have happened to him?"

"Nothing's happened to him!" His voice was steady. "He's just playing somewhere. We'll find him. I'll try again behind the rec hall."

Marcy had difficulty keeping up with him. This time they walked farther into the woods, calling his name over and over again. There was no answer, and as it grew darker and colder, her apprehension mounted.

"Shouldn't we give the alarm," she asked, "so other people can help us look for him?"

"Not yet," he said. "Not yet. We'll find him."

"Anybody could get lost in these woods! And suppose he hurt himself and can't move, and—"

"He can hear," Steve said, and he called even louder, "Davey! Davey! Where are you?"

Steve continued to call, but she heard the anxiety in his voice, and an ominous chill swept through her. She remembered his desolation that first day, when the death of his sister had really hit him. Dear God, don't let him lose Davey, too!

"Look, I'm going back to get some of the men," she said, tugging at his sleeve. "They could spread out in different directions and—"

"No!" he said. "I don't want to scare him with a lot of people converging around."

"Scare him! He's lost and he's only five years old, and he's already scared. And you are being impossibly stubborn!" Could it be that he didn't want to face the fact that the boy might be lost, really lost? She felt frustrated, angry and very, very frightened. "You just don't want to ask for help," she shouted. "You don't want people to think you can't take care of your own. And it doesn't matter to you that anything could have happened to him! Don't you realize someone could have lured him away? Some pervert could have wandered up the beach and—"

"The beach!" Steve bolted through the trees toward the beach. Marcy hesitated a moment, looking back toward the conference grounds, then raced after him. Steve was well ahead of her and she scrambled through the dunes, her heart a heavy lump of fear, as the images reeled through her mind. The tide crashing onto the shore...Davey, helpless, caught under a rock as the water pounded in, rising higher and higher!

"Davey!" Marcy heard the relief in Steve's voice before she'd even made it as far as the beach. When she got there, she saw the tiny figure some distance away, walking slowly, nonchalantly, in their direction, trailing a stick in the wet sand. Steve was running toward him.

"Davey!" he yelled again. Now there was only anger in the sound, a hot fury that lashed out at the boy. By the time Marcy reached them, Steve was holding Davey by the shoulders and shaking him furiously. Marcy put out a hand to stop him, afraid he would hurt the child. But a moment later, Steve seemed to gain control of himself. Still, he kept a firm hold on Davey and spoke to him sternly.

"Just what are you doing out here alone, young man?"

"I...I...playing." He looked up at Steve with wide, scared eyes.

"Oh, Davey," Marcy cried, tears of relief running down her cheeks. "We thought you were lost."

"I...I wasn't losted." It was to Steve that Davey spoke, his eyes never leaving his uncle's face.

"Didn't I tell you to stay in the recreation hall with the other kids and the teachers?"

Davey nodded, and he looked so frightened that Marcy wanted to cry out, "You said you didn't want to scare him!" But she kept quiet, knowing that this was something between the boy and his uncle, and remembering how terrified Steve had been. When you were that frightened you got angry!

Steve gave Davey's shoulder another little shake. "Now, you listen to me, young man. And you listen hard! When I leave you somewhere, you don't take it upon yourself to walk out. You stay there until I, or the adult I left you with, says you can go. Do you understand that?" Again Davey nodded. "You're responsible to me. Me! You don't take it upon yourself and you don't ask some other kid. You get permission from me. Do you understand?"

"Yes, sir." The same respectful salutation, Marcy noted, that she had heard Davey give his father after a severe reprimand.

"Look at you! You came out here without a jacket, and your feet are all wet! You've been walking in the water?" Steve's voice was still scolding, but more gentle now. He took off his own jacket and wrapped it around Davey. Suddenly he put his arms around the boy and held him close. "I'm sorry I yelled at you, Davey. But I was really scared. I was scared because I care so much about you." He lifted Davey in his arms and hugged him hard, and Marcy saw a glint of tears in Steve's eyes. He cleared his throat, then said, rather gruffly, "We'd better get back to the cottage and put you in a tub of hot water. And I'm not standing for this kind of behavior anymore. Do you understand?"

"Yes," said Davey, his voice muffled against his uncle's neck.

As Marcy walked up the beach beside Steve, who carried Davey, she marveled at the union that had been born between them. It was as if uncle and nephew were enclosed in a world of their own.

"Steve," she heard Davey timidly say.

"Yes?"

"They laughed at me. I didn't want to play with them."

"Oh?" Steve hitched the boy closer to his shoulder. "And that's why you ran away?"

Davey's head bobbed up and down. "They said I was a sissy. Because I was afraid of that cat. It was a big cat, Steve." He raised his head. "A great big black cat, and its eyes...ooh! And it came by me and I was scared and everybody laughed. And I don't like them laughing at me."

Marcy felt a flash of annoyance at those older boys. No wonder they looked so sheepish when they were questioned about Davey.

"Something you'd better get used to," Steve said quietly. "You can't let other people goad you into doing something you shouldn't. Like making you run away. You know what I do when they laugh at me? I just laugh with them."

"You scared of cats?" Davey moved so abruptly that the jacket slipped. Steve, never pausing in his stride, pulled the coat closer around Davey.

"No," he said. "I'm scared of snakes."

"Yes," said Davey, in a voice that indicated that surely everybody was scared of snakes. "Like those big long ones I saw at the zoo that could wrap around you and squeeze you to death?"

"Yeah," Steve said. "There are snakes that are harmless too, but I'm scared of all of them." Marcy noticed that Davey listened intently as Steve told him about his phobia and about how the other men would tease him. He said that just a few months before in Mexico, one of the men had dangled a harmless garden snake in front of him. "He shouldn't have done that. I upset the whole camp. I jumped up, kicking like crazy, threw my grub away and knocked over other food, too. I was like a jumping jack."

Davey giggled.

"See there?" Steve said. "You're laughing at me, too. Just like they did. But I didn't run away. I just laughed with them and said 'Okay, so I'm scared of snakes. Everybody's scared of something.'"

Marcy studied Steve's face, still visible through the gathering darkness. His tender concern was evident, and she heard the fatherly conviction in his voice as he told Davey, in his own special way, that it was all right to be afraid, that he need only face up to his fears and never be ashamed. She had not believed it possible. How could she have known that Steve Prescott would be the best thing that could have happened to Diane's children? She reached out and touched him lightly on the arm. He smiled down at her, then set Davey on the ground.

"All right, tiger! You're getting a bit heavy. Hold on to Marcy. She needs help getting through these dunes."

So they walked the rest of the way together, with Davey between them, the three of them holding hands.

It seemed so right.

ACTUALLY, STEVE THOUGHT a few days after he returned home, he hadn't got too much out of those lectures at Asilomar. But, remembering that day on the beach, he was glad he'd gone. He'd been so terrified, he'd lost control, but somehow he had gained Davey's affection. Somehow, that day had brought a change in the boy's attitude.

He liked it. He liked Davey coming home, shouting, "Steve! Steve! Guess what happened at school!" Or, when he'd completed a drawing, "Hey, Steve! Look at this." Or, working with numbers, "Steve, does a three go this way?" Yes, Steve decided, he liked it. Even Ginger, following Davey's lead as usual, had grown a little closer.

Everything seemed to be going well. He'd just about got their legal entanglements straightened out enough to pass on to a lawyer. The real-estate agent had sent pictures of a small, attractive country house in Connecticut. He wanted to show them to Marcy, see what she thought. But he had a feeling that this house was exactly what he'd been looking for. Then, just as everything seemed to be falling into place, two things happened.

First, Mrs. Evans, the almost-suitable housekeeper with excellent references and no encumbrances, tendered her resignation, effective immediately. She had to go back home to care for her bedridden sister whose husband had just died.

"I hate to leave you so suddenly," she said. "But you see how it is, Mr. Prescott."

Yes, Steve told her, he saw how it was, and he gave her a bonus plus a return ticket to New York. Then, inwardly cursing with frustration but resigned to the inevitable, he braced himself to start the housekeeper hunt all over again. He called Mrs. Chisholm who cheerfully agreed to return on an interim basis until he could find another "live-in." She even said she would stay nights when he was out of town, because her sister was now living with her and could look after her children on those occasions.

When he called his secretary in New York and told her to start searching again, he began to understand how things had been with his own father. He'd never had much money at his disposal, and he'd had no one to help him—certainly not an efficient secretary to advertise for applicants and then sift through them. I suppose, Steve thought, feeling more kindly toward his father than he ever had, he did the very best he could.

The day after Mrs. Chisholm's return, Steve got a call from Ginger's nursery school. Ginger had fallen off the monkey bars and hurt her arm. They couldn't tell how seriously because she wouldn't let anyone touch her.

Monkey bars! Steve frowned as he jumped into his car and drove rapidly toward the school. Why would they have such a contraption in a nursery school? And why, since they had one, wasn't it protected underneath with padding or sawdust or something? Anyway, wasn't it too cold and wet for her to play outside?

Poor little kid. So scared she wouldn't let anyone touch her. He had a sudden thought. Maybe she wouldn't let *him* touch her, either. He wondered if he should call Marcy at her office and ask her to come with him.

"Steve!" Ginger cried, running toward him as soon as she saw him. "I hurted myself, Steve!"

"It's going to be all right," he soothed, lifting her gently into his arms, careful to avoid her injury. "We're going to get you all fixed up." He decided to leave his car at the school and take a taxi to the hospital so he could hold Ginger on his lap all the way there. He held and comforted her while the doctor set her arm, which turned out to be broken. And overriding his anger that the school authorities had allowed such a thing to happen, overriding his pity for the tiny child with her arm in a cast, was the exultant thought—*she had run to him.*

"Lord a mercy," Mrs. Chisholm muttered, as she helped a drowsy Ginger out of her jacket. "You've got to be more careful, child. Now, come on and I'll put you to bed. And after you have a nice sleep, I'll make something special for you to eat. I'll even feed you myself." Still fussing tenderly, the housekeeper led Ginger to her room.

SEVERAL DAYS LATER, when the children were playing in Davey's room after dinner, Mrs. Chisholm had a talk with Steve. She poured him a cup of coffee, shaking her head in sympathy. "Lord a mercy, Mr. Prescott, I don't know what you're going to do with these children. You'll run yourself ragged trying to keep up with them. You know what I think? I think you'd better get yourself a wife."

"Ah, Mrs. Chisholm," he said, as he watched her clear the table. "Who'd want a vagabond like me?"

"Humph! Most any woman would like to get her hooks into you, the way you throw your money around!"

"Maybe," Steve said, laughing. "But hooks aren't exactly what I'm looking for."

"Oh, Lord, you're just like everybody else! You want love, sweet love! I'm not talking about love. I'm saying get yourself a wife." She picked up a pile of dishes and started toward the kitchen.

"Hey, wait a minute," Steve called, being in a teasing mood. "Aren't love and marriage supposed to go together like—"

"It just ain't so." Still holding the dishes, she turned to face him. "The way these love matches start today and end tomorrow, you'd be better off hiring yourself a wife!"

"*Hiring* a wife!" Steve had become accustomed to Mrs. Chisholm's outspoken and sometimes outlandish ideas, but this was too much. "Now, Mrs. Chisholm, surely you don't mean—"

"I meant exactly what I said. Hire a wife. You want another cup of coffee?"

"I'll get it," he said, following her into the kitchen. He chuckled as he filled his mug from the steaming pot. "No," he said, shaking his head, "I think it's easier to hire a housekeeper."

"You think so?" Mrs. Chisholm turned from the sink to look at him. "How long have you had these children?"

"Er, I, let's see." He blew on his coffee. "Maybe... almost two months."

"And in those two months you've had three housekeepers, including me twice on a temporary basis. Plus a lot of help from that social worker next door. Isn't that right?"

"Well, yes," Steve admitted.

"The thing is, Mr. Prescott—" she pointed a finger at him "—what you need is more than a housekeeper. You've been hanging around here these past two months and you've hardly been to work at all. You need somebody who can go out and get that child, take her to the hospital and get her arm fixed. And they're growing up. Pretty soon, you'll need somebody to help 'em with their homework. Take 'em to Little League and Girl Scouts. You see, I've been through this. And I can tell you there's more to raising children than keeping a house."

"You've got a point there," he agreed. He leaned against the counter and took a swallow of coffee. "Now, just in case I find somebody who agrees to shoulder all this responsibility, what do I offer in return?"

"Shoot! Any woman would be glad to settle for the kind of security you could give her." She turned back to the sink and began to load the dishwasher.

"Okay." He smiled. "So I find her, and she agrees. How is all this going to be arranged, this hired marriage business?"

"Just like any other business. You write up a paper. Sign it. What do you call that? A contract? You know more about this kind of thing than I do. You're in business."

"Marriage by contract, huh?"

"Sure. They used to do it all the time. In the olden days, and in lots of those foreign countries. Sometimes they'd contract a marriage even before the child grew up. According to what they could offer each other."

"I see." Steve, still smiling, took another swallow of coffee. "Now suppose something happens—like one of the parties just happens to fall in love with somebody else?"

"But that's just it. You've ruled out the love business, so you're both free to do whatever you please. Fall in and out of love as many times as you want. Just so long as you don't mess up your contract."

Steve choked on his coffee. Mrs. Chisholm paused in her task and looked at him curiously. "You all right, Mr. Prescott?"

Steve cleared his throat, wiped his eyes and handed her the cup. "Yes, I...I'm all right. But you...free love, too!" he exclaimed in mock surprise. "Mrs. Chisholm, you amaze me. I never thought that you...of all people—":

"Oh, go along with you! You're just leading me on. Not paying me a bit of mind. Even though I'm making good sense." She measured out the detergent, locked the dishwasher and turned it on. "You want to marry for love. Love! Probably that young Miss America whose picture you've got sitting on the dresser in there, that lady who keeps calling you all the time. She's pretty, all right, but I doubt she's what you need. I can tell by the way she talks. 'Now how is he managing with the dear little ones?'" she mimicked in tones of exaggerated sweetness and managed to sound, Steve thought, just like Trish. But before he could comment, Mrs. Chisholm gave him a gentle shove. "Now, get away with you. So I can finish in here and bathe those children. And you needn't laugh! You know I'm right."

Still chuckling, Steve went into the living room. Well, she's right about Trish, he decided. Matter of fact, she was right about a lot of things.

"I'm going now. See you in the morning," Mrs. Chisholm said an hour or so later, as she bustled toward the door. "You think about what I told you, Mr. P."

"I'm thinking, I'm thinking!" Steve protested laughingly, as he opened the promised bedtime storybook. The children, already in their pajamas, were waiting, Davey on the arm of his chair, and Ginger on his lap. She'd snuggled as close as she could get, considering that she had a cast on one arm and a tight hold on Lilli Ann with the other.

"Oh, come on in, Miss Wilson," he heard Mrs. Chisholm say. "I'm just leaving."

Then the door shut, and Marcy was standing there in jeans and a pullover. She held a basket in her hand, and she looked, Steve thought, absolutely bewitching. How did she manage to look that way no matter what she wore? The things Mrs. Chisholm had said spun crazily in his mind. Marcy! If he were going to hire a wife . . . But—he couldn't do a crazy thing like that!

Marcy's breath caught in her throat as she observed the little group by the fire. They looked so . . . so right. Her heart warmed at the thought that this man had so quickly gained the trust and affection of these children. She wished . . . What did she wish?

"What's that, Marcy? What you got?" Ginger scrambled down from her uncle's arms and Marcy suddenly noticed the cast.

"Ginger! What happened?"

"I fell and I broke it. And look, the doctor signed the cast. Will you sign it too, Marcy?"

"Oh, baby, of course I will. But you must be more careful." Marcy put down the basket and started toward Ginger. But Ginger was distracted by the mewing sound coming from the basket and ran to see.

"Marcy, you've got a kitten! Where did you get him? Can I hold him?" She ran back to deposit Lilli Ann in Steve's lap and went to kneel by the basket. "Let me hold him."

"Sit down first." Marcy placed the kitten in Ginger's lap. "Now you have to be gentle." As Ginger stroked the kitten, Marcy glanced at Davey. Making a routine call at one of her foster homes earlier that day, she'd been offered her choice from a litter of kittens. She had immediately thought of Davey. Maybe, if he began with such a tiny kitten, he could overcome his fear of cats. He did seem curious, but so far had not moved from the safety of his uncle's chair. Finally it was Steve who persuaded him to approach the kitten.

"Come on. Maybe we men had better take a look at what Marcy dragged in." The four of them sat on the floor and watched the kitten vainly trying to catch the rubber mouse Ginger dangled before him.

"No, Ginger!" Davey cried. "You're teasing him. Here, kitty. I'll get it for you."

Marcy held her breath as Davey took the mouse from Ginger and gave it to the kitten. Then, cautiously reaching out one finger, he stroked the soft gray ball of fur. Marcy felt Steve's touch on her arm and looked across to see him wink at her.

"That was a very thoughtful, very smart thing you did," he told her much later, when the children were in bed.

"I think so too," she said with a grin. "And just as soon as Davey becomes more accustomed to Mr. Kitty Cat, I'm giving him to you, litter box and all."

"Thanks a lot." Steve grimaced. "Hey, wait a minute," he said, as she started to pick up the basket. "I want to show you something." He took an envelope from the coffee table and sat down on the floor beside her, spreading out the pictures. "This is a place in Connecticut that I might be buying. What do you think?"

"Oh, Steve, it's beautiful! Look at all these trees for Davey to climb."

"And there's a small stable. See? Right here. They can have their ponies."

"It seems perfect, Steve."

He showed her the pictures and talked about the house. Six bedrooms with servant quarters, on six acres of ground. How large a staff did she think he would need to care for the place? He was going up next week to look at it and check on schools. Did she like it? Did she think it was a good plan?

"Perfect! Beautiful!" she said over and over again, through the constriction in her throat. She had to blink rapidly to hold back the tears. She smiled and talked brightly about what a lovely house it was, what a great setting. But never in her life had she felt such a wave of sadness and longing. She couldn't bear to think of this apartment empty and the children so far away. And Steve. She watched him as he talked, watched that sweet smile, the way his eyes crinkled. Steve. Oh, God! It was Steve she would miss. She...she...dear Lord, she loved him! The realization was such a shock to her that she missed his next words.

"What . . . what did you say?" she stuttered.

"I said would you like to live here?" he asked, his finger on the picture of the house.

"Oh, why, yes. Of course. Almost anybody would like to live in a place like this."

"No. What I mean is, er . . ." He hesitated. "Er, hey, Marcy, would you marry me?" He was astounded. Had he meant to say that? Still, it seemed right. Mrs. Chisholm . . .

"Would I . . . ?" She stared at him, hardly believing that he had said it. But he had. The joy welled up in her, filling her heart with so much gladness that—

"Now, wait a minute," She was looking so shocked that he felt he had to explain quickly. "I don't mean a real marriage. It would be more like . . . like a job."

"A job?" But hadn't he said *marry*?

"I know it sounds crazy. But it does make sense. Actually, Mrs. Chisholm suggested it."

Marcy listened to him explain something she couldn't understand, something Mrs. Chisholm had said about how he needed more than just a housekeeper, and what he should do was hire a wife. *Hire a wife?* His words seeped through the confusion of her muddled thoughts. She was astounded that anyone would think of such a thing! How dare he suggest that she... She had thought... No! She stifled the feeling, refusing to acknowledge the hurt and the disappointment.

"Marcy, I vowed a long time ago that I would never fall in love with anyone. I don't want... I don't believe in love, in this love-forever-after stuff." His own mother. He had loved her so much! And she had just walked away. Had never come back. "What Mrs. Chisholm said makes sense. It makes good sense. We'd both be free. Emotionally free, I mean. We could go our separate ways. You wouldn't have to answer to me for anything. If there was someone else in your life I'd... well, I'd just look the other way."

"Oh. I see. Open marriage, you mean?" She was surprised to find that she could speak so calmly.

"Well, yes. Of course, we'd both have to be discreet. But you could have, er, friends, and so could I."

"I see." *You could have as many women as you chose, couldn't you? You just wouldn't have to be sneaky about it.* She felt a rising tide of anger.

"But we'd both always be there," he said. "For the children."

"I see. For the children."

"Legally, you'd really be my wife, Marcy. You could have anything you wanted. Share everything I own."

"I see." *Everything but love.*

"What do you think, Marcy?"

"I think," she said, making her voice sound pleasant, "that Mrs. Chisholm, whom I would never have suspected of such modern ideas, has come up with an excellent plan. And I think it's marvelous of you. Such a grand gesture. Really wonderful to make such a tremendous sacrifice for Davey and Ginger. To contract a marriage for the sake of those children. And I am sure—" her voice trembled as she stood up "—I am sure that somewhere among your acquaintances, you will find a perfect woman, someone who will be glad to contract such a marriage. But it will not be me!"

"Oh, but Marcy," Steve cried, getting to his feet and gazing seriously down at her, "there's nobody else, no other woman who could love the children as much as you do. Wait," he said, as she picked up her basket. "Listen, I—"

"I've heard enough! And you listen, Steve Prescott. I'm sorry, but I'm not as modern as your Mrs. Chisholm. And I'm not as self-sacrificing as you. And I do believe in that love-forever-after stuff. And I will not enter into any business marriage."

"Oh, now, Marcy, don't feel like that. It wouldn't be... Look, you and I... we get on well together."

She stared at him, suddenly remembering the way he had kissed her, the way she had felt. Here was a man who didn't believe in love but was an expert in the physical expression of it. She was so distressed by the thought, so ashamed of the erotic sensations aroused by it, that she grabbed at the basket, frightening the kitten, who jumped out. She scrambled after him, dumped him back in his basket and ran out, slamming the door behind her, rushing to the safety of her own apartment, hurrying, before the tears came.

CHAPTER ELEVEN

SHE COULDN'T CRY! She wasn't crying. She had no reason to cry!

Safe at last in the seclusion of her own apartment,
Marcy brushed a tear from her cheek and placed the
basket near the fireplace. She sank onto her knees beside it, picked up the kitten and held him close. She
stroked him, trying to sort out the tangled web of her
emotions.

"You're a darling little kitty cat. You're going to love
living here with me," she crooned, trying to deny the
hurt and disappointment that were sweeping through
her. The shame!

No. Not shame!

*Yes. Shame! All he had to do was hold out his arms,
and you would have fallen into them before he could say
"I love you"—which, please note, he did not say!*

No. That's not true. I would not have fallen into his
arms. And I was not waiting for protestations of love!
Marcy bit her lip and shook her head vehemently.

"I can't keep calling you 'Kitty.' What am I going to
call you?" Her finger traced his delicate backbone, and
the kitten purred with emphatic contentment.

She'd planned to ask Davey to name him. Davey.
Ginger.

Marcy Wilson, you'd better keep away from those kids. They'll be gone soon. And Steve. Steve will be gone.

You're in love with him!

No. It just wasn't possible. She couldn't be in love with a man who was insensitive enough to...*hire a wife!* He was impossible! He was an idiot! What made him think she would consent to such a ridiculous arrangement? Did he imagine she was so eager to get married that she'd jump at some unconventional half-baked idea like that!

Oh! She was still furious. She felt feverish and restless. She wanted to get outside, in the fresh brisk air, and run and run and run through the park. But she couldn't, it was too late and too dark. Quickly she flung open her patio door, then tugged the minitrampoline out of the hall closet.

The little kitten purred, stretched, placed one paw over the other and watched with interest as his new mistress bounced and bounced and bounced, all the while muttering to herself, "He's crazy. Absolutely crazy! Impossible! How dare he suggest such a thing!"

WELL, DAMN IT! He had fumbled that one. Steve gave a log a vicious kick, and slammed the fire screen shut.

Maybe he'd taken the wrong approach. No, damn it! She hadn't listened.

It made sense. The more he thought about it, the more sense it made. For her, too. Here she was, working so hard at such an impossible job, frustrated because she couldn't find the perfect home for every problem child. And what did she get for all that work? Peanuts! Otherwise her bank account wouldn't be overdrawn and she wouldn't have to struggle through her bills with that Peter-Paul routine. They obviously weren't paying her enough to live on.

If she married him, she'd never have to skimp. For a moment he mused on that thought, anticipating the pleasure—to take care of her, to give her anything she wanted.

Well, damn it! What did she want? He ran a distracted hand through his hair as he paced the floor.

Love. She wanted *love*. The very word frightened him. Never, not even in the deepest throes of sensual passion, had he whispered the words "I love you" to any woman. Love meant commitment. Promise. And promise of pain when it was over. Mrs. Chisholm had the right idea. If you ruled out love, you ruled out pain. Love was a game people played, making promises of "forever," promises they never intended to keep.

Suddenly he stopped pacing, and stood very still.

Was someone making such promises to Marcy? That Gerald guy? Good old-fashioned friendship, she'd said. Horn Rims? What had she said about Horn Rims? Either one of them could be telling her *anything*! Marcy was so gullible. And she'd said it herself—she believed in that love-forever-after stuff. If a guy played the "I love you" game and played it long enough ...

But if she married him, she'd have everything to gain and nothing to lose. He wasn't playing games. He'd been honest with her. Didn't she know she'd be better off with him than falling for the love game? Didn't she know that? He reached for his phone. He'd call her and tell her, right this minute. Then, through the wall, he heard it—that rhythmic jumping. Did she get on that blasted trampoline every time she got mad?

He took his hand from the phone. Not tonight. Give her time to cool off. She'd run out of here fighting mad. And just because he'd asked her to marry him!

Tomorrow. He'd take her out to dinner. He'd convince her that it made sense. That it was to their mutual benefit. And to the children's. One thing he was sure of. If he did hire a wife, arrange a contract marriage, whatever, it wouldn't be with anyone but Marcy Wilson!

HE PHONED before she went to work the next morning. "Marcy, we need to talk."

"I don't think so." Cold. Crisp.

Damn it! She was still mad. "Look, you haven't heard me out."

"I've heard all I need to hear. And I'm in a hurry. I don't want to be late for work."

"Wait. Wait. Don't hang up. Listen, how about dinner tonight?"

"I'm busy tonight."

He might have known. "Lunch? How about lunch?"

"I don't think I can make it. I'm really busy today."

"Oh, for Pete's sake! They do let you eat, don't they? I'll meet you at your office. See you then." He hung up quickly before she could protest.

Busy! He looked out the patio door at the pouring rain. He just bet she'd be busy. Probably sitting at her desk doing paperwork. Nobody with any sense would be out in this weather. The wind whistled around the building and the rain was coming down in sheets.

He got to her office about eleven, and it was a good thing he did, for she was on her way out. In this weather? He couldn't believe it. But there she was.

Black umbrella bent against the wind, black raincoat whipping around her legs. Black ankle boots plodding through the puddles to her car. Trust Marcy to be all matched up, he thought, as he turned up the collar of his raincoat and hurried after her.

"Wait! I thought we were going to lunch."

"I told you I don't have time to go to lunch. I've got to go out and transfer this kid to another home."

"Then let me take you. We could stop for a bite on the way and—"

"No, thanks. I prefer to drive myself." She was having a struggle trying to hold on to the umbrella while she unlocked the car. He took the umbrella from her and held it while she got in, protesting that he could take her wherever she needed to go. When she shook her head and reached for the umbrella, he went around to the other side of the car and slid in beside her.

"You should always lock both doors," he said, grinning. "Anybody could get into your car."

"I can see that," she snapped.

"I'd rather drive, but if this is the way you want it, I won't complain," he said as he placed the umbrella on the floor behind his seat.

"This isn't the way I want it," she said through clenched teeth. "Why don't you get out and let me go about my business!"

"Who's stopping you? Drive on. We can have our little discussion en route."

"If it's the same little discussion you started last night, there's no point. Look, I'm already late."

"So drive on." He pushed the seat back to make more room for his legs.

"Oh!" She put the car in gear and swung out of the parking lot with such a terrific burst of speed that he was jerked forward.

"Be careful!" he shouted. "Safety first and all that—"

"Fasten your seat belt if you're scared." She drove onto the freeway, never slackening her speed.

"It's all right. Quite all right." He relaxed against the seat. "I'm perfectly willing to risk life and limb just to have a little straight talk, knowing that should I expire in the attempt, Ginger and Davey will be safe in the arms of Placer County Child Welfare."

"Oh, be quiet!" she said. But their speed diminished a trifle and he couldn't help smiling. Even so, the little Volkswagen rocked dangerously, buffeted by wind and rain.

"'Over hill, over dale! Through the wind and the hail, And those caissons go rolling along,'" he sang.

"Oh, be quiet," she said again.

"All right, all right," he said serenely. "But, if you ask me, this is a hell of a day to transfer a child."

"Life's little tragedies don't stop for the weather," she informed him crisply. "And it's hard enough for a child to be moved from one house to another, without being delayed from one day to another."

Suddenly he felt depressed. Sorry for any child who had to be shoved around like that. She had pulled off the highway now, pulled up before a neat little bungalow.

"Can I help?" he asked.

"Yes," she said, reaching behind him for the umbrella. "Get in the back seat. Angie will have to sit up front so I can talk to her."

The back seat was a tight squeeze, and he was made even more uncomfortable when Marcy returned and pushed a suitcase in beside him. Angie was a pale-faced little girl of about eight with wide frightened eyes. She was crying softly. Marcy did not start the car immediately, but sat for a time talking quietly with the little girl.

From the conversation, Steve gathered that the child had been abused by her mother, had been taken to an emergency home and was now being transferred to a more permanent foster home.

"Your mother's going through a very hard time right now," Marcy told her. "She wants you to stay with Mrs. Enright for a while, until things get better. You'll like Mrs. Enright. She's very nice, and she has cows and chickens. And she has another little girl just about your age.... Of course you'll see your mother. She'll come and visit you very soon."

Marcy finally started the car, but she kept talking, reassuring the child as she drove. By the time they reached the farmhouse, Steve felt like crying himself. How did Marcy stand it? Sad cases like this, day after day after day.

When Marcy and Angie went into the house, he climbed out of the car and stood for a moment in the steady downpour, stretching his legs. Then he got back in. The rain beat on the roof and washed against the windshield. He stared through the rain at the split-rail fence, thinking about the little girl, wondering about her future. He hoped she would be happy.

"Doesn't it ever get you down?" he asked Marcy when she finally returned. "This kind of situation over and over again?"

"Somebody has to do it."

He was silent as she drove out of the farmyard and back onto the freeway. It was some time before he could force his mind to return to his own predicament. He wanted to take a more diplomatic approach this time. Last night, lying awake, he'd rehearsed it several times. But now, everything he'd planned to say was completely gone from his mind.

"I'm going back east next week," he ventured. "To look at that place. Maybe make an offer."

"That's nice."

"I thought you might take a few days off and go with me. To help me decide."

She gave him a quick incredulous glance. "Fly to New York? You must be nuts. I think you're perfectly capable of making a decision all by yourself."

"Marcy, listen to me." He paused. Hell, what *had* he planned to say? Whatever it was, he'd meant to say it in some quiet, exotic restaurant. Not racking about in this little car in the middle of a windstorm, having to shout above the roar of traffic, the clatter of those damned windshield wipers. "Look, you haven't had lunch. Couldn't we stop somewhere and—"

"No, I don't have time," she was saying when the car suddenly swerved and began to bump along, crazily out of balance. She managed to pull to the shoulder and stop. "Darn," she said. "I think I have a flat tire."

"Darn!" he said ten minutes later, as he placed the last lug in the hubcap, then wrenched the wheel free. "No wonder it went flat. You were riding on threads, Marcy. Will you stop hovering over me with that umbrella!"

"I just want to help."

"You can help by staying out of my way," he said, lifting the wheel toward the trunk.

She followed, still trying to shield him with the umbrella. "This is awful," she moaned. "I knew I should have bought tires last month."

"It appears that you should have," he said, as he loosened the spare from its rack. "This one doesn't look much better than the one that blew. Marcy, will you please get in the car? There's no need for both of us to get soaked."

"But I want to help. What can I . . . can I hold something?"

He put down the tire, took her none too gently by the arm and herded her into the passenger seat.

"Get in," he ordered, taking the umbrella and closing it. "And take this thing with you." He handed it to her, then slammed the door. Wiping the rain from his face, he returned to his task.

"Women! 'I knew I should have bought tires last month,'" he repeated to himself. "From the looks of these she should have bought them last year. And the way she drives . . ." He cursed as he shoved the wheel into place. She could have been killed, driving on tires like these. As he tightened the lug nuts, he shuddered and it was not from the cold.

"I'm sorry," she said, when he at last slid into the driver's seat. "I knew we should have called Triple-A. You're wet through."

"You're right about that. Just as wet as I would have got if I'd walked to a telephone." He surveyed the traffic, then pulled onto the freeway. "I don't understand you, Marcy. I really don't. Driving on tires like these. It's downright dangerous. Don't you know that?"

"Yes. I know." She bit her lip. "I meant to get tires. But...well, something came up."

I just bet it did, he thought. Robbing Peter to pay Paul, and never mind about essentials like tires! That settled it. She'd better marry him. She needed taking care of.

"Where are you going?" she asked, as they turned off the freeway.

"To the nearest garage. We're not driving another mile on those threads."

"Oh, for goodness' sake," she protested. "That spare will certainly last until we get back to the office. I'll take care of it tomorrow."

"Yeah." I just bet you will!

"Really, Steve, you needn't bother."

"I'm bothering. You could kill yourself driving on these bald tires."

"My tires are none of your business, Steve Prescott."

"Now you tell me!" he said, grinning. "If you'd told me that half an hour ago, I wouldn't be all wet and half-frozen."

"Oh, you know what I mean! I...listen, I'd rather go to Pete's gas station in Auburn. I trust him." Pete, Marcy was thinking, would let her charge a tire until she got paid. But Steve had already pulled into a gas station and was getting out of the car.

"You have tires to fit a Volkswagen?" he asked the attendant.

"Sure," the man answered. Marcy's heart sank. Her Visa was up to its limit. But maybe she had enough in her bank account for one tire. How much did the darn things cost?

"We'll take five," Steve said.

Five! She jumped out of the car and ran around to confront them. "No, Steve, we don't need five. We—" Steve's lips were on her parted mouth before she could finish the sentence. Afterward, she was too stunned to speak.

"We certainly do need five, honey," Steve said, shaking her gently. "*You* didn't have to get out in the rain to change a tire. Wives!" he exclaimed, turning to the attendant. "They think all a car needs is gas." He took his wallet from his pocket and handed the man a credit card. "You'd better fill it up and check the oil. Take all the time you need. We'll be in the coffee shop across the street. Come on, sweetheart." Steve put an arm around Marcy and propelled her out of the station.

"Steve Prescott!" she said, panting as he hurried her across the street before the light changed. "I didn't want all those tires. And you told that man… You made him think I'm your wife!"

"Only way to shut you up," he said, reaching for the door of the coffee shop.

"You had no right to give anyone the impression that we're—"

"Sssh!" he whispered. "Folks will think we're having a spat."

"That's just what we are having!" she snapped. But he only smiled.

"Two," he said to the hostess. "Just my wife and myself."

A joke! Love, marriage—it was all a big joke to him. She followed the hostess across the restaurant, bright with Christmas lights and decorations. Only a few tables were occupied, since the noon-hour rush was over.

"Coffee. Hot, hot coffee," Steve said to the waitress, as soon as they were settled in one of the more secluded booths. "Coffee, Marcy?"

She nodded, her anger fading as she looked at him. His hair was still damp and his clothes were soaked, because he'd taken off his raincoat to change the tire. He must have been chilled to the bone. And he had not once complained. Suddenly, she was glad for his sake that they'd stopped. Glad they could rest for a while in the warmth of this place filled with the rich aroma of coffee and the soft, haunting sound of Christmas music. She had to admit that she was grateful to Steve. What would she have done if he hadn't been with her?

"I . . . I do appreciate your changing the tire," she said, "and everything." Oh, Lord! How was she ever going to repay him? Maybe she could borrow the money from Jennifer. "And I'll pay you for the tires as soon as I can," she added.

He waved his hand in a gesture of dismissal.

"Consider it a gift—for both of us."

"Both of us?"

"Your life and my sanity." He chuckled. "I'd have nightmares thinking of you skidding around on those tires."

"All the same," she started to say, then silently finished, *I am going to repay you,* as the waitress placed two mugs of steaming coffee before them and asked if they were ready to order.

"Steak sandwich for me," Steve said. "Marcy?"

She scanned the menu quickly. "Split pea soup," she decided.

"And soup for my wife," he said, his lips twitching.

"You should stop that!" Marcy scolded when the waitress had left.

"Stop what?"

"Joking about this wife business."

"Who's joking?" He was still grinning as he spoke, but then, looking almost serious, he reached across the table to take her hand. "Think about it, Marcy. Really think about it. It would be a good deal."

"A good deal?" she repeated, drawing her hand away. That was how he thought of marriage. A good deal!

"Sure." He took a swallow of coffee, then put the mug down. "All right. Admittedly it's a good deal for me. I'd never worry about Ginger and Davey if you were there to look after them. But it would be a great plan for you, too, Marcy. Don't you see that?"

"No. I don't think so. And really, Steve, I don't want to discuss it."

"There would be a lot of advantages for you," he continued as if she hadn't spoken. "It's funny, you know. I got the impression you were so efficient. And I guess you are—with your job and the children. But not with yourself." He shook his head. "You need somebody to take care of you, Marcy."

"I've been taking pretty good care of myself for some time!"

"That's debatable, Marcy. Anyway, I'm offering you a very practical plan."

Practical!

"I don't want to talk about it!" she snapped. "Just because you changed my tire doesn't mean you've changed my mind."

"But that's just it. You need somebody around to change your tires. To look after things like that." *Pay your bills.* He leaned toward her. "I'm not trying to shackle you or tie you down. You'd be perfectly free. And listen, I thought of something else. All that stuff you were telling me about the kind of children's home you would like to see developed? You said it could be a better alternative than the foster parent program."

"Yes." Strange he should remember that.

"Well, if you married me, you wouldn't be working in the system. And you wouldn't be under any obligation to them. You could take your time. Write up your ideas, plan the kind of program you prefer. And then make a proposal or whatever you call it. Maybe some county or foundation could be talked into starting that kind of home on an experimental basis. My company would contribute to the funding. I promise. You might accomplish more with the stroke of a pen than you could ever accomplish running around with these kids the way you do. Can't you see that, Marcy? Later on, other counties might decide to copy the idea."

"You know something, Steve? You have a point there. I wonder why I never thought of it myself. But," she added, shaking her head, "I don't have to marry anyone to write up a plan."

"But don't you see? If you're going to come up with an effective proposal, you'll have to be independent. Free to speak your own piece. Under no obligation to anyone, including me. Except for the kids, of course. We'd both be free to pursue our own interests. Wouldn't you like that?" He paused, as the waitress brought their orders. "Very quick service. Thank you." He smiled up at the waitress, and Marcy felt a stab of pain as she watched the girl glow under the influence of that smile.

Yes, she thought. He'd be free to smile, to touch or kiss anyone he wanted . . . Tricia? And I would go crazy with jealousy. No. I wouldn't be jealous. I couldn't be. I'm not in love with him!

"Marcy, are you in love?"

"What?" His question caught her by surprise, and she felt her face grow warm.

"Are you in love with someone?"

"No. No, indeed I'm not," she answered, perhaps a shade too emphatically.

"Then why not marry me?" he asked. "It might save you from heartbreak. Believe me, Marcy," he said earnestly. "This love stuff never lasts. It only leads to pain."

CHAPTER TWELVE

MARCY MANAGED TO RESIST all his arguments. She was relieved when they finally picked up her car and drove back to Auburn, where he reluctantly left her at her office. His voice with its joking, cajoling persuasions still lingered in her ears. His face swam before her, obscuring the forms on her desk, so that she accomplished very little in the late afternoon. She would have to stay away from him, would have to keep busy with other people, other things.

"I think I'll spend this weekend with you at the cabin," she told Jo. "I'd like to do some skiing."

"Oh, so nice of you to let us have you over." Jo laughed. "Are you driving up with us tonight?"

"No, I can't," Marcy said, remembering her date with Tom. "I'll probably get Tom or Gerald to drive me up in the morning. Then I'll stay over and come back with you guys Sunday night. Okay?"

"Okay," said Jo. "See you tomorrow."

At home, Marcy fed the kitten by herself, not calling Davey as she'd originally intended.

She must detach herself. She was too involved with these two children who would soon be out of her life altogether.

"Guess you'll have to be my company, Mr. Kitty Cat." She rubbed her chin against his soft fur and tried not to feel so disheartened. Still holding the kitten, she picked up the phone and called Jennifer. Jennifer, too, sounded a little depressed, but said she'd be glad to lend Marcy the money to pay for the tires. She said she was relieved Marcy had got her old ones replaced; bad tires were dangerous in this weather.

Marcy then washed her hair, and stood a long time in the shower, letting the hot steamy water pour over her. I'm pretty lucky, she thought as she toweled herself dry, to have the kind of hair that doesn't have to be set. In fact, I'm not too bad at all, she decided, brushing her hair and letting it fall into the full natural waves that framed her face.

I'm a chic size eight, and I'm smart. Well . . . maybe not too smart. I go overboard buying nice things, and I do lose track of my money sometimes. So I couldn't say I'm *smart* smart. But I'm not lazy, either. I do my job and I do it well. I'm good-natured and good company. And I can ski and swim and play a pretty fair game of tennis.

I'm *me*. I'm more than a housekeeper and a nanny, Steve Prescott!

She paused, her mind lingering on the name. She was seeing that dark hair, tumbled and wet, one lock falling across his forehead. Seeing his smile, remembering the feel of his arms around her, the touch of his lips on hers. Suddenly, her thoughts went racing wildly in another direction, the very direction she'd been trying to avoid.

I could love you, Steve Prescott! I could make you happy.

Tom took her dancing, and Marcy was glad she'd worn her turquoise silk with the full skirt that swirled so gracefully around her legs. Tom was a good dancer, and they both enjoyed the evening, staying out until two in the morning. Even so, he said he'd be happy to drive her up to Jo's the next morning.

STEVE HAD HEARD MARCY come in from work. Later, he heard the knock on her door, heard her go out with... He wasn't sure. He thought it was Horn Rims. He never paused in his reading of *A Visit From St. Nicholas.*

She'd told him she had a date. That was okay. "We'd each be free to go our separate ways," he had said. And he meant it. No ties. No commitments. He hoped she realized how he was taking it all in stride, all her men friends and her dates. He shifted Ginger in his lap and read on. "'The moon, on the crest of the new-fallen snow...'"

Of course she'd have to schedule time for the children. She was out tonight. Okay. Maybe in the morning, they could, all four of them, go down to the Nut Tree for brunch. "'And then in a twinkling I heard on the roof the prancing and pawing of each little hoof.'"

He wondered whom she was with. Probably Horn Rims. He hoped she had a miserable time.

MARCY REALLY HADN'T BELIEVED Tom when he told her to be ready at five. But there he was. And he didn't object when she explained that they had to take Mr. Kitty Cat with them.

"Mr. Kitty Cat?" he asked. "Doesn't he have a real name?"

"I'm still trying to decide," Marcy said, thinking of Davey and wondering if the poor little kitten would be forever nameless. Because part of her was waiting for Davey to name him, and part of her was keeping as far away from Davey as she could.

She liked Tom, she decided, although he did keep harping on the necessity of accumulating a stock portfolio. She didn't bother to tell him that she couldn't afford even *one* stock. Still, it was nice of him to drive her up to Jo's place. He stayed for most of the day and went skiing with her. Then she and Jo made spaghetti. The boys were ecstatic over Mr. Kitty Cat.

On Sunday, Marcy took Jo's boys to the beginners' hill, so Jo and her husband could go skiing together on the higher slopes. They drove back very late Sunday night.

There! That took care of the weekend.

WELL, DAMN! She'd been away the whole weekend.

When he found she wasn't there Saturday morning, he and the children had gone to the Nut Tree anyway. The kids seemed to enjoy the brunch and the rides. But... something was missing.

Marcy. He missed her laugh, seeing her dimples appear and disappear, watching her play with the kids.

She wasn't there Sunday, either, and he wondered where she was spending the weekend. And with whom.

MONDAY, SHE GOT UP EARLY and had breakfast at a coffee shop near the office. Her phone was ringing when she got to work. Her heart sank when she heard Mrs. Emory's voice.

"Somebody's got to talk to that boy, Miss Wilson. He's really getting out of hand."

"Jimmy? Oh, I'm sorry, Mrs. Emory. What's wrong?"

"Well, for one thing, he got in a fight at school last Thursday and got suspended. Had to stay home Friday. I tried to call you, but you weren't there. I just don't know what to do with him, Miss Wilson." The poor woman sounded at her wits' end and Marcy felt guilty that she hadn't been there at such a crucial time.

"Sorry. I was out in the field. I'll try to see Jimmy today. He's a very troubled boy, Mrs. Emory."

"Yes, I know, Miss Wilson. I've been talking to his counselor and he tells me to be patient. I want to help Jimmy, but he seems sassier than ever."

Marcy tried to soothe her, promising to talk with the counselor and with Jimmy. She was glad Mrs. Emory hadn't asked to have the boy removed from her home. At least she was still trying—even if it was as much out of financial need as concern for Jimmy.

Marcy sighed. She did sympathize with the woman, who probably had her hands full with that boy. She decided to visit the school that morning and talk to Jimmy's teacher.

"He's a very bright boy, Miss Wilson. But so belligerent. Always in a spat with some kid or other."

Marcy picked Jimmy up after school and the first thing he asked her was, "Can't I go back and live with my mom, Miss Wilson?"

"Not yet, Jimmy. You know your mother isn't well." How could she tell him that she didn't even know where his mother was?

"I don't want to stay with Mrs. Emory. They don't like me."

"Oh, Jimmy, of course they do."

"No, they don't. Nobody likes me."

"I like you. And your teacher likes you. She tells me you're very bright. And you're on the soccer team. Do you like playing soccer?"

The boy's eyes brightened. "Yes, and I'm good, Miss Wilson. Coach made me the goalie, and Sid Bates got mad. He thinks he's the best, and he ought to be the goalie."

"Sid. Is that the boy you had the fight with?"

"Yes." Jimmy looked down at his scuffed shoes, then he looked at her. "But he started it. He said I couldn't be the goalie 'cause I didn't have no soccer shoes."

Somehow, in a roundabout way, Marcy learned that soccer shoes were the immediate problem. Jimmy was the only boy on the team without them. "Mr. Emory said there was no money to buy soccer shoes." But Jimmy had run errands for the man next door, and when the man gave him five dollars he went to buy the shoes himself. Here Jimmy's eyes opened wide.

"Do you know how much soccer shoes cost, Miss Wilson? Sixteen dollars and ninety-five cents. I'm never gonna have sixteen whole dollars."

Marcy had exactly fourteen dollars and some change in her purse.

"For the soccer shoes. You'll have to put your five with it," she told him, as she gave him the money. "All I want you to do is govern your temper. Don't get in any more fights. Smart people don't fight, Jimmy, and your teacher tells me you're very smart." She talked with him a long time, encouraging him as much as she could and finally promising to look for another home.

Marcy felt like crying as she drove back to the office. She thought of searching for Jimmy's mother. But, no. If the woman had put her life into some kind of order, made any progress at all, she would have got in touch with them.

Marcy looked over the list of available homes, knowing it would be hard to find the perfect place for Jimmy. A home where he would be cherished and given the attention he craved, the patient discipline he needed. A home where he might be happy. Well, she could ensure that he had adequate food and shelter, but there was nothing she could do to ensure him happiness. She'd just better accept that.

But she could make Ginger and Davey happy. If she married Steve . . .

Ginger and Davey are happy. Steve will take good care of them. They don't need you.

She remembered Steve's suggestion that she write a proposal for the kind of children's home she envisioned. He'd said some county or foundation might fund it on an experimental basis. She should put her plans on paper, he'd said.

You don't need to marry anybody to do that. You're just making excuses to accept his ridiculous offer—of a marriage that would make you miserable.

Get your mind off yourself, Marcy, and get back to work!

She thumbed through her files. The Stevensons. Jimmy might be happier there. They already had three boys, but they might take another. She'd call them, maybe tomorrow.

After work, she went over to Gerald's and made dinner for the three of them. She played chess with Mr. Sims, and when he'd gone to bed, she listened to records with Gerald until almost midnight. She couldn't keep doing this, she told herself when she finally let herself into her own apartment. She couldn't avoid Steve forever. Well, she'd certainly try to do just that. They had to leave for Connecticut sometime.

Steve phoned her twice the next morning at the office, but she said she was too busy to talk. It was almost noon when she got the call from her sister.

"Marcy, I can't stand it! I can't live without Al."

Without Al? "Jennifer, pull yourself together and tell me what happened."

"He's left me. Oh, Marcy, what am I going to do?"

Marcy had trouble understanding her through the sobs. "Just hang on, Jennifer," she soothed. "I'll be there as soon as I can." She got emergency leave and went straight home to pack. When she drove into the parking lot, she was relieved to see that Steve's car wasn't there.

She scanned the mail and found the promised check from Jennifer. Poor Jennifer. So generous. So unhappy. Marcy decided to deposit Jennifer's check immediately, so she could repay Steve for the tires. She wrote him a check and slipped it into an envelope with a note. Then she packed.

"Oh, what am I going to do with you?" she asked, as Mr. Kitty Cat rubbed against her leg. "I can't handle you and Jennifer, too." And I won't take you next door, she thought. Board him at the vet's? No, he's too young.

Gerald. She picked up the phone.

"Sure," said Gerald. "Swing back by the office and leave your key. I'll get the kitten."

She gave the note for Steve to Mrs. Chisholm. Then she deposited Jennifer's check, left her key with Gerald and drove on to Shingle Springs. She was sorry about Jennifer's plight, but at least it meant she wouldn't be running into Steve during the next several days.

Jennifer's house was in a development designed and controlled by her husband, Al's, company. These were all luxurious custom-built homes, each one located on almost an acre of land. The grounds featured a golf course, several tennis courts, two swimming pools and a very large clubhouse. The security guard at the entrance phoned Jennifer before waving Marcy on.

Money isn't everything, Marcy thought, as she drove through the well-tended grounds to Jennifer's house.

Jennifer, still in her nightgown and robe, looked awful. She sat at her kitchen table, surrounded by dirty dishes and leftover food, cradling a cup of long-cold coffee in both hands. Her beautiful golden-blond hair was uncombed and lay in tangled disarray around her swollen face. Her eyes were red and puffy. She looked dazed, exhausted, as though she'd cried until there were no more tears. She flung herself into Marcy's arms, and Marcy held her for a long time, soothing her, saying she was not to be upset, that everything was going to be all right. Just as she had said to so many children, Marcy thought.

"Everything is going to be all right. This is Mrs. Blank. You'll be happy here." And then she always held her breath, knowing that everything was not going to be all right. But hoping the child would be happy anyway.

STEVE STOOD in his living room, drumming his fingers on the mantel, holding the note Mrs. Chisholm had given him.

> I can never thank you enough for the roadside service in the rain. But I can repay you for the tires. Thank you again.

So! She was avoiding him. That was plain.

Well, Miss Marcy Wilson, you can run, but you can't hide forever. I'll see you tonight, he thought, tearing the check and tossing it into the fireplace.

He waited for her to come home. When he heard footsteps moving toward her apartment, he quickly stepped out to confront her. It was Gerald, and he was opening Marcy's door. *Apparently with his own key.* Steve managed a nonchalant nod, then walked right past him and kept going all the way to the parking lot, where he jumped into his car and roared off.

Damned if he'd ask that smug-faced guy where Marcy was! And what the hell was he doing with a key to her apartment?

"I DIDN'T THINK Al would ever leave me. I couldn't believe it," Jennifer said.

Marcy couldn't believe it, either. Those two had seemed so happy, so much in love when they got married.

This love stuff never lasts! That was what Steve Prescott had said. Marcy shook her head, impatient to rid herself of the memory. When she turned to Jennifer again, her voice was sharper than she'd intended.

"You mean he just walked out? For no reason?"

"Well . . . not exactly. He was late coming home last night and I really lit into him. And he said he was sick and tired of me being suspicious all the time for no reason. Then he grabbed some clothes and walked out."

"Now that just sounds like a temporary rift to me. Come on. Help me unpack and you can tell me all about it. Where do you want me to stay?"

"Stay with me. I can't stand to be by myself. And it's not a temporary rift, Marcy. It's been coming a long time. I knew it was going to happen." She took Marcy's hand as they walked slowly from the kitchen to the bedroom.

Surprisingly, the rest of the house was in perfect order. Plants, sofa pillows, nothing was out of place. Not even an open magazine or an old newspaper thrown carelessly about. The living room looked like a picture in *Better Homes and Gardens*.

The bedroom was another matter. It was a mess.
Rumpled bed, discarded clothes tossed everywhere, a
pair of Al's dirty socks on the floor. While Marcy un-
packed, Jennifer fell across the bed in a miserable heap,
and her story poured out in a garbled flood of words.

She'd suspected it all along, she told Marcy. More
and more weekends out of town, late nights out when
he had to see a client, all those Sundays on the golf
course.

"Of course, I always knew. Well, you know, Marcy,
how women take to Al. They flatter him and he's so...
so... vulnerable."

Marcy picked up her cosmetic case and carried it to
the bathroom.

Vulnerable! Gullible was the better word, Marcy
thought. Al was well aware of his good looks. He knew
that women were attracted to his striking blue eyes and
blond hair and he loved every minute of it!

Unlike Steve Prescott, Marcy thought, lingering to
straighten and wipe off the cluttered counter. Steve was
absolutely unaware of his charms. He just smiled that
sweet, lazy, adorable smile, oblivious to its effect. Never
guessing how many women were enraptured by the way
his eyes lit up and crinkled at the corners.

Marcy went back into the bedroom, and sat on the
bed beside Jennifer. "...this divorcée," Jennifer was
saying, "who bought a house on the east side of the
development this summer. She calls Al at least once a
week to come and see about this or that. And when
she's not calling him, she's parading around the pool in
her bikini. She's got the figure for it, too. But I'm sure

that flaming red hair of hers is dyed! Oh, Marcy, I knew from the first that she had her eye on Al!''

Marcy listened to her sister's tearful recital and wondered about Al. It was true that he was easily flattered, but she did not believe him unfaithful.

''Has Al given you any reason to think he's interested in this woman?'' she asked carefully.

''Oh, you know Al.'' Jennifer tossed her head. ''He just says it's good business to keep everybody satisfied.''

It occurred to Marcy that Al had always worked hard, always spent a lot of time trying to please his customers. But she didn't say anything. She just sat there, holding Jennifer's hand, listening to her tearful saga of suspicions, denials and uneasy reconciliations.

What was happening to her sister's marriage? Marcy wondered. And how had Jennifer become this distraught, unhappy woman? She had always been so cheerful and loving and confident.

''Get up,'' she said suddenly. ''Go take a shower, Jennifer, while I fix us something to eat.''

''Oh, Marcy, I'm not hungry.''

''Well, I am. And I don't like seeing you looking like something the cat dragged in, when you're one of the prettiest women I know. Now, scoot!''

While Jennifer showered, Marcy made the bed and then went into the kitchen, where she emptied and washed the coffeepot, stacked the dirty dishes in the dishwasher and wiped off the counters and table. She tried to concentrate on Jennifer and Al, but Steve's image kept intruding and she kept hearing his voice making dire predictions about love.

But you're wrong, Steve Prescott, you're wrong! It's *people* who change. They become immersed in their day-by-day existence. Al, too busy making money and pleasing his customers. Jennifer, not busy enough in her picture-book house. It takes a strong love to carry a marriage through the hardships and the monotony of daily living, she thought. And marriage without love hasn't a chance, she told herself fiercely, determined to stamp every vestige of Steve from her mind.

There was little in the refrigerator but a leftover roast that looked as though it should be thrown away. We are definitely going to the grocery store, she decided, heating up a can of soup and setting out cheese and crackers.

Jennifer came into the kitchen, looking considerably better in brown slacks and a beige sweater, and even managed to eat some of the meal Marcy had prepared. Still, she continued to complain about Al. While Jennifer talked, Marcy's practical mind began to sift through the facts. As far as she could determine from what she'd heard, there was no real evidence of "another woman."

"When he took off this morning, it just confirmed what I suspected," Jennifer said, aimlessly toying with her soupspoon. "I've been watching...waiting for this to happen."

Marcy studied her sister's hurt embittered face. Suspecting...watching...waiting. Was that the key? Had Jennifer driven Al away with her accusations of imagined betrayals? Marcy remembered the Sunday she and the children had spent with a most disagreeable Jennifer.... *If I were Al, I'd spend my Sundays on the golf course too* had been her own reaction. Could it be that Jennifer, even after her marriage, had never stopped competing for Al, had never really believed he loved her, had visualized the day he would leave her?

Visualization. Marcy sat up. Funny how the ideas in that book—ideas she wasn't sure she believed in—kept coming back to her.

Whatever you picture in your mind will come to pass.

"And this morning," Jennifer was saying, "I really confronted him. I told him I wouldn't stand for it anymore. And he said he was sick of my accusations and complaining, and then he walked out. And it isn't just a temporary rift like you think, Marcy. He said he had to go out of town today, but he'd be back to get the rest of his clothes tomorrow evening."

Marcy looked at Jennifer, hardly hearing her. Attitude. How could she change Jennifer's attitude?

"Oh, Marcy, I don't believe he'll ever come back."

"He won't if you keep thinking he won't," Marcy said so sharply that Jennifer gave a start.

"Oh, Marcy, don't say that!"

"Well, you certainly can't mope him back. You've got to change the picture in your mind."

"Picture in my...? Marcy, what are you talking about?"

"I read this book about a technique called visualization. If you want something to happen, you can help bring it about by pretending it's already happened."

Jennifer said the whole thing sounded crazy to her, but Marcy caught her attention with the story about a woman whose husband had asked for a divorce, saying he didn't love her anymore. The woman agreed, only asking him to wait a month. During that month, she put her imagination to work, picturing in her mind the way things had been when her husband loved her. Pretending that he'd never stopped loving her.

"And at the end of the month," Marcy concluded, "it came true. He returned, saying he still loved her and didn't want a divorce after all."

"Marcy, that's not possible."

"It's a true story, Jennifer. It really is possible to change your life by changing your thinking." She had thought it would be difficult to convince her sister, but like a drowning person, Jennifer was grasping at any straw.

"What do I do first?" she asked.

"Start thinking how much Al loves you, how happy you are together."

"But we ... he doesn't ... he's not even here."

"Thoughts, Jennifer. Thoughts! Take control of your thoughts. In your mind he loves you and you are happy."

"Oh, Marcy. That's not true."

"Listen, darn it! You have to do it with your whole heart and mind. No negatives. Positive thinking all the way. Dwell on how you *want* things to be. Not how they appear on the outside. Say it over and over, out loud if necessary, 'Al loves me. He's coming home.'"

Jennifer regarded her dubiously, but obediently repeated the phrases several times.

"And look happy," Marcy advised. Privately she believed more in action. Al needed to *see* Jennifer being happy. "When did you say Al was coming for his things?" she asked.

"Tomorrow evening."

"Perfect," said Marcy. "Now, the first thing we're going to do is go out and buy a Christmas tree."

"Christmas tree! I can't bear to think of Christmas. And, anyway, it's not even the tenth of the month yet."

"We're starting early. And you love Christmas. Picture this—Al is here with you," Marcy said in her most seductive voice. "The two of you are sitting by the Christmas tree, and he's giving you a diamond bracelet and telling you how much he loves you."

"Oh, Marcy, do you really think . . . ?"

"It's not what *I* think that matters; it's what *you* think. Now put your coat on. We're going out for that tree."

But first Marcy called Tom. Would he come over early tomorrow afternoon, and bring a friend?

"We'll make dinner if you help decorate a Christmas tree. I'm in Shingle Springs with my sister who's going through a bad time and needs cheering up."

When Al did appear the next evening, he seemed dumbfounded to find a jolly group in his living room, decorating a Christmas tree and drinking hot toddies.

"Oh, hello, Al," said Jennifer, who had been carefully coached. "I forgot you were coming. Marcy's here to help me with the tree. This is Phil Glover, and I think you've met Tom Jenkins." Then, as Al nodded to everyone, she added, "Can I get you a toddy or something?"

"Oh, no. No thanks," he said. But Marcy noticed he couldn't take his eyes off Jennifer, who looked absolutely stunning in a green velvet jumpsuit, with her golden hair tousled just right.

"Can you manage with your things?" Jennifer asked sweetly, "Or do you need some help?"

"No. I'll manage."

Marcy couldn't tell whether he was puzzled or disgruntled. Probably both, she thought, winking at Jennifer as he turned away. Her sister bore very little resemblance, now, to the hysterical female he had walked out on just one day before.

STEVE PRESCOTT was frustrated. He hadn't been able to reach Marcy, and all her office would tell him was that she was on emergency leave. He wanted to ask her about the children's Christmas presents. And, yes, he wanted to get her final answer on the Connecticut place.

He just bet that Gerald guy knew where she was, but damned if he'd ask him!

On Thursday, the real-estate agent called and said someone else was dickering for the place he was interested in. If he still wanted it...

He took a plane for Connecticut the next day.

CHAPTER THIRTEEN

MARCY WAS PACKING to go home. Al had returned the night before and all was forgiveness, love and happiness in the household.

"Your coming made a big difference," Jennifer told her.

"Nonsense!" Marcy folded her slacks and placed them in the suitcase. "You love each other. You would have patched things up without me."

"Well, yes, I suppose. But, you see, it was our quarreling that drove him away in the first place. And it could have happened again. But it won't, because I'm different now."

"Oh?" Marcy closed her suitcase and looked at her sister.

"I was afraid to be happy, Marcy. Every time Al was out of my sight, I filled my mind with suspicions and . . . well, negative thoughts." She smiled at Marcy. "You taught me that it was all right to be happy." She had a strange way of putting it, but Marcy knew what she meant.

"Happy thinking," she said, when she kissed her sister goodbye. As she drove away she wondered if happy thinking really did change things. Or just change you inside, so that you were happy even though things on the outside weren't any different at all.

Perhaps it's foolhardy to try to change things into being the way you want them to be, Marcy thought. It's better to think yourself into being happy with the way things are. And that's what I must do, she told herself.

During the time she'd just spent at Shingle Springs, Marcy had been absorbed in Jennifer's problems, so absorbed that she'd been able to stifle her own feelings. But deep inside her, there had been a sense of hopeless desolation. Buried beneath the bravado, beneath the encouraging words uttered for Jennifer's sake, was the hurtful knowledge of her own loss.

She was being ridiculous. How could she lose something she'd never had? *I have to try to make sense of my real world,* she thought. *I must face up to the fact that I am in love with a man who does not love me, who does not want to be committed to anyone.* A man callous enough to try to involve her in a make-believe marriage for his own convenience. How dare he!

How dare you? Are you going to let Steve Prescott muddle up your life?

Definitely not. She'd been happy before she knew him. She would continue to be happy without him.

She sped toward Auburn, full of determination. Of course she wouldn't avoid the children, and she'd be casually pleasant to Steve. But she would certainly be busy, very busy. She would have to catch up on her work, finish her Christmas shopping, mail her Christmas cards.... There would be parties, too. Jo always had a party, and so did her friend, Meg. Yes, she would be busy. And she would be happy if it killed her! She would think happy, and her thoughts would not include Steve Prescott!

"Marcy!" Ginger cried, running out to meet her. "Where have you been, and where is the kitty? You promised we could feed him, and then we couldn't find you."

"I had to go away for a while. The kitty will be home soon, and you can feed him," Marcy said, as she hugged Ginger.

"Steve's gone away," Ginger volunteered. "To...to 'neticut."

"Oh!" Marcy was casual, masking her disappointment. How could she possibly feel disappointed? She didn't want to see Steve; she'd even planned to avoid him. Now she was keenly aware of how much she missed him. How much she longed to see that crooked smile. She had resolved not to be touched by his smile, had braced herself to resist his playful, teasing persuasions—persuasions that were somehow very strong, very sweet. But he wasn't there, and she was not prepared for the emptiness. It felt as though something exciting and vibrant in her life had suddenly been snatched away, leaving a terrible void.

"We're going to 'neticut too," said Ginger. "Pretty soon, we're going. And we're going to have ponies."

"How nice," Marcy said. So he had decided to buy that beautiful home. They would go and live there, and she would stay here. And she couldn't bear it!

Take control of your thoughts, Marcy. Think happy. With life as it is.

"I'm going to buy a Christmas tree," she said. "Will you help me decorate it?" No matter where she planned to spend Christmas, Marcy always had her own tree.

"Oh, yes!" Ginger was delighted. "Can we get it now?"

She bought a small tree, so heavily flocked it seemed weighted down with snow. She and the children decorated it with tiny white lights, golden bells and two white doves. She made an arrangement of frosted magnolia leaves and pine cones for her mantel, and placed a large poinsettia on her dining table. She set a fire blazing in the fireplace. The apartment looked very cheerful and Christmassy. And felt very empty.

She called her mother in Phoenix to ask her plans for the holiday.

"I'm so glad you called," exclaimed her mother, "I've got some wonderful news." She'd just received an airline ticket from Marcy's brother, Bill, along with an invitation to spend Christmas with his family in Japan.

After the call, Marcy sat in her cheerful empty apartment and stared at the fire. The radio was playing a medley of Christmas tunes, and she wondered why the sound of holiday rejoicing made her feel sad. She stood up. Enough of this self-pity! She marched briskly to the phone to call Tom and invite him for dinner the next night. He'd been so nice, helping with Jennifer, and she wanted to return the favor.

Tom said he'd be glad to come, and Marcy went to bed, thinking she might give a Christmas party herself. She thought about her guest list and what she should serve. She thought about Jennifer, happy with Al. She remembered she'd have to get a loan to repay Jennifer for the money she'd borrowed to repay Steve for the tires. That made her smile—she really was robbing Peter to pay Paul. She'd mail the presents for her mother and Bill's family, so her mother would get them before she left for Japan. She tossed and turned and finally fell asleep.

She dreamed she was running, running through the park by the complex. In the middle of the park was a giant flocked Christmas tree, decorated with golden bells and white doves. Steve stood under the tree, smiling, holding out his arms. She ran straight to him, and he gathered her close. She felt warm in his embrace. Then he kissed her, and she heard Christmas music and the bells on the tree began to ring. They clanged louder and louder.

Her bedside phone was ringing. Still half-asleep, Marcy groped for it.

"Hello?" Who on earth could be calling her at this time of night?

"Miss Wilson? Miss Wilson, can you come here?" It was a child's voice, and he was crying.

"Yes, this is Miss Wilson. Who is this? What's wrong?"

"Please, Miss Wilson, would you come and get me?"

"Jimmy?" Marcy sat up in bed. "Is this Jimmy Braxton?"

"Yes, ma'am. Would you come and get me?"

"What's the matter? Let me speak to Mrs. Emory."

"She's not here. I'm—I'm not there. I'm here."

"Where?" Marcy looked at her clock radio. 12:14. "Jimmy, you're not at the Emorys'? Where are you?"

"I don't know exactly. I—"

Marcy, very disturbed now, was about to question him further when a man's voice broke in.

"Hello, ma'am. Pete Turner here. I picked this kid up on the highway."

"On the highway!" Marcy cried. "What on earth—?"

"He was thumbing a ride. But I know damn well no kid this size should be out here this time of night. It's rough out here. All kinds of folk around. He's lucky I picked him up."

"Oh, yes, I'm glad you did. Thank you, Mr...."

"Turner. Pete Turner. I thought I'd better turn him over to the police, but he begged me not to. I ... well, I hated to get him in trouble. He said you were with the welfare department and you'd take care of it."

"Oh, yes, I will," Marcy said quickly.

"What do you want me to do? I don't want to leave him by himself. It's just not safe."

"No, of course not. Where are you, Mr. Turner?"

"Jake's Place. You know it? A truck stop on Highway 80."

Marcy said she did know it, and that she would come right away. The man promised to wait. She scrambled into a pair of woolen pants and a heavy jacket, her mind in turmoil. What was Jimmy doing out on Highway 80 at this time of night? And if he was missing from the Emorys', why hadn't Mrs. Emory called her? Then she hoped Mrs. Emory hadn't noticed his absence, because Jimmy had run away once before. If he was reported again, and the authorities took him into custody, he might be sent to Juvenile Hall—the last thing he needed. She was convinced he'd do well in the right environment.

But you knew the Emorys weren't right for him. You knew it, Marcy! And you've been so busy with Jennifer, and so busy feeling sorry for yourself, you've hardly given him a thought. Maybe he'd called when she was on leave and hadn't been able to get in touch with her. Oh, but Jimmy, why did you run away? Where on earth did you think you could go?

It was a crisp cold night. Thank goodness it wasn't raining, Marcy muttered to herself as she ran down the gravel path to the parking lot. She reached a line of parked cars and started toward her Volkswagen when she was blinded by the headlights of an incoming car. She drew back to let it pass.

But the car didn't pass; instead, it pulled up short beside her. Marcy didn't hesitate. She turned quickly, running back the way she had come, moving faster when she heard someone get out of the car.

"Marcy!" It was Steve.

When she recognized his voice, she stopped and leaned against the hood of a car, panting. Still trembling, she watched him stride toward her.

"I didn't know it was you," she gasped. "I ... I thought ... you scared me."

"Well, good!" he bellowed. "You ought to be scared. What the hell are you doing out here by yourself this late at night?"

"I—it's this kid. I've got to pick him up."

"Now?"

"And I don't have much time. I've got to go."

"Not by yourself. Here, get in." He bundled her into his car, and Marcy didn't protest. She didn't have time to argue.

"Jake's Place," she told him. "It's a truck stop on Highway 80." While he drove, she told him about Jimmy. How unhappy he'd been since he was taken away from his alcoholic mother, when she'd disappeared for a week during one of her binges. How he'd been shuffled from home to home. How he didn't seem to fit in anywhere and had run away once before. "He's not a bad boy, and—well, I don't think the Emorys really understand him." Marcy felt close to tears as she thought about Jimmy. Maybe he, too, had been listening to Christmas music and been depressed by it. He'd probably heard other children making plans—family plans.

"I should have moved him, Steve. I knew he was unhappy there." Marcy's voice broke. She was suddenly overwhelmed by the sadness and the guilt. "He must have felt so alone."

Steve's hand covered hers. "No, Marcy, he was not alone. He called you, didn't he? From the truck stop?"

"Yes, but—"

"He knew you were there for him. He knew that you cared."

"Maybe," she said, sighing doubtfully. But the weight of guilt lifted just a little as the lights of the truck stop loomed ahead. Steve drove in and parked, then turned to her again.

"No maybe about it," he said. "When the chips are down and you're in trouble, real trouble, you call someone you can trust. He knew that. This Jimmy knew he could trust you." Steve rubbed the back of his hand gently against her cheek. "Come on, let's go see about the little scamp. Brave kid to walk out on a night like this. Foolish kid," he said as they went in.

The truck stop was typical. Warm and brightly lighted, filled with the smell of frying hamburgers and coffee. The trucker who had picked Jimmy up was a short stocky man with a genial face. He said he had kids of his own and didn't like to see any kid in trouble. And he sure didn't like to see them walking the highway, night *or* day. He had bought Jimmy a hamburger and hot chocolate. But now that they'd come for him, he said, he'd be on his way.

After thanking the trucker, Marcy slid into the booth beside Jimmy, whose frightened, tearstained face was raised to hers.

"Jimmy, why did you do this? And how? Didn't Mrs. Emory try to stop you?"

"I climbed out the window," Jimmy said, "after they went to sleep. And I don't want to go back there, Miss Wilson. They don't like me."

"Oh, Jimmy, why do you feel that way?" Marcy asked. Her mind was trying to grapple with the whole situation. Jimmy had to understand that he couldn't just run away like this, that it was wrong and he could get into trouble. But she had to try to find out what was wrong at the Emorys' and either straighten things out or else move him. She could tell he was frightened and anxious, and she was torn between the need to reprimand him, and her desire to comfort. "What makes you feel they don't like you?" she asked again.

"I just know. Please, Miss Wilson, don't make me go back. They don't like me."

"That doesn't matter." The calm voice was unexpected, and they both looked up to see Steve, who had appeared with two mugs of coffee. He gave one to Marcy, then sat across from them and looked intently at Jimmy. "You are going to meet lots of people, and some of them are not going to like you. The thing is, you have to like yourself. Do you like yourself, Jimmy?"

"Er...er...what do you mean?" Jimmy seemed puzzled, and perhaps, Marcy thought, a little intimidated by this man who was a stranger to him.

"Simple question. I asked you if you like yourself. Do you?"

Staring at Steve, the boy slowly nodded.

"Why?" Steve asked. "Why do you like yourself?"

"I...I play good soccer."

"Okay. That's fine for a start. What else do you like about yourself?"

Marcy sat spellbound as Steve drew Jimmy out, getting the boy to tell him in a faltering way that he was "pretty good at school," that he "didn't beat up on anybody" unless they picked on him first and that sometimes he ran errands for Mr. Orr, who was crippled.

"Well, you sound like a pretty good kid to me, Jimmy. Lots of reasons to like yourself. You're smart too, huh?"

Jimmy, more at ease now, nodded.

"Well then, tell me this," Steve said, taking a swallow of coffee, then setting down his mug. "How come a smart kid like you would do a dumb thing like this? Run away in the middle of the night and walk down a highway going nowhere?"

"I wasn't going nowhere. I was going to find my mama."

"You know where she is?"

"Well, no. But maybe I could find her." Jimmy bit his lip, his expression mutinous. "Anyway, I was mad 'cause Mrs. Emory took the money Miss Wilson gave me."

"Oh? Miss Wilson gave you some money?"

"For soccer shoes. 'Cause everybody on the team had soccer shoes but me. And I worked and made five dollars, but that wasn't enough, and Miss Wilson gave me the rest."

"And...?" Steve prompted, but his gaze had shifted to Marcy, and there was something in the way he looked at her that made the color steal into her cheeks. Embarrassed, she turned toward Jimmy, trying to concentrate on what he was saying.

He hadn't got the shoes at first because they didn't have his size. But Mrs. Emory had kept the money for him, and he was supposed to pick up the shoes yesterday. "Only—" here Jimmy looked rather sheepish "—me and Tad were fooling around on the way home from school. He had his soccer ball and we were kicking it back and forth, you know, and...well, it went right through Mr. Burton's window. He came out real mad and he said that windowpane was going to cost him fifteen dollars and somebody had to pay for it. Then Mrs. Emory came out and said I was responsible. And that wasn't fair!"

"It wasn't fair?" Steve's eyes were fixed on Jimmy. "Who kicked the ball?"

"I did," Jimmy admitted. "But...but...Tad missed it," he said defiantly. "If he'd just jumped up..."

"Wait a minute," Steve said. "It was you who kicked the ball that went through the window, right?"

"Right. But... but that money was for soccer shoes and Mrs. Emory shouldn't have given it to Mr. Burton." Jimmy gulped. Marcy could see that he was fighting back tears. "She kept saying I had to learn to be responsible."

"She's right, you know," Steve said. "You have to take the consequences for what you do. Even if what you did was an accident." He shrugged. "It's one of life's tougher lessons—and the sooner you learn it, the better."

But Marcy's heart went out to Jimmy. Poor little kid. Soccer shoes. First he'd got into a fight over them. Then when he finally had the money to buy them, it had to go for a broken windowpane. That was hard. But, of course, she knew that Mrs. Emory—and Steve—were right. Teaching the boy responsibility was more important than soccer shoes.

Mrs. Emory! Good Lord, if she missed him and reported... I'd better call, Marcy thought, and make some excuse. She glanced toward Jimmy, who was staring at Steve, completely absorbed in what he was saying. They hardly heard her when she told them she'd be back in a minute.

When she reached the public phone, she hesitated. What excuse could she possibly give Mrs. Emory? Calling her in the middle of the night and ... She stopped. Jimmy had sneaked out of a window. Was there any chance they could sneak him back in? Oh, Marcy, what an unprofessional thing to do! Still . . .

When she returned to the booth she found Steve still talking confidentially to Jimmy, both of them eating apple pie and ice cream.

"Pie, Marcy?" Steve asked.

She shook her head.

"I was telling Steve that I want to find my mama," Jimmy explained. "She wouldn't treat me like Mrs. Emory, bossing me around and yelling at me all the time. My mama loves me."

"I don't know about that. She left you, didn't she?" Steve asked.

Oh, no! Marcy thought. That was cruel! Steve had gone too far. Jimmy was her case, and she shouldn't allow Steve to take over.

"Wait a minute, Steve," she started to say, but he broke in as if he knew what she was thinking.

"Miss Wilson doesn't think I should be talking to you," he said to Jimmy. "But I want to talk to you because when I was a little boy, I was just like you."

"You were?" Jimmy's eyes widened with astonishment.

"Exactly. My mother left me, too. Just walked out."

"She did? Was she sick?" Jimmy asked.

"No, she wasn't." Steve pushed away his half-finished pie, as if he had lost his appetite. "She just walked out." He sounded so sharp, so bitter, that Marcy's breath caught. For a moment, she felt confused. Diane had distinctly said that their mother died when Steve was five and Diane was two. Then she understood. When you were two you believed what you were told. But Steve, at five, had been old enough not to be fooled. Old enough to be hurt.

"How come?" Jimmy was asking. "How come your mama left you if she wasn't sick or anything?"

"I...well, maybe in a way she was sick." Steve swallowed. "I...I thought she would come back...and I kept waiting...." Steve's voice broke, and there was such pain in his eyes that Marcy wanted to reach out, to comfort him.

"She didn't *never* come back?" Jimmy asked.

"No." For a long moment Steve was silent. Then he said, "So you see, I know how you feel. I felt all alone, too. My dad left me with people. And some of them— I could tell—didn't like me. You know?"

Jimmy's nod was full of understanding.

"Now," Steve said, "I know you're just ten years old."

"Ten years and two months," Jimmy said.

"Okay. And two months." Steve smiled. "Well, you'd better learn now that the main person you have to depend on is yourself. And you have to make the best of whatever situation you're in."

"But when people don't like you... Anyway, I bet nobody ever took your money."

"My father took all the money I earned one summer. My real father. And that's when *I* ran away from home."

While Jimmy exclaimed in a frenzy of empathy and anger, Diane's words came back to Marcy. *Steve was fifteen. He'd been caddying all summer at the golf course and was saving to buy a car. He gave me the*

money for that coat.... The very next day, he left home.
Just walked out. Steve's father had taken his car money!
That was why he'd left home.

Oh, Steve, I'm so sorry!

"Later—much later—I knew why my father took
that money," Steve said quietly. "He took it because he
didn't make very much himself, and he had to pay most
of that to the people who looked after us. It must have
hurt his pride a great deal . . . but at the time, all I could
see was that he'd taken *my* money. I was hurt and angry, and I decided to get out." He paused, staring down
at the table, then looked directly into Jimmy's eyes. "I
made the wrong decision.

"Maybe you want to run away because things aren't
going the way you think they should," he continued.
"But before you do, you ought to have somewhere to
run. I was four years older than you, but just as dumb.
I ran away with no place to go, no money, no education and no Miss Wilson to call."

Marcy listened to Steve tell Jimmy of his precarious
existence as a homeless teenager wandering from place
to place. She knew that the episodes related were chosen deliberately and possibly exaggerated to scare the
boy out of following the same course. But Marcy listened as avidly as Jimmy and was just as horrified.
From the moment that Steve had walked into her office that September day, looking so confident and
smiling that special smile, she had pictured him a
strong, almost invincible man. Even when she had
heard some of the details of his early life—how he
couldn't get a job . . . lied about his age . . . joined the
navy—she had thought him a man who did what needed

to be done, no matter how difficult. Always confident, always in charge.

Now, as she watched him, and listened, his dark eyes serious and intent, full of compassion and determined to convince Jimmy of the dangers, she saw Steve in a different light. She saw a lonely, unhappy child, deserted by his mother—how could she have left him! She saw a frightened teenager, running, hiding to keep from being arrested as a vagrant.... Trapped in an alley by a gang of ruffians.... Always hungry, sleeping on the damp ground under a bridge, or, covered with a newspaper, huddled near the warm vent of a building. Marcy was as heartsick as Jimmy was frightened. She wanted to hold Steve in her arms, love him, make up for all he had been through. Yet she marveled at his wisdom and compassion and realized that what he had endured had helped to make him all that he was—strong and understanding. She was aware of the advice so cleverly woven in....

"Any home is better than none; don't expect it to be perfect.... Grown-ups have problems, too.... Lessons are important; I couldn't get a job because I didn't know anything.... Learn how to *do* something so you can earn money; folks always need windows washed or grass cut."

Marcy thought that if Jimmy was listening as intently as he appeared to be, sometimes forgetting his pie, he was learning lessons that could last him a lifetime. He seemed to have learned one lesson, anyway.

"Guess I'll stay at Mrs. Emory's, Miss Wilson. It ain't so bad. Nobody ever hits me, and she cooks good. And I did break that window."

So they took him back to the Emorys', where they managed to sneak him in through the same window he had climbed out of.

"Don't think of it as being unprofessional," Steve said, in answer to Marcy's qualms. "This comes under the heading of problem prevention."

"Why did you stop me from giving him the money for the soccer shoes?" she asked Steve, when she got back into the car.

"And reward him for running away?" Steve exclaimed, as he put the car in gear and headed home. "Besides, easy come, easy go."

"Oh, Steve, it's not as though he broke the window on purpose. And he wants those shoes so badly."

"That kid is on his own, Marcy. So he's got to learn to take care of himself. Handouts don't come easy. He's got to learn to work for what he wants, and learn to be responsible. It's rough out there."

Rough out there! That was what the trucker had said, too. Maybe, she thought, experience really was the best teacher. She had a degree in social work, but never could she have been as compellingly down-to-earth as Steve had been in his talk with Jimmy.

And never could she have been as compassionately honest. She looked at the man beside her, who had so exposed himself, who had dug up painful memories she knew he preferred to hide—to save a boy from making the same mistakes. She was so grateful to him for sharing his experience and his wisdom with Jimmy. But this feeling that filled her heart, flooded her whole being, was more than gratitude. It was a deep caring, something akin to adoration, for the Steve Prescott she had not known until tonight. Almost timidly she touched his arm.

"Steve, I want to thank you. It was very lucky that you came with me."

"Damn lucky!" He glanced at her, frowning a little. "It's not safe, Marcy—out by yourself this time of night. I'm glad I spotted you when I drove in from the airport."

"Oh! You're back from Connecticut." She couldn't help the twinge of pleasure she felt at the thought that he was home now. "Well, yes, I'm glad you came with me, of course. But I wasn't thinking of me."

"No, you never think of you. Some kid needs help and off you go whether it's storming or the middle of the night or—"

"Steve." She pressed his arm. "I want to tell you that what you did for Jimmy tonight was wonderful. Nobody could have talked to him the way you did. Could have made him understand so well."

"Maybe." He shrugged. "But lectures don't always do it. Guess some lessons have to be lived before you can learn 'em."

She was silent after that, thinking about lessons and life—and Steve. He was quiet, too. She realized it must have been a long day for him, and he was probably tired. Yet he had not hesitated to do what needed to be done.

When, finally, they'd walked up from the parking lot and stopped at her door, she turned toward him.

"Do you know what I think?" she said.

"No. What?" He smiled down at her.

"I think you are a very special person, Steve Prescott." Standing on tiptoe, she kissed him, surprising him so that he never let go of his bags. Then she went in, and shut the door.

WORK HAD PILED UP so that she didn't have a chance to visit the Emorys until four days later. She hadn't seen Steve during those four days, either. Though she was exhausted, she'd had Tom to dinner the next day, as promised. The day after that, she had to attend a conference in Sacramento and stayed overnight.

However, when she got home, the first thing she did was call on Mrs. Emory.

"He seems to be doing better," Mrs. Emory said. "He's not sassy like he used to be. And yesterday he asked me to let him help wash windows. Can you believe that? Said he wanted to learn how."

One night. One talk. Could it have made that much difference?

She spoke with Jimmy, too. Privately. Anxious to see if he really wanted to remain with the Emorys.

"It's all right, I guess. Mr. Prescott says one place is about as good as another."

"Mr. Prescott?"

"You know. That man that came with you when you picked me up. He came to see me yesterday and gave me his card. He told me to put it away real careful. His New York office number is on there, and he says they always know where he is and he's gonna tell them to always put me through. So I can call him collect anytime. That is, whenever I really need to."

He's got to learn to take care of himself, huh? You're a softie, Steve.

"He says I'm to write him. Let him know about my lessons. And when I finish high school, he says he'll help me get a job. If I keep in touch. Maybe I can go to college."

When Marcy left, her heart was full. Steve's interest had extended far beyond one night. She had not known Steve was so... so good. He had accomplished more in one night than the welfare department had done in three years. Washing windows—"said he wanted to learn how." Learning to depend on himself. And Jimmy's face, Marcy thought, had lost that defeated "nobody likes me" look. He had made a friend, and his face was full of hope.

She thought of Steve. He was different from any man she had ever known. Gruff and callous on the outside. "I don't believe in this love-forever-after stuff." But so tender and caring on the inside. He was the best thing that could have happened to Diane's children. To Jimmy.

And to you, Marcy Wilson. You're a fool if you don't snap him up on any terms.

But marriage is different. I couldn't bear it if he didn't love me in a special way. She thought of Jennifer, her misery when Al had left. If I married Steve, and he left me or turned to another woman... "We'd both be free. We could go our separate ways."

No, she thought. I couldn't stand it. I couldn't bear it. It would hurt too much.

CHAPTER FOURTEEN

WHEN MARCY LEFT JIMMY, she went straight home. It was still a little early, but too late to go back to the office. These past three days had been difficult, and she knew she should feel tired.

But she didn't. She felt restless and strangely exhilarated, poised on tiptoe, waiting for something to happen.

Steve.

The kitten rolled at her feet, and she reached down and tickled his belly. After she'd filled his bowl with milk, she made herself a cup of tea. The tea, hot and spicy with chamomile, warmed and soothed her. She drank it slowly and thought about Steve.

Deliberately she made her mind dart away, fasten on her mother flying off to Japan. She'd received Marcy's gifts and was taking them with her. Good. Jennifer...Jennifer was happy, now. She and Al had left for their cruise this morning. Good. Jo...Marcy hadn't selected her gift yet. Maybe tomorrow at lunch.

Steve. What to think?

The kitten had not yet mastered the steps, so Marcy lifted him up and carried him to her loft. She kicked off her shoes, changed into jeans and a pullover. Then she lay across her bed and finally allowed herself to think about Steve Prescott.

"I don't believe in this love stuff." Just how important were the words "I love you" anyway? She was reminded of one of her father's favorite expressions, "What you do speaks so loudly I can't hear what you say."

Steve. He *said*, "I don't believe in love." Yet he exhibited more love than any man she knew. He had taken over the care of his sister's children so easily and naturally, acting out of love and not mere duty. And he had taken such a kindly, loving interest in Jimmy, a boy he hardly knew.

So he's a good guy. Nice to people. What does that mean to you?

It means he's a man worth loving.

And you love him?

Yes! Yes, I love him. The thought resounded almost defiantly as she looked down at the kitten, trying to get a good grip on a tennis ball that was too big for him to handle. She remembered another of her father's favorite sayings—the poet Browning's line, "A man's reach should exceed his grasp or what's a heaven for?"

Marriage, a real marriage, to Steve Prescott would be heaven. Dare she reach for it?

You're copping out, Marcy. A business marriage would be a mockery.

The kitten gave up on the tennis ball and clawed at the bed covers. Marcy scooped him up and put him on the bed beside her, where he purred contentedly as she stroked him.

Steve. I love him. I love everything about him. That crooked, engaging smile. I love his gruff way of taking charge. I love his cheerful teasing. I love the way he goes about doing whatever has to be done, whether it's changing a tire or scolding a runaway kid. I love his gentleness. The woman who marries him will be lucky.

She sat up, startling the kitten. He tumbled confusedly for a moment, then lay calmly down, placed one paw over the other and regarded her thoughtfully.

I could be that woman! He asked me to marry him. Me, Marcy Wilson. Nobody else.

Purely a business arrangement.

Maybe. But he does feel something for me. I know he does. The way he kissed me...

When he apologized for doing it? When he immediately backed away?

Because he was afraid! It came to her in a blinding flash of understanding. He was afraid to love, afraid he might be betrayed as he had once been betrayed by his mother. Again she saw the disillusionment in his face as clearly as she had seen it that night at the truck stop, when he had told Jimmy of his mother's desertion. Again she heard the bitterness in his voice that first night she had met him—*You can't trust women.* She had thought then that she'd misheard him. But she hadn't. That was truly how he felt. Because the woman he trusted most had betrayed him. Marcy knew well how the traumas of early childhood could hurt, could linger throughout life and affect one's whole outlook.

Steve's mother had left him. His father had taken his money. And the pain had cut so deep that he hid it, even from himself. But at the truck stop, in trying to break through to Jimmy, Steve had revealed his own hurt, his own fear. Strange, Marcy thought, that what happened to Steve had not made him unloving or unkind. Only afraid. To give love or receive it. To trust anyone.

She picked up the kitten, nestled her chin against his soft fur and tried to piece together the puzzle that was Steve Prescott. Strong. Dependable. Caring. Hurt. Confused. Untrusting. She longed to take him in her arms and love him so that he would never feel that kind of pain again. If she married him, she could teach him to love. To trust.

Almost subconsciously, she *visualized* it. Pictured being Steve's wife. Living with him. Each morning seeing that crooked smile across the breakfast table. Walking arm in arm with him under those great oak trees. Touching him, loving him. And being loved by him, his lips on hers, his hands caressing. Her imagination ran riot, and for moments she was gripped in an erotic fantasy of intense pleasure. Steve, holding her, loving her . . .

Reality intruded, punctured the dream. It couldn't be a real marriage. He might never love her, might never desire her as she desired him. He might fall in love with another woman.

But overriding the doubts and the dream loomed a very real possibility. If she didn't marry him, he would gradually disappear from her life. And there would be nothing left between them but the memory of what might have been. It was a grim prospect. No matter how, she had to be with him.

She would risk loving, rather than losing him.

Making the decision seemed to make her feel more alive. Happy. She wanted to run to Steve, to let him know she'd changed her mind, and now agreed to his crazy idea of a business marriage.

She smiled. Funny, it didn't seem crazy anymore. It seemed . . . well, right. She gave the kitten a gentle squeeze, set him on the floor and put on her loafers. Then she ran downstairs to Steve's apartment.

The woman who opened the door was beautiful, more beautiful even than her picture in the silver frame. *To my darling Steve, with all my love, Tricia.* The long wheat-colored hair was coiled in a loose knot and tied with a wide black ribbon. She had a perfect oval face, and hazel eyes that glinted with gold and slanted slightly. Her skin was flawless ivory above the low neck of her black cashmere sweater.

"Hello," she said, full red lips curving in that provocative smile. "Come in. You must be Marcy."

"Yes," admitted Marcy, smiling stiffly at the woman in black, as well as at Mrs. Chisholm, who had also come to the door. Mrs. Chisholm gave Marcy a knowing wink, and retreated to the kitchen. The *vision* repeated her invitation to come in.

She couldn't just walk away. Keenly aware of her old jeans and pullover and feeling a bit too short, Marcy followed the tall, graceful figure in the smart, black leather pants that seemed to be molded to her slender hips.

"Hi, Marcy! This is Tricia. Isn't she pretty?" Davey's eyes were big, his voice full of awe. Marcy resisted the impulse to shake him and agreed that, yes, Tricia was very pretty.

"Want some popcorn, Marcy?" Ginger asked.

"Yes, do have some. And join us." Tricia, the beautiful, gestured to a big bowl of popcorn and sank gracefully to the floor beside it. The glow from the fire and the lights of the Christmas tree enhanced her exquisite features and made a halo around her wheat-colored hair. She looked not only gorgeous, but very much at home. And Marcy wanted to dump the bowl of popcorn over her head. And I probably would, she thought, if I stayed another minute!

"No thanks," she managed to say. "I'll just be on my way and—"

"Eat some, Marcy. It's real good." Ginger tugged at her hand, pulling her to the floor. Marcy took a few kernels and choked them down while Ginger watched.

"Don't you like it? Didn't Tricia make it good?"

"Yes, she did," said Marcy. Big deal! What's to do with corn but pop it?

"Marcy, look what Trish brought us! It's a puzzle from the New York zoo. It's got lots of animals." Davey carefully placed a piece in the giant jigsaw puzzle. "I think this one goes right here, don't you, Tricia?"

"How nice," said Marcy. She wondered where Steve was but didn't want to ask. It was bad enough watching this cozy threesome. She felt isolated, out of place.

"Well, I must be going," she said again.

"No, wait," Tricia urged. "Steve went on an errand, but he'll be right back. Did you want to see him about something?"

"Well, I . . . it . . . it's nothing important."

"Why don't you wait? Here, let me get you a glass of wine."

"No," Marcy said quickly and firmly, feeling a flash of irritation at the way this woman was taking charge—as if she, Tricia, were mistress of the place. Offering her wine. Steve's wine! What gave her the right?

Marcy felt suddenly ashamed. What was the matter with her? She had never in all her life taken such an instant dislike to anyone. She made herself smile, made her voice congenial.

"It's nice to finally meet you, Tricia. Are you enjoying your stay?" *How long will you be here? Don't ask!*

"Oh, yes, I'm enjoying myself very much."

"We're going to 'neticut," Ginger said excitedly. "And Tricia's coming, too."

Marcy felt a stabbing pain of apprehension.

"And we're going to have ponies," Davey added, looking up from his puzzle. "And Tricia's going to teach us to ride. Aren't you, Tricia?"

The apprehension turned to despair. Steve had hired his wife! Tricia. Tricia would be there. Living with Steve, with the children. Marcy wanted to stand up and run out of the apartment, but her knees felt weak and she couldn't move. She just sat there, all the will gone out of her.

Ginger said she was going to name her pony Bozo. And Davey said that wasn't any kind of a name for a horse, was it, Tricia? He was going to name his pony King or Captain. Tricia asked if Marcy had seen pictures of the Connecticut place, and she took the photographs from the coffee table and began to talk about them. She said she thought the stable should be enlarged, and if it was, then the paddock could be placed here. She pointed a slender finger.

They all seemed to be talking at once, and the words flowed around Marcy, confused and sounding far away. She kept saying "yes" and "no" and "how nice," and she couldn't find the strength to stand up, to run. Finally, she did manage to pull herself to her feet.

"I must go," she said. "I have to... to buy some cat food."

"Oh, I'm sorry," said the vision. "Steve did say he'd be right back but... Could I give him a message?"

"No. No. It's not important." And all the way out of the door and back to her apartment, she kept telling herself that it really wasn't important. It didn't matter. It was best this way.

She sat on her sofa, staring at the ashes in the cold fireplace. She felt as though she were drowning. As though she were floundering in a dark empty sea, and there was nothing, no one, to hold on to.

Steve.

She told herself she was lucky. Lucky to have seen Tricia first. Before she'd had a chance to run to Steve and babble her heart out.

Oh, Steve! How could you!

You are a fool, Marcy. You thought... *He asked me to marry him. Me, Marcy Wilson. Nobody else*. But she had refused, so he asked Tricia.

A thought struck her.

Maybe he'd asked Tricia first, and *she* had refused! Of course. They had been friends... lovers?... long before he ever met Marcy. And now Tricia had changed her mind and accepted him. And probably not for hire. For real! She would be Steve's wife—living with him and loving him. Marcy turned her head against the sofa pillow, trying to block out the thought. The desolation.

Again she told herself she was lucky. It couldn't have worked out. She couldn't have been happy with Steve. Loving him, and not being loved in return.

But she wasn't happy now. Without Steve, there was a crying, aching emptiness. She couldn't bear it. She couldn't.

Marcy lifted her head. Jennifer. She was acting just like Jennifer. Dependent. Desolate. Unhappy.

Well, she wasn't going to live that way! She would be perfectly happy without him. Marcy Wilson's life did not revolve around Steve Prescott.

The cat pulled at her pant leg, and she reached down to pick him up. Cat food. She had to buy some cat food. Wearily she got up, plugged in the tree lights and watched the tiny beams appear against the white flocking and the golden bells.

Christmas. A happy time. Jennifer would be away with Al, her mother with Bill and his family in Japan. Maybe, Marcy decided, she'd fix Christmas dinner for Gerald and his father. No. She might go to the cabin with Jo and her family. She would think happy. And be happy. After all, she had good friends, a good job, a lovely apartment....

The phone rang. She put down the kitten to answer it.

Tom. At first she said no, she was just too tired.

"Please," he said. He had to talk to her.

So she said yes, he could come over for a little while.

STEVE PUT DOWN his coffee cup and smiled at Trish. He thought it must be almost time for her friends to pick her up. He liked Trish, and when she'd called, saying that she was in San Francisco for a modeling job and that some friends were driving up to visit relatives in Auburn, he'd told her sure, come along, he'd like to have her come and visit. But now... He wouldn't look at his watch.

"That was a delicious dinner, Steve."

"Yes, Mrs. Chisholm is an excellent cook." Wasn't it six yet? They had said they'd be back about six. Marcy. She had the darnedest way of disappearing. He hadn't seen her for several days, and he needed to talk to her.

"Will you be taking her with you when you move?"

"I sure hope so. I..." He stopped. Tricia was speaking of Mrs. Chisholm. "Well, that is, I'd like to," he hastily amended, "but she has a family here." Mrs. Chisholm would be through bathing the kids soon, and then she'd be off. But he desperately wanted her to stay, and Trish to leave, so he could go over to Marcy's.

Trish snubbed out her cigarette and poured herself another cup of coffee.

"More coffee, Steve?"

"No. No, thank you." He realized he wasn't being a good host, so he remarked very heartily that her career certainly seemed to be taking off.

"Yes," she said. "I have a shoot in Paris next month." She talked about her modeling jobs for a while, then began to fill him in on what all their friends in New York were doing. He listened with half an ear, his mind on his own problems. He had finally made an offer on that place in Connecticut, and now was wondering whether he'd done the right thing. He hadn't had time to check on schools. He wasn't even sure that Marcy had really liked the place. She'd been so reticent that night he'd shown her the pictures. He wanted to talk with her anyway. He wanted to see her. Darn it! Sometimes she could be so evasive. Abruptly he stood, motioning for Trish to accompany him to the living room. He tossed another log on the fire, and dusted his hands. Tricia came up behind him and slowly, sensuously, began to massage his shoulders.

"Oh! Did Mrs. Chisholm tell you? The little social worker from next door stopped by."

"Marcy?" Steve moved out of Tricia's reach, and turned to face her. "What did she want?"

Tricia shrugged. "She said it was nothing important. But I have my own ideas."

"What's that supposed to mean?"

Tricia moved close to him and trailed her fingers along his jawline. "She's just like the rest of us. Charmed beyond our good sense by a man named Stephen Prescott."

"You're wrong about that. She's given me no reason to think I'm charming. And Marcy's not like anyone I've ever known."

"Oh?" Tricia raised an eyebrow. "Would you care to elaborate?"

"Well, she's . . . very . . . very officious." He fumbled for more benign words, not wanting to share with Trish all that Marcy was. "Unselfish. A truly dedicated social worker." The doorbell rang. Thank God, Trish's friends were here!

They didn't stay long, and he rejoiced when he finally closed the door behind them. Tricia had hinted that he might drive her down to San Francisco, spend a few days there. Steve turned down her invitation, and she did not persist. They parted, as always, uncommitted.

He asked Mrs. Chisholm to remain at the apartment while he went on an errand. She agreed, reminding him to pick up some milk for the children's morning cereal.

Steve went out, but just as he started toward Marcy's door, he saw her walking down the steps with Horn Rims. They didn't see him, and he watched them walk on toward the parking lot. The guy's arm was entwined around Marcy's waist. She was laughing and looking up at him in a way that made Steve's temples pound. His pulse raced and there was a peculiar feeling in the pit of his stomach.

Jealous, old buddy?

Hell, no! It was just that every time he needed Marcy, she was unavailable. And he was getting pretty sick of these guys always hanging around her. When we get married . . .

If you get married.

For a moment he was seized by a feeling of near-panic. Then it was replaced by a spurt of angry determination.

Not if! When. I will convince her and I don't care how long it takes. No way will I go off to New York and leave Marcy here.

Horn Rims. The nerve of that guy! Holding on to Marcy as if he owned her!

Steve realized that he was standing with his hands thrust in his pockets, staring after the two people who had already disappeared. He turned to go back to his apartment, then remembered Mrs. Chisholm's request for milk and turned again to walk toward his car.

He felt restless, ill at ease, and...well, abandoned. He told himself that was crazy. Just because he hadn't been in touch with Marcy for a couple of days, and she had a date tonight... Well, damn it, he needed to talk with her. He wanted to get things settled! He slammed the door of his car, shoved it into gear and drove out of the lot with an unusual burst of speed.

The way Marcy had looked up at Horn Rims... *I'm not in love with anyone*, she had declared when Steve asked her point-blank. But she sure could give a guy the wrong impression. Marcy was too trusting...and too giving, and people could take advantage of her.

Friendship, she called it. Good old-fashioned friendship. That was what she'd said about Gerald. Gerald, who had a key to her place and slept over at his convenience! I bet there's more than friendship on his mind!

Steve was only dimly aware that he had passed the cutoff to the supermarket, and that his speedometer was creeping toward seventy, until he heard the siren and saw the flashing light.

"Going to a fire, buddy?" asked the good-natured patrolman who gave him the ticket.

"More like a funeral." Steve sighed, unable to rid himself of the feeling of abandonment. He pulled back onto the highway at a more moderate speed, now feeling more emptiness than anger. The lights of Jake's

Place loomed ahead and, without knowing why, he turned into the parking lot.

Inside, the waitress asked if he wanted anything besides coffee. He said no, and sat there in the booth, the same booth he had shared with Marcy and Jimmy. He tried to recapture the slightest fragment of all that he had felt that night. They had been so close, he and Marcy. So in unison. Together. And later, when he had stood at her door, the way she'd looked into his eyes and stood on tiptoe to kiss him.

You are a very special person, Steve Prescott.

Even now he remembered the warmth of that moment. The sense of belonging that he had never known before. The love that had shone in Marcy's eyes. *Love for him.* And she had said she believed in that love-forever-after stuff. . . .

Steve Prescott, you're a fool! You don't want to *talk* to Marcy. You want to hold her in your arms, kiss her until she's breathless, be with her forever.

Hire a wife! Who are you kidding? You love Marcy like crazy and you're afraid to admit it to yourself. You want the whole thing—love...honor...cherish...cleave to me only. Yes, damn it! No Geralds. No Horn Rims. And no Tricias, either.

I've got to see her. I've got to tell her. Steve tucked a dollar bill under the saucer and hurried out.

MARCY PLACED a half-dozen cans of cat food in the grocery cart.

She was very fond of Tom and never wanted to cause him pain. But she couldn't love him the way he deserved to be loved. She couldn't lead him on, allow him to hope. It would be unfair.

And so she had turned down his proposal, turned down his plea to think things over and join his family in Sausalito for Christmas.

Christmas.

"Excuse me, please."

"Oh, I'm sorry." Marcy realized her cart was blocking the aisle and pushed it out of the way. What would Christmas be like this year? Without Steve or the children. Without her dreams.

But she had to stop dreaming and go on living! Dinner. She hadn't eaten. But she really wasn't hungry. Still, her mother's voice echoed in her thoughts... "Have something warm, and you'll feel better." The fresh oysters in the fish section ahead caught her eye and she reached for them, almost smelling the aroma of homemade stew.

WHY IS THE MILK always at the back of the store? Steve grumbled as he threaded his way through the aisles. Why do things that seem so right go wrong? Why was Marcy with Horn Rims when she ought to be with him? *He could never love her as I do.* No one could.

I love her! And she loves me, too. I know it.

He did truly love Marcy in a way he had never thought possible. And she didn't know, because he had never told her.

Damn it! He would tell her. He'd make her understand.

MARCY'S HAND HOVERED over the jars of oysters. Three ninety-five each! She'd have to put back some of the cat food in order to pay. . . .

"Marcy, I've got to tell you something. Put that down!"

The voice had boomed out of nowhere, and automatically, Marcy answered. "I am. I'm going to put back some of the—" Marcy spun around in sudden realization. "Steve!"

"Did you hear what I said? I've got to tell you something."

"I don't want to hear it!" Marcy became conscious of a woman watching them and lowered her voice. "There's no need to tell me." She didn't want him to tell her. She couldn't bear to hear him say, "I'm marrying Trish."

Steve looked at her in surprise. "Marcy, you have to listen to me. You have to know—"

"You don't need to tell me. I already know."

"You know? How could you when I didn't know myself?"

"The children told me." She bit her lip. "And I'm very happy for you." She turned her head away. Dear Lord, don't let me cry now.

"The children told you what? Wait a minute." He shoved Marcy's cart aside. A woman standing nearby clapped her hand over her mouth and scurried away. "I'm trying to tell you I love you and you keep babbling about something the children said."

She wasn't sure what she'd just heard. She took a few steps back to look up at him. Her shoulder brushed against a pile of cans stacked for display and they came crashing down. Several people turned to look.

"Oh, hell." Steve got on his knees and began to re-stack the cans.

Marcy sank down on her knees beside him. "Steve, what did you say?"

"You keep babbling something about the children."

"No, before that. Did you say you love...?"

"Yes, I love you, Marcy. And I want you to marry me. To really be my wife."

"But I thought... Tricia..." She stopped. What did Tricia matter now?

Steve was holding a can of tomatoes and he was looking into her eyes, telling her that he loved her, and those were the sweetest words she had ever heard him say. She was laughing... and she was crying... and she felt giddy and excited... and wonderful. She moved closer, cupped his face in her hands and kissed him.

"Lady, this don't look like no fight to me."

They glanced up to see the woman and two strong clerks grinning down at them just as the store lights dimmed.

"Never mind about those cans, folks," one of the clerks said. "We'll take care of them."

Marcy hardly heard. She could only gaze into Steve's eyes and see that her dreams were coming true.

Steve stood and clasped her hand, pulling her to her feet, and into his arms. He held her close. As she felt his lips on hers, waves of exaltation and happiness flooded through her. Her heart sang in joyous rhythm with the Christmas music that echoed through the store.

The crowd around them applauded.

"Come on, folks," a clerk pleaded. "Time to go. It's the end of the day."

Steve and Marcy smiled at the people around them and walked out, arm in arm, knowing it was the beginning of a lifetime.

If you enjoyed this book by
ELISE TITLE
Here's your chance to order more stories by one of Harlequin's great authors:

Harlequin Temptation®

#25609	*DANGEROUS AT HEART	$2.99 U.S.☐	$3.50 CAN.☐
#25613	*HEARTSTRUCK	$2.99 U.S.☐	$3.50 CAN.☐
#25617	*HEART TO HEART	$2.99 U.S.☐	$3.50 CAN.☐

*Hart Girls Series

(The following stories are part of the Fortune Boys series)

#25512	ADAM & EVE		$2.99 ☐
#25516	FOR THE LOVE OF PETE		$2.99 ☐
#25520	TRUE LOVE		$2.99 ☐
#25524	TAYLOR MADE		$2.99 ☐

Harlequin Superromance®

#70478	TROUBLE IN EDEN		$3.29 ☐

Harlequin Intrigue®

#22180	STAGE WHISPERS		$2.79 ☐
#22209	NO RIGHT TURN		$2.89 ☐

Harlequin® Promotional Titles

#83258	JUST MARRIED		$4.99 ☐

(short-story collection also featuring
Sandra Canfield, Muriel Jensen, Rebecca Winters)
(limited quantities available on certain titles)

TOTAL AMOUNT	$
POSTAGE & HANDLING	$
($1.00 for one book, 50¢ for each additional)	
APPLICABLE TAXES*	$_____
TOTAL PAYABLE	$_____
(check or money order—please do not send cash)	

To order, complete this form and send it, along with a check or money order for the total above, payable to Harlequin Books, to: **In the U.S.:** 3010 Walden Avenue, P.O. Box 9047, Buffalo, NY 14269-9047; **In Canada:** P.O. Box 613, Fort Erie, Ontario, L2A 5X3.

Name:_____

Address:_____ City:_____

State/Prov.:_____ Zip/Postal Code:_____

*New York residents remit applicable sales taxes.

HETBACK3

◆HARLEQUIN ®

MILLION DOLLAR SWEEPSTAKES (III)

SWP-H495

Fifty red-blooded, white-hot, true-blue hunks
from every State in the Union!

Look for MEN MADE IN AMERICA! Written by some
of our most popular authors, these stories feature some
of the strongest, sexiest men, each from a different state
in the union!

Two titles available every month at your favorite
retail outlet.

In April, look for:

FOR THE LOVE OF MIKE
by Candace Schuler (Texas)
THE DEVLIN DARE
by Cathy Thacker (Virginia)

In May, look for:

A TIME AND A SEASON
by Curtiss Ann Matlock (Oklahoma)
SPECIAL TOUCHES
by Sharon Brondos (Wyoming)

You won't be able to resist MEN MADE IN AMERICA!

Harlequin invites you to the most
romantic wedding of the season.

Rope the cowboy of your dreams in
Marry Me, Cowboy!

A collection of 4 brand-new stories,
celebrating weddings, written by:

New York Times bestselling author

JANET DAILEY

and favorite authors

Margaret Way
Anne McAllister
Susan Fox

Be sure not to miss Marry Me, Cowboy!
coming this April

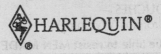

MMC

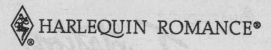

HARLEQUIN ROMANCE®

brings you

More Romances Celebrating Love, Families and Children!

Harlequin Romance #3362

THE BABY BUSINESS

by

Rebecca Winters

If you love babies—this book is for you!

When hotel nanny Rachel Ellis searches for her lost
brother, she meets his boss—the dashing and gorgeous
Vincente de Raino. She is unprepared for her strong
attraction to him, but even more unprepared to be left
holding the baby—his adorable baby niece, Luisa, who
makes her long for a baby of her own!

Available in May wherever Harlequin Books are sold.

KIDS12

THREE GROOMS:
Case, Carter and Mike

TWO WORDS:
"We Don't!"

ONE MINISERIES:

GROOMS ON THE RUN

Starting in May 1995, Harlequin Temptation
brings you an exciting miniseries called

GROOMS ON THE RUN

Each book (and there'll be one a month for three
months!) features a sexy hero who's ready to say,
"I do!" but ends up saying, "I don't!"

Watch for these special Temptations:

In May, **I WON'T!** by Gina Wilkins #539
In June, **JILT TRIP** by Heather MacAllister #543
In July, **NOT THIS GUY!** by Glenda Sanders #547

Available wherever Harlequin books are sold.

New York Times Bestselling Author

CHARLOTTE VALE ALLEN

Three women, three haunted pasts.

DREAMING IN COLOR

Bobby Salton is a woman on the run. With her young daughter, she finds refuge in a rambling house on the Connecticut shore. Alma Ogilvie is a retired head mistress, who, with Bobby's help, wants to regain the independence she lost following a stroke. Eva Rule, Alma's niece, is a successful writer who is trying desperately to put the past behind her—until Bobby shows up.

Now as they all begin to hope for the future, will past threats ruin everything?

Watch for *Dreaming in Color*, this April at your favorite retail outlet.